PRAISE FOR
AMNESIA OF JUNE BUGS

"Jackson Bliss paints with words. He is the Kendrick Lamar of the literary world."
—**Regina King, Emmy-award-winning actress & director**

"*Amnesia of June Bugs* is a lush, kaleidoscopic love song to the city. Jackson Bliss's voice is original, and intricately wrought. It is cerebral and tender. There is so much passion and love in these pages. I love how central a role identity and mixed race experience play here, and how this thrilling story keeps you gripped all the while, like a train underground in a storm, headed for what you can't know but can't stop reading to find out."
—**Tommy Orange, Pulitzer Prize winning author of *There There***

"In *Amnesia of June Bugs*, Jackson Bliss has written a bold, innovative masterpiece. I luxuriated over every sentence of this smart, zeitgeisty novel. At once tender and acute, Bliss deftly captures the multifaceted lives of his diverse cast of characters. The amalgamation of honest characters, stylistic feats, and shrewd social commentary makes this singular novel a must-read."
—**Amy Meyerson, bestselling author of *The Bookshop of Yesterdays* and *The Imperfects***

"In *Amnesia of June Bugs*, Jackson Bliss delivers a hip, intimate, and heartfelt exploration of our multicultural, cosmopolitan world, one full of promise and yet under threat. He is one of the great advocates and defenders of such a world, so urgently embodied in this very necessary novel."
—**Viet Thanh Nguyen, Pulitzer Prize winning author of *The Sympathizer***

"I love this book. Word for word, sentence for sentence, page for page, Jackson Bliss is a narrative and syntactical wonder. And in this novel—a cultural takedown that is at times gentle, at times furious and incisive—he takes no prisoners. Each character is both an ordinary individual navigating an unforgiving 21st urban landscape—Paris, Seattle, Chicago, New York—and an indefatigable warrior committed to love, to art, and to dispensing with the racism, hatred, and violence they encounter on the daily. *Amnesia of June Bugs* is a howl and a call to recreate the world one friendship, one lover, once chance urban encounter at a time. I will read it again and again."
—**Bonnie Nadzam, author of *Lions and Lamb***

"A virtuosic feat of storytelling with fire on every page. It feels prophetic, like a meditation on aspects of identity and pop culture that haven't even been invented yet."
—**Jamie Ford, *New York Times* bestselling author of books not as well written as this one**

"In *Amnesia of June Bugs*, Ginger Lin, Winnie Yu, Aziz Al-Wahnan, and Suzanne Gupta are trapped on the C-train in the NYC underground. Hurricane Sandy swirls above. In this brief rupture in time, their rebellious metamorphoses intersect, stories emerging from hybrid bodies, woven cultures, translingual narratives at play with graffiti, screenplay, questionnaire, lyric lists. Jackson Bliss, diasporic hapa-Whitman, has written a protest poem, manifesto, and anthem. A 21st century love song to America."
—**Karen Tei Yamashita, author of *Translation of Memory & Sansei & Sensibility: Stories* and *I, Hotel***

"Jackson Bliss is as verbally exuberant as any writer I've come across in years. *Amnesia of June Bugs* is beautifully conceived, powerful, affecting, hip, comedic, and as close to being of-the-moment as it is possible for a novel to be."
—**T.C. Boyle, award-winning author of *The Terranauts***

"A kaleidoscopic and polyphonic novel that vividly portrays a multicultural, Pan-Asian world while reflecting, in smart and moving ways, on the complications and complexities of art, identity, love, and belonging."
—**Jenny Bhatt, author of *Each of Us Killers***

"A visionary novel that boldly invents a new American patois to light the way. Jackson Bliss is hellbent on telling the truth about the lived experience of his diverse characters and the result is haunting and shot through with weird pathos. Cutting edge but timeless in its preoccupation with the human heart and the grace notes found therein."
—Gabe Hudson, author of *Gork, The Teenage Dragon* and *Dear Mr. President*

Ingenious in premise and wise in execution, this novel explores how lines of class, race, and nationality divide us in real and painful ways. Both tough-minded and generous, it finds us also capable of forging connections with great tensile strength. Bliss offers a portrait of American culture both true and unlike any I have encountered."
—Elise Blackwell, author of *Hunger* and *The Lower Quarter*

AMNESIA OF JUNE BUGS

a novel by

Jackson Bliss

7.13 Books
Brooklyn

Printed in the United States of America

First Edition
1 2 3 4 5 6 7 8 9

Cover art by Alban Fischer
Edited by Leland Cheuk

Library of Congress Cataloging-in-Publication Data

ISBN (paperback): 979-8-9853762-0-3
ISBN (eBook): 979-8-9853762-1-0
LCCN: 2022932849

この本をお母さんに捧げます
For my mum

"Life can only be understood backwards, but it must be lived forwards."

-Søren Kierkegaard

"Add a ladybug/transformation is complete.
For the metamorphosis from the box to the jeep.
And it's good to be here gettin' fly with the raps.
We love it where we from/but we kick it where we at."

—Digable Planets

"Cafés, (day) dreaming, travel, and reflection are the
cultural spaces where humans tend to violate the sacred laws of linearity,
making anything possible: suspended animation, counterfactual
narratives, cyclical timelines, parallel worlds, even speculative romance."

—*Time Travel in the Insect World*

"I don't know what I'm supposed to do/
Haunted by the ghost of you."

—Lord Huron

ADULTHOOD

1. BROKEN PIECES OF MEMORY

Somewhere between Fulton/Nassau and High Street, Hurricane Sandy obliterates the tri-state electrical grid, beating New York to a Mesozoic pulp. The storm knocks the C train unconscious and fractures the cityscape with black-eye rain and face-slap wind, ripping out the electronic dreams of Manhattan and casting a curse of car accidents, street operas, and traffic jams over Queens and the Bronx. It scrapes the glean off Brooklyn's shiny surfaces. It disperses storm clouds of black locusts that slowly engulf the whole region, their diaphanous wings glistening in the unlit streets like shards of wet stained glass. Without electricity, there is a cool vulnerability in the city that is impossible to ignore, the portentous rain nags New Yorkers, reminds them of the thin boundary separating civilization from catastrophe, enlightenment from obscurity, thriving hive from colony collapse. In the gloomy and wet streets, people speak in frantic whisper, calling out to each other in the cool air, dread overshadowing expectation, their ricocheting words ping like dropped coins. Deep underground, somewhere on six hundred miles of train tracks, the lives of four passengers intersect briefly on the halted subway. We are their only witnesses. We are their only readers. We must do the work of understanding them and cohering their incoherent world. As we read, we will connect and collate their torn stories together like heartbroken book-binders. We will survive on the crumbs of starved language and the ashes of burnt memories. The following chapters are their forgotten songs, their broken pieces of personhood, describing everything that happens before and after this moment in time.

PUPA

2. THE HUNGARIAN DIVORCE IN SEVEN MOVEMENTS (GINGER LIN)

1. Europe: When she'd graduated from Cooper Union in 2000, Ginger Lin decided to travel through Europe with her girlfriends after they catwalked through their graduation ceremonies. Chelsea and Meredith were yang guizi, but cool enough, or so she'd thought at the time. In retrospect, it's so hard to nail anyone down in college since students are masters at shifting their identities depending on who they're with, but Ginger thought her friends cared about her. As it turned out and as she'd feared all along, they only cared about themselves, centering their upper-class whiteness above all else.

2. Paris: Before the great split, they went out clubbing at glitzy boums (aka discothèques), sipping on delicate café au laits, the foam in their mugs forming hearts and arrows, portraits of le Pont Neuf, the Musée d'Orsay, and La Défense. During their last two days in the city of the golden apple, Meredith and Chelsea dragged her around town as they went on lavish shopping sprees on rue du Faubourg, Saint-Honoré, and l'Avenue Montaigne, a spendathon that started at Cartier and Chaumet and ended at Piaget and Van Cleef & Arpels, the 8eme and the 16eme arrondissements pillaged by her rich friends who were intent on taking Paris's boutiques by storm like Navy

SEALs decked out in leisure wear, platinum grey highlights, blood lotus red lipstick, and Jason Wu sunglasses. While Ginger looked on with embarrassment and unrepressed class envy, her friends bought identical animal print blouses, half-transparent harem pants, daffodil dresses, dad jeans, flesh-colored blazers, Burberry trenches, and matching yellow wedge sneakers, all delivered safely to their parents' Long Island homes.

3. Paris & New York: It's not that Ginger hadn't planned on going shopping in Paris either, she just didn't have a family credit card with a whopping $70,000 spending limit like Meredith and it's not that Ginger didn't have spending money to buy new clothes in Europe either because she'd busted her ass through college as a freelance graphic designer and had saved enough to buy her own airfare, pay for her own food when they ate out, and even splurge on a Louis Vuitton change purse, literally the cheapest thing they sold, but who's counting and who fucking cares, anyway? The issue was that Ginger's white mom was a public school teacher and spent most her money on an exorbitant mortgage and an extensive grocery list of charities she contributed to every month: the ASPCA, the UNHCR, Goats of Anarchy, Oxfam, the Humane Society, and Trees for Trollops, so she didn't have money to give Ginger once she'd graduated, just a Starbucks gift card and a jade Buddha necklace, which Ginger loved and wore like an acolyte, even in the shower. Chelsea's parents, on the other hand, gave her a check for $20,000 for her graduation, just a little chump change for her in case of an emergency. As the three of them took a car service to JFK, she watched Chelsea toss the check into her Gucci tote like it was an ATM receipt. Ginger just couldn't relate with that kind of cash flow or that disregard for money.

4. Budapest: After Paris, the three of them took afternoon trains to Milan, Amsterdam, Vienna, and Madrid, five cities in twenty days, surely that was a record somewhere, but it was

at the ever-so-hip and ever-so-gaudy Jack Rabbit Slims bar in Budapest that the three of them had their inevitable falling out. It was a pivotal moment in Ginger's life because she'd been waiting for it since their friendship began at a crowded West Village party where a bunch of coked-up Tisch, Columbia, and Parsons students were speaking in obnoxious industry acronyms about the movie festivals they were entering and campaigns they were designing for. The three of them left together and walked to SoHo where they split two bottles of overpriced rosé and discovered they were all art students at NYU. Now, Meredith and Chelsea were preparing for adulthood as fashion interns, complaining about how dirty Budapest was, a comment Ginger found ironic coming from New Yorkers who lived in the dirtiest city in America, even dirtier than LA, which was hard to out-dirt. She stood there and sorta half-listened, stabbing her one-dollar rum and coke with a thin red straw, scanning the bar for pretty Hungarian boys, wondering why she felt so lonely in the company of her friends.

That's when Chelsea cleared her throat. —So, um, Ginger?

—Whazzup?

—Okay, Chelsea said, giving Meredith a conspiratorial glance, so Meredith and I have been talking.

The hairs on Ginger's neck stood up like a spiked neck collar.

—And, Chelsea continued, we decided we're leaving tomorrow.

—What do you mean? Ginger asked. —We're all going to Istanbul.

—Actually, we're not going.

—What are you *talking* about? Ginger asked incredulously.

—We're *sick* of Europe, Meredith said.

—Yeah, and we *totally* miss the city, Chelsea said.

—But we're flying *out* of Istanbul, Ginger said.

—No…you are, Chelsea said, we already changed our tickets.

Ginger had never felt so betrayed like this and she'd been fucked over plenty by juice-fasting white fuckboys with dragon and maritime tattoos and affected melancholy who used to tell her how cute and exotic she was, by hot androgynous bi-racial rocker chicks who used to flick their stinky cigarette butts down the broken stairwells of their Lower East Side apartments and order terrible Chinese takeout before claiming she wasn't really Asian anyway, by old-money, East Coast editorial assistants with unmanageable beards and perfect skin who tried to pay for everything with free softcover books and tote bags they'd snagged from the Take Shelf at their Big Five imprint until their monthly allowance kicked in. It was bad enough that Ginger always felt too poor to be friends with Meredith and Chelsea, always the hapa ghetto star with more intelligence, natural beauty, spunk, work ethic, and color in her blood line than their two pasty, flatulent, rosy-cheeked genealogies combined, but now she felt like she was too poor to travel with them. She'd known her social function from the very beginning, she'd always been their street cred, their token hip half-Asian friend every rich white girl on the Sound longed for and fought for in college, posturing urbanity, vague social liberalism, and anti-capitalism for the tacit approval of their intellectual classmates. In truth, Ginger had always been their link to the other side of hegemony, but now the field trip was over.

5. Budapest, Belgrade, & Sofia: When they'd left Ginger out of the travel logistics in Europe, she was devastated because logistics aren't even a class thing, just spending habits. The Hungarian Divorce, as she later tagged it, merely proved her greatest and most primal fear, that she was on the outside of that country club looking in, that she'd always been on the outside of their friendship peering through the tiny plastic windows of another girl's dollhouse. In college, they'd just given her a hall pass to the auditorium of the 1%, but college was done now and

her class rejection in Budapest was absolute and final, leaving her only one choice to salvage her dignity: she took the train to Istanbul by herself. She felt a little badass doing it alone, even had the compartment all to herself. A few Italian guys knocked on the doors from the dark corridors of the train and gave her *ehi, bambina* eyes, insisting they had tickets, one even started singing a Verdi aria to her, which she found slightly romantic but also incredibly cheesy. Still, she didn't budge. She didn't make eye-contact either. Making a quick deduction inside her head, she calculated that the Italian pickup artists were lying both by context and facial expression. Chelsea and Meredith were rich, impatient, and brash, but they weren't thorough, so there was no way in hell they'd canceled their train reservations because money didn't matter to them, they were the kind of rich white people who threw five-digit checks into their purses like used Kleenex. Logistics were for the middle-class, something only people who weren't rich had to deal with, that's what she'd learned observing them every time they demanded something from the concierge and palmed a twenty to the Maitre D,' so she locked the compartment door during the aria, skimmed through a shitty travelogue written by a white woman who "found" herself in Morocco that Suzanne had bought impulsively at JFK, and then she thought about her life. Really thought about it. As she looked through the window, her eyes couldn't distinguish between Hungarian, Bulgarian, and Serbian villages, she didn't know Belgrade from Sofia, but when the train finally creeped into the Haydarpaşa Station like a scene from Indiana Jones, she woke up from an empty and hollow sleep, her dreams all fallow and soggy. She just knew she'd arrived in Istanbul. As vividly as she'd visualized Meredith and Chelsea dumping her ass on the curb someday, she knew with the same before-the-moment-clarity that she'd arrived in Istanbul even before the first merhaba, before she could smell the Bosporus or taste her first chicken döner kebab. For the first time in her shifty life, she already knew where she was and why she was there, which was more than she could have said about her fake-ass friends from Long Island.

6. Istanbul: Ginger visited the Blue and Yeni Mosques, the confusing Aya Sofia, the Topkapı Palace Museum, the Palace Wall, the Harem, and the royal Spoon collection. She walked over the Attatürk Bridge every morning, got ripped off *twice* at the Spice Bazaar, and ate döner sandwiches obsessively. In İstiklal Caddesi, Ginger bought Europop CDs, kitschy T-shirts, and glass nazars to ward off the evil eye for her family, the good luck charms reminding her of blue sunny side eggs.

One day, as she was exploring the side streets of Taksim, a group of shoe polish boys harassed her, which is where she experienced her first real adult trauma. They smeared shoe polish on her shoe, apologized, and then said, *we wipe for free, no charge*, but then they did it again on her other shoe, giving her the same line, *so sorry, no charge.* Once they'd finished, the leader of the shoe polish runts, a small gangly boy with a snaggletooth and black shoe polish streaks on his cheeks pinched her T-shirt shirt with his finger and said, *you pay me now or I hurt you.* She laughed at first, but snaggletooth was dead serious. They closed in on her, grabbing her clothes with their dirty little paws that were caked in dried polish. They yelled into her face, *Come on, you pay us now! This not free. Pay us you bitch, you steal from us, this not free!* Her heart was a nuclear meltdown. She handed them a 1,000 Turkish Lira in a daze and they laughed in her face, their spit ricocheting on her cheeks as they held tightly to her T-shirt and made throat-cutting gestures and pulled their eyes back, *You joke with us*, they shouted, *pay us now you Kung-Fu* bitch, *pay us or we stab you!* Never in Ginger's life had children treated her like garbage before and she was a teaching assistant, but here in Istanbul the shoe polish boys made throat slitting gestures and shouted at her, *Give us your time, Kung-Fu bitch!* Snaggle-tooth's nostrils flared with every exclamation point. The other boys mirrored him, shouting at her, pulling their eyes back and outlining their bodies with their own hands as if to say, *Look at her body, look at her eyes.* Snaggletooth grabbed her watchstrap and wrapped the end of her T-shirt around his fists, exposing her blue bra strap to the world. She pushed him away and tugged at her T-shirt, her heart skipping frantically like scratched-to-hell vinyl. She tried to create separation for a second to give herself the room to breathe, but her breath was lost in her body. She saw their threats for what they were—the training wheels for racist misogyny—and she felt helpless and exposed in a country without the amulet of language.

But just as she felt a scream slipping out of her throat, just as she pictured her hand slapping five boys in perfect succession like a scene out of *Enter the Dragon*, her fave movie as a teenager, an old Turkish man placed his body between Ginger and the boys. He was almost bald with a few strands of entangled gray hair covering his brown scalp like malnourished vines. Dressed in grey pants, brown sandals, and a black button down, he carried a newspaper tucked underneath his arm. Ginger was a New Yorker and could take care of herself in New York because she knew the rules of her existence, but here in Istanbul the rules weren't hers. The old man yelled at the shoe polish boys in Uzi-fire Turkish, wagging his finger in the air and shaking his head in disapproval. Their faces plummeted to the ground as the ringleader looked around for help, his eyes scanning the crowd, glaring at her defiantly out of the corner of his eye. When the old man was done berating them, he led Ginger to a nearby restaurant, looking over his shoulder until the baby gangsters had disappeared like a cloud of cicadas floating to another crop. Of course, she felt sudden loyalty for this Turkish grandfather, whoever the hell he was, but she worried that her gratitude could make her vulnerable, and that her vulnerability could make her disappear.

The old man paid for two chais, stirring a dissolved sugar cube inside the slender beak of his tea glass. He took a slow sip and then looked up at her. —Çinli mısın? he asked.

—I'm sorry, yok türkçe.

—Amerikan?

—Yes.

—Oh.

For an hour they talked in two broken languages using sentence fragments, botched infinitives, air sketches, regressive charades, moments of sympathetic listening, fill in the blanks, napkin illustrations, polite confusion, and sometimes blind intuition. It was a whole conversation of conclusion jumping. Ginger had never been good with foreign languages. Her Mandarin was for teenyboppers and her English grammar totally sucked, but somehow, she and the old Turkish man understood each other because they wanted to and the desire to understand is always a precondition for empathy. For one singular hour, they were two travelers trying to cross the great cultural divide, two human beings dialed into each other after spending their whole lives translating their feelings for people who didn't listen and didn't understand. It was only after he'd shaken her hand one last time and grinned, his crow's feet crawling up his temples like enchanted ivy, carved into his leathery skin like Roman aqueducts in Foça's streets, it was only after he'd walked towards Taksim Square that Ginger felt a sickness in her stomach. She suddenly noticed the polish stains on her favorite BKI T-shirt, the one she'd bought in Williamsburg one rainy spring day. She gazed into the bottom of her chai glass and noticed clumps of sugar like the ruins of Troy, or at least the postcards of them she'd spotted near the Pudding Shop. It was at that moment of averted crisis and sudden isolation that she felt a deep, almost spiritual debt to the old man for his kindness. Ginger walked around the city center until she got lost, the sun bowing its head in the call to prayer, honeycombed streetlamps shed soft and wan geometries on the cobblestone sidewalks across the street from the Blue Mosque.

7. New York: The next day, almost in a trance, she left Istanbul like a bullied teenager leaving an impenetrable high school. She felt relieved, regretful, ashamed, and longing all at once for all the things she didn't do. How could a city make her feel so many complex emotions? How could this be the end of her trip? When she made her way through customs at JFK twenty-two hours later, New York had changed on her like an unfaithful mutation. Its streets were dirtier, brighter, and larger than she remembered. She felt like a stranger in her own city with a corrupted memory of her childhood and a narrated memory of her birth. Ginger remained in this daze for a couple weeks until the new pieces of her life fit into place. First, she got a full-time job at a fashion magazine she fucking detested, then she went to grad school for graphic design, and finally she began the flawed science of adulting. One day, she ran into Winnie at Astor Place just as the sun was setting, fireflies glowing around his head like a troupe of electric apostles preaching their incandescent gospel of love to the fallen city, their sermons floating above him like a tiny star map of salvation.

3. GHOST WRITER OF THE VOID (WINNIE YU)

IT WAS A COOL and cloudy day, just a couple days before Hurricane Sandy crashed into the Eastern Seaboard, when Winnie walked between cars stuck in traffic in Fort Greene to the subway station. Dressed in a blue G-Star hoodie, denim jacket, and matching 3d slim jeans, he had a man bun that Ginger had basically forced on him, a two-week-old beard, and X studs in both his ears. Winnie had just peaced out of Brooklyn after rolling with his homeboy and apprentice, M-Boz, and was headed to Harlem now to see Ginger so they could eat dinner at their favorite pho joint on 81st Street. Truth is, he'd do almost anything in the world just to hear her voice, hold her hand, and taste her lips that were smooth and sweet. Gotta be the vegan gummy bears. Winnie needed to see Ginger every day, she was the metaphysical puzzle piece that filled his kong xu that couldn't be translated into English or erased with magical thinking. It was the spiritual intersection where his emotion used to be all frozen inside, where qi needed to flow like morning traffic in Chengdu.

Earlier that day, Winnie had jetsetted to Greenpoint with M-Boz when he saw his neighbor, Mr. Li, on the subway platform playing his guqin again. It was the first time Winnie had seen him since the teenage gangbang on 116th Street, since the day the old man had carried his punkass to a brand-new Chinese diner, since the day he'd told Winnie about the Invisible Dress and the Chinese girl who sang for him inside a Xinjiang reeducation camp. The world was caving in, man.

—Yo Winn, isn't that your neighbor? M-Boz asked.

—Nah, Winnie said.

—Gēmen, you sure?

—Not really. Truth was, Winnie didn't wanna retell Kwan Li's story. He felt intense loyalty and affection for the old man, so avoiding him right now seemed like the easiest way to honor his confession and prevent their two worlds from colliding.

The G train pulled up, breaks screeching, the sound so toxic that passengers covered their ears. A few even left the platform in protest. When the train doors opened, Winnie sat down and looked at Kwan Li through the window. There was no one listening to his music, almost no one on the platform except a homeless woman sleeping on a heating vent and a group of Korean tourists pointing at the MTA map, but Kwan Li kept playing his song anyway like an OG and truthfully, Winnie loved him for it, he loved the old man for not abandoning his craft. This was a legit artist right here, someone who fought for their art, even when they were the only person giving it the attention it deserved.

Winnie had lived on the Bowery his whole life, didn't even know that New York was in America until he was six. His parents spoke Cantonese and Taiwanese, everyone in his fam did. The market signs on Grand Street where his mom bought her groceries were written in simplified Chinese, his neighbors watched Cantonese soap operas in the afternoon, old guys hung out at Mr. Chang's corner store at night, playing dominoes and drinking ginseng tea and viper whiskey, cracking jokes in Wu.

His super was Fujian, cheapest motherfucker he'd ever seen. Dude tried to fix everything with duct tape, tin foil, and DAP. For the longest time, Winnie thought he lived in Asia. He thought (still thinks) that white people were the cultural tourists, but in one day, Mama changed the rules of his storytelling.

She'd taken him on the subway to Brooklyn over the Manhattan Bridge, giving him emotional distance from their apartment. As a kid, he didn't realize that New York was connected together by bridges, the vertebrae of the urban body. He didn't realize that subway lines were veins, the major lines arteries, and the streets capillaries. Until that fateful and transformative day, Winnie hadn't realized that he would always live in a fractal world, that every borough was its own city of billboards, insects, damaged vascular systems, and wandering spirits. Their subway ride to Brooklyn together confirmed what he'd always suspected, namely that New York was an ethnographic sponge absorbing the screenplay of immigration. New York was a megapolis, its streets, highways, and bridges resembling the human nervous system. New York was an urban hive imploding with refugee stories, diasporic longing, bustling multiculturalism, and inherited wealth. New York was also a collapsing urban space where culture danced between neighborhoods and history intersected ethnicity, creating abstract forms that interacted but didn't touch each other like a kaleidoscope.

Until that fateful day, Winnie thought New York was just ten blocks, from Mr. Chang's bodega all the way to Good Times Dry-Cleaners. He kinda thought New York was the unofficial capital of Taiwan, a nation in an island, and a freaky global village. He was half right, actually. The straight shit is that the day they took the train over the Manhattan Bridge, Mama was showing him the way to St. Ursula School where Asian, Latino, and Black kids wore unforgiving white polo shirts with stiff collars that dug into their necks like plow yokes and old man pants that resisted wrinkles and refused to be rolled up at the ankles. It was a school where Asian, Latino, and Black girls were forced to wear skimpy plaid skirts, even in the winter, poor students of color pretended they were rich, rich white kids pretended they were gangsta, and white teachers spoke Midtown English. That school was an academy of impersonations. A theater of the restless mind. When Mama enrolled Winnie in Catholic school and filled out the paperwork for a "St. Martin de Porres scholarship for immigrant students," a detail he wouldn't even understand until he was in high school, Winnie realized his mom had radically altered his own identity and shoved him into a chrysalis of her own making. As they passed over the Manhattan Bridge again, he didn't understand how the alternate world he'd traveled to that day could still be New York, didn't understand why his home disappeared and then reappeared again, why no one spoke his family's languages at his new school. Even now as a late thirty-something, he still couldn't figure out how his parents had managed to sequester him from the class struggle, the racial conflict, and the spatial tension of inner-city life for as long as they did. After Mama had enrolled him for classes, smoothed his hair in the back for his school ID, bribed him with Feng Li Su cakes from a Taiwanese baker to celebrate his enrollment, and then led him back to their apartment, pineapple paste caramelized in his teeth, Winnie realized that he didn't know shit about America. He only knew he wasn't living in Asia and he mos def wasn't Catholic. As far as birthdays went, turning six fucking sucked, the worst thing to happen to him until explosive acne in tenth grade, until his ba peaced out of his life for good, too quick and too soon.

On the subway, Winnie studied passengers when he noticed a viejito, his face wrinkled like a tubby Puerto Rican bulldog. He only had a couple sprouts of hair like weeds sticking through sidewalk cracks, but his face radiated some kinda goodness, it was calm and weathered like old leather as he talked to this Arab American kid like they were old friends or something. They seemed so open, so receptive to each other, laughing the way only strangers could without history or expectations. Winnie's heart still hurt inside. He felt a familiar tightness in his chest, a gaping emptiness where his spirit wanted to escape, the very place he'd been locking out his emotion with police tape since the day his ba abandoned them to the spirt world.

Last year, a bunch of heavy shit hit Winnie in the heart, one thing after another like a bad telenovela. First: Kwan Li and his family moved in downstairs. Most families in his building set up shop years ago as relatives touched shore or arrived in skinny caravans, moving from one town to the next, working just long enough to buy an airplane ticket to New York. They showed up with a muted child, a plastic bag full of Zongzi buns, Yuanxiao dumplings, Niangao cakes, and a small suitcase of heartache. The Kwans moved in one week after the Yangs moved out. After his daughter ran away, Mr. Yang lived by himself for six months, waiting for her like an abandoned groom, but she never came back because she'd found her own happiness outside. They say she got hitched to a Black model in the New York ballet who was the next Baryshnikov. They say Mr. Yang begged her to find a nice Chinese banker from 重庆市 (Chongching) or a brain surgeon from 上海市 (Shanghai), but she wasn't hearing that shit because America is always the soundtrack of self-invention—everyone knows that—so when he tried to quarantine his daughter from the American supervirus of the ego, he lost her forever.

Dude should have known better, should have understood that this country of intersection, this site of cultural hyphenation, was a death sentence to the motherland, but he couldn't see it coming because his eyes were closed shut like every dreamer. She packed her bags one night and slipped through the window like a trapped fly. Winnie could hear her crying down the block. The next morning, Mrs. Yang shunned her husband and moved in with her sister. Their siblings and nieces moved down the street. Finally, Mr. Yang bounced too, his memory of the homeland stomped on and beat up by filial haunting. Less than a month after Mr. Yang finished mopping the busted-up hardwood floors in his apartment, the Kwans moved in and Winnie stopped thinking about Mr. Yang's daughter, wondering why she left without a word or why her father pretended they lived in Shanghai until the day she woke up from her Confucian daze and realized her father's spirit was still in Jing'an Park and hers was in a Julliard dance studio. The Yang Scandal foreshadowed The Kwan Drama. The building where Winnie lived would always be a place of mourning for the living and the lived.

The second thing that happened was actually the first, except Winnie didn't know how to deal with it: his ba got shot in the temple for the cost of a small pizza. That's all he had in his pockets. The dude that ganked him ran three blocks, tripped on a box of cabbage, and knocked his dumbass out in a stairwell. Lights out, sha bi. To this day, Winnie wished he and his uncle had found him because they would have sunk their shoes into that motherfucker's septum, broken the cartilage in eulogy. When his ba died the next morning from head trauma, Winnie and his family lost everything except their bodega. All that paper, small bonds, and family heirlooms were locked in his American Steel 510 safe and no one knew the combo. It was all they had that separated them from the FOBs. That's how his ba liked it too. He'd bought it at the Saturday Market one day— used but not registered—to protect their future, he'd explained, so their future prosperity wouldn't be stolen by their past. No one even had a receipt for that shit. On his last night on earth, Mama stayed up late into the shadows for Ba, his whole life was waiting for him on the kitchen table: the teapot filled with water that went through the various temperatures of their own marriage, the sesame noodles in a glazed green bowl covered with a chipped, second-hand plate, and his favorite black rice bowl emblazoned with red Han Dragons, beads of condensation dripping down the sides from old steam. Mama tried to stay up, watched re-runs of her favorite Taiwanese soap opera, *The Barons of Taipei*. Eventually she crashed, the remote still in her hand, snow falling on the screen.

As M-Boz listened to his cell, a big ole grin cut into his cheeks. Winnie looked away and let him have his moment.

—Yo man, it's your bae, M-Boz said, laughing, —she said to get a smart phone.

—Gēmen, Winnie said, smacking his lips, tell her to get a job that involves manual labor first and then we'll talk.

The first time Winnie crashed into Ginger's world he was sixteen, his head full of anime designs and color swatches. She was trying to break up a fight in the hallway between her friend, Kayisha, and this Vietnamese gangster known as Vipermouth who had mercury teeth when Ginger got popped in the mouth, blood trickling between her teeth. The next thing Winnie knew, she was in her friend's face shouting, *Don't ever fucking hit me like that again, even by accident, you hear me?* And that was that. Ginger was superdirect and courageous. You *had* to respect her because she was hard and sweet and everything rolled off her like an everlasting gobstopper. She hated ignorance, smug white people, and violence, and she couldn't deal with gangs, but she knew how to deal with people. She knew how to make them listen. That was her secret, why people lodged themselves into her like delirious ticks.

—Where she at? Winnie asked.

—Hudson and Reade

—TriBeCa?

—Yeah. She wants us to go meet up.

—Hell no. You *know* how I feel about The Triangle. I'd rather rot in Long Island with all the Gin Blossoms.

—Winn, why you tripping? M-Boz clicked off his phone and shook his head.

The day Winnie learned that the words graffiti and confetti weren't related, he was floored. He was a naïve graphie when he first started, he can admit it now. He once believed his throw-ups would still be there a month later, which never happened, there was a vulnerable part of him even now that still hoped if his technique was legit enough, his art might be immune to bad cover-ups by paint-by-number patzers. Some vain part of him hoped, even now, that the raw, untested toys of the world would take a step back when they saw his work and say, *Yo man, this shit is too damn tight to cover it up with my sad-ass scribbles. Let's bounce!* But that shit never happened. There was no artistic conscience with graffiti because it was an illegal and decentralized gallery. Graffiti was expropriated art, its individual design created for the visual consumption of millions of commuters, so the instant you combined street creds, artistic ego, illegality, and danger, integrity was always the first thing to go. Good urban graphics always got worn quick, covered up by amateurs who never got the memo that your shit better be better than the shit you covered up, otherwise, it was a desecration against the church of urban design. But young and brash artists always liked to burn the history books they never read. They couldn't accept, wouldn't believe, and didn't understand, that there was an entire artistic discourse that came before them that they were speaking to in their own work, even if they didn't know it.

Winnie remembered his first throw-up. He was shadowing

Kareem, one of the original Bronx CM3s. Dude was the most audacious, talented, and controversial culture jammer in the city before Giuliani's goon squad locked him up for good for stealing a loaf of sourdough and some organic peanut butter from a bougie co-op in Park Slope. It was some crazy *Les Mis* shit, three strikes and you're out kinda thing. Before that predictable injustice happened, though, K. had taken Winnie to the Inwood tunnels near 207th Street. He'd made a quick outline for him and said, *A'ight kid, this is you. Show me what you got or retire the ink.* Winnie pretty much butchered his first throw-up in twenty minutes of floundering: his shading was off, he didn't match his background combos at all, his center axis was floating, he picked the wrong contrasts, his font was generic as hell, his layering misaligned, his tag stupid as fuck, and his contour lines, totally wack. He'd taken a clean, perfectly tight starter and fucking massacred it. Winnie was mad ashamed and everything he did afterwards just made it worse until finally he just stopped trying, his hands hanging at his sides. It hurt too much to look at K., who busted out laughing, his face electrified with amused sympathy, but right when Winnie was about to whitewash his first and biggest tragedy and start over, K. stopped him.

—Nah, leave it man, K. said.

—Wait, why? Winnie asked.

—This way, you'll *never* make that mistake again, bro. Cats be busting jokes about this nauseating piece of bubble gum for months and that'll keep y'ass humble. You need *humility* to tell other people's stories, you need *strength* to jam corporate fascism, you need *hunger* to push your craft, you need *perspective* to see the big picture, you need *silence* to hear your own voice, and you need *openness* to understand the world.

—Damn, okay, Winnie said, confused, humbled, and strangely inspired.

—Also, you need *shame* to bring y'ass back out in the wintertime.

—Wait, why? Winnie asked.

—If you're *made* for this, K. said, you need to create a *studio* of your mistakes. That way, when all those motherfuckers are cozy and warm, hiding in their houses and watching YouTube videos, you gonna evolve on the DL and show them what's up when they least expect it, you *feel* me?

Winnie had nodded, trying to keep up. Winter separated artists from taggers, it cultivated rebirth, froze the gallery, and inspired self-creation in the subarctic darkness. The battlefield of style in the summer was a different beast, it caused suffocation, became an orgy of cover-ups, wannabe kings, and wallflowers. After years of figuring out his own brand, Winnie eventually realized that K. was right about everything. Truth was, Winnie's first graffito *did* bring him back outside. When he knew that piece of shit was out there for everyone to diss, he became deeply self-conscious, even obsessive about his artistic flaws, limited vision, and primitive craft, slowly becoming aware of his technical weaknesses, his shit work ethic, and his superficial imagination. It took Winnie a condensed lifetime to respect the majesty of language, the power of the graphic imaginary, and the psychology of font. It took him even longer to recognize the crucial but transitory value of public art, the way it could express a gritty realism of the city and give an existential vocabulary to the invisible struggle of silenced people living in concrete Legolands. After that first night with K., the city became Winnie's sensei and the streets became his workshop, helping him slowly transform into a cement poet who would dedicate his life to reifying his own political stylistics for the cultural hyphens of Chinatown, a graphie for the chained spirituality of the Bowery, and a ghostwriter for every void that had no name.

4. COMMUNITY SERVICE

Ginger wasn't normally monomaniacal, but it was hard not to obsess about the things she didn't understand and she really didn't understand her own body. She got out of bed, walked to the bathroom in her underwear, peed, and thought about her kids at school. She thought about the time she'd held Winnie's hand and smoked the stickiest blunt as they strolled across the Brooklyn Bridge with M-Boz for the first time in ages and gave each other hip-hop hugs just because they were happy to be alive. She thought about the expanded family she'd been advocating for since January and the late-night arguments she and Winnie got into every time she fired the same blank from her antique gun, telling herself that her ultimatum to start a fam wasn't an act of coercion. She thought about her reproductive endocrinologist who wouldn't call her back even after she'd left three frantic voice mails and the results Ginger feared and fantasized about almost every waking moment after being off birth control forever. Ginger wondered why doctors were always playing God, why Dr. Park was ghosting her at the peak of her vulnerability, why Winnie was so unfazed about every missed period, why everyone seemed so damn optimistic about the family they didn't have. Did she lack imagination? Had she become too cynical for her own good? As a hapa woman used to alienation, disqualification, and erasure from both the white and the Chinese sides of her fam, had she learned to be pessimistic about the power of her own mixed-race body? Would she feel like a terrible mom if she realized one day that she didn't even like her own kids? Would she feel like a terrible person if she realized one day that motherhood was just unpaid labor for the population explosion? Even when she let herself daydream about holding her future daughter in her arms for a second, Ginger wondered if she could possibly love her hypothetical kids as much as she loved Winnie, the only man, the only person who'd ever tattooed her heart with his own lyrics.

She sat on the toilet, underwear lassoing her ankles, and blew on her cup of green tea that smelled like cut grass and plucked garden vegetables. Tea was her magic spell to cast away the future. As she sipped, she wondered for the twentieth time that day if she was finally going to enter the Mom Sweepstakes. After a series of invasive and unpleasant tests, did she finally get to enter the raffle contest? She flushed the toilet, washed her face, brushed her teeth with an electric toothbrush, and put on her Asian Daily 4 (toner, Korean serum, squalene oil, and Lush moisturizer) before sitting down on a turquoise sectional in front of the window. The trees outside were a series of brush-fires in different stages of containment, the infernal leaves burning bold and beautiful in hues of dirty gold, cinnamon red, and bonfire orange in the window. Filaments of the afternoon sun bled between the treetops and entered the living room window like melting copper wire. Ginger wanted to grab a piece of the windowpane at the exact spot where the sunlight was trapped like fire inside honeycomb, but she respected the two worlds that all windows separated and refracted like an ongoing conversation between space and light. Who was she to interrupt such a beautiful conversation?

Eventually, she rolled up her area rug, unrolled her yoga

mat, and played Chopin nocturnes on her Bluetooth speaker (Artur Rubinstein all the way). After she finished the Corpse Pose, she tried to exhale all the porn she'd watched earlier that morning. Inhale. Porn had become a guilty pleasure. Sometimes, Ginger had to take care of her business with Winnie's unpredictable graffiti schedule, but she noticed there was something vital missing from porn nowadays. It lacked a sense of urgency. It lacked credible female pleasure, a late-night argument as foreplay, a bloated tummy, a facial scar, the sparkling chemistry of new lovers, or the giddy exploration of the human body she loved so much. Porn lacked the innocent laughter of two people trying to figure out how their bodies fit together. It lacked the sweet kisses Winnie gave her on the neck, the lacework of their entangled desire, or the soft intensity of their slow lovemaking. Breathe. Porn in the digital realm had sped up too much, felt too degrading, and involved too much acting. It bore no relation to Ginger's own desire.

Her iPhone sang Erykah Badu's "Baby You Got Me," which was Winnie's ringtone. She reached for her phone and stretched her arms underneath the couch, her fingertips grazing the keypad. She scooted her body up the floor until she could get a grip and then pressed the talk button with her thumb.

—What's up, butterfly? Winnie said.

—Hey baby beetle, she said, inhaling.

For as long as they'd been together, Winnie and Ginger gave each other insect nicknames based on a longstanding origin story they'd made up one night while gobbling down vegetable biryani and channa masala at a restaurant on East 6th Street, high as hell and drunk as sin. According to their own creation myth, Asians and other people of color were the insects of the animal kingdom. Sure, they might seem tiny, they might seem small, they might get crushed by dumb white giants every day (their tiny exoskeletons littering the sidewalks), they might be the enemies of exterminated white spaces, and they might not be as sexy as fluorescent poisonous frogs burning the flesh of assaulters or hypnotic serpents spitting their syllables out at invaders, but insects were the hardest workers in the food chain economy and they got no credit for the shit they did. The world depended on them to survive and the world didn't even know it. If their colonies collapsed, the world died. Simple as that, ladies and gentlemen.

—Where you at? he asked.

—Chez moi, she exhaled.

—Cool. Whachew doing?

—A little tea, a little yoga.

—'Bout time you busted out that mat.

She snarled at him.

Winnie chuckled. —Listen, shorty boo, this piece of shit phone is gonna die soon.

She laughed because Winnie was a fool. He was the only person in NYC who insisted on using the same burner flip phone. Talk about NSA paranoia. —Kay, stinkbug.

—Boz and I gotta head back to Manhattanville tonight.

—Uh huh.

—No, for real.

—You be *good* Winnie Yu.

—Nah, fuck good, I want to be great.

—I'll leave some dinner for you.

—Xie xie. You a dime, Ginger.

—I love you.

—You too.

—No, *say* it.

—Ah, man.

—I'm waiting, she said, crossing her feet.

—I love you.

—Me too. Peace, baby.

—Peace.

She ended the call and glanced at her phone. The screen said:

2:43

September 25th, 2012
73° Cloudy

Ginger lay on the floor for a shameful amount of time, her body spread out and mangled like a Staten Island bike accident, her interlocked hands cradling her head. When she got up, she fine-tuned the shower to just the right temperature and stepped into the blue tiled shower. Today, her heart was beating like a blown subwoofer because it was time for goal #1,000, holler! Originally, her list was called "A 100 Good Deeds," but it had grown like a bamboo shoot since an old Turkish grandfather in Istanbul rescued her, simply because he knew what it felt like to be a stranger in Germany.

After the subway had passed 103rd Street, she unfolded her list and reread it between the wrinkles, which reminded Ginger of her nainai who shrunk slowly with age, her body whittled down into a bony microcosm of itself by the pen-blade world. Now, she looked around the subway and noticed an Asian woman sitting in her sadness. It was practically soiling her. In her mid-fifties, her face was elegant but deflated like a Filipino mask left in the sun for forty years. Her lips were wilted cherries. Her eyebrows were ellipses. She nibbled on her cuticles. Ginger wrote three inspired lines of a metta prayer on a piece of paper and then folded it into a slender rectangle. Suddenly, she was transported back to the agonies of middle school, when she used to pass notes to boys with palpitating sentence fragments, strange acronyms (SSS=sorry so short, something only girls wrote because they'd been taught to apologize for taking up other people's time), and romantic either/or fallacies like:

Do you like me?
  □ yes?
  □ no?

When Ginger stood up and walked over to the Filipino woman, Ginger saw that she was devouring her lips and staring in the window (at the passengers? At her own beautiful brown face? At the tunnel lights?). Ginger hesitated for a second. She felt suddenly invasive, misguided by her new project. Her lime green Velcro sneakers stuck to the floor, protesting. It felt like everyone on the train was watching her, but she had to be fierce (and maybe insane). She held out the folded blue note with her teenage confession scribbled like a geometry proof, her fingers shaking. The woman sitting in her sadness did what New Yorkers did so well, she pretended Ginger was transparent, waiting until Ginger stopped existing. Ginger felt erased before she could disappear. *Here*, she finally said as the subway doors opened. The woman's eyes bounced from intruder back to window like a game of handball as she ate her cuticles, seemingly in love with glass and keratin. Ginger was no match to her willful ignorance. Finally, she flung the note at the seat next to the woman, which crashed to the ground like a nosediving warplane. The woman stayed faithful to her reflection and her appetite, stuck inside the chamber of her denial. Ginger ran through the open doors and slipped between the rubber brackets at 72nd Street. Twelve minutes later, before she got psyched out, she boarded another 2 train. She noticed a Black woman in vintage jean shorts, a Dolce & Gabbana mesh sweatshirt, and a fuzzy yellow overcoat. Her frizzy hair had sections of green, blue and yellow, like frozen fireworks. The woman could have been an iridescent blowfish lost in the urban stream. When Ginger got close, the woman screamed, *I don't want none of your bullshit!* into her phone. Ginger ignored her intuition telling her that cell phones didn't work in this stretch because the woman was having a heated argument. Ginger scribbled a modest paragraph of Buddhist prayers on her Hello Kitty stationery, folded the note, this time in the shape of a flattened fortune cookie with the words *please read me* written in hasty cursive, and then walked up to her and cleared her throat. The woman looked up with a scowl burned into her face, her forehead stamped by wavy postage lines.

—This is for you, Ginger said, feeling like she was in eighth grade again when she asked Rodrigo Yamamoto out for the Tropical Paradise prom.

—Hold on a sec, the woman said, holding her phone in the air. Her eyes gleamed with soft intensity. —Whachew want?

Ginger handed her the note when she caught a glimpse of the cell phone and realized there was no backlight, no illuminated numbers. The phone was just a prop for her subway monologues.

—Bitch, I don't *know* you, she growled.

At 66th Street, the doors opened again.

Ginger placed the note on her lap.

—Getouta my fucking *face!* Get the fuck *away* from me! she screamed, swatting the note away, which wobbled to the ground like a paper football.

Ginger flew through the subway doors as if her lime green shoes had invisible wings. Standing on the Lincoln Center platform, she scratched her head with both hands. She sat down and cried, that's the truth. After Istanbul, being called a bitch by strangers hurt more than it used to because the term was loaded. She wouldn't apologize for her sensitivity. The world had made her sensitive, dammit. A Native guy in an expensive suit passed her a Kleenex, said *here*, and left without a word. *Thank you,* she said to the empty platform. Ginger finished crying, blew her nose, and stood up. When the next subway stopped at the platform, the faces of passengers bled into each other like a state fair funhouse mirror. It took her a while to shed her shame, but she did. She always did. She assembled new courage from old desire and a free Kleenex. Of course, goal #1,000 was way harder than #109 (becoming a vegetarian), #347 (sponsoring an African child), #620 (serving Thanksgiving food at a shelter for women and children), #705 (design a culture jam), or #881 (inviting a homeless woman home for Christmas). Goal #1,000 involved the possibility of public humiliation, which Ginger liked about as much as swallowing glass.

Inside the next subway, she took a deep breath and cleared her head. She observed passengers and this time, she let her intuition guide her. Instead of searching for clues of sadness or despair, she tried vibing people and then she saw it: a pregnant mamita flanked by two kids. Boricua maybe. The mom rocked a little girl back and forth in a plastic pink stroller. She wore a stained T-shirt that said *Daddy's Girl.* The second kid was pouting, punching the metal pole with his little fists. The young mamita told him to stop. The little boy paused, looked around for a response, and punched the pole again. The young mom squeezed his fat little leg. He fidgeted, hitting the pole with his palm a third time. She raised her voice at him, scolding him in short bursts of trilling Spanish. Ginger wrote her metta prayers in one continuous stream of affection and love on blue paper. She folded the third note into another rectangle and got up. Once she was standing next to them, the boy looked up at her suspiciously, the girl in the pink T-shirt closed her eyes, and the mamita turned her head. Ginger noticed razor-thin eyebrows that resembled microns, turning the Latina's eyes into long vowels. Her soft, delicate features and angular eyebrows were framed in a soft layer of sepia with an elegant outline of pink lips and thoughtfully sculpted hair that curved into an elegant percentage sign at the temple. The lighting inside the subway was perfect for her self-portrait. In that moment, she looked gorgeous to Ginger, a mom in love with the pain and the struggle of motherhood, even the grimy part she couldn't handle. She placed the note in the woman's open palm and walked away. The little boy looked at Ginger confused when she jumped off at Columbus Circle. Halfway to the staircase, the subway began crawling. Ginger was in full stride when she noticed the glowing mamita staring at her for a perfect second from the other side of the train. Her palm was placed on the glass. She held the boy in her arms and mouthed something to her, something that penetrated window and defied glass. For one single moment, the women saw each other on the inside, not as the world saw them, but as they saw themselves before the violence of the translation. They were women who imagined and hoped and fought and felt and analyzed and worried and feared and loved their way to this moment. They were their own witnesses. They held their heads up and kept going, even when it hurt to be in love, even when the world hated them for their happiness. The train became a wet blur, a snapshot framed in slow shutter speeds. Ginger walked up the staircase to the food-stained streets, wiping the crystalized tears from her eyes and swallowing the beautiful noise in her chest.

5. BLANK SHEET OF PAPER

WINNIE WAS ALL ABOUT pushing the limits of political graffiti, especially when it came to pushing back against corporate greed, police brutality, institutional racism, and white nationalism, but tagging a tombstone was straight up wrong unless it was Hitler's. For Winnie, there were rules to graffiti:

1. You don't tag tombstones. Oscar Wilde's grave has lipstick marks, not some stock AT. All heavyweight graphies know you don't dishonor the dead with your author tag.

2. You should critique the fuck out of cultural brainwash—not to be confused with that French toy who shadowed Banksy like an epigone bitch—and provoke introspection, and elevate the mental in your graphic reality, but you don't disrespect our shared humanity.

3. You always punch up, you always wear a ring, and you always leave a bruise.

—Yo, you believe this shit? Winnie asked, pointing to the tag.

—Saddest thing I've ever seen.

—Definitely a toy, Winnie muttered.

—Most def, M-Boz grunted.

It was early evening. The lingering September heat had finally buried its head into the concrete like a celestial tick. Winnie and M-Boz scrambled through Trinity Cemetery on 155th street towards the Double H P, which was a paradise of virgin billboards and whitewashed subway tunnels as if Manhattanville were stuck in cultural amnesia. It was a brave new world for culture jammers. Winnie was pumped that they'd finally made it to this all-white Apple billboard after vowing to critique the human rights abuses of the IT sector. They knew it would be easy to jam and hard to cover up. Winnie was feeling this moment big time.

Winnie's grandparents came to America in 1966 with $57.45 worth of Yuan tied into little stacks with silk handkerchiefs. It looked like Monopoly money to the American eye. They brought two musty old suitcases, a cookie tin of Wenshan Baozhong, Taiping Monkey King, and White Hair Peony tea, and a list of English words written in phonetic Mandarin. They promised their family that the first thing they'd do after passing through customs in San Francisco and making the great trek to Penn Station was find their neighbor from Guangzhou, some dude they'd been wiring money to each month to set up an apartment for their new life in America. When they finally made it to the city, however, they discovered that Mr. Deng Xi had vanished like a ninja smoke bomb. The neighbors in the building he supposedly lived in had never heard of him before. Ask the cobbler, they said, he knows everyone. His grandparents looked down at their shoes and walked away, their soft landing into America gone like a lipstick mark on a button-down collar that was washed, scrubbed, and steamed away at the dry cleaners.

Every time Winnie was about to do a major burner, he got this moment of intense euphoria. He wanted New Yorkers to taste his free sample, which would be both a beautification project and a drive-by curation of color in the republic of gray squares. His culture jamming was the one good thing he could give them. Art had become a class performance for the bourgeoisie, a class marker for large Japanese corporations, Upper East Side soirées, SoHo studios, and undergraduate lecture halls. The instant you made art accessible and free to everyone, art lost its value according to the gatekeepers because "real" art required private property and economic rent, something artists never had, something they never got, but this throw-up they were working on right now would settle the score for a couple days and then some, which almost felt enough for Winnie.

After his zu had started a new life in the Land of Ghosts, they were mad ashamed at how poor they were. In their old neighborhood in Guangzhou where they'd met as teenagers after their families relocated from Hong Kong and Taiwan to the mainland, everyone lived in a continuum of brokenness, but in America, some white people suffocated in obscene wealth while everybody else lived in counterfactual daydreams and invented genealogies. Everyone seemed to be waiting for their first big break here, waiting to win the Mega Class Lotto or score a job promotion or stumble upon a duffel bag crammed with narcodollars, their minds always window-shopping a better life, always imagining an alternate universe borrowed from window displays, glib TV commercials, and billboards larger than entire buildings. Work was the skeleton key to unlocking inequality, everyone knew that. Winnie's grandparents vowed not to write back home until they had their own crib, until they'd walked through The Great Mirage, until the price of stamps was lower than rice. It was years before they wrote their first letter to their parents in Guangzhou and their cousins on the islands. Back then, NYC was a bold and sometimes discordant symphony of immigration. It was a time when Uptown yang guizi took the subway to Chinatown to watch the pandas in their invisible cages, eating bamboo shoots in restaurant windows, and sipping the dirtiest water in the city (and all New York water was dirty). That wasn't the reason, though, his grandparents never went out.

The problem for Winnie was that beauty had become the prerogative of museums, advertising firms, social media posts, and marketing campaigns, not the by-product of spiritual aspiration. Beauty was no longer a trait, it was cultural capital that people purchased and that companies owned, controlling our attention span every millisecond, muscling social structures, bullying public space, and injecting brains with mutating images of artificial lifestyles, appropriated style, anglonormative beauty, and rented bodies of color. New Yorkers weren't shareholders of the cityscape. They couldn't hoist their own signs in Times Square or change the graphic reality in the subway because corporations owned public space now. They implanted feelings of envy and deformity, self-judgment and inadequacy in order to weaponize social inferiority. As Winnie had argued in his MA thesis in social ecology, advertisements were cultural midwives delivering embryonic appetites for consumer identities. They blurred the lines between desire, necessity, and social imprinting until any fool with heat was willing to cap a hapless bystander, just to avoid drowning in class resentment. Winnie's culture jamming was first and foremost, an attempt to monkeywrench both the marketing firms working for multinational corporations and also the machinery of market capitalism itself.When his zu moved into their first apartment four blocks from the Confucius Plaza, it was right above The Golden Temple restaurant and massage parlor. There were cockroaches and ants, a broken kitchen sink, and no happy endings, but they didn't care. His grandparents laid out pieces of day-old bread dipped in honey and meadow saffron. The bugs died with X's for eyes and his grandparents washed their dishes in the bathtub. When you were poor AF, to dream was to innovate. That's what Winnie's mama always said.

Because city life meant muggings and high-rises, turf wars and bull markets, poverty and glitz, roaches and models, low-end players and ostentatious high rollers, identity flare-ups and class contempt, New Yorkers fought for the American markers of prosperity. They wanted the lifestyle that billboards invented, they wanted their own false idols delivered to them in cardboard boxes, they wanted props for an imaginary world that felt more real than the one they toiled in, a life supposedly at their beck and call that kept slipping through calloused fingers. The good life was viscous, aromatic, and slippery like papaya shavings.

Winnie's yeye used to sneak into NYU lectures just because he could. He had no idea what the fuck was going on because his English was sketchy. After he'd returned home, Nainai would ask him what he learned and he'd say shit like, *Oh, so much I don't even know where to start.* She'd raise an eyebrow to say, *As if, mofo* and then they'd eat rice, expired tuna fish, and spicy douchi sauce in front of the stove, huddling together to defy the winter draft that was always recruiting poor immigrants for the common graves.

Winnie felt like he created something beautiful *within* a community with graffiti, like he gave the crayon box back to the barrio where art came from. Poverty was its own palette and he used it to paint and reclaim art from the studio gallery. Most of the people he knew were pervious to marketing, their broken hearts wheezing in gray slabs of prison concrete surrounded by littered streets and police strobes. Winnie's Buddha Maos were a visual counternarrative to billboards, his very own act of public resistance to corporations. Whatever Giuliani declared, graffiti was a silent and decentralized riot for Winnie. It was the taking back of public space, a permanent street revolution of visual culture, and the graphic reinvention of reality. Graffiti was the creation of a new class iconography, giving down-and-out people the power to decide how they depicted themselves and how the world saw them, reifying non-white space to contest cultural occupation and provide testimony for injustice, street poetics, and visual activism. Graffiti was the celebration of class struggle and the redefinition of selfhood outside the semantics of consumption. In his graffiti, Winnie thanked New York for its bustling multiculturalism, its language of dreaming, and its bold experiment of racial reimagining. In every jam, he strove to create his own visual language that could stand tall and glow like a benign plutonium mountain. As an alphabet of resistance, Winnie used graffiti to (re)create visual narratives that picketed this marauding empire, turning advertisements against themselves one block at a time. It was the way he could mute, tag, and mock every CEO. At least, that's what he planned on telling *Adbusters* for his upcoming interview.

Winnie's yeye learned English from a Chinese dude who only half-spoke it, interjecting his Wu, Mandarin, and fakeass English into his lesson. That's why Winnie's grandfather spoke English like a kid Hooked on Phonics, pounding out each syllable like he couldn't hear his own voice. Sometimes, when he was lucky, he learned a real word that tough Uptowners understood like "thank you" or "I need water," but he still said "hell . . . ohh!" to strangers until the day he passed to the spirit world. Most of the time, Winnie's yeye just made shit up, creating a language that only made sense to bilingual Chinese immigrants whose first language was Wu. He became the first revolutionary in Winnie's American fam to stretch, create, and sabotage words that didn't exist exclusively in American or Chinese culture.

M-Boz cocked his head up and clicked his mouth. —Hit me up, kid.

—Black Panther? Winnie asked.

—Nah. Just the Valentine Red and that Orange Crush you were using.

—Here, Winnie said, throwing him the spray paint, but diet the orange. It's all we got.

—For real? M-Boz asked.

Winnie nodded sadly, like he just realized he'd made a miscalculation of color.

—How you feel about a fade out around the legs? M-Boz asked.

—To what? Winnie asked.

—How about that Some Kinda Blue we swiped today?

—For background?

M-Boz nodded.

—Cool, Winnie said.

—Bust it out, baby.

Winnie tossed him the new can. M-Boz caught it like a veteran tight end. Inside Winnie's head, the crowd went wild.

Yeye's tutor was fronting like some egg-headed punk to get some cash money, but his gramps didn't care. He paid that dude every week religiously just because his face reminded him of his sepia toned hamlet where he'd lived with his family in Taipei, the former Japanese colonial city, then Fuzhou, and finally Guangzhou when the Great Leap Forward starved tens of millions of peasants and turned herbalists and yam farmers into industrial steel workers overnight. Before rakes, furnace pieces, and kitchen knives were melted down into scrap metal and everyone joined a commune or migrated to the mainland or moved to the nearest city in search of cooking oil. His yeye was like that, wasting his time to protect a fuzzy memory of the homeland that was unfaithful, impossible, and dangerous like a dull scalpel.

Graphies helped communities of color reclaim their artistic self-worth from the cocaine-encrusted countertops of SoHo loft apartments and the stagnant vaults of Hudson Yard boutiques. When all the toys were taking notes about Winnie's army of Buddha Maos, he and M-Boz would already have gotten ghost, planning their next installation, hawking the next untouched surface, and locating the next dollar-store throw-up to challenge. For this particular joint, Winnie and Boz had to climb up an apartment building fire escape and then long jump from the roof to the billboard ladder. It was some acrobatic shit Winnie definitely wasn't ready for. In fact, he almost missed the ladder, banging his wrist against the rungs before he finally got a grip. The eighteen-wheelers on the Henry Hudson looked like windup model trucks to Winnie and the humid and cool evening smelled like the cardiomyopathy of blighted diesel engines and run-down pickup trucks as they cut through the night, their metal bodies slicing the congested air like swinging cleavers, the kind Winnie's parents used to decapitate ducks with.

For a long time, his yeye did odd jobs like shining shoes on Canal Street and mopping trattoria floors in Little Italy, making dead surfaces shiny again like freshly oiled woks. He even worked at a Chinese apothecary that sold traditional—and supposedly legal—Chinese tinctures from tiger flesh and Yin Qiao San. He helped a friend unload chickens from a rusted pick-up truck that came from some house on the prairie in Pennsylvania. He even tried selling H-69 vacuums to his neighbors, but no one could afford them. Besides, sponges were cheap and a broom could be used to hit children, especially the ones that cried too much or looked elders in the eyes. As far as Winnie was concerned, Chinese immigrants invented the daily grind in the city.

The height and the vulnerability of this culture jam was starting to take its toll on Winnie and M-Boz, who both felt light-headed after going at it for hours. They'd run out of snacks, their blood sugar was low, and their adrenaline had peaked. They took turns wiping their foreheads with Chinese silk handkerchiefs, sipping water from thermoses, and looking down on the busy highway with a nervous gulp.

—Gēmen, your sky's looking dope as fuck, Winnie said, wiping his forehead with the back of his hand. —You gonna make my Buddha Mao look tighter than Bruce.

—Xie xie, M-Boz said.

Winnie nodded back.

—You know, Winn?

—Whaddup?

—It feels good, what we do. I feel bent, you know?

Winnie pivoted one of the floodlights toward him.

M-Boz waved his hand behind his head.

—This is how I look at it, Winnie said, art is the greatest pheromone because beauty is the most dangerous and elusive thing of all.

Before Boz could respond, Winnie's burner vibrated in his pants pocket. He knew it was Ginger. He could tell she was worried but he couldn't answer. It was a rule: he never talked to her until he was done with his throw-up. He was crazy superstitious like that. Fortunately, she never called twice because she knew what's up. Winnie only had to look down to know that speed was for highways and bodies never bounced back from their hubris.

Winnie's nainai got lost in New York's multicultural fever dream where ethnic Chinese faces passed her dressed in the visual vocabulary of the American upper-class: consignment tweed coats and earth tone turtlenecks, shapeless drop dresses with contrast-collars, tennis V-necks and polo shirts, Jackie O pillbox hats, khaki bush jackets, and baby dolls in matching Mary Janes. New York was an exquisite corpse for Chinese faces, their outfits changing radically with a flick of the wrist. Winnie's nainai found Midtown bewildering, Wall Street cold and hostile, and the Lower East Side and Riverdale inauspicious after getting mugged once in each neighborhood. Eventually, Chinatown became the only place where she felt safe, the only enclave where people reminded her of her legible past. She stayed inside the half-furnished apartment like an agoraphobe choking on space. The air was different here, she'd written back home. It didn't smell like Kowloon. It was dirty and insoluble. Her impeccable Hong Kong City accent (where she'd studied to be an artist and had learned seven types of calligraphy as a teenager, one for each day of the week) was treated with indifference in New York where Taiwanese, Southern Min, Fujian, and Wu were spoken without apology or explanation.

For Winnie, every installation was different. Sometimes, his Buddha Mao had parachute pants and glam specks, winking playfully or laughing like a badass, ready to airbrush insurrections from the scrapbooks of history. Sometimes, he gave the Buddha Mao a hint of a goatee, a couple of moles, a bruised cheekbone, a spliff dangling from his mouth, or a gold tooth à la ODB. Other times, the Buddha Mao looked like he was in a Broadway musical, a streetwear campaign, or a hip-hop video, surrounded by Asian American poets, Latino activists, Black MCs, Native artists, NYC ballers, and punk-rock ballerinas. But each Buddha Mao had his trademark brand: the face of a mischievous Buddha, a Yankees cap spun at an angle like the earth's axis, fingers peacing out, a quote from the Little Red Book, and his very own AT. That'd been his trademark since forever and he didn't even like (what) Mao (did to his own people).

Winnie's grandparents were legit shocked at how disrespectful Chinese Americans kids were. They had no respect for their elders, even the ones that had crossed the international timeline. These little Chinese American punks didn't greet his nainai or help her with her groceries as she passed, a wicker basket wobbling in her transparent arms. She left home only to go to the market on Mott Street or to bring her husband his lunch. Other than that, she felt chained to the kitchen table like a guard dog protecting its poverty. There she prepared rice dishes in Taro leaves. Whenever Yeye brought home three quarters, she made noodles with pork and vegetables, both of them scarfing down their food until their bodies stopped pulsating from the hunger.

Graffiti was Winnie's bloodless Cultural Revolution. He got crazy shout-outs from Staten Island to Co-op City, from Forest Hills to Hell's Kitchen. New Yorkers had an eye for controversy, culture, and politics, and they loved it when jammers busted out cold design behind the backs of corporations. Culture jamming was a decentralized campaign of political resistance and one of Winnie's strengths was that he knew how to infiltrate social, corporate, and print media sources incognito. Even more importantly, he could pop his shit up faster than the Jakes could tear it down.

His nainai used to write graceful letters of false consolation and irrevocable despair to her three cousins in Victoria, the former British capital, and Guangzhou, each of them now married with sovereign families of their own to care for. While Yeye had traipsed from Little Italy to the Lower East Side doing odd jobs for pennies, Grandma became an avid arranger of flowers, composing delicate gushi of stems and petals that gave resonance and brightness to an empty kitchen with bare plaster walls. She was the first writer, revolutionary, and graphie in the Yu family in America. She was also the first of many women to barricade her husband from the lanterns of Midtown and the jì nǚ (妓女) of Lexington Avenue where other Chinese families were destroyed and men rejuvenated and made penniless out of lust and for everything they couldn't have.

This Buddha Mao was one of Winnie's faves. It had all the standard qualities of his copyright, but M-Boz did such a tight background that the burner looked fucking sick. It just lunged out at you like a bulldog high on gunpowder. The Manhattan-ville Buddha Mao winked at passing cars like a shyster as he did a badass flying kick through the air, aimed at a group of bankers with demonic robot eyes all dressed in SWAT gear. In the distance, Winnie painted a dove hovering above two squad cars with a sheet of blank paper tied to its little ankle that read:

Poverty gives rise to the desire for revolution. On a blank sheet of paper, the freshest and most beautiful characters can be written, the freshest and most beautiful pictures can be painted.

—Mao Tse-Tung, The Little Red Book

Their burner was tight as shit, the product of hours of artistic collaboration, but after Winnie looked at his watch again, he lost it. —Boz, I'm bugging out, man.

M-Boz nodded and tossed the remaining spray cans into his backpack and then threw it on. They climbed down the ladder, attached the snap link, and then rappelled the climbing rope until they hit the ground like some black ops shit. For just one brief moment, they felt unknown and unseen. It was the only time they craved invisibility. But thirty seconds later, a police cruiser was nipping at their heals, its flashing lights drowning the pavement in a dizzy strobe. Winnie and M-Boz raced down a narrow alley, sprinting their asses to 157th Street where the subway stairs in the distance disappeared into the underworld and Charon was a subway turnstile. A few gurp peeps walked up the staircase, scowled, and covered their eyes, dazed by the blinding high beams of the approaching cruiser. Winnie and M-Boz's kicks were gliding above the ground like a backwards can-can as the blue and reds chased them down the street and smashed into a rotting trash can. Their only goal at that point was losing the alphabet bois, so Winnie and M-Boz ran for their fucking lives down the staircase and over the turnstile, the air exploding through their nostrils like old racing horses fleeing the needle.

6. JUST NIBBLE THE MOON CAKE & SHUT THE HELL UP

GINGER USED TO THINK Winnie was way too young to have old-man rituals, but the longer they were together, the more she understood the importance of protecting something stable and familiar in a life of endless change and betrayal. It made Winn incredibly happy and one smoke a day wasn't gonna kill him. Outside on his stoop, Winnie sat on the second step, his legs crossed half-lotus style, leaning back on his elbows. He held Ginger's hand softly with tenderness she found reassuring after her near-death experience with the falling safe. Ginger was full of baked tofu, joy, and harmony as they watched the transformation of the gold leaf sky as it slowly contused into the evening.

Winnie kissed her one last time and disappeared. He said he'd be back soon but Ginger knew he was going to the bodega where he'd work until his depression-binging shūshu showed up. If he showed up. Sometimes it took his uncle an hour to get his shit together. Sometimes, it took a month, especially when he felt particularly guilty about his brother's death, which he told himself he could have prevented if he'd just showed up to the bodega on time, something he'd never done since it opened. Other times, Winnie escaped into his bedroom to make stencils on his architect desk for future jams or he invented new tags or he snuck into their living room and played *Final Fantasy XIII* on his PS3 or he went into the kitchen and read books on social ecology, the prison industrial complex, visual culture, and relativity that made his head spin. Ginger remained on the stoop and sighed. The weather was finally calming down. She was full, sleepy, and in love with the evening. She felt blessed to be alive, as idiotic as that sounded inside her New Yorker head. She could have been a starfish on the ocean floor, soaking up the desperate rays from the dying sunlight.

As Ginger was about to get up, she heard tables screeching and dishes shattering in one of the apartments above. Had to be the Kwan Drama. Ever since they'd moved in, it'd become the *Barons of Shanghai*. Not the original Cantonese version either, which was crazy vulgar, but the badly dubbed Mandarin version. She could make out a few words through the buzz of air conditioners, Chinese game shows, and NFL announcers. She'd learned from Winnie's family words like *tao jiang hu* and the Cantonese word for *lazy ass* and *disgrace* and *idiot*. Or was it ugly? Cantonese insults could make a smashed Irish shoreman blush and Mrs. Li was the worst. She spat poison darts at her husband upstairs. Winnie said Mrs. Li screamed at the top of her lungs. Sometimes, she even threw stuff at her husband: cheap plastic dishes (from China, no less), musty, old books from Salvation Army bins, misshapen shoes that didn't fit her Asian feet, plastic kids chopsticks, cans of expired jackfruit (and how the hell did jackfruit go bad?), basically whatever was lying around. Ginger sat up and cocked her head to the side but couldn't hear them anymore. Truth was, she didn't want to listen anyway.

Ginger grabbed her beat-up, crimson Goyard tote she'd splurged on for her thirtieth birthday and slung it over her shoulder when she heard little footsteps coming down the staircase like one of those radio dramas she heard as a kid. Mr. Li walked through the front door in his slippers and looked around. When he saw her, he attempted to smile, but the pretense seemed too painful for him.

—Ni hai hao ba? she asked in her 16-year-old Mandarin.

He nodded, putting his hands in the pockets of his cardigan. Ginger looked at him and felt conflicted. He was such a gentle old man, definitely not the type of person you'd expect to break up a fight in the subway or play a guqin on the scorching subway platform for twelve straight hours. He looked demoralized now and she didn't know what to do.

—I think it's finally cooling down, she said in English to break the silence.

He nodded again, looking up at the sky that she and Winnie had admired only ten minutes ago, now welted with hues of indigo and blood orange. She knew that as a younger Asian woman, she should follow hierarchy and defer, offering her seat or disappearing so he could have the night all to himself, but the bicultural American in her wanted to understand him. Like all mixed-race people she'd met along the way, she wanted to hear Mr. Li's story. As a hapa woman living in America, stories were sometimes the only thing she had that connected her to the motherland.

—You wanna sit down? she asked in Mandarin, you can take the next step.

He shook his head and kept looking up at the skin-damaged skyline. Ginger wondered if he saw something she didn't, something that wasn't there or something only he could see. Sometimes, your pain was a radar for lost objects and sometimes you were the only person who saw what you saw because you were the only one looking for it.

—Mr. Li, Ginger said at last, please sit down. You're making me nervous.

He looked down at her and smiled faintly. It was the saddest smile she'd ever seen. The kind of smile you gave as ransom.

Kwan Li sat in the middle of the stairs, one step below her, something she knew would never have happened on the mainland.

They stayed there for a good twenty minutes in awkward silence. An occasional car whizzed by them, hip-hop bass vibrating its windows. A few tenants in their building greeted them as they squeezed their bodies up the stoop and through the front door, but the two of them sat there in silence, sucking on the gradient darkness like a fat tin of lavender pastilles.

—Are you a student? he asked out of the blue.

She shook her head. —Graphic designer, part-time idealist, and bad feminist, she said.

—So, you're an artist.

She laughed. —I guess so.

—That's good. Art is spiritual food.

—Huh?

—*Book of Odes.*

—You can read that stuff?

—Shi.

—That's impressive. Ginger didn't have the knowledge of Chinese characters to read anything, not even a coupon written in simplified Chinese.

—That was my life once.

—I see.

—I was a professor.

—Are you teaching here? Ginger already knew the answer, but her question was mortar for him to build back his dignity brick by brick. She knew that Kwan Li played in the subway platform every single day, even on holidays. Every time she ran into the old man, Kwan Li always smiled at her without looking as if he could sense her presence but couldn't afford her pity. As if by not looking at the people who knew him on the platform, Mr. Li shielded himself from the hailstorm of his own poverty he was constantly seeking refuge from.

—No, he said, my English is pathetic. I sound like a stuttering child.

—It's humbling to lose your fluency, she said.

—Embarrassing too.

—Yeah, I know what you mean. My Mandarin sucks.

He nodded, smiling.

Ginger knew that his lack of contradiction only confirmed it. —But you know what? It's like that saying: Don't eat the whole moon cake, just nibble at it until it makes you sick.

He chuckled. —I've never heard that before.

—I think it's a Taiwanese expression, though I don't know how to say it in Taiwanese.

Mr. Li nodded before looking up at the sky again. Ginger wondered if the invisible stars grounded the old man or disoriented him from everything he used to know before he left China. Whenever she felt lost, Ginger found herself searching the sky for stars she could never see. But now she wondered why she still had so much faith in those celestial bodies when none of her dreams had ever come true. Well, except falling in love. What had the stars ever given her anyway? Why did everyone assume they sparkled for this smashed-up, curb-stomped planet? What if stars were just the souls of dead planets? What if she and Winnie became stars after they died and no one saw them because of New York's pollution? God, her thoughts could turn dark quickly, especially with all the fertility tests looming over her.

A window screeched open above their heads. —Where ARE you? a woman's voice shouted.

The skin on Mr. Li's face tightened into a canvas. His eyes were downcast now, heavy with shame but also a determination to hide it.

—Are you . . . looking for Mr. Li? Ginger asked in stuttering Mandarin.

—Yeah, Mrs. Li grunted, where is that pok gai?

—He left, Ginger said in English, maybe he went for a walk.

—He doesn't go on walks, Mrs. Li cursed, her voice drenched in contempt.

Ginger tapped her feet.

Kwan Li looked sideways.

—Well, Ginger continued, I don't know what to tell you, but he left a while ago.

The window slammed shut, echoing above their heads.

Mr. Li shook his head and stood up. —Thank you, he said, I needed someone else's voice inside my head for a little while.

—You're welcome, Ginger said.

—I should go now.

Ginger felt a cloud of desolation pass through her. She couldn't imagine living with someone who loathed her. She thought of the hopelessness, panic, and self-hatred he must feel every day of his life. She stood up. —You know, Mr. Li, it's wrong of me to say this, but you don't deserve to be treated that way.

—I married her, so the mistake is mine.

—I understand, but that doesn't mean you deserve to be treated like shit. I think you're a kind person and a talented musician, so if you ever need anything . . .

He nodded with a pensive look in his eyes.

—Just let me know if I can help you. That's all I'm trying to say.

—Xie xie.

—Good night, she said in English.

—Goo nigh, he echoed. He paused, and then shook her hand before walking through the front door. She waited until his shoes stopped dragging up the staircase and then walked to East Broadway where she knew there would be lights and people and the smell of fried noodles, fermented douchi, garlic, vinegar, and flaming woks, just as summer was singing the last notes of her swan song.

7. DANGLING PARTICIPLES

Ginger volunteered at PS 47 as an art teacher's assistant. In her spare time, she did a lot of random things during dead hours like paint portraits of psychedelic butterflies, do yoga in the nude, read books on deep ecology and the collapse of late-stage capitalism, and take pics of Winnie's Buddha Maos whenever she stumbled on a new one. Mostly, though, she enjoyed the perks and the heartaches of the freelancer's credo, which allowed her to do what really mattered to her: seeing art reborn and recultivated in her students, holding hands with Winnie, getting lost in MOMA, finishing her list of good deeds, traveling to new countries, and spending time in her gloriously fractal city.

Today, the kids were fingerpainting family portraits with earth tone smudges. Some made their moms really fat and angelic or gave them a third leg or a macaroni wig. Others painted their siblings with gingerbread legs, balloon arms, Robert Crumb asses, or volcanic zits gushing with blood and bacteria. Ginger pretended everything was a pocket. It was just easier that way. The alarming thing about childhood art was the way kids expressed their suffering so clearly in the clumsy fluorescent lighting of their own lives. Ginger saw drawings of fathers clubbing their kids with cutting boards, cousins handcuffing neighbors with telephone receivers, teenage girls stabbing each other with freakishly long fingernail shivs, boys nailing wooden pegs into the wrists of Dracula figures that looked like incarcerated older brothers, saint portraits of Nintendo characters, superhero pugs, and J-Lo analogues, girls reinventing their tíos as cholo Christ figures, boys redrawing the carcasses of alcoholic stepdads with a halo of robot flies. That's what Ginger found so beautiful and tragic and moving about her students, they didn't know how to cover up their feelings. They were what they felt.

As Ginger made the rounds around the classroom, Angie waved at her. The little girl was dressed in boyfriend jeans, a tank top, and a flat top.

—Ms. Lin?

—What's up, girl?

—When is Winnie coming back?

—I dunno, sweetie.

—Are you too, you know, like still together?

—Of course. He's my boo.

—Um, do you love him?

—Yup, Ginger said, chuckling.

—Then why don't you marry him?

—I might someday, but marriage isn't the only way to love someone, you know. Honestly, sometimes marriage is just an ugly catsuit shipped to you in the wrong size.

Angie looked confused, then concerned, and finally skeptical.

Ginger rubbed the girl's head softly. Every time Angie asked about Winnie, she told him his girlfriend missed him and then he said, *which one*, and Ginger would bite him real hard on the bicep until he shouted.

At the Westerly Market, she picked up marinated seitan, a bag of organic carrots, a bundle of celery, two heads of garlic, a small forest of broccoli, and some porn star zucchini for dinner along with peanut butter cookies. Ginger hopped on the Q to Chinatown until she got to the Bowery, her grocery bags getting heavier after every block. She stopped to take a break before pushing herself a few more blocks. Once she was close to the stoop, she noticed Winnie on the rooftop screaming at the top of his lungs. They'd been together for twelve years now and she'd never heard him yell like this before, not once, but his voice was all falsetto now like a Vienna Boys Choir solo as he waved his hands furiously to the side like an umpire. *Foul Ball*, his hands said emphatically. That's when she spotted a large metal object spiraling from the sky in slow motion like a cartoon anvil, the classic object of comic relief and sanctioned violence that was always a split second behind the Road Runner. Winnie was telling her in his primitive sign language to get the fuck out of the way because that large black metal object was plummeting towards her little hapa face. She had to make a decision right there and then about her own existence, whether she wanted to exist, whether she thought her existence mattered, whether she should fight for her life before she was crushed into Asian sponge cake. For a split second, she considered giving up. Life had damaged her so bad and yet she kept finding new reasons to love it all over again, which she hated about herself.

But that large metal object spiraling from the sky wasn't a cartoon anvil because those things didn't kill people, they just caused red mountainous bumps and a tiara of circling stars. Cartoon injuries were cute and short-lived, they healed quickly, and always made children laugh hysterically because violence was so deeply American, both as comedy and tragedy. But Ginger saw what she saw, her whole life flashing before her eyes like a million-dollar K-drama. Ginger had always thought that humans had primordial firmware that kept them alive in life-or-death situations, but the truth was she just froze when she saw that thing falling from the sky. She closed her damn eyes as one of her grocery bags got ripped out of her hand, followed by a series of tiny wet explosions on her face that felt dense and gooey like a tired Nickelodeon trope.

The front door of Winnie's apartment slammed open. When Ginger opened her eyes, she saw:

1. Winnie running down the stoop
2. Winnie's neighbors all peeking their heads through their windows

And then she saw that:

1. The huge black metallic thing was six inches away from her.
2. The huge black metallic thing had crushed most of her groceries.
3. Chunks of zucchini, celery, and hummus covered her face and arms.
4. The black metallic box was the same goddamn safe Winnie had been trying to blow up with dynamite or puncture with high-tech drills since his ba passed away.

Safe crêpe. What an embarrassing way to die! For Ginger, that was right up there with impaling yourself on a plunger or getting electrocuted while having sex with a vacuum cleaner. Death was supposed to be tragic, but if your death was comic relief, then your life became a travesty. It wasn't death exactly that Ginger was afraid of, so much as it was the dishonor of dying without significance, the burning shame of her mom thinking her life had been pointless every time someone asked how her mixed-race daughter died. Ginger thought, *Let me die helping to smuggle HIV drugs across the border for old people, let me die teaching orphans how to weave baskets so they could sell them in the Fair-Trade Market to guilty West Coast philanthropists and white liberals, let me die protecting an old woman from a purse thief or saving the environment from Monsanto Round Up or protecting polar bears from global warming, let me die in any way besides a cartoon death. And if my boyfriend had to kill me (and WHY DID HE HAVE TO KILL ME?), let it be with dignity and devotion. Let it be a bold gesture of love for the whole wide world to witness and record and create memes out of once I'm gone.*

Winnie ran over to her and wrapped his arms around her waist.

—Ginger Lin, oh my fucking God!

She blinked hard.

Winnie hugged her tight enough to squeeze the air out of her lungs. She could feel his body heat through her wet clothes. She could smell his sweat, Chanel Bleu, and ramen through his T-shirt. Winnie smelled like home, like a place big enough for her to stretch out into herself.

—Honey. Baby. Ginger.

—Winnie *Yu*, she said in her best teacher's tone, what the hell, boy?

—I know, that was wack.

—Yes, it was.

—That was totally my bad. I didn't see you. I thought—

—You crushed my groceries.

—I know, I—

—Is *this* how you get out of eating vegan food? Are you protesting my stir-fry?

He snickered. —*No.* That shit's funny though.

—You almost killed me. Is *that* funny?

—Come on girl, you *know* that's not what I meant.

—I'm really pissed at you right now! she shouted, wiping the liquefied zucchini from her eyebrows. —Maybe I should go home. She clawed the veggie sludge out of her hair and sighed.

—Boo, I'm *so* sorry. He tried kissing her.

—Don't *touch* me, she snapped, one hand pointing at him in anger, the other clearing the mush from her cheeks.

—Ginger. Butterfly. I'm so sorry.

Winnie kept his distance but smiled secretly to himself because he loved it when Ginger got angry, which, of course, only made her angrier.

Winnie stayed where he was with his mouth stitched shut while Ginger pointed at him accusingly, shaking her head and zipping his mouth shut every time he tried to open it and carbon copy his apology. She made him stand there, hugging himself for five whole minutes until her heart thawed. It was the first time she'd punished him in public before and she really enjoyed it, almost too much. She apologized for nothing.

Eventually, Ginger calmed down, but on her own schedule and in her own way. Winnie carried her squashed groceries into the kitchen and then he kissed her real sweet all over her face, temples, and eyes because he knew her sweet spots. It was like his lips operated on some mysterious point system. He kissed her nose and flushed cheeks. His lips incinerated her neck with silent and soft intensity. He knew how to raise her pulse and then console her troubled soul with the same pair of lips, opening her up like a bottle of Bully Hill. Ginger found it kinda infuriating, but comforting too because it proved he knew her, understood and valued her emotions, and respected her needs and saw them as clearly as highway flares. Sometimes, she wished she didn't know how to forgive him, but she's not spiteful. Besides, she knew that holding on to her fire for too long always consumed her from the inside out until both the fire and the receptacle were annihilated. After ten minutes of ridiculous semi-sweetness, she was as good as uncorked. Sometimes, love was a serendipitous, volatile, and fragile thing for her. There were worst things to discover in your thirties, frankly.

Every time Winnie tagged some prize building or painted a new Buddha Mao, every time he got chased by the alphabet bois or walked out of a street fight without a scratch or swiped new spray paint from factories, Winnie loved her just a little bit more because he'd had to fight the world just to look into her eyes again, each time with a little more urgency and humility. Of course, part of her wanted to resist Winnie's newfound love, but being reminded of her mortality turned her on. Maybe, she was fucked up that way. Maybe, she'd had bad role models growing up on a steady diet of Whitney, Michael, Nirvana, and 10,000 Maniacs, but the arousal from her own survival and the risk of permanent loss made her see Winnie clearly. It helped clarify the meaning of everything she felt in this morally shattered world and everyone she needed in this miniscule life for it to have meaning. For Ginger, love was always the amnesia of time/space and the erasure of the ego, always the renunciation of selfishness and the intrepid long jump over the downed power line. Ginger didn't give two fucks about what the rules were, because she'd been hurt bad and cheated on enough to know the sanctity of love when she stumbled upon it, and no person, no man had ever made her cry the way Winnie did just by seeing her soul every day. No person, no man understood the conflict she'd felt as a hapa woman pulled between two impossible worlds wanting to claim, qualify, erase, and exclude her. You're not Asian, you're not white, you're a fake Asian, that's really your mom? No man, no person understood the never-ending fragmentation Ginger felt inside because she grew up in racial limbo without a dad or a direct link to her Asian genealogy or a story of passage or a lineage to persecuted boat people or an immigrant narrative she could whip out every time someone told an endearing Asian mom story she pretended to understand. And no person, no man knew how to transform and refract their life in their art in a way that made her feel like she belonged, even in an alternate world. Ginger had learned how to construct a space in their relationship where she could create an entire galaxy for herself that she didn't have to share with anyone, not even him.

After they'd kissed right there in front of everyone, Ginger realized how turned on she was by her near-death experience. She wanted to go inside and make love right now, so she pulled Winnie up the stoop, dragged him up two flights of stairs smelling of sesame oil and cabbage, through the front door, past the kitchen, and into his bedroom. She ripped off his jean shorts, inhaled him, thrust his head between her legs, and then she rode him until she felt raw inside, her pleasure sparking into fireworks.

Winnie lugged the big mysterious safe back into the elevator and into the basement like a dirty secret and then made dinner for the whole family, clearly overcompensating in Ginger's mind. He was extra-affectionate with her. He gave her the best piece of oven-baked tofu, he sliced lemons for her water, he refilled her glass like a bistro waiter, he squeezed her hands under the table, and he told dad jokes with a soft glow in his eyes. Tian Tian and Winnie's Mom laughed, delighted by his focused affection. They loved these special occasions when he flaunted his love for his fam without explaining its conception. Only Ginger knew. For two hours, they shared a moment together as a family not defined by negative space or emotional fragmentation. They were a coherent and transitory astronomy of orbiting bodies, a family of cycles and trajectories, all intertwined but concentric, circling a bright star.

ADULTHOOD

8. MYSTERIOUS POINT SYSTEM

1.

AFTER THE EMERGENCY LIGHTS flicker on inside the subway, two teenagers in Knicks jerseys start freaking out. *Get me the fuck out of here! Help us!* the white teenager screams, punching the window. Everyone looks up. Then, the Latino teenager pushes him and tells him to shut the fuck up. They break out into a violent skirmish, their fists smashing each other's cheeks and noses, removing chunks of skin like bulldozer claws tearing down walls of condemned buildings. The white boy's face starts bleeding profusely. The Latino boy's nose seems to hang from his face, the blood pooling on the floor.

2.

Passengers gasp in horror. Some shout, *Oh my fucking God!* Some start recording the fight with their phones. Others pretend not to notice, the New York game par excellence. Winnie turns to Ginger and tells her to stay where she is using his hands. He walks over and grabs one of the kid's blood-splattered arms before he can punch the other kid again. Ginger yelps. Someone mutters, *Well shit, that was scary as fuck.*

3.

As the white teen tries to free his arm, Aziz, with his two missing teeth, comes over and seizes the kid's other arm and pegs it behind his back, bending it backwards until the boy howls, *Yo, motherfucker! You're hurting me. I said you're fucking hurting me!* The boy tries to twist and contort his way out of Aziz's grip. He flails his body. Then, he tries headbutting a nearby woman in a pink jumper. He wants to smash dense frontal bone mass into sweaty female skin in the final seconds of his battle royal with the world, as if violence operates on a mysterious point system. Aziz pulls him away and restrains him.

PUPA

9. DRUNK SPEED (AZIZ AL-WAHNAN)

As he crossed the Brooklyn Bridge on his last day of training, Aziz looked south. Instead of ripples of polluted water and awe-inspiring bridges running parallel lines across the East River, he spotted a Lego congregation of glittering skyscrapers, huddling together in the cool autumn shade. From a distance, the Manhattan skyline sparkled like gigantic spears thrown from an Olympian perch. New York wasn't classically beautiful the way that Paris was in October, but he had to admit there was an electric current he'd felt immediately inside his ribcage as he walked around Manhattan. The energy he felt here was an urban caffeination that never ended. The streets here were so moody, godforsaken, dirty, and overcrowded one minute, then charming, upscale, multicultural, and cosmopolitan the next. He just couldn't keep track of New York's rules, couldn't resist its blunt cultural force or its relentless ambition. In this fractal city of diasporic communities, in this magnificent city of grime, style, attitude, and heartache, every long walk was a dizzying cocktail of joy, estrangement, and longing.

Once Aziz passed the halfway point, he felt a slight breeze blowing between the steel cables. With the humidity bouncing off the tarmac, the soft wind was a merciful respite. Spandexy bikers, one-mile joggers in sweat-stained East Coast college T-shirts, lawyers in slim fit navy suits and stilettos, college students in Adidas track suits and bucket hats and patterned wrap dresses and overalls and Chucks and farmer hats, creative types in black blazers, rolled up black jeans, Bape T-shirts, white beanies and Brooklyn T-shirts, tourists in straw hats, tank-tops, and jean shorts, teenagers in double-breasted suits and fedoras, executives with afro puffs and septum piercings dressed in pleated miniskirts and sleeveless denim button-downs, interns with lip piercings, torn jeans, ribbed sweaters, and massive tri-tone cashmere scarves, publicists in Bebe suit jackets, black tights, and black jean shorts passed him by in changing snapshots of self-care, class flex, beauty flaunt, and aerobic catharsis. Aziz had grown accustomed to the freestyle jazz of New York fashion, as if every person played their own solo at the same time. New York might be fast, expensive, and blurry, but its people were sharp and clear. Aziz spent most of his free time studying people through café windows in the West Village, Long Island City, Williamsburg, and the UWS nursing vanilla lattes (Americans love this shit), eating Jollof Rice and Chicken in the Bronx, chowing down on Cubanos and chimis in Washington Heights, watching his neighbors gossip in Spanglish from the windows of his loaner, eating avo-toast at a Fort Greene diner, buying poetry anthologies in a Park Slope stoop sale, taking pictures of a Buddha Mao in Jamaica, devouring toro rolls in Midtown, and gorging himself on Indian buffets in Jackson Heights. He never took a single day for granted. He couldn't afford to. Who knew the next time he'd be in New York?

Once after walking around Midtown, smashed on gimlets and romantic nostalgia, Aziz realized there were so many women in New York he could have fallen in love with, killed himself for, and written love-drunk poetry fragments on cocktail napkins to in another life. But in this life where he divided his time between corporate publishing training, sightseeing, and brief but intense periods of social isolation, he felt contagious, ugly, and invisible as he ate dim sum in Chinatown and ordered lattes at Soho cafés. He felt self-conscious and repellant passing brownstones in Brooklyn Heights. He felt foreign, suspicious, and unlovable exploring Coney Island at night. He felt spurned, erased, and disoriented navigating the Union Square Whole Foods, Penn Station platform rushes, and subway transfers at 42nd Street. Aziz wasn't culturally fluent in the New York language of cool, he wasn't relentlessly ambitious the way they were, he had no psychological mission to "make it," and he wasn't sold on the city's cultural mythology either. Mostly, he wanted to tomber d'amoureux and watch the world crumble into chaos with the love of his life by his side. He felt like such a French cliché.

The longer he stayed in New York, the deeper Aziz slid into self-doubt and self-loathing. He found himself thinking about old totems to comfort him, like snapshots of Hassan's laughter that came all the way from his diaphragm when Aziz told him jokes about racist Parisians. Aziz thought about the faces of his friends, who were always lighting up cigarettes and exchanging conspiracy stories about the Iraq occupation. He thought about Yesha sleeping in the sunlight on a blanket in Champ de Mars, the last copine of his to sever his fucking heart with a plastic spork. She had been such a fucking coward and yet he loved her foolishly and feverishly anyway. Even years later, he would never understand why she gave up so easily, why she never fought for their relationship the way he did, if only she'd had bigger dreams than the Paris citadel she was trapped in. If only she would have run away with him to an unknown city like New York where they could have become strangers to their own lives, emancipated of the pain, disappointment, and betrayal that bound them together like a vengeful Santería spell. Now, he felt trapped inside someone else's dream. It was the dream of an older version of himself when the only thing he cared about was getting out of Paris. He felt lost all the time in this Borgesian library of stories within stories within stories like a narrative matryoshka. New York was unforgivably exciting, but it was also haunted by its own polyphonic beauty, class conflict, cultural intersection, and sublimated grief.

The longer he stayed in New York, the more questions Aziz had. Did New Yorkers even stop to admire their own city? Did anyone even date in New York anymore? Could anyone even afford to live in Manhattan? Did anyone ever fall in love here? Sometimes, New York was just a wrestling match with his own breathlessness, invisibility, arousal, and disconnection. It made Aziz think obsessively about falling in love precisely because New Yorkers were too busy for it. It was one thing Paris did better than anyplace in the world. Since the day he'd arrived at JFK, Aziz realized he would always be unlovable in New York for the simple reason that love served no purpose in this city. Love highjacked your professional ambition, threatened your family, and subverted your life goals. New Yorkers were too impatient, too practical, and too overworked to fall in love. They were too pushy to be that vulnerable. And love, for all its hype, mythos, and capitalist performance, was meant to be inconvenient. It forced you to make impractical decisions about your life.

The last time Aziz had wanted to be in love, he was a thirteen-year-old boy wandering through Casa in the late afternoon after a fire-and-brimstone storm, the sky honeycombed into tiny gold medallions of sunlight. His papa had taken him and Sakina, his sister, to the Bab Marrakech market where Aziz had experienced his first teenage daze. She wore a creme-colored coatdress with two embroidered green turtles on the outside pockets, her hair wavy and elegant, graced by agave highlights, and fragrant like a pine forest, her curls spilling out of her matching green hijab. Her taut butterscotch skin glowed as if she'd traveled all the way from the stars above. As she walked in the broken rain-damp streets of Casablanca holding her blind aunt's hand, describing each item in sing-song French, narrativizing the bustling market into libretti for the older woman who sighed after every description, the young girl compressed every kiosk, every basket and table, every texture and scent into a series of fragments and ellipses with a voice sweet and dense like crushed pistachio candy. Aziz had watched with a transfixed expression, stuck in the liquid dream of his own inebriation: *Et puis tantine, ici on a de belles mangues d'or . . . et juste à côté, chez Monsieur Lahyani, il vend de l'aile superbe comme des bulbes d'hyacinthes violettes . . . et ensuite . . . and here auntie, we have some beautiful golden mangoes . . . and in the next stall, we have Mr. Lahyani's garlic, like purple Hyacinth bulbs . . . and then.* Aziz wished he could have stayed there and listened to her "and then" forever. He never found out what her name was, which neighborhood she'd lived in, or how old she was, but he always remembered the brushfire she lit inside of him, which blazed on and on like a pyromaniac's love song.

That day in Casa was the only time he'd wanted to be in love because only a dumb teenager would ask to be sliced open in front everyone. Aziz never understood how or why he'd loved that girl instantly, why he could never let go of the way she'd made him feel twenty years ago. He'd never know why as a teenager, he surrendered immediately to a complete stranger in a way that he never could with Yesha, a woman who always loved him with one eye open, always obsessed with the front door, always worried about bumping into reality, always fixated on the judgments of her racist papa who hated Arabs, immigrants, and gay people like the piece of shit he was.

The one thing Aziz learned as an adult was that falling in love had nothing to do with what you wanted, it just happened out of the blue like a natural disaster annihilating a village. Since

Yesha's excommunication, Aziz was afraid to fall in love again, he disliked walking in the dark, and despised eating alone in New York. Every time he wandered through Strand, he got distracted by one book after another, always making promises inside his head, always wanting everything and committing to nothing like some literary fuckboy. At night, he fell asleep reading books he'd swiped from the take shelf and woke up to pages he couldn't remember. He left for lunch to go to his favorite food cart in Midtown called Dougga Delish and ate his shawarma on the subway to be surrounded by people he didn't have to talk to. When training was done for the day, he sometimes saw Yesha's face in the crowd as he wandered aimlessly into other people's trajectories on the sidewalk. When he was alone, he could see their last day together, could see the deadness in her eyes that reminded him of an interrupted lamb dangling from a butcher hook. The way she'd looked at him then had made him feel like he was a monstrosity, as if his organs were hanging on the outside of his body, dangling and dripping, bleeding and pulsating on the ground like an eviscerated war hero who didn't know his life was gone. After all, being in love meant being disemboweled by someone else's sword. Maybe, that's why samurai loved the little sword so much, because it reminded them of how ephemeral their lives were. After a month and change in New York, it hurt Aziz too much now to spend his last days alone and stuck inside his head, but it also hurt too much to think about Yesha in Paris who saw him as a breaking and broken thing, even before she broke him.

Near the end of the bridge, Aziz noticed two men entangled in harnesses and belay devices. They looked like they were part of an alpinist documentary as they changed billboards in the sky. He only caught a glimpse before the words were gone:

in the

Colonial

Army of   **Fatigue**

ding & Occupy

id Assault

In a flash, the words were wiped clean from the visual memory of New York. The billboard became a blank page again, its message erased by the janitors of American culture. Aziz wished he'd arrived just a few minutes earlier, if only to understand what an id assault was. There was so much you could do with an extra hundred and twenty seconds in this country.

Once he was back in Washington Heights, Aziz went to Mami's again and ordered a Cubano to go, which had become his favorite sandwich in America. Definitely a worthy contender to a Gruyère and ham crêpe in Paris. While he waited for his order, he looked at the bright mural of famous Latino pitchers on the wall, all of them winding up for their next throws. There were American and Cuban flags above their heads in patriotic coronation. Underneath one picture, a banner read, *Hernandez 26, gracias por tenerme*, but then the writing got blurry.

Aziz turned to the cashier. —Oye, ¿quien es este tipo en la foto? he asked.

—¿Qué? En serio? Es *El Duque*, cabrón. ¡El mejor lanzador del mundo!

—Ai, discúlpa.

—El error más grande that Chicago ever made.

—Wait, why?

—They traded him like comemierdas.

—Why?

—Coño, who the hell knows why smart people act stupid?

Aziz shrugged his shoulder because he didn't know much

about baseball or American sports rivalries. The only thing he remembered growing up was that despite all the money in this city, Michael Jordan had brought New York to its knees for ten glorious years, one of many reasons why he'd loved the Bulls as only a French person of color could.

—But I'll tell you one thing, the cashier continued, leaning forward on the counter and speaking in a conspiratorial tone, when El Duque was on, fuck, it was lights out, cabrón. Not a man left standing with that arm of his. I saw him twice in Yankee Stadium and when he pitched, ¡bomba!, it was like something in comic books.

—His strength?

—Nah man, his speed. His whole body was a giant blur. When you watched him, you felt like a jumo. Like you was drunk.

Aziz understood. No one could knuckleball the world that much and not get vertigo eventually.

10. ANOTHER LINGUISTIC QUARTET OF SELF-IMPLOSION (SUZANNE GUPTA)

Because recently her ABCD mind had become a dizzying swirl of intense loneliness, emotional upheaval, and philosophical speculation, which may or may not have been related to spending three months in three cities, Suzanne bought a digital SLR camera two days before she left New York because she felt inspired but also why the hell not? She'd spent all of October in New York, the leaves were starting to incinerate, but Richard Gere hadn't hit on her in Central Park and she hadn't made a single friend either. Even the acquaintances she'd made in Brooklyn cafés as she'd nursed her morning almond mochas (an ephemeral community of college students, writers, chatty extroverts, Bluetooth Tigers, and depressed tenants escaping their 250-square-foot studios) had slowly disappeared or acted too busy and too cool to chat now. She couldn't wait to return to Chicago and show her friends her new boyfriend. Everyone, she'd say, *this is Nikon. He's smooth, versatile, and brilliant. Being a person of color, he has a phenomenal sense of perspective of white spaces, he knows how to codeswitch flawlessly, and he's knows injustice when he sees it [rimshot]. Plus, he's got a photographic memory and his megapixels are out of control!* She'd been waiting her whole life to buy one of these evil geniuses and for good reason. She had absolutely no talent when it came to taking photos but also would never have splurged on something so technically demanding if she hadn't stumbled upon a huge fall sale at an electronics store filled with quiet Hasidic boys and Japanese tourists asking for help using Google Translate on their Samsung phones. With her new assault rifle of a camera, Suzanne was an artiste, an editor of visual culture, and possibly, a genius! Maybe, she should start wearing scarves, get a septum piercing, and start vaping really potent weed at family get-to-gethers to survive every invasive question posed by a vicarious auntie about her "wasted eggs," her mysterious aversion to med school, and her conspicuous bachelorhood. That could be like her own branding, the desi culture photographer with a nasty weed habit and a brilliant sense of perspective. Now, if she could just figure out how to rotate pictures.

At Union Square, Suzanne took shots of the color tour, capturing the amber, saffron, and flamingo-pink leaves in the treetops while stylish interracial couples sat on benches and fiddled with their phones, groups of multiracial teenagers in jean jackets, black jeans, and beanies cracked jokes as they smoked blunts and drank gin and tonics from engraved flasks, Black and Asian breakdancers performed blurry backspins on pieces of greasy cardboard, moonwalking over concrete and circling the boom box, eventually coalescing into one body of movement as their skinny bodies did the wave in perfect synchronicity like a slow electric current. After she'd taken enough photos to make her trigger finger pulsate, Suzanne bought a bottle of mineral water and a vegetarian salad roll from the deli, devouring both like a stowaway. When was the last time she'd eaten?

She fiddled with her camera and walked to the other side of the park (how the hell do you rotate pictures?) as the sun dipped into the Neapolitan sky, a pleasant breeze casting a wide net over the park now. Couples zipped up their jackets and pulled up their hoodies, some headed for the subway or walked into the bougie mosh pit known as Whole Foods. Filtered in half-light, Union Square looked like a cinematic still she'd examined at the Fine Arts Theater on Michigan Avenue as a teenager waiting for her friends so they could sneak into the R-rated movies and rip open Ziploc bags full of popcorn. New York was the only city besides Chicago (and okay, maybe Seattle) that made Suzanne feel like her life was a beautiful accident requiring no deeper interpretation to be meaningful, something she could never take credit for but still love anyway for its serendipity. Just then, a troupe of capoeira dancers formed a circle in the square, all of them, blurry, graceful, and dripping like a series of choreographed one-night stands. Suzanne ignored the pain in her fingers and the goosebumps on her neck as she clicked the shutter release button over and over again, fighting the fading natural light to capture their graceful movements. In groups of two, they defied gravity with their ripped bodies, lifting and flapping their pristine white pants into the air like small flags as their torsos twirled into half circles. They were illusionists, landing on the ground without falling, their bodies glowing and glistening under the slow cloud of dusk while a Brazilian band played music that felt both spontaneous and cyclical and other dancers chanted songs in Brazilian Portuguese and new dancers replaced old ones, dueling out of love, lost in the infectious rhythm. Every few minutes, the dancers replicated themselves in the middle of the circle as fresh bodies spun around each other, invoking duality, symbiosis, and collaboration. Suzanne couldn't take her eyes off their fluidity and lightness and gracefulness and strength. The capoeira dancers were everything she'd hoped to be growing up, everything she wasn't in real life, their performance too fast and too graceful to export to the digital realm.

The next day in Central Park, Suzanne took pictures of a spectacle that in any other city would have been ridiculous: hot New Yorkers roller-skating in a circle to really loud '80s music like it was no big deal. Part nostalgia performance, part fashion show, and part post-hipster reunion, somehow it just worked. Maybe, it was just the power of double and triple meta. Maybe, they were stuck in a time warp and she was the time/space invader.

Later that afternoon, Suzanne went to the Met, which was just too much for her crowded head (and too big for the memory chip in her camera). She couldn't see that much art without having an aneurysm, so she closed her eyes and listened to people talk about art, which was kind of nauseating. Was everything in New York going to be meta today? She wondered as she headed to Chelsea to make her reservation at Blossom.

On her last official day in the city, Suzanne walked to Hipstonia armed with a brand-new memory chip and a why-the-fuck-not sense of optimism she had no right to have whatsoever, as she took enough photos to rival the Getty Photo Archives. She figured it was the perfect way to say ciao bella to New York and besides, Williamsburg was kinda like the Wicker Park clusterfuck, so her last day here could be the foreshadowing for her return to Chicago. She bought a straw hat at a boho store called Sun Freckles and a customary BKI T-shirt (gray and burgundy) at Brooklyn Industries, because why not? She didn't know yet whether her tiny shopping spree was a baptism or a memento, whether she'd return to New York in five years for grad school or to pursue the illusive—and self-gratifying—dream of "making it" in New York, whatever that meant (*If you can make it here*, said one ad inside the subway, *then you can make it anywhere*), or whether this would be her last time in Brooklyn. Maybe, she had too much faith in her intelligence to figure it all out. Maybe, that was the problem with every U of C student.

After strolling up and down Bedford Avenue for as long as she could bear, she ate lunch at a little vegetarian café called What's Love Got to Do with It? where she ordered a *Who Needs a Heart Bowl?* and a *Secondhand Emotion Smoothie*, channeling her inner rock'n'roll melancholy. She pulled out some stationery she'd bought in the UES (is that how they abbreviate it?), and started writing her fifth letter to George, something she'd been postponing since the day she left Chicago on a whim and a scorching sense of intuition. She'd been avoiding this letter but couldn't avoid her guilt. The time had come to purge herself of this Georgian sickness.

```
21 October 2012          WLGTDWI                Café,
Williamsburg
```

```
Dear Gengé,
    Long time no write. How are you? Hi.  I
know I know I know it's been way too long.
I should have written this letter years ago
in Chicago.  I should have written you  in
Seattle. I should have written this at every
café I loitered in, stargazing at brightly
colored maps of the world where I played
"what-if" counterfactual games with spinning
antique globes and alternate worlds. I know,
I know, my imagination can be a huge defense
mechanism.  The problem is,  every time  I
thought about writing you but failed, I felt
guiltier because I was thinking of you but
not creating anything material to reconnect
with you. I've spent so much time thinking
about Bossie, Lil' Zye, and Samba, wondering
```

if they lick your face in the morning. I've spent so much time wondering if it still hurts inside for you, whether you hate me, possibly even more than you did when you woke up and found my note under the pillow, whether I even deserve to be forgiven for leaving without a word (something I still can't believe I did).

The truth is, there is a big part of me that hopes you believe in counterfactual and/or parallel worlds, the mind-bending postulate of quantum mechanics that claims single atoms cannot be pinpointed in one specific time/ place because they're flashing between time-lines in the multiverse. I hope you believe this like I do, because maybe in some other universe you already know my intentions or you've already read everything I can't tell you in this one, not because I'm emotion-ally lazy or because I hate you or because you don't matter (because I'm not, I don't, and you do), but because I don't know how to say goodbye to the us in this non-theoret-ical world. I mean, does anyone? I find it extremely comforting—and a total cop-out, I know, I know—to believe this letter is redun-dant. I want to believe you already know everything I'm saying right now. It's such a beautiful idea to imagine that in some other universe, you already know everything I'm struggling to write in this one. It's ridicu-lously comforting to me to think that in more than one universe, you've already forgiven me, I've already told you, and you've already moved on. ~~Argh, I haven't written one thing~~ ~~that is making sense right now and that's a~~ ~~bad sign for a fifth letter.~~

~~I'm not in love with you, Gengé and after~~ ~~being away for two months, I can say with a~~ ~~lot of guilt-ridden certainty that I never~~ ~~was, but I miss you terribly, and I can't~~ ~~explain that paradox. A big part of me feels~~ ~~like I'll never come back to Chicago, at~~ ~~least not as the same person, and definitely~~ ~~not as your girlfriend, I'm sorry (but also~~ ~~absolutely relieved) to say.~~ Still, I miss the way our relationship used to be, back when I still lived in Hyde Park, when we couldn't take each other for granted. I miss the way you used to love me Gengé, the way you'd hurry to my apartment during your lunch break so we could have passionate sex on the kitchen table, my head just inches from the ceramic bowl filled with calcified lemons. I miss the way it used to feel to love you but not own you like a sentimental tchotchke. I miss the way it felt to not be forgotten. I miss the comfort of being needed by you. I miss the conversations we used to have in the dark layers of my musty bedroom, the way you were always asking me why we met in this universe, what it all meant to love someone by accident, without asking. ~~I miss the inquis-~~ ~~itiveness you used to have, Gengé. I miss~~ ~~the way you used to pledge allegiance to the~~ ~~question mark, back when I was a subject of~~ ~~insatiable intrigue and harrowing desire.~~ I miss that look in your eyes when you saw me in the lobby of the Drake, waiting so we could eat sushi at Ginza (our secret sushi joint in The Loop) or when I dragged you to the CSO to listen to Shostakovich and Mahler against your will, a look in your eyes that said I was a brilliant dreamer, a complex hetaera of storytelling, a delusional optimist, and a beautiful quirk in your normative life of khakis, car payments, and Bears games. Sometimes, I was just a woman who wanted to be listened to, respected, supported, and believed. Other times, I just wanted to be your temporary object of lust as long as my subjectivity was fully acknowledged and fully celebrated. I expected you to check in with me and not treat our relationship like some vapid formula you could just plug in values for. When we first dated, you used to act like I was a flash mob of beauty, subversion, and impossibility in your perfectly calibrated world. I was the thunderstorm for your agoraphobia, speaking to you in camera flashes and rooftop drum rolls. All those things we once shared at the beginning used to make me wildly, unsustainably happy. ~~What happened to that? What happened to us? What happened to the semi-solid postulates of our relationship?~~

~~I used to crush hard on you, George, even though you weren't my type, even though you're the only white guy I've ever dated. Precisely because you weren't my type, in fact. That was how I knew how to appreciate you in my own flawed way. Maybe it still is.~~

But I'm not in love, I can't pretend, and you shouldn't want me to. I guess what I'm trying to say is that you and I weren't supposed to last, despite your delusional ideas about our honeymoon in the Tambelan Islands and the number of kids you wanted. And you know, or you should have known that I will wait until I'm thirty-five at the earliest to start a family. How could you forget that? How could you forget me?

The truth is, you were too stable for me and my love wasn't stable enough for you. You became complacent and I became precarious. You took me for granted and I rebelled against you, pushing back on the very stability I'd created in our relationship. I mean, we've all been programmed to want things that make us unhappy (thanks late-stage capitalism!) and now that I'm alone, I mean, really alone, I'm an itinerant mess. I can't commit to a city, an idea, or way of life (which are all the same thing). My daydreams are jetlagged, my thoughts keep skipping between timelines and experiences, and I daydream every single day. Sometimes, my daydreams smash into my night dreams and I become nostalgic for something that never happened, at least not in this world. God, I can be so vain. ~~But I'm not apologizing for how I feel (nor should you). I'll never feel the way I did during the Age of Innocence. We can't go back to the beginning of this plot structure unless the beginning is the end, unless Chronos's bracelet is broken. If I were still happy,~~

~~if I could love you, if I still knew how to carry on like a good soldier of inertia, I wouldn't want to go back to the beginning. But the fact that I do, the fact that I want to start over again only proves that I can't grasp our relationship as it really is anymore because it hurts too much to separate myself from you with box cutters, but it also hurts too much to bury us alive with our smug self-certainty and stagnation.~~

In a strange and a deeply flawed way, I supposed I do love you, George. Or maybe, I love a version of you at a fixed point in time. Either way, this love has become obsolete, nostalgic, unreal, and misplaced like an old Discman. A part of me doesn't know how to stop needing you because stasis is a crude scientific analogy of how I felt in Chicago, a feeling I still hoard sometimes like a quiet addiction, which will never disappear unless we go backwards in time to the beginning of our life cycle. Our relationship has fallen apart, Gengé, and the chemical romance has changed. My entire world erased itself this summer and while I feel really bad admitting this, my eyes, my eyes have become wide and clear now, and I won't ever let you put me to sleep again. I'm supposed to be awake, feasting on the succulent sunlight like a famished orphan sucking freshly plucked sugarcane. I was never supposed to sleep without dreaming. Save that for the *Upanishads*, save that for another ballad of longing, for another linguistic quartet of self-implosion. Forget about me,

```
George, that's the best thing you can do for
yourself, not because our relationship didn't
matter, but because it's a dead shell now and
you can't bring back its soul.
     The only thing I ask of you is that you
please love my babies as I used to. I think I
have that right, at least, until we can figure
out joint custody for them.


With love and enormous conflict,


—Suzie Q


p.s. Sorry so long!
```

When her order came, the smell of warm food suddenly made Suzanne famished. It was the perfect diversion from her own regret. After she slurped her straw and scooped the last mouthful of quinoa, tahini sauce, and roasted broccolini into her mouth with a spoon, she dropped a couple twenties on the table and walked to the subway with her shopping bag in one hand and George's letter in the other, carrying it like a trapped spider in a glass. When the Manhattan-bound L train pulled into the platform, her hands suddenly crumpled George's letter into a small globe, entire continents and bodies of water reduced to globs of slanted cursive in permanent marker. The train doors opened dramatically (ta-dah! they sang) and stylish commuters poured out of the car in swaggering droves of affected coolness. Somewhere above the shellacked hairdos, tight black jeans, still-bloody tattoos, and stylish salon cuts, a paper globe traveled in a great arc from Suzanne's palms to the trashcan that overflowed with half-eaten pizza slices and iced coffees, the straws vandalized by a continuum of lipstick kisses that missed their mark as kisses so often do.

11. THE CLARITY OF FARAWAY PLACES

A PLASTIC BANNER WITH glazed donut fingerprints on top hung above the entrance of the main conference room, clinging for life, its corners flopping over on both sides:

COME TO *L'Éditions Pont Neuf's 2012 Training & Orien*

in alternating purple and yellow letters that were supposed to convey energy and excitement. After three weeks of training, Aziz learned that the banner's Mardi Gras color scheme was just one of many lies of corporate publishing, which was all glam on the outside, but number-crunching tedium on the inside, no matter how sexy the industry pretended to be. He slogged through orientation for weeks and was incurably bored now. While the other trainees disappeared into their smartphones, Aziz became nostalgic for a life he didn't miss in Paris and critical of a life he didn't understand in New York.

He sat in a half circle with entry-level copy editors, personal and editorial assistants, bright-eyed secretaries, disheveled web and graphic designers, fresh-off-the-bachelor-press book-keepers, and fat-cheeked interns all trying to look grown-up in layers of baby flesh and new pinstriped suits with stitched front pockets. He couldn't help but notice that virtually all the trainees were white women with a modest splatter of white men. Aziz did count one Black guy and two Asian women, which was a shitty ratio.

Out of boredom and insecurity, he wanted to say fucked-up, totally obnoxious things during presentations and small group discussion just so he felt like he was putting up a fight against corporate brainwash. Among the bitchier thoughts he had were:

1. The sale rack is your mortal enemy.
2. Cologne isn't self-defense.
3. Ambition doesn't make up for inelegance.
4. No one cares about your Princeton degree.
5. Stop telling college stories.
6. That's not what *eschew* means.
7. Pont Neuf didn't publish that book.
8. This isn't a sorority.
9. You're one sleezy look away from sexual harassment, bro.
10. We're not your drinking buddies.
11. There's a fine line between confidence and delusion.
12. You just repeated the same thing she said, only with less panache and originality.
13. That's not what mot juste means.
14. You just regurgitated this week's *New Yorker*.
15. You just said three sexist things in one sentence.
16. She's not straight.
17. He's married.
18. No one here cares about Lacan except me.
19. This isn't your pulpit.
20. Your transparent blouse is a masterpiece of distraction.
21. Wrong John Updike novel.
22. You've got specks of glazed donut on your tie and everyone knows you're wearing your roommate's sport coat.

23. Wow a JD from Penn and you still don't understand institutional racism.

24. Trou de cul! That comment was Islamophobic!

But what the hell did Aziz know anyway? He was just a Parisian polyglot with a broken heart, two missing teeth, and a major chip on his shoulder. But at least he knew when to keep his gaping mouth shut (theoretically).

White plastic chairs used for country club engagement parties formed six parallel rows, forming a half-moon around a guy from Leeds who used a flowchart to explain the impending corporate merger between Gallimard, Old School International, and ÉPN. Dude just prattled on forever about the intricate web of editorial hierarchies connecting the London, Paris, Moscow, Tokyo, and New York offices. Aziz found the presentation soul-obliterating. The other trainees sat there, fidgeting and shifting their feet and coughing during every Q & A, fondling their phones, checking their text messages obsessively, and doodling on notepads. The camaraderie was forced and circumstantial. Aziz thought about pocketing the free croissants, bracket-shaped melon slices, and jelly-filled butter cookies, folded into little napkin bundles from the always-half-empty buffet tables in case he became poor again. His self-preservation instincts died hard and also il s'en fiche. Aziz felt like *someone* had to clear the snack trays, it might as well be the Moroccan French guy with the broken teeth. He remembers the first stomachache he got from picking food out of the trash. Maman was furious. She told him they weren't poor enough for him to be excavating the trash bins for his afternoon snack, but he was sick of eating the same lamb tagine every day. Just the thought of that dish used to make him furious as a boy.

After another hour of corporatese indoctrination, Aziz

started doodling pictures of the Brooklyn Bridge and Montmartre staircases on a yellow legal pad, nodding every so often when
he felt the speaker look in his direction. *Whereas ÉPN Tokyo
has transfuhed thee majoritee of thee Anglophone publication proejects in the Pacific Rim to the Hanoi Office, thee Paris Office on thee
othuh hand has seen a mahked increase in thee numbuh of bi-lingual
poetry proejects, as we can see in diagram 5.* More than anything,
Aziz wanted a smoke, a real glass of Moroccan mint tea, and two
piping hot Cubanos bundled in tin foil like little babies.

At five sharp, he took the A train to High Street and then
walked back to Manhattan on the Brooklyn Bridge. On a high billboard in the distance, he saw a large Buddha dressed in military
fatigues, lipstick, and a sports coat, flashing a peace sign to the
world. Aziz thought about the Paris riots in the Arab neighborhoods that were on all the TV stations now. He thought about
Wafi, Ousmane, and Michel. He thought about Hassan's saintly
face, how happy he would have been to see Aziz walking over the
Brooklyn Bridge (that puissant symbol of human language), just
as they'd talked about months ago. Hassan had always understood
the redemption that Aziz saw in this magnificent bridge, always
nodded when Aziz gave his spiel about the power of verbal ingenu-
ity, the adaptability of colloquial speech acts, the cultural morphol-
ogy of dialect, slang, and class jargon, and the vibration of words
when someone sang them in a perfect cadence. As long as Hassan
had known him, Aziz was the consummate linguaphile who saw
endless companionship, infinite potentiality, and the building
blocks of human connectivity in every word. While computer
engineers might understand the world in terms of zeroes and
ones, Aziz understood it in terms of phonemes, irreducible units
of language that when put together became words, sentences,
paragraphs and then prayers for every lost soul and every crushed
insect. The whole world was just a decillion magnetic clusters of
letters of the alphabet written in 6,909 languages.

After he dodged overzealous bikers and practically stage-dived into small groups of clustered joggers that refused to split up, even on the wrong side of the bridge, he looked out across the East River. He saw Wall Street and Navy Yard, Fulton Landing, East River Park, and the Jehovah's Witness building, all the things his Routard mentioned, but it was the nauseatingly sublime New York skyline that really hit him in the knees like a mafia trope. The view from the Brooklyn Bridge, where Manhattan looked like a pin cushion island and the pulsating sun sizzled into the horizon, its metallic light transmogrifying the Financial District into a national mint of gold bars and silver obelisks, turning skyscrapers into gigantic lightbulbs, the ground into a broken chandelier of modernism, the splintered sunlight into fragments of deliquescent crystal, it all gobsmacked him. Aziz felt like the city was a colossal container of energy for the expanding galaxy, a captivating blur of glimmering orbs raining down on the ground as far as the eye could see, the horizon like an incendiary dream trance. It was only the distance that helped him see the smallness of his life and grasp its delicate and illusive beauty, helping Aziz understand—if only momentarily—that his life was in flames, had always been in flames, and that everyone who wasn't frozen in time was slowly burning to death.

12. OFF SCRIPT

SUZANNE GOT OFF THE W train at Prince Street station dressed in a wrinkled, second-hand trench coat and Gucci knockoffs she'd bought on Canal Street several days ago, her cheap umbrella strapped around her wrist. She reapplied Bleeding Commie red lipstick that had faded after her juice breakfast, using her phone as a mirror. As she walked down Broadway from SoHo to Tribeca, the smell of warm rain and unidentifiable croissants in the air, she realized that she'd accidentally stepped onto a film set. A white production manager dressed in black jeans, a Metallica T-shirt, black baseball cap, black sunglasses, and headphones wrapped around his neck, waved her away to the other side of the street.

                                            FADE IN:

EXT. RAIN-COVERED STREET - TRIBECA - DAY

SUZANNE, a 33-year-old Indian American/desi woman who is visiting New York, walks through Tribeca and looks into shop windows as the sun comes back out. The streets are still wet.

> FEMALE BRITISH NARRATOR (V.O.)
> For Suzanne, New York was the
> loneliest place on earth once the
> urban buzz became an ontological
> hangover.

DISSOLVE TO:

EXT. EL PLATFORM — THE LOOP - DAY

Suzanne looks out the El window as it travels
north to the Addison stop.

> FEMALE BRITISH NARRATOR (V.O.)
> Suzanne's first love would always be
> Chicago, a working-class city of brick
> and mortar that was big and bold,
> but also basic and bankrupt. She found
> comfort in the city's grid even though
> she detested it. She knew that Chicago
> was a city of parallel worlds connecting
> the North Side and the South Side. She
> also knew that the one place where these
> separate worlds connected was the Loop
> where all addresses started at zero.

DISSOLVE TO:

INT. SEA-TAC AIRPORT — DAY

Suzanne walks down the terminal carrying
a leather satchel, ladybug backpack, and
suitcase. She takes the escalator to the ground

level where PUNK WHITE GIRL WITH LIP RING, a
31-year-old white woman dressed in stylish
black clothes, Doc Martens boots, with a blue-
dyed pixie cut, runs over and hugs Suzanne.
Suzanne and Punk White Girl with Lip Ring exit
the airport.

                                DISSOLVE TO:

          FEMALE   BRITISH   NARRATOR   (V.O.
          carries over)
     Even though Seattle was insanely white
     compared to Chicago and New York,
     Suzanne never felt blue there the way
     she did in New York's enchanted and
     dirty streets. She wondered if she'd
     made a mistake leaving Seattle on a
     whim after a drunken session with a
     grumpy psychic.

SEATTLE MONTAGE:

  … Suzanne drinks tea and laughs inside a
Chinese tea shop.
  … Suzanne raises her hands in the air and
screams as she gets splashed aboard the
Vashon Island Ferry.
  … Suzanne walks around the University of
Washington campus and takes pictures of
squirrels with her phone.
  … Suzanne eats dim sum with Punk White Girl
with Lip Ring in the International District.
  … Suzanne buys giant salmon at Pike Street
Market.

… Suzanne sings karaoke with Punk White Girl with Lip Ring inside dive bar.
… Suzanne chats with a psychic in run-down studio.
… Suzanne dances with Punk White Girl with Lip Ring at night club in Capitol Hill.

END OF SEATTLE MONTAGE

                              DISSOLVE TO:

EXT. NEW YORK CITY — TRIBECA — DAY

Suzanne walks into a throng of people on Chambers Street, holding her pistachio ice-cream cone in one hand and her phone in the other. AGGRESSIVE NEW YORKER, a forty-some-thing white man in a pin-stripe suit, bumps into Suzanne as he passes and knocks her ice-cream to the sidewalk. Suzanne looks down at her ice-cream.

                    SUZANNE
          Jeez, that was a shitty thing
          to do!

                    AGGRESSIVE NEW YORKER
               (without turning around)
          Welcome to New York!

                              DISSOLVE TO:

                    FEMALE   BRITISH   NARRATOR   (V.O.
               carries over)

The real problem for Suzanne was her expectations. She liked New York, but her expectations had become unruly and unreasonable after listening to New Yorker friends of hers talk about their city for years as if every neighborhood was a movie or a music video or a Norton anthology of world literature.

NEW YORK MONTAGE:

… Suzanne walks past Radio City Music Hall.

… Suzanne has a picnic in Central Park where she feeds squirrels.

… Suzanne writes a letter inside a Williamsburg café called What's Love Got to Do with It?

… Suzanne sips coffee and makes calls at Caffe Dante.

… Suzanne leaves MOMA holding her head in her hands.

… Suzanne takes photos of Capoeira dancers in Union Square.

… Suzanne eats a vegan gyro in Long Island City.

… Suzanne takes pictures of several Buddha Maos in the Bronx.

… Suzanne gets pushed by commuters on the C, F, Q, and L trains.

END OF NEW YORK MONTAGE

                                    DISSOLVE TO:

EXT. NEW YORK CITY — TRIBECA — DAY

We are back at Chambers Street. Suzanne is still looking at her ice-cream on the sidewalk when she suddenly becomes aware of the camera.

                    SUZANNE
                 (to camera)
          Let's be honest, the people in this
          city are stylish and cosmopolitan, but
          they're also rude and impatient. And
          they'll knock over your pistachio
          ice-cream just to get ahead of you in
          the line for the subway. And for the
          record, the rats here are longer than
          Proustian sentences.

Suzanne starts walking again down Chambers Street and looks at her phone.

                    FEMALE BRITISH NARRATOR (V.O.)
          Eventually, Suzanne felt like she was
          living in a book pretending to be a
          dream pretending to be a screenplay.
          She felt like she was living in a
          metafictional, polyphonic, hyper-real
          novel about novels where the roles of
          author, character, narrator, and
          audience collapsed into each other.

Suzanne stops suddenly.

                    SUZANNE

                    (to camera)
          I guess you could say I'm a character
          in search of my own arc.

Suzanne walks again.

               FEMALE BRITISH NARRATOR (V.O.)
          After spending two weeks in New York,
          Suzanne craved an honest non-linear
          storyline. She wanted a clearer sense
          of what she was supposed to do with her
          life. A new boyfriend would be nice
          too.

Suzanne stops, looks at her phone again, and
re-applies her lipstick.

               SUZANNE
          (looks at herself on her phone)
          Don't listen to her. I'm just tired of
          all the traveling I've done in this
          novel. Also, I refuse to be another
          English subject any longer, if you know
          what I mean. And if we're being real, I
          really miss my mum's mushroom biryani.

                              DISSOLVE TO:

EXT. NEW YORK CITY — STREET IN WEST VILLAGE
— DAY

Suzanne tosses her phone into her satchel and
asks for the check. OLD ITALIAN WAITRESS,
a seventy-something Italian woman dressed

in stilettos and a black leather miniskirt, stomps to the table. Suzanne hands Old Italian Waitress a fifty-dollar bill. The waitress winks at Suzanne. Afterwards, Suzanne walks around the Village where she eventually sits down on a bench in Washington Square. She takes a couple of pictures of squirrels with her phone and then opens up her book, *Forgetfulness of Butterflies* by Jackson Bliss, which

transported her back to the time and place where she felt happiest, to the genre that had always felt like home to her: a contemporary novel about mixed-race identity, multiracial urban spaces, counterfactual longing, and class consciousness. Once Suzanne was done reading, she looked around the park to see if Zadie Smith, her favorite author of all time, was passing by because you never know. After all, she taught at NYU, which was just across the street. Suzanne knew it was ridiculous, but she couldn't help it because fangirls gonna fangirl. She left the park, entered a graphic novel store near Astor Place, browsed new releases, and eventually bought several volumes of high school romance manga before making her way to the Bowery where she bought vegan gyoza and wibbled (walked and nibbled at the same time) a good forty blocks until she came to an electronics store filled with Hasidic men dressed in short-sleeve button-ups, matching vests, and yarmulkes. She threw her to-go box in the trash and stepped inside, ready for the next paragraph.

Normally, Suzanne found bright stores oppressive. Normally, she found megastores spatially intimidating. Normally, there were too many people trying to help you and they always asked you before you remembered what you came for and even when you knew exactly what you wanted, even when you were *holding the thing you were about to purchase in your hand*, they still wanted to help you. And during those rare instances where you really did need help, the megastore became a ghost town, tumbleweed blowing through the aisles, abandoned televisions showing synchronized commercials for slasher movies, a haunting jingle echoing through the aisles. In addition to Suzanne's extensive psychohistory with megastores, this place was heinously large, practically Texan in scope and aspiration, but something had pulled her inside like a tractor beam. Maybe, it was the industrial strength AC or the fact that she was pickling in her own sweat. Maybe, there was something inside this place that was calling to her like a distress signal (*Help me, fellow Jedis, you're my only hope*). Much like the past two months, Suzanne wasn't sure what she was looking for as she wandered from aisle to aisle in a blind autumn daze like her spontaneous itinerary from Chicago to Seattle to New York. The only thing she knew for sure was the charred colors of ignition in every leaf and treetop silently raging through the store's windows. Suzanne grabbed the tag for the fanciest and most high-tech SLR she could afford and then moved with indecent swag to the cashier where they retrieved her dream camera for her. For possibly the first time in her life, Suzanne wasn't worried about buying the wrong thing. At least with electronics, you could return them if they malfunctioned. They came with warranties that anticipated every disaster, which was more than she could say for her relationships.

13. MY HEART IS AN OLD PARISIAN GHETTO

THE NEXT THREE WEEKS were a cultural mood swing and miniature time-travel between the vibrant and chatty streets of Washington Heights where la gente sat on stoops in baggy jeans, track suits, sweat shorts, and tropical-colored dress suits, listening to hip-hop, Reggaeton, and Spanish language radio, gossiping in Dominican Spanish and the stubbornly sterile world of Wall Street with its monochromatic streets and squadrons of white サラリーマンslow-roasting in their suits as they chewed on their Blackberries, shouted at taxis, elbowed passengers on the subway, and avoided eye contact on the sidewalk, huffing in disgust and reeking of coke, hundred-dollar-bills, antacids, and Aqua di Gio. Aziz found the class anxiety absolutely stifling. His good friend, Michel, was right: Washington Heights was just like Saint-Denis. Only Parisians didn't eat late-night chimis and they were stuck in racial gloom.

Aziz walked inside the conference room cautiously and pulled out his nametag, pinning it to the breast pocket of his rose-colored button-up that said:

Hi, my name is

<u>Aziz!</u>

Paris Office

The weird thing was, he'd never used an exclamation point in his entire life. *J'ai horreur de ça*, he'd always told his friends about any punctuation besides the period. Full stop.

Dressed in ironed khakis, a Brooks Brothers oxford, a perfectly-trimmed beard, and brown tortoise shell glasses, an editorial-looking man in his late forties made a hazelnut coffee on the public Keurig, grabbed his Styrofoam cup, and started gabbing to Aziz like they were frat bros. —Hey, how's it going? he asked.

—Meh, Aziz replied.

Aziz looked at his nametag:

Hi, my name is
<u>Andrew!</u>
Boston Office

—Let me guess, you're <u>Andrew!</u>

The editor grimaced. —You can call me '<u>Drew!</u>

<u>Aziz!</u> nodded.

—So what department are you in? <u>Andrew!</u> asked.

—Translation, <u>Aziz!</u> said.

—Oh, very cool.

<u>Aziz!</u> nodded again, becoming self-conscious of his two missing front teeth. —What about you?

—Editorial all the way. It's wicked fun.

—Wicked? You mean, it's fun but also evil? <u>Aziz!</u> wondered whether he was having another cultural misunderstanding. He'd had a rash of them recently.

—Kinda, the editor said, downing his coffee and tossing it in the trash.

—Or do you mean Wicked as in the musical? <u>Aziz!</u> asked.

<u>Andrew!</u> pulled an ancient-looking Danish out of his pants pocket. —You know, your English is excellent, he said, nibbling on the edge.

—Thanks, <u>Aziz!</u> said, sipping his cold Parisian blend, which he'd chosen just to understand American stereotypes of France. He grimaced after every sip.

—Where did you study it? <u>Andrew!</u> asked, chewing in small circles.

—In London. Also, at uni.

The editor chewed and smirked.

—What? <u>Aziz!</u> asked.

—I just love that Anglicism, *at uni.*

—Oh, right, Americans don't say that, do they?

—No, we use our definite articles.

—Pretty sure the English do too.

—Of course.

—I mean, they invented the language we're speaking right now.

The editor laughed before inhaling the rest of his pastry and wiping his mouth, large crumbs shipwrecked in his beard. — Touché, <u>Aziz!</u>, but it's *our* language now.

<u>Aziz!</u> gulped. —America's?

—God no, <u>Andrew!</u> said, pieces of caramelized sugar sticking to his teeth. —I'm not some yahoo, <u>Aziz!</u> I mean the publishing industry.

—Oh.

—Sadly, we've become the Stalins of the literary world. We control what people read, since we decide what gets *published*, and that's mind-blowing if you think about it for too long.

—Yeah, I guess you're right, <u>Aziz!</u> said. —That's not what I thought you were saying.

—I don't know, the editor continued, I guess that's just how I console myself. He wiped his mouth with a napkin and filled a Dixie cup with orange juice. —I always tell my wife: sure, we publish a lot of drivel by ghost-writing celebrities, premature MFA burnouts, and talentless hacks who don't have an original bone in their overfed bodies, but at least no company, no country, and no industry has a monopoly on storytelling anymore. At least I can still fight for important books, smart characters, and beautiful language, if only in my own acquisitions.

—Also, indie presses are really killing it right now.

—Oh, tell me about it. I'm shocked they don't win every award every year.

<u>Aziz!</u> nodded at <u>Andrew!</u>'s admission.

The editor nodded and gave a little wink. —Anyway, I have to go abuse some interns now. I'll see you later, <u>Aziz!</u> from Paris.

—Bye, <u>Andrew!</u> from Boston. <u>Aziz!</u> shook his hand. —I'll look for your name in the next celebrity memoir.

<u>Andrew!</u> stopped and laughed before turning the corner.

At the buffet table, Aziz grabbed the last two Danishes, wrapped them up in napkins, and sat down in a banquet chair. He nibbled on unripe melon slices that were hard enough to be horseshoes. When he was done, he opened his orientation folder and sighed:

Today's Events (29 September 2012)
- Getting to know your affiliates
- Understanding the grievance policy (& why you'll never need to, wink wink)
- How to use health insurance abroad
- We are quite woke
- Great moments in ÉPN and Old School publishing history
- Diversity in Publishing: More than Just Race
- Ice Breaker: Hot Potato and Human Machine

A slender blond woman from Austin named Candy Bellinger gave the first presentation with an accent Aziz couldn't quite place (Toronto? Johannesburg? Maine?), winking every time she said the word *bedazzling*. Aziz admired the fake bird of paradise pinned in her coiffure, a spectacle that was nothing short of miraculous. Bedazzling, if you will. When Candy's PowerPoint presentation began, smooth jazz sighed in the surround-sound speakers, the lights dimmed, and then she said, *Behold the bedazzling history of ÉPN*, with a wink. Aziz's eyelids dropped and his heart slowed to a crawl almost immediately.

When the lights turned back on again twenty-five minutes later, Aziz wiped his eyes and stepped into the common hall, passing long conference tables crammed with Subway six-inch sandwiches, massive éclairs, and premature fruit slices fanned across giant plastic plates. He grabbed a handful of unripe strawberries and walked across Sixth Avenue to a popular shawarma cart called Dougga Delish. Aziz started chatting with the vendor in Maghrebi Arabic, a chubby guy dressed in a Tunisian flag apron and Yankees cap. After one sentence, he knew Aziz was Moroccan French, a huge smile plastered across his face.

They talked about the Africa Cup, Barça's draw with Chelsea in the Champions League, and the 2003 bombings in Casa, which he expressed deep sadness for, even though it'd been nine years. Mehdi lived with his wife, two brilliant girls (one at Cooper Union and the other at Brooklyn College), and his cynical uncle, all in Crown Heights. Aziz wasn't sure where Crown Heights was, but it sounded far away. He handed Mehdi a twenty, but the vendor shook his head.

—Yella, Aziz insisted, cocking his chin in the air.

Mehdi smiled, exposing three gold teeth that made Aziz aware of his own gap. —No, brother, he said in Maghrebi Arabic, your money is no good here.

Aziz patted him on the shoulder, shook his hand, and nodded. —Be in peace Mehdi.

—You too, bro, Mehdi said in Arabic before turning back to the impatient customers crucifying him with their eyes. Aziz tossed his twenty into his tip jar. —Okay, Mehdi shouted in perfect New York English, hitting the grill with his skillet, who's next?

Aziz walked without a destination, lost in his own thoughts, absorbed in the endless energy of the city, reminiscing about Yesha's breath on his chest, thinking about his father who'd told him never to look back, picturing Hassan's wheezing body as it breathed its last breaths inside his convulsing arms. Aziz thought of his friends back home who sent him pervy text messages in the middle of the night about J-Lo and hysterical emails about random Banksy sightings, he thought of Sakina, his sister, who was still in mourning, just as he was supposed to be. As he dodged a platoon of corporate infantry in navy pinstriped suits by walking into the street between parked cars and idling taxis on Nassau Street, he crossed the street and ran down the subway stairs. On the A train, he ate his shawarma that dribbled down its tin foil chemise into the paper bag, breaking up the sandwich's heat with a cold can of Coke, his teeth rotting with every sip. As Aziz ate his lunch, he thought about Mehdi and his two brilliant daughters, he thought about his fave place to eat in Paris, a tiny kiosk that served crêpes de Gruyère, scrambled eggs, pesto, and ham a few blocks from the Montparnasse subway station, he thought about Hassan, his incorrigible optimism, and his love of proverbs, Ovid creation myths, and Amina El Bakouri's poetry, especially the line, "Open up your arms to the wind," he thought about falling asleep with Yesha in old movie theaters in Paris and Sakina trembling to the Arabic prayer of the dead, Aziz thought about Duke Ellington's "In a Sentimental Mood," which he used to hum as a kid when walking to school, and then he thought about how long it had been since he'd kissed a woman who'd kissed him back with the same passion, urgency, and surrender that he did.

He walked up the staircase to street level and crossed the Brooklyn Bridge, unbuttoning his collar and untangling his tie before it became a silk noose. For a second, he considered turning around and making it to the one o'clock training session, but something pushed him forward, something connected to his own isolation and nostalgia. His heart felt like an old Parisian ghetto, full of displaced tenants, grounded imagination, collapsed buildings, and shiny Starbucks sprouting from the ground like nightshades. He felt displaced, violated, and bullied by his life in Paris. He felt estranged, disfigured, and liberated by his life in New York. He felt overwhelmed and overstimulated by his emotional reality. But mostly, he felt alone. Aziz was drowning in the city's energy, gagging on its billboards, and burning up in the contagion of numbers. His lips were silenced by fire and his heart held hostage by triage.

ADULTHOOD

14. FLOWERS ARE THE CLUMSIEST METAPHORS

I.

After Hurricane Sandy slams into the tri-city power grid, wiping out the electricity in all five boroughs, the city becomes a giant cocoon of shadow and artifact. The C train is knocked unconscious. Aziz sees no way out of his New York nightmare now. He smells salt and broken chrysanthemums. He realizes in a moment of deadline-clarity that he has no other choice but to stay alive for his family. Whether New York gets submerged in rising sea levels, whether brainwashed Jihadists attack New York again using suicide bombers and remote-controlled dirty bombs inside a Penn Station locker, whether the former megalomaniacs of the Soviet Union and the People's Republic of China launch ICBMs from hidden silos in Beijing and Moscow after a night of drinking and a trillion-dollar poker ante, whether his paralysis underneath the Hudson River is temporary or his final resting place, Aziz needs to survive this agony and fucking stay alive. His family needs him now more than ever. For the first time, his family relies on him not just emotionally, but financially. It's a seminal moment in his life and he's not ready to give it up. He literally arm-wrestled his own nihilism to get this job. Hassan isn't ready yet to meet him in paradise and Aziz needs to shed fresh tears for another meuf besides Yesha. He needs to kiss a woman who will close her eyes when they make love and not hide him in the closet because she has a racist father who hates Arabs, intellectuals, communists, and brown people. Aziz needs to keep Hassan's dream alive. He needs to remember the smell of wet cedar wood, girlie shampoo, and freshly baked houbz araby. He has too much to live for, too much to fight for, too much to let go of. He can't die before he falls in love again and he can't die in New York, a city he doesn't love, a city he doesn't even understand. He can't die this way, not in isolation, not anonymously, not without the chime of another woman's voice inside his head, without her teeth imprinted on his nipples, not before he discovers her scent hidden in old towels and lingering in unwashed pillowcases. This cannot be his time to go. He will reject everything except his own survival.

2.

Suzanne doesn't understand why the New York subway is stuck, practically constipated inside the tunnel, but it's strange and terrifying. Sitting in a silent and dark subway has become a street fight inside her brain between the educated side that's calculating new itineraries and rationalizing alternate worlds and the reptilian side that's freaking out like a paranoid schizophrenic amped on meth. She feels like at any moment, she could be a train wreck inside a train wreck. Can tragedy be melodrama, irony, and fractal, all at once? She wants to cry or maybe kick out the subway window or hug a stranger or run into another car for safety. Maybe, her mum was right after all. Maybe, getting stuck on the C train is what she gets for flying to New York on a whim after listening to a malnourished psychic in Seattle tell her what she clearly wanted to hear. Maybe, this is what she gets for rebelling against inertia in Chicago where her destiny was plotted and cast before she'd opened her eyes. Maybe, this is what she gets for thinking that traveling is just an elevated metaphor for love.

LARVA

15. LOST IN THE SPIRIT WORLD (WINNIE YU)

It was a strangely cold day for New York for the middle of September and there were stunned, half-frozen insects blanketing the windshields of parked cars like discarded ingots. Winnie got off the subway at Fulton and strolled down the street in his twelve-bar Spike-Lee stride when he heard someone screaming in toxic Cantonese up above like she was assaulting the clouds. He unlocked the front door of the building when the furious voice crashed down the stairwell like a grand piano.

—Sha bi! Sha bi! Why don't you go back to the subway then?

—I'm doing the best job I can.

—Tao jiang hu!

—Stop yelling in my face!

—You're a pathetic loser! You can't even provide for us.

—What do you expect? Only one of us is working.

—You call that work?

—I call it survival.

—You used to be a professor in China. Now, look at you!

—Honor is a luxury, not food.

Inside his bedroom, Winnie closed his window and pulled down the blinds, but the words invaded his bedroom, crawling down the walls through the vent like long red centipedes until they entered his head space. He threw on Adidas sweats and a long-sleeve T-shirt and pulled the covers up to his chin, his heart trembling in the darkness.

—You're a failure. Just like your ba.

—I brought us here, didn't I?

—An airplane could do that.

—If you hate your life so much, why don't you help out once in a while?

—Your job is to be the provider and bring home money for us to live.

—My job is to play music that no one listens to. Besides, New York is too expensive and America is too modern for you to be that old-fashioned.

Patriarchy is a bitch, Winnie thought as he covered his head with a pillow.

—I can't even look at you.

—You don't look at me. You're too busy yelling.

Winnie pulled out a j from his nightstand, took a couple drags, and turned off the lamp, his pillow covering his head, his blanket draping his body. The back of his eyeballs hurt and he could feel his legs slowly drifting into soft dreamy ether, but sleep couldn't happen fast enough.

The next day, Winnie made veggie lo mein noodles with bok choy, sesame oil, and tofu for Tian Tian, the little vegetarian. About a month ago, she'd declared that she was a "no-hurt-at-arian" at the dinner table, so now they had to cook meat in a separate pan that Winnie had drawn a cartoon pig with X's for eyes on the handle. Part of Winnie wondered if Ginger had gotten to his sister somehow because his boo could be fucking persuasive when she got on a roll about animal rights. They ate their noodles with huge chopsticks in the TV room, watching

Hong Kong game shows, Mexican soap operas that made Tian Tian laugh hysterically, and French cartoons about mice. When they were done, he brought out a plate of coconut cookies, the ones Mama bought every week at the Saturday market. He threw one at Tian Tian, which she dropped on the floor.

—Yo, open your mouth, kid, Winnie said. She opened it real wide like a blowfish. He could see her silver fillings in back, the ceiling lights bouncing against the metallic lining. He threw a perfect Jason Kidd lob. The cookie disappeared into her little black hole, her mouth moving in a happy circle like she was chewing on a smile. Every time she swallowed and gestured for more cookie with her hands like a kung fu heroine, he threw another piece her way. Sometimes, it ricocheted against her lips or hit her square in the forehead. Other times, it landed on her dry feathered bangs or bounced off her ear. She giggled with every miss, picking up the tiny chunk off the couch and nibbling on it afterwards. Winnie held another piece of coconut cookie in the air one final time. Tian Tian opened her mouth, her eyes sparkling with animated laughter like little marbles. Suddenly, there was a knock on the door like a slow break beat. Winnie kicked his bunny slippers behind the coffee table, stuck the piece gingerly in her eager mouth, rubbed her head, and then unlatched the front door.

—Whaddup, Boz?

—'Sup, Win?

They gave each other hip-hop hugs. —Just chilling. You wanna come in?

—Nah man, throw on your kicks. We going to Harlem, baby.

—What's there?

—You gonna like it. And we got wheels.

When they got to Ginger Lin's condo, the scene was booming. People were talking up a storm, passing around blunts and playing dominoes, a DJ was spinning Mathematics, Black Star, The Roots, and Madlib, Winnie smelled sticky weed and

C-bombs, there was a group of people shaking it in the living room, and a whole lot of shorties were in the kitchen, sipping Henny and bougie red wines, laughing like mermaids, conjugating joy. It felt like everything had been flipped on. Winnie greeted some of his homies that he hadn't seen since the world was flat and then he tapped the Henny to a Wu-Tang song, beating his head, smiling at the serendipity, taking it all in.

—Hey, Winnie Yu.

He turned around. —Ginger Lin. They hugged and kissed, short and sweet like a one-two punch. —What's up, baby?

—You know, kids, cunts, and crayons. My kinda Pez.

He started laughing. —Shiiiit.

—I saw another Buddha Mao of yours the other day.

—Which one? he asked defiantly, a tiny smirk dimpling his cheek.

—Jamaica.

—The F or the J line?

—F?

—179th or 212th street?

—What is this, an interrogation? 179th if you must know.

—Girl, that's older than Chia Pets.

—You're a genius Winnie Yu.

—Xie xie. Takes one to know one.

—It's good to see you, baby. I've missed you.

—You too, Ginger Snap.

Ever since Winnie had shown her his Long Island City masterpiece, a sprawling and intricate love song for her and his family created with manga linework and a pointillist background of Chinatown, Ginger has felt an emboldened and rewired love for Winnie. It's not that she doubted her importance in his life, but seeing herself in his work for the first time changed how she felt about him, about their relationship, and about the emotional voltage of his artwork. —You look tired, boo.

—Man, I'm so tired, he sighed in Mandarin, but you've been on my mind all week.

She smirked the way he loved, a little wicked, her mouth twisted to one side, halfway between a pout and declaration. He noticed she had some crazy *Charlie's Angels* shit going on with her tight turquoise pants, one exposed shoulder that showed off her freckles like chestnut constellations, her hair gelled to one side, a little chichi scarf tied around her neck like some hot little Frenchie. He'd known Ginger forever, it seemed. They'd been friends since the zit invasion, even hooked up once in a friend's basement after arguing passionately all night about Biggie versus 2Pac, Nirvana versus Jesus Jones, *Dragon League* versus *X*, *Reservoir Dogs* versus *Dazed & Confused*, Tommy versus Polo, Mamoun's Falafel versus Dougga Delish, Brooklyn versus Manhattan, Wo Hop versus New Wong, Prospect Park versus Central Park, Knicks versus Bulls, just jumping from one debate to another like archnemeses secretly in love, but something changed when Winnie ran into Ginger at Astor Place back in 2000, both of them suddenly in full bloom. That moment was where it all began for them as a couple.

Ever since his ba died, Winnie needed her now more than ever, though he never told her enough. Ginger felt him because she'd also lost her dad, who was just a Chinese intellectual and eloquent dissident, or so they said, just a casual fling with her white mom who'd wandered into an upscale bar in Beijing one night to order Chongqin hot pot while on assignment for *Nation*. Based on the stories her mom had told her, the memory of her ba lingered in the family legend like the silent tragedy, shame, and denial of a stillborn child. Supposedly, he got shot by one of his own students at Tsinghua University where he'd taught econ, snipered right in the eye like he was a raccoon raiding the trash bin of democracy or something. Ginger's father had been an activist and supporter of Hu Yaobang, one of the most vocal critics of the Chinese government who had demanded major reforms back in the day. Ginger said he'd died execution-style in Tiananmen Square demonstrations when she was just a baby. Nowadays, it seemed like they were the only Asian Americans they knew in the city without dads. How sad was that shit? They shared the same kong xu, they struggled with the same family void, the same cultural amnesia, the same obsession with empty stairwells and dark hallways, the same vulnerability to haunted altars, broken pictures, and vacant chairs in school auditoriums. Sometimes, Winnie felt like it was just a matter of time before he started falling for Ginger as a grownass man. After all, her ba was lost in the spirit world too, funneled into a myth by time, reduced to an overdeveloped portrait inside a scuffed bamboo picture frame now, his inscrutable face, his ageless features, all adorned by plastic leis and glistening garlands, his memory immune to the changing world, sometimes aspiring to infinity in every retelling, but always frozen to the touch since she was a hapa girl in race denial. For the first half of Ginger's life, she pretended she wasn't Asian and now she routinely forgot she was white. Classic hapa girl blues.

When the DJ started spinning "You Got Me" by The Roots featuring Erykah Badu, they both smirked like fucking dorks. This song was their anthem after they'd started dating. Winnie grabbed Ginger's hand and lead her to the dancefloor. He placed his hands on her waist, his fingers inside her belt loops, pulling her against him, their bodies moving together, legs and waists collated, his hands sliding down to caress her ass as she put an arm around his neck and raised her other arm in the air before dropping it to hold his hand with soft pressure. Winnie felt her pulse in his hand. Ginger's smell was sweet and bitter like pickled ginger, green tea mochi, and spearmint leaves. Their stomachs rubbed against each other as they danced, gliding back and forth, faithful like a mirror. Their dads might have abandoned them, made them orphans in this country, but Winnie and Ginger were a family when they were together. They were their own refuge, their own zip code. As they moved in sync to the break beats, their thighs rhymed in sticky couplets. Together they formed a complete erotic. Winnie felt himself get hard in the semi-darkness as he swallowed Ginger's sugary plum scent and inhaled the heat of her skin, the music connecting them both sexually and nostalgically as they became parallel forces of desire, their hips expressing a synchronicity of longing and joy and belonging. He felt awake in her arms now. His blood was a marathon. Her kisses burned his throat like kerosene.

The next morning, Winnie washed his face and brushed his teeth with Ginger's fancy electric toothbrush, something he just started doing recently after the dentist said he had three cavities that looked like tiny mines, the enamel pillaged by too much late-night boba. Winnie looked in the mirror and noticed his eyes were bloodshot and his cheeks were puffy. He really needed to lay off drinking for the rest of the week. In the bedroom, he kissed Ginger's neck, smelled her hair, and thought about last night. After everyone had left, they'd picked up stained wine glasses, encrusted hors d'oeuvre plates, and Turkish ashtrays crammed with blunts all around her place and then made love on the area rug with a fierce and candid urgency that had been missing recently. Their jam-packed, always-on schedules had cockblocked their intimacy most of the summer, their professional ambitions both inflaming and threatening their relationship in ways they both hated but couldn't avoid right now.

Ginger woke up, threw on one of his dirty Supreme T-shirts, made vegetarian dumplings and dan dan noodles in her fancy wok, poured them the rest of the leftover Miraval, rolled a j, lit it and hit it, and then passed it his way as they chowed down.

The weed was better than MSG, it made Winnie wanna throw her ass on the table and fuck her sweetly again, but he resisted that temptation. They got dressed, looking at each other in the mirror as they held each other, watching their reflections with fierce tenderness. It was bad feng shui to have a mirror in the bedroom, but Ginger didn't fucking care, they both liked the mirror because it replicated them, multiplied their family by two.

They walked to the subway on 116th Street. After Winnie passed the turnstile and looked for Ginger, he heard music playing on the platform. He *knew* this song. It was the "March of The Dancing Spirits," the song they played every Chinese New Year. He tried to pull Ginger in the other direction, but she tugged back.

—Winnie, where you going, boy? We gotta go *that* way, she said, pointing right at Mr. Li. —Besides, I wanna hear him play. You know I've got a soft spot for this old man.

Winnie did too, but he wasn't in the right head space to see his neighbor. —Nah Ginger, he said, the hookup is that way.

—Baby, we'll *never* get a seat there. Trust me.

He shook his head, but she yanked his glum ass down the subway platform before he could think of an excuse until they were standing right in front of Mr. Li. She nodded her head to the music and smiled at Winnie like they were sharing some magical fucking moment together. She tossed a five-dollar bill in his instrument case that swayed like a feather until it landed on the velvet interior, its lithe green body reminding her of an ampersand. There was a little sign tacked to the instrument case that Winnie tried not to read. It said:

Mr. Kwan Li
Professional Player of guqin.
I play song for
Thanking you.

Mr. Li was dressed in a thin yellow sweater vest and a white button-down, creased gray pants and polished black shoes. His face was somber, sweaty, and sad, but he kept playing his song, filling up the subway tunnels with music most Americans had never heard before, playing for his family that couldn't hear him, playing for all the passengers who didn't listen, playing for his wife who didn't see him, and playing for a girl in Western China who was probably dead, a story that still broke Winnie's heart when he thought about it. Winnie wasn't sure what happened, but the next thing he knew, he put his hands in his pockets and took out all his dead presidents, dropping everything he had in the instrument case: eighty-one dollars and eighteen cents, a pretty numerical palindrome. Ginger's eye's opened wide. Winnie and Kwan Li exchanged glances, but the old man kept playing like an OG.

When the train doors closed, Ginger turned to him. — Winnie Yu, why you so goddamn beautiful?

—Yo, it just broke my heart. That guy's someone's ba too, you know?

—I do, baby, she said, hugging him with intuitive tenderness. —I definitely do. She kissed Winnie's hand and bit her lip because she knew what was going on.

Winnie tried hard to control his emotions on the train, but he couldn't do it, he just couldn't do it, he didn't know why. As he laid his head on Ginger's lap and tried not to cry, she scratched his neck and rubbed his hair, told him it was okay, told him she was there for him, told him that his ba heard everything he said as she backhanded the petulant glances from commuters with an angry look that made them turn away quickly. She'd never seen Winnie like this before. He was always trying to control his shit, even when he didn't need to, even when he shouldn't have, because he felt like he needed to be available to the people he loved, so that his own issues didn't sabotage their needs, but he couldn't do that forever. Before this moment, Winnie thought he was done with everything, thought he'd worked it all out inside his head, but then he saw Mr. Li playing his music for passengers who didn't notice, didn't care, and didn't listen while the old man told his story of heartache and cowardice to a world both indifferent and immune to his pain. Winnie just lost it. He bawled on Ginger's lap until there was nothing left of him. Some tiny, delicate part of him broke inside when he saw Kwan Li all by himself on the subway platform, confessing his grief in his music and translating his sadness that would never get fixed.

16. FALLING FROM ROOFTOPS (GINGER LIN)

FOR AS LONG AS Ginger could remember, she'd wanted her condo jam-packed with precocious bambini. The living room would be a war zone of creativity, love, and personality. She pictured their kids playing the violin, the guqin, and the piano at school concerts. She pictured them with illustrious careers like chaos mathematicians, internationally famous slam poets, Art Nouveau architects, and house DJs. She pictured them teaching art therapy to pissed-off tweens from rough backgrounds, rescuing stranded whales off the Australian shoreline, and climbing mountains in Nepal for their honeymoons. She pictured them at their hip-hop, tap, jazz, and meringue classes after school, going to their recitals with Winnie and watching their babies shake their asses on stage. She'd turn to the other parents very casually and say, *Those are* our *babies, the ones tearing it up on the dancefloor, and they don't even practice, that's the odd thing. It just comes naturally to them like every art form they've ever studied. Their IQs are technically off the charts, but after 165, who's counting, am I right?*

Ginger could picture it all so clearly. Their kids would play make-believe in their bathrobes, speak in Russian accents for no reason whatsoever, and go back and forth yelling at each other in Taiwanese, Cantonese, Spanish, and English without a second thought. They'd go to trilingual private schools and Chinese school on the weekend. She'd find a way to get them in to the UN Lycée so they could earn their IB at the ages of sixteen before taking a gap year, something neither she nor Winnie had ever done. She'd take them shopping in the city and buy them butterfly barrettes from SoHo, little hats from Norway, jumpers, sequined tights, and brown pleated skirts from Repetto, kung fu slip-ons and plastic nunchaku from Mott Street. She'd buy her (hypothetical) daughter hip little blue sneaks with blinking lights in the soles, black hoodies, and a Yankees cap. She'd buy her (hypothetical) son hip little pink chucks, grey cardigans, and tweed pageboy hats. And for Christmas, she'd buy them state-of-the art electronics from Hong Kong and Tokyo, yoga mats from Delhi, green tea from Taipei and Kyoto, elaborate marker sets that smelled like farmers markets, pottery wheels that spun like turn tables, a reflector telescope that unpacked the whole universe, and boxes, so many damn boxes of Lego sets, enough Legos to barricade themselves from reality or recreate the Louvre in eight-bit style or build a rainbow igloo for their gay and trans friends.

Ginger and Winn would write their kids love haikus and then stuff them in their Christmas stockings along with hard candy and mochi from the Ichiban store, making them read the notes out loud before their first piece of candy. They'd spend the weekends and the evenings together as a family, something neither of them had growing up. None of that quality time crap. And they'd play charades, watch the Superbowl, Jeopardy, K-drama, and Taiwanese soaps, cheering for the overpaid Knicks every year when they lost. They'd stroll through the Bowery, hit the Yu-Lin connection every month to see their overworked moms, and travel to Asia, Europe, and Canada every two years to burn incense at their ancestors' graves in Taipei, Hong Kong,

Vancouver, and Beijing, even though their Chinese in-laws told them they were American, even when they felt like they didn't belong anywhere except with each other.

Ginger wanted her kids to sleep with them in bed when they had nightmares and take baths with them when they're tiny as tadpoles. She wanted to go to their Christmas concerts and take them to Central Park in the summer for multicultural picnics, teach them to cook veggie zongzi dumplings and mock Peking duck rolls. She wanted them to know what it was like to have a dad who wasn't just a story or a tenant living in their picture frames. With Winnie, they'd have a ba they could hug and laugh with and talk to and love and paint with. He'd be a dad that picked them up, twirled them in nauseous circles, and carried them to their bedrooms when they fell asleep on the couch. A ba that would play handball with them in the Lower East Side and draw space aliens with them during creative time. A man who would dress up as Asian Santa and take them out trick-or-treating when the air started to bite. Their ba would be a good man, a lovable man who'd carry his babies in his arms and let them sleep on his chest as he walked down Ninth Avenue to meet her at the Spice Market.

Winnie had been AWOL for three whole days when he showed up at Ginger's apartment like a lost package, his eyes full of zest and mystery again, making it impossible for Ginger to hold a grudge. She tried hard though, just out of principle. They spent the weekend watching Wong Kar Wai DVDs and ordering spicy salmon rolls, vegan cheeseburgers, and pineapple fried rice. They made sweet sweet love in the TV room, on top of her shoes in the walk-in closet, even underneath the dining room table. They danced to Rihanna, Starr Chen, MIA, Stevie, Killer Mike, Kelly Rowland, and Bebel Gilberto in their underwear and sat in the sunshine on the kitchen floor drinking cucumber water.

Sunday morning as they ate vegetarian chicken and waffles at a nearby Harlem joint, Winnie told Ginger that he wanted to show her what he'd been working on for the past month. Whatever it was, she was in. Winnie never showed her his jams. She always discovered them a couple weeks later where she'd yank out her phone and take as many photos as she could like a Banksy Bitch since Winnie's art always got covered, removed, or reproduced into Etsy projects before the paint was dry. Sometimes, Ginger could get M-Boz to give her a few clues about the next installation, but Winnie never showed her his street art because he didn't want her to worry about him, didn't want her to get in trouble, and he didn't think his art deserved all the attention. Ginger called it implausible deniability. The only things Winnie showed her was the shit he drew on napkins for Tian Tian, the galleys he worked on for graphic novels, and the caricatures he'd made for the kids in her class. For Ginger, it was never enough.

Winnie once made a love poem collage for her out of old Chinese newspapers and surreptitious sketches of her from old photo albums he'd rummaged through while she slept, he transformed a cabbage salad into a replica of the Forbidden City and sculpted a small-scale version of the Temple of Heaven out of Daikon radishes and Vietnamese squash, but tonight Winnie was opening up the streets to her for the first time in their whole relationship, which felt like a watershed moment. She'd been waiting for an invitation since the day they fell in love and started walking across the Brooklyn Bridge, smoking weed and binging on samosas and malai kofta in Jackson Heights, took the Greyhound to Montréal for long weekends, and saved up money to see their favorite MCs at Irving Plaza as two crazy-in-love twenty-somethings trying to work it all out inside their heads. She's been waiting for an invitation since they'd made space for each other inside their lives, since Winnie ran to her on 9/11 and held her so tight, he practically crushed her as he cried into her neck, since Winnie waved goodbye to her at JFK to go to Tokyo for his first exhibition in Asia, smack dab in the middle of Roppongi. Ginger had loved him ever since her return from Istanbul. Now, she was just waiting for Winnie to come and pick her ass up.

There was finally a knock on the door like the break beats in Immortal Technique's "The Illest." Ginger knew that Winn had been going through a Technique phase again and she recognized him just by the beat. Right before she let him in, she waited just a split second, just long enough to prolong her sadness and stoke her desire. She knew her whole life was on the other side. After she opened the door, she gave Winnie a big sloppy hug. Winnie started cracking up when she wouldn't let go of him, but he never let go of her until she was done getting her hug on. He was sweet like that. Ginger looked at his face and sighed, touching the bruises on his cheeks and temples, the busted-up skin on his lips, all with her fingertips. She kissed his pain slowly. Every time her lips grazed a bruise, Winnie said *Ow!* with a smirk. On the 7, they gabbed about the past week like besties. When was it gonna cool down, how long had it'd been since they'd walked through the city together, why had Winnie given Mrs. Li the cold shoulder at the bodega, when was the next movie date at Union Square, and what was the next midlife crisis for Ginger's mom (last year it involved sending dirty texts to barely legal young men on an app called CCBB—*Cougar Cougar Burning Bright*—and now it involved changing her hair color every week from Electric Mango to Anarchy Red like a wounded sk8tergirl). Winnie led her from the Court Square stop to the stairs and then down the street, holding Ginger's hand the whole way, his fingers interlaced with hers like a teenage cliché.

—Kuai dian, he said, zipping up his G-Star hoodie.

—I'm coming, I'm coming, she said, wondering why Winnie was dragging her all the way to *Queens*.

—Yo, if we do this, we gotta be shady.

—Kay, boo.

—Because I can't deal with alphabet bois right now.

—Got it.

—And don't get mad, but I got a brick of Indo with me.

—Win-nie-Yu!

—It's M-Boz's! He's gonna pick it up tonight.

—Then you're gonna call him, right now!

—I'll call him later.

Her face became an angry Bian Lian mask. —What the hell were you thinking? Call him now!

—Don't boss me around, he said, irritated, this weed is *his* problem, not mine.

—If they stop and frisk you, she huffed, it's *everyone's* problem,

—So, in other words, I shouldn't break the law because the war on drugs is racist AF?

—Baby, there's culture jamming and then there's carrying enough weed to get your cute little ass thrown in jail for fifty years.

Winnie smiled sheepishly. —Bloomberg is a little bitch. Point taken.

Ginger shook her head at him in disbelief.

They crossed the street in silence. A hot wind blew into their clothes, smelling of grilled lamb and too-sweet wine. Ginger threw on her hoodie, even though it was still humid. Slight overkill.

They passed a Greek flag dangling in a restaurant window. Ginger was still feisty. She couldn't believe that Winnie had brought a brick of hydroponic weed with him. He must be crazy distracted, but why?

—Soooooooooo, what are we doing in Long Island City anyway? she asked.

—You'll see. It's gonna be off the chain.

Ginger shook her head and he smacked his lips back. They walked in silence down the sidewalk until they were standing in front of a perfectly ugly abandoned building that rubbed right up against the N/W line. A third of its pale-yellow walls was covered in tags, caricatures, and bright bubble fonts. Somehow, though, all the windows were perfectly intact and there were lights on inside. She'd never seen anything like it before.

—What is this place? she asked.

—It's called 5 Pointz, he said, before that, it was known as the Phun Factory.

—Fun factory? Where's the factory? Where's the fun?

—No, he said, chuckling, this place is legit. You can sign up for space here.

—For real?

—Tight, right?

A big part of her didn't want to give him the satisfaction because she was still annoyed with him about the weed, so she stayed quiet, but she was kinda impressed by so many different graffiti styles all plastered like a creative marketplace of design. How any of this was legal, she had no idea.

—This isn't the show, though, Winnie said.

He grabbed Ginger's hand again even after she tried letting go and then led her to a fire escape. Winnie walked up the rusty staircase and jumped on to the roof, pulling her up. For a moment, she was dangling in the air, her body full of fear and joy as he pulled her up to the rooftop with him. As her head spun, her anger blew away like a million pieces of confetti. Winnie covered her eyes with his hands before she could orient herself and led her to the middle of the roof. There was a lukewarm breeze that smelled like old bath water and roasted garlic and burnt olive oil, blowing her hair into her lips, tickling her ears, whispering on her skin, every sensation accentuated by the altitude and the blindness. Ginger felt like she was gliding through outer space, an astronaut hovering above the planet in a distant swirl of time. Winnie removed his hands, pivoting her body like a ballet instructor teaching good posture.

—Okay, open your eyes now! he said.

But Ginger just stood there, listening to the train curving in the August sky like a giant mechanical dragon. She could picture its steel scales rising high above rooftops, flying over busy streets, its long metallic body twisting and curling into a creaky capital S as it soared to Manhattan or glided to Astoria. She stood there for twenty tiny seconds, just to prolong her weightlessness and surrender to the joy she didn't feel she deserved. When Ginger opened her eyes, she gasped. Winnie had laid out a rooftop picnic for her using one of her missing blankets from Turkey with candles scattered between entrées, blue paper plates, and empty wine glasses. She spotted teriyaki salmon for Winnie, grilled asparagus, pine nut couscous, sunflower cutlets, and an endive salad with cranberries, goat cheese, and pralines for her. Cradled by gold candlelight, she noticed loaves of multigrain baguettes, stinky cheese, Israeli falafels (holla!), Italian olives, imported mineral water, bars of dark chocolate with mint filling, and a bottle of her fave Bordeaux, a Chateau Léoville Barton 1989. Ginger couldn't believe it. Five months ago, she'd told Winnie about getting drunk with Kayisha on the best damn wine she'd ever had, but didn't think he was listening. He even remembered the year.

—Winnie Yu, why you so damn beautiful?

He smirked, pulling a corkscrew from his back pocket and opening up the wine with a flick of the wrist.

—Yo, this is for us, he said, filling up her glass.

—Baby, this is so sweet I could fucking scream.

—I know I'm gonna be AWOL soon with that jam in Manhattanville with M-Boz and that *Adbusters* interview in October, so, I just wanted to spend time with you while I could. You're always on my mind, Ginger Snap, even when I get consumed in my work. He took a small, delicate sip of wine and looked into her eyes with such vulnerability, affection, and openness. The love in his eyes was a switchblade slicing through her body.

Ginger took a big gulp and wrapped her arms around his neck, her eyes glimmering like fresh bling. Winnie smelled like a humid spring shower, like corky Bordeaux, like the city, like aerosol and old bath water and green tea and garlic and mint chocolate. She planted hard kisses on his sunburnt face. She thanked him with the wetness of her lips. She kissed him with the fiery tannins in her mouth. She told him everything she felt for him at that moment in the language of wet lips, in the translated vocabulary of dark rooms and lost time. She wanted him to know that she loved him with all the heat in her body, with all qi in her veins, and all the break beats in her ventricles. She loved him at the deepest elemental level of her existence. The steel dragon train was her witness. As they kissed, her body became buoyant, floating above the roof. They could have been dragonflies, their bodies connected together, hovering above the East River until their exoskeletons ejected their souls, their hearts locked in the unchanging grammar of desire.

Sometimes, Ginger got carried away in her head and in her heart, but she didn't care. She'd learned never to apologize for love because love was courage, vulnerability, and mutilation, like ripping your rib cage open so the whole world could see your insides.

They heaped piles and piles of grilled asparagus, sunflower cutlets that tasted just like fried chicken, Carré de l'Est, garlic-filled olives, falafel balls covered in sweet tahini, and chunks of still-warm multigrain bread on their plates. They devoured their food. Sometimes, Winnie paused to remove fish bones from his mouth or Ginger took a massive sip of Bordeaux. When they were done, she laid her head on his lap. Winnie rubbed his hands through her hair while she nibbled on squares of chocolate and sighed. She almost fell asleep, practically fainted from intoxication.

—You want some chocolate? she asked, extending her arm.

—Nah, he said, maybe later?

—Baby, you okay?

—I'm cool.

—Sure?

—Yeah. I just . . . there's one more thing I gotta show you.

—Okay, she said, sitting up. —What is it?

—Stand up, he said, pulling her up by the arms.

—Kay.

—Kuai dian. Over there.

They walked to the edge of the roof, away from the candlelight picnic and back into the darkness. Ginger grabbed Winnie's arm and leaned against his shoulder, stumbling and a little dizzy from the wine. She couldn't bear to look down, it was too much. Winnie put his arm around her and kissed her head, pointing to the other building. At first, she didn't see anything except a subway platform in one direction and a few neon signs in the other, but when she scanned the yellow warehouse covered in a thousand types of graffiti, she noticed a huge mural of a new Buddha Mao hidden in the middle of a melting pointillist cityscape of Chinatown, Hong Kong, Paris, and Taipei. The Buddha Mao was dressed in camouflage pants and a BKI T-shirt, surrounded by bubble Chinese characters with English translations that said, *My family, my art, and my life are three strokes of the same character*. The Buddha Mao was dressed in a white Yankees cap and K Swiss shoes. To his right were Tian Tian and Winnie's mama. To the left, M-Boz. Underneath the Buddha Mao, Winnie had even painted himself, something he never did despite his appreciation for Manet's meta tendencies.

In the mural, Winnie's arms were wrapped around . . . her. It was her. Winnie had painted her for the first time in public, tiny hearts fluttering between their heads. Ginger couldn't believe it. Winnie had painted a graphic love song for everyone he loved and she was his centerpiece. The way Winnie had painted her, the way he captured her, made Ginger look dazzling, glimmering, even mesmerizing. For a second, she saw herself as Winnie saw her, she saw herself as only Winnie could paint her, hovering over a pointillist lake like a sea nymph with big glossy lips and huge chocolate eyes. She was both mundane and miraculous, her hair streaked with glimmering stars and tiny moons glowing in a tiara around her forehead like a celestial coronation. The dimples in her cheeks were craters, her lashes were feathers. He made her more beautiful than she'd felt inside, the way she wished she looked like to the world. How was that even possible? Winn loved her so much he'd declared his love to eight million commuters and published his graphic confessional to the city, decorating an entire building with the graffiti strokes of her little squishy face. Winn loved her so much he'd multiplied her, offered her to the city as a frozen piece of music. This mural was the way he held onto her, the way he saved her from death and old age, the way he filled the void inside him and healed his broken soul by creating a visual mixtape of color, design, and adoration.

—You beautiful little fucker, Ginger said, why are you so . . . but she never finished her sentence. She never could when she got clobbered by emotion. Winnie pulled her closer to his body as she cried into his T-shirt. Ginger clawed him with her purple fingernails and slobbered on his chest. Sometimes, she loved him so much it felt like she'd broken all the bones in her body, suffocating in the pain. They stood there and examined Winnie's mural for a good half an hour, sipping wine, and fitting their lips together like jigsaw pieces. He held her close, smelled her hair, rubbed her neck, but didn't say a word. He didn't need to. She felt everything he said in the language of his art. They returned to the candlelight dinner holding hands. Only a few candles were still lit, burning bold and bright, fighting the army of darkness until the end.

They cleaned up the rooftop and then took a final look at Winnie's mural, holding each other tight.

Ginger turned to him. —You know Winn, this Buddha Mao is different than your other ones.

—For real?

—Uh huh.

—You dissing my style, boo?

—Baby, you know I don't hate.

—Well ... who then?

She grabbed his hand and lingered on his knuckles with her lips, opening his palm and slowly kissing his Mount of Venus. —Baby, he looks like your ba.

Winnie gulped hard, turning his back to her like there was something painful stuck between his teeth, like she'd just pointed out something he wasn't supposed to understand about himself. After all, she was the only person who could help Winnie come back to himself when he tried to run away. She looked at him as the wind blew in his eyes. He seemed to surrender, looking down below at the hard-knock ground like he was trying to understand how dead things bounced back so quickly into his life. Winnie knew what it felt like to fall from the rooftops, he'd been freefalling since the day his ba got shot in the face and he'd never climbed back out of the shadow pit he'd fallen into. Only she knew that he was trapped, looking up at the 8-bit cityscape with sadness and longing, too afraid to yell for help, too damaged to climb back up, and too proud to give up. She would probably be the only person who could pull him out when he was ready. Ginger wrapped her arms around his waist and wiped her drippy nose and wet lips against his neck. He smelled like home to her. She felt his pain, felt the heaviness of his soul, felt the dirge beating in his pounding pulse, felt the accumulated debt of all the mistakes he'd committed in his life and all the things he'd never said out loud to his ba before he died, the words cluttering his ventricles and cutting off his blood supply. She understood the pain of loving a cataracted memory because her ba had always been a fuzzy memory. She knew it hurt Winnie to live in a splintered dream and lose the only loving male voice inside his head. But she also knew that as long as Winnie's feet stayed on the ground, he would keep creating art to navigate the human and the spirit worlds because that was what he did.

Winnie created community through his art. It was the one perfect thing he could give his ba when everything else came out wrong, got crushed by time, or died in his hands. For Ginger her community would come later with the family she and Winnie were trying to start. Maybe along the way, she'd heal some of the recurring pain she'd felt her whole damn life living in racial and cultural purgatory. Ginger's (future) family would be the matrix of her joy, she just knew it, the one place where she would always belong, where love could also be a homeland. As she nuzzled Winnie's chest and slobbered her incoherent love like a drunk bridesmaid, she suddenly remembered the fertility tests she'd signed up for, which filled her heart with irrational hope and gleeful determination.

EGG

17. THE INVISIBLE DRESS: A STORY TOLD IN **AAPI GRAPHIC SLANG**

BY EARLY AUGUST, THE summer had changed songs so often on the meteorological jukebox that Winnie lost count of which season it was. When his train to 116th Street finally arrived, he'd never needed some **Buddha** so bad. His nerves were shot, his two-tone **Stüssy** T-shirt clung to his back, and he kinda smelled like his strawberry smoothie after spilling it on the subway. Winnie got off and walked halfway up the staircase when he heard Kwan Li's music again, stopping dead in his tracks. Dude was fucking ubiquitous. Winnie listened to the music coming from his **guqin**. Nothing he knew, but it was **a'ight**. The melody was slow and sobbing. It hit the morphine wavelength in his brain somehow. It was a song about exile and amnesia, a song about the words diasporic people lost when they migrated, words Mr. Li would never hear again. Winnie didn't know why, maybe he was projecting his own voids onto Kwan Li, but instead of **dipping** like he normally did when he ran into the old man and just wasn't in the right headspace to feel so vulnerable, for some reason, Winnie went back to the subway platform and stood a few feet away from the old man. Mr. Li was wearing creased black pants and a starched blue button-down even though it was oppressively hot that day. There were sweat stains under his arms and his salt and pepper hair was groomed all neat like a Korean preacher, parted on the left side with new muted silver streaks above his temples like tendrils of smoke. Dude had *maybe* two **Georgies** and a couple silvers in his case, but he kept on playing like he had a full house. Winnie admired that about him. It's like Mr. Li offered his art to the world whether people wanted it or not, whether **peeps** appreciated his **mad skillz** or not. The old man played each musical phrase with his eyes closed, concentrating on every single note like it mattered deeply to him, as if his **fam** could hear him all the way from the Chinese countryside or wherever they were in 2012.

The 2 pulled up and its doors opened, passengers exploding on the platform like a particle accelerator, their paths intersecting and splitting into a million crisscrossing trajectories before scattering, sucked up by exit signs and stairwells. It was like watching fireworks at half their natural speed. After the dust cleared, a group of high school punks in cargo shorts and tank tops stopped in front of the MTA map. They were awkward white kids, too young to keep it **trill** and too old to swat away, all standing around like they wanted to **open up shop** right here, their hair gelled and spiked up like potted wheat grass, their faces scarred with fast-food acne that reminded Winnie of tiny red volcanoes. Like all punks with shitty role models, they tried too damn hard, they **copped attitude** without adversity, they demanded respect from strangers without sacrifice or reciprocity, and they said yo way too fucking much. Winnie disliked them. He wanted them to **peace out** like now, but then one of them cocked his head to the side at Mr. Li like he was saying, *Yo, check out this Asian bitch with his* **wack** *instrument.* They circled the old man like it was a prison yard fight and started **talking smack** about him in front of his face like he didn't exist. As a **graphic**, there was nothing Winnie hated more than people **dissing** art because of personal taste, cultural ignorance, or peer pressure, and white kids (white people) were the worst.

—Yoooooo, check this dude out!

—Yo, **whachew** playing, pops?

—Yo, that an Asian banjo?

—**Word up**, yo.

—Yo, play something **hot**.

—Yeah, you know any Bow Wow, yo?

—40 Glocc?

—Three 6 Mafia, yo!

—Chingy?

—Sticky Fingaz, yo?

—Choclair?

—Mac Dre, yo.

—Paperboys?

—Fiddy?

Winnie **mad-dogged** them, mostly because those were some horrendous fucking **MCs**, but also because he didn't like the way they were treating an elder, something he literally only saw white kids do, screaming at their parents, telling them to fuck off, demanding money, cars keys, and designer jeans from them, blaming their professors for their shitty work ethic, asking for gifts from grandparents just for existing, talking to old people like they were feeble children, and just being all around assholes. **That kinda shit** just ignited a fuse in him, made him wanna **smack-shame** these little bitches.

Mr. Li ignored the white punks.

The leader of the pack, the one who looked like a zitty blowfish, got into Kwan Li's **grill**. —Gramps, I'm talking to you. You know any **legit** shit? Fiddy? Da Brat? Lil Jon and the East Side Boyz?

Kwan Li looked up at him but kept playing his **guqin**, his arms wobbling to the vibrato.

Winnie wasn't saying it was his fave music or anything, but he respected Mr. Li's craft. It wasn't top 40 **radiocrack**, thank

God, and it wasn't trying to be either. Why couldn't these **motherfuckers download reality** for a **sec**?

—Yo Glitz, let's **bounce**.

—Yeah man, this shit's lame, yo.

—**Hold up**, Glitz said, I'm almost done. Gramps, I'm talking to you. I'll give you ten bucks if you play Ashanti right now. You can buy a hundred Top Ramens with **that shit**.

That's when Winnie lost it. —Yo **gweilo**, he said, it's time for **youz** to **bounce** the fuck outta here.

—**Mofo**, this ain't your problem.

—**Mofo?** Who you calling **mofo**? Winnie asked, his face painted in a gloss of disgust.

—Yo, why you **tripping**? one of the boys asked. —Glitz is just playing.

—You don't do that shit to your elders, Winnie said, it's disrespectful.

—Yo Glitz, let's **bail**. This dude's **wack**.

—Yeah, come on, man.

—**Smoke** this dude.

—Yo, **hold up**, Glitz grinned, we gonna leave in one goddamn minute, but not cuz of this Chinese bitch.

—Don't call me a bitch, Winnie warned, taking a step.

—Bitch, Glitz dared.

Winnie turned to Glitz's posse. —Yo, tell your **punkass** friend to back the fuck up or I'm gonna **lay him down**. The truth was, Winnie didn't believe in violence for the simple reason that it never worked. The infinite regress of revenge was some serious Hegelian shit and he wasn't particularly good at **scrapping** either, but sometimes, he had to pretend he **fucked shit up** to keep **peeps** off his back because America was such a primitive fight club when it came to gender performance, especially for men, so his choices were **straight-up** limited.

—Glitz, drop this sucker.

—Dude, let's **bail**. He's got like fifty pounds on you, Glitz.

—Bruh, knock this **buster** down.

—**Nah** man, let's get the fuck outta here.

With a defiant look, Glitz took a step towards Winnie, his hair all puffed up in adolescent rage. He looked Winnie smugly in the eyes and said: —Bitch, **whachew** gonna do? I'm like five across and **youz** like one and a half, you **chinky*** motherfucker.

*Not graphie slang, just racist garbage from another white kid who grabbed fruit from the lowest hanging branch on the tree of white supremacy.

Kwan Li's instrument made a scratching sound like in the movies and then **shit went down**. It was a sticky blur of upper-cuts, crunching bones, broken skin, elbows to eye sockets, flying feet to swollen lips, throbbing knuckles rammed into skittish diaphragms, kneecaps into nuts, and blood jacksonpollocked on dirty concrete. It was a concatenation of male rage for every generation and style. And somewhere in that morass of human bodies, Winnie was trapped in a teenage mob frenzy, pushing those teen punks off the old man, trying to protect Kwan Li like he was his own **yeye** or something when those chumps bumrushed him, stomping on Winnie's ribs and kicking his face with their overpriced sneakers and extracting the **motherfucking qi** outta him until he **peaced out**, a visitor in his own shadow world. His last memories were a sauna, all hot and foggy, his tears burning his eyes. For a brief moment before he zonked out, though, Winnie could have sworn he saw Mr. Li giving those **motherfuckers** the **smackdown**, his palms forming a tiger claw or some shit like that, performing crazy moves like the Jumping Over the Moon and the Praying Mantis techniques. Winnie could have sworn he saw the old man striking those rent-a-thugs with his fists, circling the air with his feet like a pissed-off Shaolin warrior, giving them a **heaping plate of asskicking** like a kung fu master **fucking shit up** old school. Winnie would never know whether his vision was a hallucination or legit. By the time he woke the hell up, he was sitting in a Chinese diner he'd never seen before. Kwan Li stared at him all bug-eyed like a physician looking for vital signs. His face told him that Winnie was a lost cause and maybe he was, maybe he'd always been since the day his **ba got jumped**.

Winnie looked around the diner before touching his face. His cheeks fucking throbbed. —Kwan Li? he asked in English, rubbing his eyes with the back of his hand.

—**Shi**, the old man replied.

—Yo, Winnie said, switching to Mandarin, my head is killing me, **fam**.

—Here, drink some tea, Kwan Li said. He poured green tea into Winnie's mug and then looked at him again. —This'll help.

Winnie slurped the maroon teacup with blue Swallowtail butterflies on it until it was almost empty.

Kwan Li stared at him without blinking.

—How long I been out? Winnie asked.

—A few hours.

—Fuck, Winnie moaned. He took a few more sips. —What time is it?

—11:41.

Winnie looked around the diner that was too fancy for his tastes. The waitresses looked **brand new**. —How'd I get here anyway?

—I carried you.

—What? he laughed, **for real**?

—**Shi.** Kwan Li said, blinking. The old man looked thin and malnourished. From certain angles, he resembled a large glue stick in a sweater vest, so how in the hell did this dude carry Winnie? The idea seemed fucking crazy to him. They sat there for a couple minutes, mulling over things. Winnie felt uncomfortable wading in the silence, his jaw ached, his eyes were puffy **AF**, his head felt screwed on wrong, and he felt tired and hungry but exhausted too. He gulped down his tea, filling up both their cups. He didn't know what to say to his neighbor who kept staring at him, so he kept drinking his tea.

—You have some cuts and bruises on your face, Kwan Li said, I cleaned them as best as I could, but they'll need to be re-cleaned tonight.

—**Xie xie**, Winnie said, wincing as his hands grazed the bandage outlines above his temple and over his cheek. In his Asian American brain, there was a division between thank you and **xie xie**. When he felt obligated to thank someone, when it wasn't a choice, when gratitude was a mandatory social game he was forced to play with strangers who **didn't mean shit** to him, then he **busted out** the *thank you* like it was fucking punctuation, like it was a long period to end every prosaic sentence with: *Yo. Mrs. Lin, the egg salad was very good thank you, Dear Uncle, your birthday card was very thoughtful thank you, It's cold enough outside to freeze your fucking synapses thank you, Your daughter keeps making obscene gestures at me, Mr. Yang, thank you*, but when Winnie felt humbled, surprised, or when gratitude bubbled up, **xie xie** always came out of his mouth before he could think about it. It was always that word and nothing else because his gratitude sprang up from his Asian identity, not his American one, that was the cold hard truth. White people were only grateful for tax cuts, distant wars, invented enemies, and faceless veterans.

—Why didn't you walk away? Kwan Li asked suddenly.

—What, you mean from those punks?

The old man nodded.

—I dunno, Winnie said, taking another sip.

The old man gave him a pensive look. —Were you afraid?

—Nah, just pissed.

—You were seriously outnumbered.

—I know, it was stupid of me.

The old man nodded again. —Sometimes delusion is a necessary part of courage.

—**Gēmen**, I just went **703**.

—**Shénme?**

—I **lost my shit.**

Kwan Li shook his head in confusion.

—I went crazy.

—At least you tried. The odds were unfair, that's all.

—Yeah. Also, I'm not a scrapper.

—Thank you for trying. I didn't expect your help.

—You don't have to thank me. I'd do it again in a heartbeat.

Kwan Li blinked hard and sipped his tea.

—Thing is, I got jumped. No pride in that.

The old man smirked. —True bravery has no reward. It's an accessory for virtue.

Winnie gave him a skeptical look and finished his tea.

—Ginger's your girlfriend, right?

—Yup.

Kwan Li looked him square in the eyes. —And your name is Winnie, right?

Winnie nodded.

—Isn't that normally a woman's name?

Winnie blushed and shook his head. —Yeah, my parents named me before I was born and then they just said, fuck it, our son will understand women better now with this name. Kinda cruel if you ask me.

The old man started laughing, his eyes watering in the corners like Winnie's **ba**.

—Interestingly enough, Winnie said, I've got an auntie in Vancouver and a cousin in Hong Kong named Winnie too, so there's a history to that name in my fam.

Kwan Li wiped his eyes and then his face turned serious. —Winnie, I want to tell you a story. It's the kind of story you can only tell a stranger because it has no place in my life anymore.

—Go for it, man.

—When I was your age, I once met a girl I loved very much.

—You mean Mrs. Li?

The old man gave a disgusted look. —No, definitely not her. Winnie **busted out** laughing.

—We grew up in the same village. When I studied at the university, we met each other in the city every weekend. After a while, our love became strong like a Chinese knot. Solid like platinum rings. Our relationship was our own public vow and everyone in the village knew it.

Winnie refilled Mr. Li's teacup, astonished to hear the old man opening up.

—She was my childhood sweetheart and I was going to marry her after I graduated.

—So, like, what happened?

—One evening, Xiulan and I ate dinner at The Friendship Lounge. It was our favorite restaurant. As usual, it was filled with the same drunk PLA soldiers and their paid female companions, but it was a cheap place in those days and many locals ate there so we always felt safe. They had the best **baozi** steamed buns and the best **shao long bao** soup in all of Beijing. I paid the bill and then we walked down Qianmen Street together to gaze at window displays. The old man took a big gulp of tea and swallowed. —One of our favorite things to do when we window-shopped was to talk about the imaginary gifts we'd bought each other with our imaginary **yuan**. *I bought you a really nice globe*, she'd say. *Where is it?* I'd ask. **Right here**, she'd say, holding out an empty hand. I love it, I'd tell her. And I meant it. Once, I bought her an invisible Chinese dress. It was mint blue with white flowers and teal buttons. *Here*, I said, *I bought this for you.*

She asked me to describe it in detail to her, so I did. She nodded with approval and then repeated my words: mint blue, white flowers, teal buttons. *I love it,* she'd said, *and I'm not taking it off. Ever.* Before we'd gone out that night, I'd even asked her, *Are you still wearing the dress?* And she'd said, *Of course. I'll wear it until it's real.* Those words made me so happy, I almost cried in gratitude. About five blocks from the restaurant, we stopped to look inside the window of a jewelry store to look for new imaginary gifts when a group of PLA soldiers stopped us. I recognized one of them from the Friendship Lounge. He searched us and then called us Robbers of the State.

—Wait, why?

—He claimed we'd left the restaurant without paying. Of course, that was a lie, unless he'd pocketed our money. Anyway, after that, he asked us for identification. Being a student, of course, I had ID. Xiulan didn't, so they took her away. She was trying to stop herself from crying so I wouldn't worry about her (I knew how she thought), but it wasn't working because she kept trying to turn around to look at me one last time as they dragged her away, and every time she did, her eyes pleaded with me, *Please find me, Please don't give up on me.* The soldiers were so violent with her, it made me sick to my stomach. They grabbed her head with their hands and turned her around like she was a doll before shoving her into an unmarked car like some common criminal. And then she was gone. It shattered my heart to lose the love of my life. I didn't eat for a week. I skipped class. I wandered the streets looking for clues about where she might have gone, but it was like chasing a ghost with a dirty mirror.

—So, like, what happened?

—I never found her again.

—Fuck, man. Winnie wiped his mouth with his hand. —I'm sorry.

Kwan Li shook his head. —Years later after I'd given up

hope of living a normal life, I received this strange letter from someone living in the Xinjiang province.

Winnie stopped to think. —Wait, that's on the other side of the country, right?

The old man nodded.

—Was it your **shorty**?

—**Shorty**?

—Sorry, girlfriend.

—No, it wasn't her, but he knew her.

—A friend?

—A prison guard.

—Wait, what?

—It was a prison guard who'd fallen in love with Xiulan.

—Oh, man.

Kwan Li paused, looking down at his shoes, and then back at Winnie again, his eyes brimming with barely controlled emotion. —There was only one sentence written on that sheet of paper, Winnie. It was a single line, but I collapsed instantly after reading it. I tried starving myself to death afterwards. I even went to the apothecary to buy a vial of **gu**, but I couldn't do it because I wanted to live like all cowards too attached to this broken world.

—Do I even wanna know what it said?

—No, but I'll tell you anyway. The letter said:

```
I'm still wearing your dress.
```

Winnie felt tears welling up. He wiped them with his forearms, hoped Kwan Li hadn't noticed, but the old man's eyes looked like frozen puddles of water.

—The truth is, Kwan Li continued, I should have stuck up for her. I should have fought them all with my bare hands, just like you did today, using my fingernails as penknives.

—You would have died, Winnie said, sipping an empty teacup.

—I know, the old man said smiling, that's the point, Winnie. That's exactly my point.

The old man's pain really hurt Winnie's heart for days afterwards.

He thanked Kwan Li and took an Uber to Ginger's place. Winnie snuck into the condo as quietly as he could in case she was sleeping. The foyer was cool and comforting and he smelled Vanilla-cedar candles in the living room and baked sweet potatoes in the kitchen. When he got to the loft bedroom, Ginger was already in **camp Snoopy**, her legs straddling a plum quilt, her wet hair splayed on a gray silk pillowcase, her hands held in prayer, her slow breath diffusing the room with her dreams. Winnie looked down at her and felt his heart pounding in his chest, his love for her an expanding and uncontainable equation.

After his run-in with the wannabe gangsters, Ginger was his refuge, the place where he felt safest to be hurt. He rubbed her wet hair, kissed her temple gently, flicked off the lamp on his nightstand, and tried to sneak into bed without waking her, but it didn't work, it never did because she was sensitive to changes in energy fields. She rolled towards Winnie, kissed him in the changing darkness, and touched his face. He winced. Ginger sat up. She knew right away **something was up**.

In the bathroom, Winnie broke it all down for her as she cleaned his wounds with cotton balls dipped in warm water and hydrogen peroxide. She applied a thin layer of Neosporin, even though he told her not to bother. Ginger really liked the part about the letter sent from prison, especially the invisible dress that Kwan Li never bought that his ex-girlfriend still wore. As Winnie finished story-talking, he found Ginger's reactions, her effortless authenticity, and her solicitude incredibly comforting after the white thug mosh pit. When the two of them finally fell asleep, Ginger's head resting on his chest, he held her tight like he was afraid she might disappear. Time became blurry inside his head as he slept. The next day, Winnie woke up late in the afternoon, Ginger busy typing away on her keyboard like some coding prodigy as she photoshopped a series of her photos and wrote twelve future Instagram posts, each one sponsored by a different company. When she was done, they ate Everything Bagels with avo smear and drank strawberry lemonade, and then they made out on the couch. When Winnie was halfway out the door, he looked Ginger in the eyes and told her he loved her. She looked totally startled. Maybe, he didn't say it enough out of the blue. *Gotta get better with* **that shit**, he thought to himself.

—Are you feeling alright? she asked, did you bump your head when you woke up?

—**Nah**, he said, but you can thank Mr. Li for that one. He lingered at the door and smiled at her before walking away.

Ginger gave him a dirty look and then shouted down the hallway. —Winnie Yu, why you gotta ruin a perfectly good moment like that?

Once he was home, Winnie ran into Tian-Tian who was pretending to conduct in the kitchen. She had divided the fancy red Hong Kong bone plates into six piles, forming two choir rows with tiny teacups, her little hands imitating her choir director's. When he sat down at the kitchen table and asked what she was doing, she said she was practicing for the summer recital.

—You know Mama's gonna kill you if she finds out, he muttered, cuz you're using her best china.

—This is a *secret* practice, Winnie! She held up her index finger to her mouth. —You can't tell anyone.

He held his hands up and chuckled. —Fair enough, girl, so what you doing?

—Singing songs.

—What songs.

—The pretty ones.

—Like?

—"Old Macdonald"

—Man, anything but *that*.

—"Leaping Dragon."

—Next.

—"The Alphabet Song."

—Okay. Hit it.

—A has five friends and they all wanna B, close to C, D, E, F, and G.

—That's **bumping**, he said, keep going. Winnie walked down the stairs to the basement. *H, I, and J, have nothing else to say. L, M, and N will never come again.* Winnie pulled out M-Boz's drill and poked it into his ba's American Steel safe, but he either broke the drill bit or just made a symbolic scratch on the surface. Winnie tried one last time, slowing down the drill speed, aiming the drill head on the bottom of the safe. *O, P, and Q, R still with S-T-U.* When he pulled the trigger, sparks exploded until the bit splintered. Finally, he dropped the drill on the floor and cursed. The safe was probably empty anyways, he hoped/rationalized/feared/pretended/hypothesized. He might have to throw this damn thing off the roof.

At his parents' bodega, business was **slo-mo**. Winnie watched K-dramas on the little Sony TV in back, worked on some stencils, and heated up Korean instant kimchi noodles, the spicier the better as far as he was concerned. After watching two episodes of *Dream High 2*, the good luck bell above the front door rattled. A stocky woman waddled up to the counter dressed in black Capri pants and a white T-shirt that said *Old Navy* like an ad for geriatric sailors.

In a nanosecond, Winnie realized it was Mrs. Li aka The Cantonese Screamer.

—Ni hao, she said dryly. Her face looked stern **AF** as if someone had told her that Winnie had **kicked it** with Kwan Li last night, but Winnie knew he hadn't told her shit. Hell, he wouldn't. In his unhumble opinion, she didn't deserve anyone's stories of love and heartache. She didn't even deserve their pain.

—Ni hao, he said, nodding once, trying not to mad dog her but failing.

—I need a calling card, she continued in Mandarin, the fifty-dollar one for Asia.

Winnie glanced down behind the counter. There was a small library of calling cards with pictures of the Great Wall of China, The Taj Mahal, the White House, Fourth of July fireworks with soaring eagles, a random savannah in South Africa, Kenyan women with lip rings, Big Ben standing tall, Bolivian tobacco farmers in slick Derby hats, and a picture of Jesus **bringing down the house** in Rio de Janeiro like an apostolic raver. The cards had different rates, connection fees, and small print. Winnie flicked the ones she wanted with his fingernail, a whole row of them swaying back and forth on the rack.

—Did you hear me? she said impatiently, switching to Cantonese. —the fifty-dollar one! She gave him a supercilious look that ignited a defiant and protective reaction in him.

Winnie looked at her for a moment, the mango sticky rice beeping in the microwave, the TV murmuring in the background, and he decided she didn't deserve Mr. Li's music. That must be the true source of her anger and resentment, she didn't deserve his kindness or his spirit or his music. Winnie could see the old man's face playing in the subterranean heat of the subway platform, cobbling together enough money for a modest dinner every night. Winnie thought about the way Kwan Li insisted on wearing **cheapass** sweater vests as he performed, even when the subway was infernal, he thought about the way Mr. Kwan kept playing his **guqin** that no one understood, filling up the tunnels with sobbing string music, playing for his family that couldn't hear him, playing for passengers who didn't listen, and playing for a Chinese girl who sang along with him all the way from the Western border of China where she'd probably died years ago of dysentery along with Uyghur prisoners, her ghost probably dancing in the same streets they'd walked down when they were in love, back when they were both so young and so unafraid of the annihilation of the future.

—Yo, Winnie said in English, we're all out. Sorry about that.

Mrs. Li scowled at him in disbelief. Winnie walked to the storage room in back, grabbed his dessert out of the microwave, pulled a pair of lacquer chopsticks out of his shirt pocket, and sat down to watch another episode. When she slammed the door, the good luck bell rattled and shook extra-long this time, the sound vibrating through the whole store like a meditation gong. Pops always said that was a good sign.

18. THE WAR ON REALITY

TODAY WAS ONE OF those scorching July days in Harlem when Ginger didn't wanna do anything except watch *Breaking Bad* in her underwear, eat homemade strawberry Zinfandel basil popsicles, and drink lychee lemonade mixed with Pinot Grigio. But summer school was the cross she bore to give art to today's little people and she was (mostly) okay with it. On her lunch break, she and Winn walked to a nearby park and ate lunch on a bench in the shade. Because he was the sweetest thing since the XL Slurpee, he brought them falafel pitas for lunch. Unfortunately, they were horrendous, but Ginger loved every bite because she'd forgotten to pack a lunch. When your boo brought you lunch out of the blue, it didn't matter how it tasted.

—Yo, this falafel is nasty AF, isn't it? Winnie said, taking another bite and grimacing like he should have known. He was wearing a gray pageboy hat, gray skinny jeans, burgundy Adidas kicks, and olive-green tank.

—I wasn't gonna say anything, Ginger said, adjusting the strap of her tan, punch-red, and turquoise dress, matched with a straw hat and cork sandals for just the right boho aesthetic.

—It's cool, he said, I can taste the truth.

Ginger kissed his neck with a mouthful of pita.

Winnie smirked, took out a chocolate almond milk shake

from a paper bag, and handed it to her. Ginger's eyes lit up like she'd taken a hit of acid. Winnie noticed she destroyed the milkshake like it had personally wronged her.

Thirty minutes later, Ginger cleared her throat to get her students' attention inside the classroom. She tried not to laugh when they looked up, their T-shirts and cheeks all covered in paint splats with funny names: Mouthful of Crickets Green, Frank's Red-hot Red, Phonebook Yellow, Oops I Did It Again Brown, and Set a Drift on Memory Bliss Blue. Her students looked like they'd just left a paintball tournament.

—Hey everyone, she began, we have a visitor today.

—What? Elena asked.

—Is he famous? Jawan asks.

—Kinda, Ginger said.

—Is it the billionaire mayor again? I don't wanna see his stupid face, Cristal said.

Ginger tried not laugh.

—Is it a clown? Madelina asked.

—I literally just asked that question, Cristal said, shaking her head.

—A clown? Shaquilla echoed, smacking her lips. —Why the hell would it be a damn clown?

—Wull, today's Cristal's *birthday*.

—I don't want no clown, Felipe said.

—Fuck clowns! Cristal said.

—Is it Brooke Lopez? Benji asked.

—Nope, Ginger said.

—Nas? DeSean asked.

—No, but that would be cool, Ginger said, okay, I'll give you all a hint. He's a talented artist, he's kinda cute, and he's the poutiest man alive.

—Winnie! They cried.

—Yup.

—Yeeee! They shouted.

Ginger opened the classroom door and Winnie moonwalked into the classroom like a superstar. The kids yelled and stomped their feet in an instant beat while Winnie did some locking and popping that made them all cheer. Her students just adored him. Every time he visited it was like that last chapter in *The Brothers Karamazov*. There was something really authentic and pure about Winnie that children understood instinctively. Even if he was Public Enemy #1 according to the billionaire clown mayor, her kids were good judges of character. They were intuitive. Part of it was that they knew Winnie loved them. Part of it was that he was very playful, loving, and super-sweet with them but still had a quiet authority about him, which Ginger couldn't help extrapolating made him perfect dad material (though she kept those observations to herself). Plus, Winnie knew a million different graffiti fonts and characters. Her kids just loved his graphic wizardry.

—Hey Winnie, Angie said, can you help?

—Sure thing, Mrs. Bling, he said, whaddya got there?

—A singing squid.

Winnie nodded. —I like it!

—But *these* are velocidancers, she explained.

—Course, what else could they be?

—Dinosaurs are hard to draw though.

—Ain't that the truth.

—I guess they could be triceradancers.

—Yo, *now* we're talking. Let's start with the shoes.

—Okay, Angie agreed with a smile.

For the next half hour, Ginger walked around the classroom and gave the kids lots of love and attention, telling them how awesome their drawings were, encouraging them to keep at it. Sometimes, she gave them suggestions of things to add or colors to consider as they did their best to impress Winn. After they'd finished, they started migrat-ing to Angie's desk to sneak a peek at Winnie's newest creation. Only Marilena stayed true to her artwork. God bless her little soul, Ginger thought, glancing down at her drawing of a carnival with a Ferris wheel, cotton candy cloud and corndog stands, a funhouse, and clowns passing out balloons that looked like severed heads. She patted the girl on the head and told her how much she liked the colors in her drawing. Marilena smiled without looking back, painting like an artist possessed. At Angie's table, the rest of the class watched Winnie do his magic on a landscape sketchpad.

He drew Washington Heights with thin sharpies and his favorite Derwent watercolor pencils Ginger had given him for Christmas and a hapa kid listening to hip-hop on his headphones. Winnie always created places and people her students could vibe. As mostly students of color, they really valued seeing their own world recreated in caricature. It was a way of graphically centering themselves.

Ginger remembers this one time, Winnie had made a cartoon strip of multiracial ballers in Brooklyn, all the characters climbing on top of each other to be closer to the moon and the stars. It was called *Earth, Wind, and Sky in Gray Bed-Stuy*. Her students fucking *loved* that. Winnie even made color copies for them, which Ginger had handed out, all her kids throwing their copies back on her desk and insisting that Winnie sign them first. They acted like Winnie was LL Cool J and they didn't even know that Winnie was the general of the Buddha Mao army either, which many of them took photos of before posting on their IG accounts.

Another time, Winnie drew a series of sketches of break-dancers at Union Square. By the end of free drawing, the whole class was doing a walk of fame to Snoop's "What's my Name?" playing on Winnie's Bluetooth speaker. Still another time, Winnie had painted the whole class as *Fat Albert* caricatures. He told them about Albert Jackson, Russell, Weird, Mushmouth, Ms. Berry, and the Brown Hornet, explaining why each *Fat Albert* character was so important to Black culture, but also to people of color forced to watch cartoons with white voices and white cartoon characters who did shit they couldn't relate to. Sometimes, Ginger couldn't get her students to listen to a single word she said, but everything Winnie said they just gobbled up like gourmet cupcakes. God knows she didn't have the same powers of persuasion. Being the cool uncle was so much easier than being the tough mom. Sometimes, she resented Winnie for having it so easy.

Six hours later, Ginger, Winnie, and M-Boz watched a Japanese movie at DUMBO's Outdoor Spring Film Festival called *Untitled* (虫の声) on a picnic blanket outside surrounded by pretty mixed-race couples, Russian and Ukrainian models, boat club yuppies, trigger-happy Japanese tourists, loud Tisch students, carbon copied white hipsters, and editorial interns live-tweeting their every thought (each one armed with an ÉPN tote bag that bulged with free softcovers from the take shelf). The three of them devoured their vegan dim sum, their chopsticks a collective blur of aggression, focus, and desire as they navigated take-out boxes and palates, the sun sizzling into the East River like a freshly welded gold disc. Afterwards, they sipped on frozen hot chocolates and sighed. M-Boz grabbed Winnie by the T-shirt.

Winnie looked sideways, confused. —Whaddup? he asked.

—Yo, what do you say we hit the Brooklyn Bridge? M-Boz said.

—Hey, I like that idea, Ginger chimed in, we haven't done that in years.

—I'm in, Winnie said.

They walked towards the bridge as the sun's halo expanded through the sky, dragging the horizon down with it. The spring had accelerated into a hard and breathtaking summer in a telegenic downward spiral. Ginger was grateful that she had people in her life who could push everything to the side for one night and just cele- brate their fleeting life together for

a few hours. The truth was, when New Yorkers walked over the Brooklyn Bridge, they could view their city like tourists for a few brief moments, their familiarity bending into intoxication. For Ginger, it was like walking over water for the first time all over again. Fifteen minutes later, the three of them reached the halfway point when M-Boz stopped.

—Hold up, he said, I wanna blaze, pulling out the largest blunt Ginger had ever seen from his satchel and lighting it. M-Boz took a few massive drags and then handed it to Winnie as a small group of desis passed by dressed in jean shorts and oversized block color T-shirts. They snickered when the smoke hit them in the face. One guy even held out his hand as if to say, *Can I hit that, please?*

—Damn, this thing is phallic, Winnie said, inhaling.

Ginger laughed. Winnie passed her the massive blunt. She took a few honest drags and then handed it to M-Boz.

—That's it, girl? he said, you don't have to diet this shit. I just bought a brick of it in bulk. Next time, I might even go for the Indo.

Ginger made a mental note to Google "Indo" when she got home.

—So yo, Winnie said, is this why you wanted to hit the Bridge?

—Nah, fam, M-Boz said, we're celebrating.

—Celebrating what? Ginger asked.

—I'll show you, M-Boz said with a mysterious glean in his eyes.

—You're a jack-in-the-box today, Winnie muttered.

They walked down the Gothic limestone and granite bridge, their feet creating a perfect beat on the wood planks. Winnie and M-Boz passed the blunt back and forth like a primitive sign language. Ginger took one more hit, her body a warm and fuzzy euphoria now.

—Bro, I'm blunted as hell, M-Boz said.

—Same, Winnie said, I'm about to nom nom again.

For a split second between joy and laughter, Ginger thought about her OBGYN's advice that she and Winnie take a series of tests in the next couple of months. She wondered why she'd waited so long to get answers. It had taken her years to convince Winnie that the time to start a family was now or it would soon be too late. They both hated ultimatums and she didn't like giving him one, but her thirty-something body was changing radically, her periods were getting more and more irregular, and she worried that he might be trying to run out the clock. Winnie said he wanted to wait until he got his Masters, then he wanted to wait until his first exhibition in Asia, then he wanted to wait until he'd put ten stacks in savings (still working on that one, buddy), and then he wanted to retire the Buddha Army first so that he wouldn't get arrested, but then his ba died and Winnie went into shock. Ginger didn't bring it up then. She knew it was too much for Winnie to deal with losing a dad and simultaneously becoming a dad, so she cooked him Taiwanese food, cleaned her condo, and forced him to go on walks with her to get him outside. She made him smell the sun and taste the clouds, even when he complained. Meanwhile, her window of opportunity became a rocket racing into space, becoming smaller with every stage. When she and Winnie made love now, it was out of urgency and desperation and sometimes obligation, depending on the mood. Ginger kept track of her periods, which was tricky considering how erratic they were and she knew all the signs of ovulation (she could rattle them off in her sleep), but month after month, nothing changed. Not even when her body checked every box from breast tenderness all the way to cervical mucus. Seeing a fertility specialist was her first and last solution. After losing hope, Ginger became hopeful again when her OBGYN referred her to a reproductive endocrinologist who told her he was cautiously optimistic about her chances of being a mom. But, he stressed, that her test results would be their guide.

—Yo Gingersnap, Winnie asked, where'd you go just now?

Ginger tried to smile away her confusion. —Nowhere. I mean, I just got lost in my head.

—Yeah, M-Boz said, this haze shit will do that to you.

Ginger smiled at M-Boz for inadvertently covering for her.

They walked in silence for a little bit, a slight breeze blowing on their faces, cars whizzing by on the lower level, seagulls bursting through the clouds above, multiracial joggers passing by, and cyclists blurring the periphery. Time evaporated like hot mist. Eventually, M-Boz stopped again.

Winnie and Ginger put their hands on the railing, leaning forward and taking a close look at the ad. The top part had the army logo (a star in a square) and a cropped photo of a serious-looking white guy with a pretty jaw line in a helmet. When Ginger read the text, she realized that M-Boz had jammed the recruitment ad using the same font to make it seem like it came from the Army. She recognized her own words too.

> There's Strong**men in the US Wearing Police Uniforms** &
> then
> There's **the Colonial**
> Army **of** Strong**men in Military Fatigues, both Groups**
> **Protecting the 1%, Invading & Occupying Non-White**
> **Spaces, Usurping Public Resources, & Intimidating,**
> **Assaulting, Dehumanizing, & Killing PoC**

—Daaaaaaamn, Winnie said, is that *you*, Boz?

M-Boz beamed. —The art is me, Winn, but the text is your homegirl's.

—Hold up? Ginger Lin, you wrote that? Winnie asked, his eyes bleeding joy.

Ginger shrugged. —Boy, that's old news. It was actually one of the rejects from my Oscar Grant campaign years ago.

—Man, that shit is *slam*ming, Winnie said, you guys are a dope team! Winnie admired the balance of graphic and narrative elements, nodding his head as he studied the billboard. —How the fuck did you get up there though?

—It's a longass story, M-Boz said, laughing.

—Dude, spit it out, Winnie said.

M-Boz paused for added drama. —I jumped off a skyscraper!

—You did *what*? Ginger asked. —Which one?

—I think it was Deutsche Bank, M-Boz said, or maybe the Brown Brother Harriman building. Shit, I don't remember. It was late at night and I was jacked when I made the jump, but—

—Hold up, Winnie interrupted, how did you not die though?

—Are you an apotheosis? Ginger asked.

M-Boz winked like he'd been waiting for that question. —I used a parachute.

Winnie and Ginger shook their heads in disbelief and then the three of them started laughing hysterically at the idea of M-Boz jumping off a skyscraper with a parachute. *Oh my God,*

Ginger thought, *that boy is crazy*.

M-Boz smiled big. —I've got some swag after working with Winnie for the past year, so maybe we should hit that virgin billboard in Manhattanville.

—Dude, fuck yeah, Winnie said, I'm into that shit.

And it was there at the intersection of a perfectly ordinary New York day and the singularity of a strange and unforgettably soft summer night that they laughed and cheered, giving each other hip-hop hugs like it was New Year's Eve all over again, even though the snow was long gone and the days were long, sticky, and bright. For one moment, they laughed and hugged each other like there was nothing they couldn't do when they found the right balance of rage, inspiration, vision, and fearlessness inside themselves. Ginger wondered if art was just a declaration of war that artists waged on reality as payback for the war that reality had already waged on art.

ADULTHOOD

19. PRISONERS OF DARKNESS & COINCIDENCE

I.

AFTER NEW YORK BECOMES a giant cocoon of blank space, Winnie is the first passenger to stand in the kaput C train. He needs to stretch his legs anyway, maybe do some yoga later on, so he stands up and looks around, surveying the subway for gang-bangers, tourists, and cops (the three groups always shutting down his creativity flow). He makes sure everything is cool in the perimeter because Ginger is with him and he's protective of his joy. After all, she's the reason he falls asleep slowly at night and the reason he wakes up slowly in the morning. She's the only woman, the only person he has truly loved more than himself. More than clean October air, more than jamming manifestoes or MC shout-outs, more than a standing army of Buddha Maos or hip-hop hugs to the color spectrum, more than fresh street creds or family dinners or the *Adbusters* article he's supposed to star in today, even more than the sickest burner he once plastered on the fiftieth floor of the Bloomberg Tower. This snap revelation freaks him out. With Ba gone, Winnie's relationship with Ginger is the one perfectly flawed and necessary thing in his life. As an artist with an infinite vocabulary of emotion and imagining, she is his world now, his madness and his muse.

2.

Ginger watches Winnie and realizes he's so different than how he used to be in high school, back when they were both self-obsessed teenagers who thought beauty and sass was a birthright and the future a giant spliff. She loves that Winnie has become a true cement poet, a low-key feminist warrior of ideas, and a jammer with millions of IG followers who think he's the next Asian Banksy. Sometimes, though, she feels engulfed by his art which is an insatiable and endless thing. She worries there's not enough room for Winnie's art and her motherhood. Even though he's affectionate and loving and kind and perceptive, Ginger worries that Winnie doesn't need her the way she needs him. She worries that his art is all he needs. Of course, she worries about dark parking lots, small elevators, and moldy cheese too, but that's not the same thing. She wonders if Winnie might someday resent her for making more money than he does. She worries about all the tests they took because she can no longer take her fertility for granted. While Winnie has become a student of the artistic revolution, transcending his own trage-dies and trauma to write an immigrant graphic novel in the key of New York, Ginger has fallen deeper in love but also become less sure of herself. She worries that she's the only person in their relationship who doesn't know what to do. She feels confused and empty sometimes and doesn't want to lean on her love but she knows she does. She knows how to love every part of Winnie, even the parts that don't match or fit together. It is her love of him that makes it possible for him to fall apart in the in-between where both of them have been living since they were children, snagged between languages, races, cultures, and life stories, but Ginger needs that too. Sometimes, Winnie forgets to ask and Ginger forgets to demand. She knows it's because she wants his love without asking for it. She wants Winnie to fight for their family the way she does. She thinks about her kids at school. She hopes they're safe. She hopes she gets to tell them about the day she and Winn visited the underground cathedral to worship the buried sun, to pay their respects to the underground city, and walk through the tunnels that their ancestors built. She hopes Winnie will still love her even if she can't be a mom. She hates herself for knowing that the answer doesn't change anything.

LARVA

20. FAST MEN IN PATENT LEATHER SHOES (SUZANNE GUPTA)

Once Suzanne saw the window seat, she realized she might actually get her nap on for a change, which felt auspicious, like a confirmation of her decision to leave Seattle and fly to New York on a whim. She pulled out a Ziploc of mixed nuts and dried organic mango, a cold Klean Kanteen of water, and her iPhone. She opened an old playlist on her phone when an old Dido song came on, one she'd been obsessed with in high school when her papa had dropped hints on the daily about the family legacy of attending Northwestern. It was a crazy time to be a brown teenager in America: The US invaded and then occupied Iraq based on shoddy intelligence, the Terminator became governor of California, the DC Sniper was found guilty, Al-Qaeda drove bomb-filled trucks into two Istanbul synagogues, SARS spread through Hong Kong, China, Vietnam, and Singapore, poor Keiko the Orca died, and the Great North American Blackout had turned half the East Coast and Canada into the summer of negative space. There was so much trauma, hatred, and violence taking place in the background as she snuck out of the house with Aditi, Valentina, and Destiny on the weekends to crash Loyola Academy, Whitney Young, and Latin School parties, looking like the next multiracial girl band. Inside the airplane,

Suzanne curled up in a little ampersand with her back to the aisle, lost in the time travel of her flashback.

Suzanne listened to "Life for Rent" three times in a row, which made her nostalgic for her teenage idealism, rage, and rebellion. Now it felt like both a personal anthem and a spiritual indictment of her life. She'd been second-guessing herself to death all week after getting a "reading" from a psychic in a dirty Bon Jovi T-shirt, but eventually she'd embraced her decision to leave Seattle not because she was convinced it was the right decision, but because for the first time in years, she felt like she had the space to make mistakes in her life and New York was worth making a mistake about.

There was some commotion in the aisle when a passenger in a royal blue button-down, gray "trousers," (there was no other word for them), and shiny patent leather shoes sat down in the other seat, staring right at her ass. His hair was mop-thick and chemical-black, parted in the middle like an '80s jock, the sides branching out into gray wings like a '90s dad. Suzanne ignored his lascivious peripheral glances, the way he adjusted his seatbelt and pulled the strap like a floppy nylon penis. She leaned closer to the window, practically hugging it, and closed her eyes, replaying the Dido song again. He moved his elbow past the armrest boundary, transgressing the common law of legroom until their thighs brushed against each other. Suzanne cringed at the dude's wide stance—the trophy of male privilege—and turned the volume up on her phone, closing her eyes again. After a few minutes, she felt a tap on her wrist. She opened her eyes with dread.

—All electronics are supposed to be off, he said with a shrug.

—Yeah, thanks for the reminder, Suzanne muttered, rolling her eyes.

—Wouldn't want to jam the airwaves.

—Tell that to the guy over there on his cell phone, she said, pointing to a loud business bro in starched grey pants, blue crewneck sweater, and a yellow button-down, shouting corporate acronyms into his phone as if the people around him were keeping score of his petty feuds.

—If I was sitting next to him, he said, I would.

—If I were, she replied.

—Sorry?

—Subjunctive past. It's the mood used to express what could have been, what we wished had happened, like me wishing I had a different seat. For example.

The man smiled like she was his entertainment.

Suzanne sighed and turned off her iPhone.

—So, he said, are you in college?

She shot him a dirty look. —Nope.

—Where you from?

—Chicago.

—And your parents?

—Chicago.

She knew what he wanted to know and refused to satisfy his racial curiosity. Life was too short for another *So, what are you?* conversation from a clueless white guy.

—What's in New York?

—I'm sorry, she said, but I'd prefer not to talk right now.

He pulled back his head as if someone had just punched him in the nose. —Okay, fine. Just trying to make conversation.

—Well, try less hard, please.

Within a few seconds, SeaTac was a wet blur of runway lights and muscular clouds as the plane pulled up into the sky, slowly erupting into the troposphere. Suzanne put her earphones back in when the man tapped her on her wrist again, his hand sliding just slightly over her fingers in a way that creeped her out.

—Sir, please don't touch me!

He raised his eyebrows. —Sorry. Can I buy you a drink?

She shook her head.

—You're so relaxed. What's your secret?

—My mind is calm, she lied.

—Oh, like a Zen thing.

—Kinda, but without the Zen.

—Well, you got any suggestions on helping me relax? he asked, staring at her breasts like an entomologist who'd just spotted a rare insect he wanted to capture before it flew away. Suzanne noticed his eyes trying to X-ray her nipples through her purple and gray Adidas track suit, his double entendre held tightly between flaky smirking lips.

—None that involve my body, she said, putting her headphones back on.

He opened his mouth in shock.

She played the Dido song one more time and let the music fill her ears with melodic recollection, the musical notes like tiny slabs of raw sugar dissolving inside her brain. Every time he tried to get her attention afterwards, she ignored him until he finally gave up, playing solitaire on his clunky IBM ThinkPad.

At JFK, Suzanne picked up her suitcase and her ladybug backpack at the baggage claim, set her satchel from Delhi on top of her suitcase, and looked for the AirTrain terminal, but got lost wandering around the airport. Eventually, she took a taxi to Williamsburg. Inside the mustard yellow Mercedes, a sign read:

Your Taxi Driver is:
Hashmat Hashmat

Hashmat was an old Afghan man. Suzanne could tell by his features (and his name). That was one of her gifts, she could always tell where someone was from, it was one of her residual gifts from being a former geography nerd and lifelong anthropology minor. From the taxi window, she saw men in kufis, Asian students dressed all in black from Parsons, some in face masks, Black hipsters riding their bikes through traffic, Hasidic families congregating on the corner, and a death metal couple in studded jean jackets and Doc Martens. Suzanne saw clusters of cafés, boutiques, and ironic bars she wanted to check out while she was here. Finally, the taxi arrived at the address listed on Suzanne's Airbnb app. The building looked desolate, practically abandoned. There was trash on the steps of the garden unit and an illegible tag above the intercom.

Hashmat turned to her. —Is this it?

—I don't know, actually, Suzanne said, it looked different in the picture.

Hashmat looked concerned.

—It's fine, she said, handing him two twenties.

—Thank you, he said, covering his heart with his hand and bowing.

Hashmat jumped out of the car, opened her door, and pulled out her luggage with a gusto that scared her. He smiled boyishly, and of course, she forgave him for carrying her luggage to the doorstep because his smile was grateful and disarming. Suzanne thanked him once more and pulled out her phone to follow the instructions. She located a padlock hanging on the front door, entered the code, caught her key that tried leaping to its death on the sidewalk, and then opened the front door, dragging her luggage inside.

—I've arrived, people! she shouted to the empty studio. —I've arrived!

21. SOUL LAG (AZIZ AL-WAHNAN)

Assis had no idea why ÉPN booked him in first class. He was just your run of the mill polyglot with strong atheistic tendencies, a distrust of nationalist rhetoric, a long and painful history dealing with anti-Maghrebin racism in France, and a soft spot for cross-cultural dialogue, what the hell did he know about the hoi polloi? He felt so self-conscious and out of place sitting in these spacious seats like the one percent. He felt like he was betraying all the other passengers with mocha skin waiting in line at the Air France counter dressed in soccer jerseys, baby-blue button-ups, and Lacoste polos, their conversations gliding back and forth between French and Maghrebi Arabic with unconscious dexterity. To be honest, he felt guilty for a lot of things: For leaving Paris, for abandoning Maman, for dropping Sakina like a burning handgun, for ditching Hassan's funeral and running away from his father who would mourn for an entire year while Aziz traveled to New York with a new suitcase of new clothes and a cleanly shaven face and two missing teeth. The only thing that felt familiar about leaving Paris was the chronic shame, but Papa insisted, he practically ordered Aziz to pack his bags. He said Aziz could thank Hassan by going to training and not rotting in Paris. When Aziz had said that it was wrong to walk away when his family needed him, his dad wiped the tears from Aziz's cheeks and looked him right in the eyes and said:

—Aziz, you're going to New York and that's final.

—Papa, this is ridiculous. How can I go now?

—By packing your bags.

—Et les obsèques?

—Aziz, the only way you honor Hassan is by going to New York and succeeding.

—He would want me to say goodbye.

—He would want you to make something of yourself.

Aziz closed his eyes and wrapped his arms around his dad, kissing him on the cheek and fighting his tears. His father hugged him for a brief second, but not long enough. It was never long enough.

The cabin smelled like a simulacrum. It made Aziz nauseous, so he kept going to the restroom like a guy with an enlarged prostrate. The red-faced white guy sitting next to him in the navy-blue pinstriped suit and yellow paisley tie kept staring at him whenever he sat back down like he'd never seen a Moroccan Frenchman in first class before. Maybe, he noticed Aziz's missing bicuspid and molar. Aziz had to admit, the gap in his mouth was fucking affreux. It made him feel really Eurotrash coming to America with missing teeth. Even though his family was lower middle-class, Aziz could always be proud of his strong straight white teeth, but not anymore. Eventually, he ignored the passenger just like he ignored racist white teenagers in Paris whenever they stared at him in the métro and snickered. Aziz tried to read the *International Herald Tribune*, but his brain wasn't registering the words. The sentences kept piling up on one another. He had so many things on his mind and one of them was his pathological fear of flying. The airplane motors hummed in the cabin and Aziz choked on his complimentary mineral water.

Flight attendants in tri-colored scarves and fresh sparkly lip gloss sashayed down the aisles with puffy eyes, passing out pre-prandial croissants, twice-washed grapes, and plastic cups full of cheap white wine that smelled like old vinaigrette, speaking in high voices with vacantly cheery eyes that Aziz distrusted. His curious/socially awkward/non-straight/racist neighbor took three plastic cups of wine vinaigrette. Every time Aziz asked questions to one of the flight attendants (it was his first time in first class), they blinked mechanically at him like they were holographic projections of women who lived in a prison on the moon working remotely, as if every one of his questions was bizarre, like asking for a barf bag, some Benadryl, or a glass of seltzer water. Wait, were those weird questions? Aziz didn't have the slightest clue. As the flight attendants fed him pieces of rubber sushi, half-frozen shrimp cocktail, a mysterious Stew with an unpronounceable Norwegian name, and pieces of microwaved bread covered in acidic boeuf bourguignon sauce (supposedly, standard first-class fare), Aziz wondered why his life had changed so radically in the past month, what he did to deserve such good fortune, and why he felt like un tel lâche. As the flight attendants continued sauntering down the aisle holding trays of bitter black tea, canned tomato juice, flat champagne, and strange wine spritzers that exploded after being opened, Aziz wondered if rich people paid more money for first-class tickets because they had insatiable appetites, because their hunger was always a cautionary tale. He also wondered if the flight crew was trying to get him drunk before he understood where he was (currently, flying over Cork). It might sound paranoid (yella, he was Moroccan French after all), but he felt like the flight attendants were sideglancing him to death. They laughed every time he fumbled with his seat belt or rushed to the bathroom, returning with his face drenched in water. Was he a cultural spectacle and they the audience? When he passed the first-class passengers on his way to coach, they seemed so professional, so smug, so vapid, and so impatient. He was none of these things, neither in life nor on this flight. He felt acutely aware of his skin color and class deviation surrounded by so many blasé white people.

Halfway through the flight, a period of time that really sludged by, Aziz scrolled through the movie library and found to his dismay that most of the movies were dubbed Hollywood flicks, which he hated. The Dark Knight should never speak in an obnoxious Parisian accent. As Aziz waited for the bathroom in coach, a large group of French teenagers clogged up the aisle dressed in patriotic jumpsuits, listening to rap on their headphones and making dramatic stabbing gestures in the air. They laughed in echo wave, drooling on each other's shoulders and shouting in a mix of céfran, American hip-hop slang, and French proverbs. By his fifth trip to the toilet, he read the patch on one girl's jacket. Evidently, half the Junior National Fencing team was on this flight, ready to stab people in the name of sport. Just the thought of these hormone-raging thirteen-year-olds stabbing the crap out of each other with épées was scary enough to keep Aziz in his seat until dinner. Teenagers shouldn't have that much power They were too young to understand adulthood or the fragility of the human body.

In the car service to Hussein's apartment in Washington Heights, Aziz watched New Yorkers shouting into their cell phones, pedestrians swarming crosswalks in a flash mob of power ties, peplum, and little black dresses, form-fitting suits, brand-name handbags, and designer jeans, sunglasses, leather pants, and hair sculptures. The streets were saturated with twenty-somethings in pageboy caps and hoodie tank tops, shaggy bike messengers in rolled up pants, tough-looking students in short skirts and tattoos, preppy types in Lacoste polo shirts and popped collars, hip-hop aficionados in Adidas track suits and New Era caps, and mutant toy dogs yelping from pricey totes. New York was nothing like Paris, which had a specific prototype that everyone's style was judged by. Here, everyone had different rules for the same game.

The other thing Aziz noticed was that New York went on for miles in every direction like an obese epic poem 338 volumes long. It was so hard **Ecumenopolis** to get his mind around the *size* of this place. There was a Greek word for this, but he couldn't think of it. New York was the whole world encapsulated in a single city, which is why it was both exhilarating and exhausting. Once the black car passed a string of little magasins, Aziz noticed storefronts covered in yellow and blue awnings, walls exploding with island-themed murals, he smelled beans and sancocho, plantains and flan. There were boutiques filling the sidewalks with racks of cheap clothing and bizarre ass mannequins advertising women's jeans (n'est-ce pas?). At Hussein's brownstone, there was a block party going on. People were hanging out on the stoops and talking to each other in Uzi-fire Spanish, eating popsicles, and playing baseball in the alleys. Aziz could actually hear meringue and hip-hop blaring out of open windows, neighbors were having loud conversations on stoops, and this might sound ridiculous, but there was a couple *dancing* in the streets. Washington Heights was like that bad Lionel Richie video he'd seen once late night at a Casa hotel. He pulled his luggage out of the trunk, paid and thanked the driver, and walked up the stoop.

One of the neighbors leaned her head out the window like a chismosa. There was a pretty eggplant glean to her lips and her blush looked like dagger scars, her hair was silky, twisted into tight corkscrew curls, practically springing to life. —Dímelo lindo, she said, waving her fake purple and glittery nails into the air as she winked, her lips smacking as she chewed her gum.

—Hola, he said. ¿Cómo andas?

—Oh, she said in English, you're not Dominican.

—No, estoy francés, he said in his best Madrileño accent, pero siéntese libre de hablar conmigo en español cuando quiera.

—A'po'ta'bien.

Aziz smiled and unlocked all five deadbolts in the door. He opened up the windows in the living room to let the shy breeze and fading sunlight into the musty living room, giving fresh life and humid air to old coffee tables. Aziz looked around the apartment and smelled Saint-Denis. He made some green tea. The oily, nasty-looking tap water gurgled on the stove and the smell of garlic and mint invaded the apartment like a great genie, transporting him back to a lost world he'd never loved and that had never loved him back.

22. YOU'RE SERIOUSLY GONNA BLAME THIS SHIT ON THE PSYCHIC?

SUZANNE AND HER BROTHER, Samir, snagged the last empty table at the Still Life Café, his favorite lunch spot in (the Republic of) Fremont. She decided to wait until he returned from the bathroom before dropping the bad news on his lap like a skillet on fire. She was fidgety.

Samir sat down, wiping his hands on his jeans. —So, what's up? You look fidgety AF.

Suzanne shook her head in quiet awe of her brother's perceptiveness. —I'm leaving tomorrow.

—Wait, what? I thought you were gonna look for apartments in Queen Anne or something.

—I know, I know.

—So, what's the dealio, sis?

—I'm stuck.

He shook his head and grabbed his fork. —Who says you have to decide right now?

—Because I know that once I find an apartment and sign the lease, I'm committed.

—Suzie, this is Seattle, not an asylum.

—But you know what I mean, right?

He shot her a dirty look. —Course.

—The only reason I've *considered* moving here is to start over again and spend more time with you and Ali.

Samir sighed slowly, sinking his fork into his veggie omelet. —For my own selfish reasons, I think you should stay.

Suzanne skimmed her coconut yogurt nervously. —So, let me tell you about last night.

—Ali already told me.

—The whole story?

—Yeah. You guys got fucked up on Jack and Sevens and went to some biker karaoke bar. He took a huge gulp of orange juice. —And then one of you sang "Bittersweet Symphony." Badly.

—That was me.

He smiled.

—Okay, but did Ali tell you about the—I don't know what to call it—*afterparty*?

—I thought that was the whole story.

—Au contraire, mon frère, she said in an unconvincing Lisa Simpson voice. They grew up watching *The Simpsons* together, so Suzanne's inside joke was a complex flashback, both deeply comforting and disturbing now.

Samir half-laughed, forking his omelet with a quiet vengeance.

—Actually, she said with a more serious voice, I got up and sang The Verve *five times* in that crowded little bar. Then Ali took an Uber home and I walked around Seattle by myself.

—I already *hate* this version, he said, shoveling a mouthful of omelet into his mouth.

—You guys okay? the waitress asked.

—All good, Samir said.

—Thanks, Suzanne said.

—Okay, cool, the waitress said.

—So, you know where I ended up? Suzanne asked.

—Lemme guess: The Erotic Bakery?

—.

—Babes in Toyland.

—Way off, bro.

—Slave to the needle?

—No, but now that you mention it . . .

—Well, *where* then?

—I went to a psychic, she said, spooning yogurt and blue-berries into her mouth.

—For real?

She nodded and chewed.

—And what did she say? That you're destined for great things? That you were a Japanese empress in a past life?

Suzanne shook her head in disapproval. —Nooooooo, she said it wasn't time for me to go home yet because I was entering a new phase in my life.

—That's so generic, it's actually insulting you gave her money.

—Okay, that was the précis. The long version is that I'm going to meet the man of my dreams.

—Bore-ring.

—And the pièce de resistance: he's waiting for me in New York!

—Ah, man. *New York?*

She nodded.

—So, let me get this straight, you're going to New York because a *psychic* told you to.

—Wow, for a DJ, you're pretty smart.

—You little beatch, he said, pinching her earlobe.

—Hey!

—So why not visit New York and then come back afterwards?

—Well, I'm open to that. I just wanna go there and see destiny calling.

—Fair enough, he sighed again, sipping his juice, but I'm gonna miss you. Ali too.

—Me too.

—Have you told Mum yet?

—God no, she said, waving at the waitress for the check.

—I'm gonna wait until I'm already there. Otherwise, she'll guilt trip me into coming home.

—Smart move, girl.

—Oh, by the way, Papa called last night.

—What he say?

—He said and I quote, *Your mum keeps buying these spider plants and then hiding them in the garage. It feels like a slow invasion, Suzie.*

Samir laughed.

—And then he recited some poem in Tamil that went on for five minutes. I think it was the *Manimekalai.*

—Man, I love Pops.

—Me too, even when he speaks with trees.

They both laughed.

—So, Samir said, I forgot to call Papa on his birthday—I know that's totally lame of me—and you know what Mum said?

—Lemme guess, that you were killing him?

—Yeah, that's *exactly* what she said! She claimed that every time I forget Papa, he gets sad and every time he gets sad, he becomes depressed, and every time he's depressed, he wants to buy a one-way ticket to the Grand Canyon so he can leap to his death.

—That's quite the slippery slope.

—So I said, *Please put him on the phone* and she tried to back track, said he seemed *fine right now* but in the future I might wanna remind him that I'm still alive. And I was like, *Put him on the phone. Now!* And she did.

—Reluctantly, I bet.

—Of course. She sighed real loud and then went in the backyard with the cordless. But he was totally fine. He talked about his garden and about his goldfinches. Then he passed the phone back because he needed his daily dose of prana. Samir grew pensive. —So, you're really gonna leave, huh?

—You and Ali are beautiful together. You don't need a third.

—Wow, how is that *even* the fucking point?

—Are you mad?

—No, I just like having you around, you know? It feels like old times in the Chi. Also, there's like five desis in all of Seattle. It's fucking depressing how white this city is.

—Maybe you should move back to Chicago.

Samir shook his head. —No way. Let's ditch this lassi stand, he said, grabbing the check.

As they walked to the counter, Suzanne hugged him from behind and smelled the different half-lifes of Vera Wang. In fifth grade, after she'd thrown up Mum's dal, it was this shoulder that had given her the greatest comfort. And when Papa had disappeared for seven days and forgot to tell them about his meditation retreat in the Catskills, it was Samir's shoulder first and then her mum's lap that calmed down the tempest raging inside her temples. Since they were tiny creatures of their own imagination in the backyard, since they were bony children in Rogers Park, addicted to gulab jamun, Gushers, Ranch Doritos, and peanut chikki, since they watched *The Simpsons, Yo! MTV Raps, The Real World* in Seattle and New Orleans on the old beige canopy bed, since they were tiny lower-case letters dancing across the computer screen, this shoulder was the safest place in her family.

23. SLAUGHTERHOUSE FOR THE BEAUTIFUL, LEVIATHAN FOR THE POOR

PARIS HAD A SPLIT personality: a flashy urban identity and a hidden suburban one. There were skeptical white masks, upbeat Black masks, and frustrated brown masks. Paris's dissociative identity disorder was temporal too: the winters in Paris were cold and rainy and the summers were hot, overcrowded, and sticky. For two summer months, Aziz counted overweight Americans in baggy shorts and waist packs inundating tourist traps and silently patting themselves on the back for V-Day, groups of Swiss teenagers gossiping to each other in their incomprehensible German, and stylish Japanese tourists with spiky haircuts and high-tech gadgets taking pictures of everything:

La Tour Eiffel √
Montmartre Carnation Lights √
Le Pont Neuf √
Dead pigeon √

For two months, it's nothing but hordes of fair-skinned Berliners with dyed hair, thin waistlines, and colored jeans, shouting things in the street and Italians, Polish football hooligans, and red-faced

Englishmen swarming the streets like mosquitoes, hovering above crowded métro stations and buzzing in the ears of tipsy girls at swanky nightclubs. As a Parisian of color, Aziz saw it every goddamn year without fail. For two months, his city was invaded by slutty white tourists across the gender spectrum who wanted to fuck, fight, or out-French French people without understanding the country's colonial history, linguistic hegemony, questionable foreign policy, systemic racism against North Africans, or rampant classism. By the time starry-eyed tourists arrived in bus platoons with thick wallets, thicker waistlines, expensive digital cameras, and execrable French language skills, the Parisian bourgeoisie had already thrown their hands in the air and abandoned the city sans rien dire, changing their license plates and itineraries in secret. For one month, Paris got taken over by tourists, footballers, and the dispossessed in that order.

Aziz promised Wafi (who was one generation removed from angels as far as he was concerned) that he'd go with him to his interview in Les Halles, the most godless place on earth. He gave Wafi a pep talk and then hugged him before they roamed around the underground shopping mall looking for the chain bookstore that Wafi had applied to. Les Halles was such an easy place to hate halfway between Notre Dame and the Louvre, history and art. The boutiques were gaudy, the porn stores were chelou, and the FNAC was so large it had its own postal code. Les Halles was a sardine tin of pickpockets, child molesters, tourists, and one-stop shoppers, a place where culture came to die, but a job was a job. Fortunately for Aziz, there was a great café southwest of the gardens called Comptoir where he liked to people-watch until the DJ started spinning brainless Europop. After Aziz wished Wafi good luck, he walked to the café and grabbed the last open table. The dark interior and kitschy décor were comforting. He ordered thé à la menthe, which always consoled Aziz when he was navigating white spaces. He took a sip and shook his head like a petit con. Moroccans knew how to do sweet green tea so much better than the French. The trick was fresh mint, organic sugar, and an old atai that refined the gunpowder green with every repour. He took another sip. It wasn't horrendous, at least for a French café. Maybe, the barista was Moroccan.

Aziz took a few more sips when his ringtone started playing "Et Alors!" by Shy'm, the caller ID revealing an American phone number with a 212 area code. He took a deep breath and pressed the *Accepter* button.

—Allô, he said.

—Allô, the voice said, je voudrais parler à monsieur Aziz Brahim . . . Al-Wahnan.

—A l'apareil.

—Bonjour, my name is Édouard Girardieu. I'm head of human resources at ÉPN. Is this a bad time?

—Bah non, Aziz said, not at all. He wiped his mouth with a napkin and took a swig of meh tea.

—Très bien. So, we examined your CV and sample clips.

—Oui.

—If it's not too much to ask, may I ask you a few follow-up questions?

—Certainement.

—Excellent, so we were very impressed by your academic credentials: *licence* at the Sorbonne, Masters at the University of London, translation certification from Oxford, but just to verify something, exactly how many languages do you *speak*? There appears to be a typo in your cover letter.

—Fluently or passively?

—Well, both I guess.

—I speak nine languages fluently, but I can understand around fifteen.

—I'm sorry, did you say *quinze*?

—Oui, quinze.

—Oh, la la, the voice said, inhaling into the phone. There was a long pause followed by surreptitious typing on the other end. Aziz assumed he was verifying his CV in real time. —It also says here that you graduated at the top of your class.

—Soi-disant.

—I have to say, the HR employee continued, while I'm impressed by your credentials, I find all of this just all a bit . . . what's the word I'm looking for . . . déroutant. I don't understand how anyone could have studied all those languages.

Aziz wanted to ask if the problem was that the HR department had shamefully low standards for maghrébin applicants or that they were just used to Americans who couldn't order fast food in French even after studying it in high school for four years. Or was the real problem that he was brown? Aziz decided to say nothing, internalizing his objections like every person of color he knew. —Well, Aziz, said, some of those languages I studied in uni and others I learned on my own. I'm nerdy like that.

—I see.

—To be honest, I've always been fascinated by linguistic anthropology, heteroglossic vectors, and transmorphology, the futile policing of grammar, the way languages follow certain grammatologies and indiscriminately violate others, depending on the level of orality, education, code-switching proficiency, and colloquial familiarity of the intra-class speech community. And I also think urban sociolinguistics are fasci—

—Très bien. I think you've answered that question more than adequately. If I may ask a follow up question, what would you rank as your top—je'n sais pas—three foreign languages?

—Well, excluding Arabic.

—Bien sûr.

—I'd say probably English, Russian, and Cantonese. Or maybe Spanish.

—Oh, la la. Le cantonais?

—Oui.

This time, the sound of furious typing. Open and unapologetic.

Aziz smiled.

—Ensuite, I've been skimming your clips.

—Zut alors.

—Is that damn because I'm *skimming* or damn because I'm skimming your *clips*?

—I don't know. I just feel like they're uninspiring.

—Actually, our editor-in-chief of English Translations found your work very impressive. She thought your translation of Teju Cole's *Open City* was quality work.

—Oh, merci.

—And your excerpt of Natasha Tretheway's *Domestic Work* impressed her greatly.

—Glad to hear it.

—To be honest, monsieur Al-Ahnan—

—Al-*Wah*nan—

—O, pardonnez-moi, monsieur Al-Wahnan. Anyway, this call is purely a formality.

Aziz's heart sank. —You're not going to hire me, are you?

—Bah, non—

—I should have *known* that French egalitarianism has an exception clause for Moroccans. If only I were Senegalese or *anything* besides Arab. If only I were—

—Monsieur, je vous en prie.

—Sorry, what?

—We'd like to offer you a job with an initial salary of € 45.000, but that comes with a signing bonus of € 5.000, use of a company car, subsidized lunches, and a company credit card.

—Putain de merde!

—I'm sorry, is there a problem?

—Just with my mouth.

He politely ignored Aziz, as so many white French people had done before. —We happen to have an excellent pension program, provide salary increase incentives and top-of-the-line dental and health insurance and of course, all house publications are free.

—You must be out of your *fucking* mind!

—Pardon?

—I don't know what to say.

—Bah, how about yes?

—Oui, absolument, oui!

—Fantastique. We'll send you a welcome packet in the mail sometime this week to the address listed in your application. In the meantime, you'll want to pack soon.

—Pack?

—Your training starts in two weeks.

—This is fucking insane!

—I'm sure it is.

—I'm sorry. I don't usually swear this much.

—Happens all the time.

—Vraiment?

—No, not really.

—Did you say where I'm training?

—I didn't, but it's New York.

—New York City?

—Correct.

—*Alham*dulillah.

—Pardon?

—This is fucking amazing! Aziz shouted.

—Glad to hear it. Our travel agent will contact you in the next few hours to book your flight. In the meantime, please stop by the front office sometime this week. You'll need to fill out some formulaires, pick up a temporary company card, and open up a company account so we can directly deposit your signing bonus.

Aziz shook his head in disbelief.

—And please don't forget to pick up your ticket.

—D'accord.

—Eh bien. Well, glad to have you on board monsieur . . . Aziz . . . we look forward to meeting you soon.

—Merci. Merci beaucoup! I really appreciate this.

—De rien, monsieur. Bonne journée.

—Oui, bonne journée, Aziz said, closing his phone in utter astonishment. He sat in his seat like an absinthe portrait, not moving and not looking at anyone in the eyes inside the café. He was afraid of losing this moment, afraid of losing this joy. Maybe, because he'd been reading too much SF, he decided he must be in a coma right now, inventing this all up in his mushy skull as food traveled through a G-tube and fake tears dropped into his IV drip. This couldn't be real, but it was. He started crying and then became embarrassed, wiping his eyes with a napkin just as the DJ started spinning his first set, a single, unadorned break beat that sounded like broken glass vibrating the café windows. Aziz almost felt like dancing.

It was a big teuf, so they all celebrated at Hassan's café, everyone except his papa, who was in the city *doing errands* when everything was closed. Aziz tried not to let it bother him, but his father's absence always wounded him because every void throbbed. Maman and Aziz's sisters, Sakina and little Sophie, arrived at Hassan's café bearing gifts of Moroccan bocadillos, sesame-covered honey cakes, khaab el ghzal pastries, and tajines de mrouzia. They moved around the café serving food, the smell of lamb, raisins, and almond paste blending with fresh tobacco leaves, mint tea, cinnamon, coriander, and slivers of saffron. Aziz smelled Casa, he smelled teenage nirvana, he smelled a country he visited once every few years so the paint would never dry, even though he was Parisian, brown, and atheist through and through.

After Maman forced everyone to eat second and third helpings of tajine, they drank strong Turkish coffee and *real* mint tea outside on the terrace. It was a beautiful summer evening in St-Denis for so many reasons that made no sense to Aziz at that moment. His joy was a delicate and tenuous thing, unfit for survival, impossible to protect, too delicate to thrive.

—I can't fucking believe it, Ousmane said, shaking his head and exhaling dramatically.

—*See*, Michel said, I *told* you guys something would work out.

—Well, Aziz said, no one believed you, we were just being nice.

Everyone laughed.

—I believed him, Wafi said.

—Allez va, Ousmane said, Aziz won the racial lottery. That's how hard it is to succeed in this country. Ousmane opened a new pack of Gitanes. —I guess the little guy *does* win sometimes.

—And Aziz *is* little, Nizar said.

Aziz stuck his forearm in the air and slapped his bicep to let Nizar know how he really felt.

—So, what's the first thing you wanna see in New York? Ousmane asked.

—Statue of Liberty, Michel said.

—Empire State, Wafi said.

Ousmane tossed Aziz his pack of cigarettes.

Aziz made a one-handed catch—more instinct that dexterity—that looked badass. —That's easy, he said.

—Et c'est quoi? Michel asked.

—The Brooklyn Bridge, Aziz said, holding up Ousmane's pack of cigarettes in the air like a bridge.

Ousmane look confused. —What's so amazing about that? It's just a bridge. We've got *tons* of those in Paris.

—It's one of the *largest* suspension bridges in the world, Aziz said, and it's also one of New York's most important cultural signifiers.

—I'm confused, Michel said, I don't know what it signifies.

—The Brooklyn Bridge, Aziz said, was a structural leap of faith for its builders because nothing like that had ever been built before. He took out a cigarette from Ousmane's pack and tossed it back to him, which deflected off Ousmane's hand and fell on the ground.

—Il faut élucider, Wafi said.

Aziz lit his cigarette with a match from Comptoir. —We all know that I love languages.

Ousmane bent down to pick up his pack of cigarettes. —Bah oui, who else can bribe the waiters in Chinatown and the flower merchants of Belleville?

Aziz smiled. —But I don't think I've ever told anyone besides Wafi why I studied languages in the first place.

—To pick up les meufs? Nizar asked, giggling.

Ousmane and Michel chuckled.

Aziz shook his head. —Not even close. For me learning a foreign language is like building a bridge between two disconnected cultures. Before the Brooklyn Bridge, Brooklyn and Manhattan were separate islands. You had to take *ferries* to get from one borough to another.

—Quel horreur, Ousmane said, shuttering. —I hate boats.

Aziz had seen Ousmane's dog paddle and it was a thing of wretched and clumsy beauty. —So, with one magnificent bridge, the people living on both islands were connected forever in space and time.

—Attend, Nizar said, so you wanna see the Brooklyn Bridge because it's a symbol of urban innovation?

—Comment? Ousmane asked.

Aziz exhaled. —Because it's a signifier of language and cultural symbiosis. It's a suspension bridge, which means it's not rigid (i.e., it's not grammatical) but conforms to its environment, just like language does morphologically. Just like culture does sociolinguistically. And that bridge is the medium by which two separate cultures (Brooklyn and Manhattan) formed their connection.

—Je comprends rien de rien, Nizar declared.

—The Brooklyn Bridge, Aziz continued, is a construction conceived out of faith and necessity, beauty and separation, functionality and chasm. It literally helped create interconnectivity between cultures, spaces, and people, just like language does to fill in the spaces in a lexicon. Languages must be flexible and adaptive to survive, otherwise they die. I mean, think about it, we speak French when Ousmane's here and Maghrebi Arabic when he's not. And learning a foreign language is the ultimate signifier of human empathy, which makes that bridge a necessary part of American multiculturalism.

—Attend, Attend, Michel said, je comprends pas.

—Aziz, did you smoke du shit before coming up with this theory? Ousmane shouted.

Everyone laughed.

Aziz pulled his cigarette a few times and grew pensive before he spoked again. —What's really cool about this metaphor is if you analyze 9/11 from this perspective, you learn that New Yorkers of every class, identity, and race, walked home together, which doesn't seem like a big deal, but walking is the traditional way that mystics discover transcendence, the way that abled Muslims fulfill the Five Pillars of Islam when they go on Hajj, and the way that many Buddhists meditate, but what is home but the Sufi concept of divine reunion?

—And so? Wafi said, his eyes twinkling.

—When 9/11 happened, New Yorkers walked over the Brooklyn Bridge *en masse* because they needed to be home, but if you translated this semiotically, what we're *really* saying is that Americans needed language (i.e., the bridge) to overcome the abyss that trauma creates. Since we need a leap of faith and a chasm to create language (i.e., create a bridge) and since language is the medium that helps us reunite with the broken land of our gods (Buddha, Allah, Jesus, whatever) through spoken prayers, mantras, and meditation, this means that language intricately links our fragile and fragmented humanity together with our unarticulated spirituality. The Brooklyn Bridge is the most spiritual invention in the whole world!

Nizar scratched his head. Ousmane exhaled dramatically. Michel nodded.

—Now, Aziz said, looking around, before you tell me I'm ouf, remember that the first thing Allah told the prophet Mohammed to do was *read*. Reading is the way we learn to speak, the way we learn to understand language and interpret reality, and after 9/11, language was the only thing left in the world. It was the only way to exorcise our pain and lament the sickening loss of order, the only thing left in our vocabulary of infinite loss. We've all used language to denounce violence, to overcome despair, and to criticize both terrorism and American foreign policy. So, the Brooklyn Bridge (i.e., language) was the only way out of that site of collective trauma, the only thing connecting people together in a world fragmented by seething hatred, religious self-righteousness, and orgiastic self-destruction. Language was the only thing bridging the spaces between our separate worldviews. It was our way back home not just for New Yorkers, but for the world.

—Al*ham*dulillah, Wafi said, knocking his hand on the wooden table and smiling, —T'es chanmé, Aziz.

They all paused to put out their cigarettes and sip their tea.

Sakina, Aziz's older sister, came over to buss the table when Aziz's friends protested. —Guys, she said, it's okay. I don't mind. Really.

—The food was delicious, Wafi said, alhamdulillah.

—Bla jmil, Wafi, she said, can I get you guys anything else?

—We're fine, Michel said, merci beaucoup.

—Oui, merci, Ousmane said.

—Cimer, Nizar said.

—Shukran bezzaf, Aziz said, standing up. —Why don't you sit for a second and let me take this stuff.

—No way, Sakina said, laughing, my feet need to move or I'll get restless.

—Take a break, sis, Aziz said, you've been working all night and the least we can do is clean up a little.

—I just, she said, okay, *fine*. Sakina plopped down in Aziz's chair, her mouth opening in shock. —Mon *dieu*, Aziz, this chair is burning! Is your ass on fire? She laughed at her own joke.

—He's been preaching, Ousmane said.

—Hmph, she said, shaking her head, from Sorbonne to shariah!

Aziz's friends all roared with laughter.

Assholes, Aziz thought. He grabbed a pile of dirty dishes and walked to the kitchen, placing them inside the sink. His friends laughed outside, which made him smile.

Aziz began washing dishes. —Hey, Hassan? he asked in Darija.

Hassan was busy watching a World Cup Qualifying match that had just started between France and Finland. —Oui, mon fils?

—Did Papa return from his *errands*?

Hassan shook his head gently. —He went home. Il était fatigué.

—I see, Aziz said, pretending not to be hurt, what's the score?

—Still 0-0, he said, evidently no one told the Finns to take the day off.

Suddenly, there were three deep baritone explosions in the distance, the sound of glass particles splintering against the pavement, and car alarms chanting polyphonically as a flutter of young voices screamed in a mix of North African Arabic, verlan, English, and French.

Hassan's eyes opened wide like a blue nazar, but he forced a smile on his face. —Everything's fine, he said to the old men inside the café, just some football hooligans.

—Ces voyous, someone muttered, they don't know when to stop.

—First Casa, then Cairo, and now Paris, one of the wrinkled men muttered before lighting a cigarette.

—It's just football hooligans, Hassan repeated.

Aziz peaked his head out the front door and down the street, but everything looked calm. That was the problem with Paris, everything was always quiet until the guillotine crashed down on your brown head.

—Aziz, Hassan said.

—Nam? Aziz said.

—I think you better walk your family home.

—You think it's serious?

—Lla, Hassan said, patting him on the shoulder. —But it's better to be safe.

—Entendu, Aziz said.

—I knew you would.

After Aziz had walked Sakina, petite Sophie, and their maman home, kissing them each on the cheek, he wondered about the explosions. Even though there were protests off and on in St-Denis, the explosions seemed portentous. Aziz felt like there were sickly moons in his cheeks and a plague of moths beating frantically inside his chest, their wings coating his lungs with a stale white powder that made breathing impossible, his fears multiplying inside his mind like sprouting polypores. Somewhere between his house and Hassan's café, Aziz broke into a blind sprint down La Rue Dominique, getting lost in the maze of his own cortisol until he felt like he was dragging a second body down the streets, his stomach loaded with rocks, broken bottles, and daggers. Somehow, he went the wrong way in his own hood.

Aziz retraced his steps past Hassan's café, looking down the street in horror. In the distance, the street was covered in flames, the spaces between cobblestone bricks, plastic garbage cans, tiny mom and pop shops, and piles of decomposing trash were all burning like a gigantic spiritual conflagration, the pavement engulfed in a spectral blaze. The rioters' fury burned from inside as they screamed in fear and rage in the humid September air. Angry students dressed in kaftans, blue jeans, buttondowns, kufis, backwards baseball caps, and Les Bleus football jerseys, all hurled rocks at the end of the street. They cursed in frantic Arabic, busted-up Darija, and weaponized French, their voices trembling with exclamation marks. They released years of gagged fury, liberating the captive spirits inside their ribcages underneath the testimony of burnt sky. Aziz saw poison in the protesters' eyes, dilated with pain, defiance, and righteous anger. The protesters grabbed chunks of blazing sidewalk with their scrawny pitching arms and hurled them into the air with furious strength, launching pieces of rubble, chipped cement, and petrol-filled carafes into blank space, throwing blocks of energy back into the ominous night as if honing their violence at an invisible army of darkness. Tonight was the tipping point, a microcosm of French subjugation and collective defiance. Tonight was just the most recent intifada against French police brutality, racial profiling, and state-sanctioned terrorism against brown and Black people that had been going on for centuries in the country. Everyone knew that and no one cared, least of all the French nobility. Aziz sometimes felt like protesting too, but he worried about his family and about Hassan, whose café was just six or seven blocks away. For all he knew, Hassan was probably talking with the protesters and giving out free tea.

Once Aziz had caught up to the throng several blocks away, he heard Hassan's voice. Aziz peered between men in chambray button-downs and Barça jerseys, but he couldn't place the old man's pansita in the smoke and darkness, his most distinguishable characteristic.

—Boys, Hassan said in Standard Arabic, listen to me. Listen! I know you're angry and I know why you want to fight, but they're wearing riot gear and they have live ammunition.

Aziz pushed his way through the thick crowd of men, most of them smoking, a few of them recording everything from their phones.

—Get outta the way, old man!

Aziz tapped a young student in a taqiyah on the shoulder, who turned around and let him pass. Aziz pushed forward.

—Whose grandpa is this?

—That's the café owner, you fool.

Aziz slid between a fat man in jeans and button-up and a reedy old man dressed in a cream djellaba.

—Vite! Voilà les keufs!

—I'm gonna destroy those motherfuckers.

—Hassan, get out of the way or I'll strike you!

—Boys, écoutez-moi, s'il vous plaît. Some of you are like sons to me. I understand your anger because it's my anger too. We all deserve justice and we all know the French judicial system will never give it to us, but this isn't a fair fight. We have rocks and rage, they have guns, batons, shields, police dogs, and whiteness. Their VBRGs have machine guns. We can't win the war by fighting blindly. We have to organize. We have to strategize.

—Hassan! Aziz shouted, Hassan!

—We cannot win this war with our hands, Hassan continued, has the prophet Mohammed taught you nothing?

Aziz pushed his way through another thick throng of men smelling like tobacco, sugar, and shoe polish.

—Get out of the way, a young student in a light blue oxford said.

—The prophet Mohammed was a fighter! someone else shouted.

—The prophet Mohammed was Allah's *servant*, Hassan said, and you are trying to be his bodyguard.

—Enough of this bullshit, another man said, waving a curtain rod in the air, his eyes glowing with pain and determination. He pushed Hassan out of the way, who collapsed to the ground. The invisible barricade splintered. Protesters erupted down the street like a fight club high on Cristal. An army of Pumas, dress shoes, Adidas, and sandals trampled on Hassan's face, jumping over him, racing around him as he covered his eyes with his arms. Aziz saw clouds of kerosene and cigarette smoke and a hailstorm of a million rocks, chunks of concrete, and an occasional Molotov cocktail thrown into the air at once. Aziz almost expected, he half hoped, that the protest was a purely symbolic act of resistance, simply a flash mob of performative defiance, but just as he reached Hassan and cradled his head, he noticed a platoon of French riot police at the end of the street marching through layers of poisoned smoke and serpentine flames, dressed in crisp blue uniforms, their bullet-proof vests adorned with big red patches. The gendarmes were a moving wall of violence. Their combat boots stomped in common time, hitting the ground in a thunderous bass beat of destruction. With riot shields and protective headgear, they looked like a platoon of Kevlar knights, suddenly transforming St-Denis into West Jerusalem. Aziz thought instantly of the crusades, of Palestinians trapped between checkpoints, of Lebanese civilians trying to flee bombed roads and walls of white phosphorus. These were CRS gendarmes, the object of St-Denis' most intense and elaborate hatred, the Compagnies Républicaines de Securité fascists, otherwise known as *The Cars of Raging Monkeys* as they were called in this neighborhood. The riot police continued marching down the street like unrepentant Stormtroopers, punching little kids in the face, knocking cell phones out of hands with their plastic shields, pistol-whipping bony adolescents whose necks practically snapped from impact. The CRS kicked praying Muslims on the sidewalk and smashed two-foot batons into the faces of grandfathers and university students whose eye sockets bled profusely as they screamed. It was another day of police occupation and power asymmetry.

—O mon dieu, Hassan, Aziz cried, trying to lift him with shaking hands, someone help us! Please, he's injured. Au secours! Aziz yelled to no one in particular, to call witness to the invasion of their neighborhood he'd seen so many times before wielded against brown and Black and Muslim bodies on Twitter and on TV5. It was the same shit he was witnessing in his own streets now, one-way state-sanctioned violence that citizens legally weren't allowed to resist or use themselves since violence was the prerogative of the state, one of the paradoxes of liberal democracies. Aziz tried ignoring the enormous weight of Hassan's body. He tried lifting him in his arms, but they wobbled every time. Aziz's knees buckled when he stood up, his body staggering every time he attempted to flee from bedlam.

In the distance, the thick phalanx of CRS officers floated towards him like a death cloud vaporizing everything in its path. Aziz tried one last time to lift Hassan's body that was still warm, the old man's diaphragm contracting, his life force still clinging to his body. Aziz pushed Hassan up by his knee, off the dark streets covered in cigarette ash and petrol, he lifted him with the last bit of strength that he had. Underneath the contusive sky, the scorched street covered in what looked like burgundy, black, and lavender Holi dye, Aziz's body trembled with fear and muscle failure. Hassan was way too heavy. He didn't have the upper body strength to carry him to safety, he was an intellectual, after all, not a gym rat, so he cradled the old man's head with his arms as combat boots crashed into the pavement, hovered above every injured face in judgment, and crushed each new brown and Black body with ferocious efficiency, the steel toes soaked in human sweat, extracted plasma, crushed enamel, and bloody spit. Aziz watched in slow motion as the fleur-de-lis patterns in their soles quickly swooped down on the two of them, imprinting their faces with the symbol of French Republicanism. A split second before the combat boots knocked them both unconscious, Aziz closed his eyes as if he'd fallen into a dream of crushed skin and broken teeth, swimming in a suspended animation of the grief-stricken, the daydreaming, and the traumatized.

After an alternate life had expired inside his mind, Aziz woke up in a strange bed. His head floated like a giant, tethered zeppelin. His teeth ached, the pain vibrating in his gums. There were pieces of gauze in his mouth where straight, white, perfect teeth used to be. When he removed the bloody wad from his mouth, there was a big gap in his front teeth. His teeth used to be the one thing about his body he was proud of, even a tiny bit arrogant, but they'd stolen part of him like everything else he once valued about himself. He felt like brown trash. Was that even a term? Aziz couldn't decide. He rubbed his eyes and winced every time he patted his jaw masochistically, trying to gauge the damage of his body. What the fuck had happened? There were huge gaps in his recall, spaces in his mind where the nightmares he'd just woken up from had smashed into false memories he couldn't erase. He looked around the eerie and dimly lit room. A soft blue candle burned on a small bread plate at the edge of a second-hand nightstand. Aziz heard the frantic whisper of sadness on the other side of the apartment, the words both undetectable and intuitive, their voices chock full of deep emotion, the cadence of their words frightening to Aziz. As he looked around the drab and unkept room, he felt disoriented and dizzy, alternating between pain, confusion, and nausea. His tongue felt heavy, his mouth bitter, his body like a giant bag of broken bones. As he stood up, the bedsprings groaned elegiacally, a sharp pain shot up his back and through his ribs and gumline. His legs wobbled as he stumbled to his feet. He heard soft footsteps in another room and then the parting of a rhinestone curtain. Sakina stopped in front of him, her cheeks stained by an entire cycle of tears. Her eyes were decimated by unrequited grief.

—Azizzzzzzzzzz, she wailed.

—Sakina, Aziz said, opening his arms, where the hell *are* we?

Sakina stumbled towards him. —Aziz. She collapsed into his chest. —Il est mort. Hassan est mort.

—*Quoi?*

—He's dead, Aziz. They trampled him to death.

—Non, non, non. C'est pas vrai. Je l'ai porté dans les bras.

—Aziz, you know I would never lie to you.

—Non! Aziz implored, his gums throbbing. —I don't believe it!

—Ask the Imam. They're reciting the Salat Al-Mayyit right now.

Aziz's eyes prickled with angry tears. They warped into shards that burned his pores like hangnails as they shot down his cheeks. He felt a deep and fantastic shame for his weakness and his agony. He held Sakina and pressed his forehead against hers before hugging her tightly. They both shook and shivered as if tragedy were a terrible draft. Sakina's hair was a field of black lines raining from her scalp, smelling of raisins and cinnamon, witch hazel shampoo and vanilla soap. The tragedy poured out of them as they sobbed. Aziz pretended he was consoling her as his lips trembled and his teeth clenched, the pain pouring out of him, the pain bleeding out. He felt like he had no control over his own body as he sobbed on his sister's neck and apologized for his weakness. Sakina told him it was okay to cry as she cried. She paraphrased Kahlil Gibran and said crying was a form of jubilation. She said they were celebrating Hassan's life through their messy tears, but Aziz kept apologizing as he sobbed in her arms. He was ashamed for his body and ashamed for his agony and ashamed of his inability to console her, but most of all, he was ashamed that he couldn't save the one person who'd believed in him when no one else would.

Aziz wondered what the point of survival was when the best people were always taken from this world? When the weakest, most selfish, and least courageous people were the ones that always inherited the earth? In this life, joy was just a tiny interest payment on the outstanding debt of tragedy, grief, injustice, and suffering. And when life was tragic, it hemorrhaged through us all: the broken memories, the surreal tears, the viral self-loathing, the whispering counterfactuals, and the prayers of regret and self-forgiveness.

There was no golden thread, Hassan, Aziz thought to himself. *You lied to me so I wouldn't lose hope.*

There was only a maze for the broken-hearted, Hassan. There was only a slaughterhouse for the beautiful and the maimed.

24. HULA DANCING IN THE BRONX

AFTER SUZANNE WOKE UP in the spare bedroom, she did some yoga, flipped through IG, took a long, guilty shower, and got dressed in light blue Capri pants, a long, flowing navy kurta with embroidered sunflowers, a layered gold and turquoise necklace, navy headband, and yellow sandals with little Taj Mahals between the toes. When she looked at herself in the mirror, her face radiated something she'd been missing in her former life as a formulaic girlfriend, dog mom, waitress, and frustrated daughter operating on autopilot in Chicago. The truth was she needed to need more from others and she needed others to need less of her. But who deserved such power inversion?

She'd been in Seattle three weeks now. Suzanne was astonished at how white the city was. She was equally astonished at how much free time she had suddenly, more than she could handle. Suzanne had been the type of student, for example, who'd once scheduled every hour of her waking life her first year of college (even sex) so she could graduate with a double major in English and gender studies in four years. Now, she was practically drowning in disposable time even though she wasn't convinced that time was disposable or that she had the right to dispose of it. Ever since she'd left George, she'd been sleeping nine hours every day like a tween on the cross-country team. Nine!

There was a knock on the door. —Suzie Q, you wanna get a bite to eat? Ali asked.

—Sure, Suzanne said.

—Girl, you're not depressed, are you?

—God, I wish. It would simplify so many things in my life.

—You know how long you've been *sleeping* for?

—Six cigarettes! Suzanne was now completely familiar with Ali's method of measuring time.

—Not even *close* bitch! Try ten.

—I'll be out in a second, Ali. I just need to finish navel-gazing.

—Look, you're gorgeous enough to make every straight girl question her sexuality, so get out here!

Ali forced a laugh and marched through the hallway in high-heeled boots that would end up drawing attention to her fierceness like an accidental dominatrix the whole day. Suzanne sprayed herself with perfume that had notes of sandalwood, vanilla, and Freesia, and then walked into the living room as Ali was taking a dramatic drag from her eleventh cigarette. She passed it to Suzanne, who grabbed the American Spirit and took a baby drag, exhaling through the open window. As she passed the cigarette back, Suzanne felt light-headed. She suddenly wanted to tell Ali everything about her dramatic departure from Chicago. Suzanne had a desperate need to feel understood right now by someone who didn't need her blindly or know her categorically. Ali didn't care one way or another whether Suzanne stayed with George, so she was an impartial judge, which Suzanne craved. Every other person in her life had already returned their verdicts on her love life:

We the jury find the defendant guilty as charged.

An hour later, Suzanne was hunched over a slab of wood at a taquería in Capitol Hill called K Padre, nom noming on chips and guacamole, sipping bottles of Tecate with lime, and erasing a slew of voice messages on her phone almost gleefully (with a healthy dose of guilt, always guilt). She'd emailed Badawi, her former manager, right before she'd hopped on a plane at O'Hare, apologizing profusely for leaving the Indonesian restaurant out of the blue and now she was trying frenetically to find her replacement. The problem was Suzanne and George had become a broken mirror and there was only one thing you could do once that happened, sweep up the mess and throw it out. So she left Chicago, but her manager couldn't accept her apology. He called every week and yelled at her. He said it would take him forever to find a waitress that spoke English, Hindi, and Spanish. He said that she'd screwed him over, *big time*. He said that he was at *his wit's end*. He said he was *angry, hurt, and confused*. He said that she had acted like an *impulsive child*. He said that he was *deeply sorry* the next day. Suzanne felt liked she'd broken up with two men. Of course, she felt really bad about leaving her job with no advanced warning. She felt like she deserved Badawi's criticism (everything except the infantilization), but she also knew that leaving on a whim was probably the first irresponsible thing she'd done in her adult life and honestly, it felt fucking great. It was so out of character for her that no one believed it at first.

After there was a stockpile of empty beer bottles on their table, Ali slid them to one side with her forearm. The jukebox was playing a saccharine song about heartache, the lyrics glowing like a distant moon in a background of polka-dancing tubas and coronet players slurring their brassy melodies in unison. Ali bumped Suzanne's bottle, the foam rushing upwards, which Suzanne swallowed before it overflowed. She wiped her mouth with the sleeve of her kurta because she'd rather get drunk than make a mess, which was the story of her life.

—'Scuse me, Ali muttered to their waiter, what's the word you taught me?

—Joven, Suzanne said.

—Joven? But this guy is way older than I am.

—Doesn't matter. That's what they say in México.

—Perdón, joven . . . God, that fucker's *still* ignoring me and I'm wearing my tit-tank. The truth was, he'd been ignoring them since they ordered chips and guacamole, so now they ordered their beer from the bar like real cowgirls.

—What's this guy's damage anyway? Ali asked, shaking her head.

—Ali, finish what you were saying.

—Sorry, okay, so I just, I just don't fucking get it. I mean, if you still love George, why bail on him?

—Because I love him rationally.

—Whaddyamean?

—I mean, I have this impressive list of reasons why I love him and they're all so, I dunno, impressive.

—What's wrong with that?

—It's like the set-up in Pedro Almodóvar's *Habla con Ella*. It's easy to love someone abstractly who doesn't talk back and who doesn't contradict your imagination.

—So, he doesn't have any backbone?

—No, he does, especially when it comes to money, he just doesn't have that je-ne-sais-quoi. That hard-to-define quality that makes life feel deep and rich and strange and surprising again. That's what I want. That's what I've always wanted.

—Oh, I got you.

—Basically, I want my heart to buzz and glow like an old neon sign.

—That's very specific, Suzy-Q.

Suzanne shrugged her shoulders and dragged a tortilla chip back and forth in the guacamole bath. —Well, *I'm* very specific.

—Honestly, you guys sounded way too functional anyway and that's just not how love is. It's a curse. It's a sickness. It's mass delusion. It's glorified hypertension, but it's *not* functional.

Suzanne sipped her beer even though she was totally buzzed, the recessed lighting reminding her of floating gold bubbles.

—I feel like love can be almost anything *except* rational, Ali said.

—You know, Suzanne said, I think you may be right.

—Bitch, of *course* I am! I'm crazy and I'm *totally* in love. She nodded triumphantly.

Suzanne wiped her mouth with her sleeve. —You know, the last guy I was in love with was such a klutz. He was the first boy I ever argued with in college. I hated him because we always got in these ridiculous arguments at dinner about Walter Benjamin, diasporic literature, and institutional racism.

—God, what fucking *geeks!*

Suzanne ignored her. —But one day, I realized I'd fallen for him and it was right after he dropped a plate of Belgian waffles on the floor a foot away from the kitchen table, tears in his eyes, the floor covered in blueberries and maple syrup.

—See, I *feel* you, Suzie-Q. That shit's cute AF.

They both stopped to think, sipping their warm beer, clearing their throats, and wiping their lips with their wrists. The jukebox shuffled to another mariachi song that was bound to break someone else's heart. Ali looked at her phone. Suzanne's head swayed back and forth as she looked around the restaurant at burly white hipsters, dotcommunists in matching Banana Republic button-downs, nose-pierced women in Patagonia fleece jackets, and Latino employees clearing tables and cracking jokes with each other. Suzanne looked through the windows as the sun was crashing through the sky like a sabotaged chrome vessel.

Ali leaned her head on Suzanne's shoulder and sighed. —You know what's really freaky? Love just *happens* to you like the

Ebola virus. One minute, you're just chilling with your friends at a bar and the next thing you know, there's blood gushing through your eye sockets.

Suzanne laughed.

—Sometimes I can't *stand* your brother, Ali continued, I wanna kick his ass for not calling me when he crashes at JB's or when he drives home totally smashed on Cuba Libres or when he wakes me up in the middle of the night playing "Far Cry" through the stereo. When he does shit like that, I wanna throw out all his B-side vinyl, toss his expensive shoe collection in the hallway with a "Free Kicks" sign, and make him sleep outside in his skivvies.

—I'm shocked you haven't already.

—Don't think I haven't *thought* about it a million times, but what's crazy is, none of that shit has any goddamn effect on the snap he's got on me. And that *really* pisses me off.

—Of course, it's like you're not in control of your feelings.

—I know, Ali grunted, and I fucking hate it.

They both sat there, mulling over things, quietly wondering when the music would die. That will be their cue to leave, the death of the mariachi band.

Outside, the sunset was an electric peach halo in the tissue-paper sky. As they walked to the bus stop, Suzanne noticed Ali swaggering a little bit like it was sidewalk meringue. Every time she did a slow stutter step, her hips jutted out to the side. From the back, you'd think she was the prize dancer of margarita ranches. Suzanne wondered if Ali still heard the music in her head, the way her brother the DJ did, the way every person in love did. Ali plopped down on the bench and sighed. In the distance, the Space Needle looked like it been built for a science fiction movie and then quickly abandoned. Suzanne saw the body of a giant ballerina hovering over the city with long, thin, muscular legs and an intrusive chignon. Ali passed her a smoke. Suzanne placed it behind her ear like a flower.

A few minutes later a Jeep Cherokee pulled up beside them, mumble rap blasting through its open windows. A tiny part of Suzanne died inside. A red-haired white dude in a ratty backwards baseball cap leered at them, elbowing his friend behind the wheel.

—'Sup, ladies?

—'Sup, Ali said flatly.

—My name's Vick.

—Wanna cookie, Vick? she asked, hitting her cigarette and looking away.

He smiled for no reason. —What're your names?

Ali exhaled and stared at him. —I'm Notta and she's Chance.

—Great fucking names!

—You idiot, Ali said.

—Hey, *fuck* you, he said, pointing his finger at her.

—Dude, the driver said, shut the fuck up. You're embarrassing me.

—Dude, fuck these snotty-ass bitches.

—Hey, Ali said, here's an idea: why don't you go fuck yourselves and leave women alone for a change?

Suzanne chuckled.

Ratty Hat smirked like Ali had just said the most adorable thing when the Jeep screeched away. Ali snickered and told Suzanne to sit down. The sun had become an introvert and she had nothing left to stand for anyway, so she plopped down on the bench and sighed just like Ali had done. Ali rested her head on Suzanne's shoulder. She smelled like DKNY and lime pulp and American Spirits and wet flowers.

—Sometimes, I really wish I were gay, Ali said.

Suzanne nodded. —Why don't we get our Master's in Library Science? We'd literally get paid to organize the world!

—No way! Give me *passion* and eccentricity.

—Okay, you're right.

—I mean, why can't they just look like Jude Law and act like John Cusack?

—I'd switch'em, Suzanne said, Jude Law is pretty, but he's *rationally* pretty. John Cusack, on the other hand, would make you laugh all day. He's what I call IB.

—You call John Cusack your irritable bowel?

Suzanne snorted. —Nooooo, it stands for idiosyncratically beautiful.

—What's that?

—It's when someone is beautiful in an unconventional, strange, or unique way that hits your heart.

—IB. I like that. I'm gonna use it.

—You should.

—Samir's IB.

—Um, I guess so, Suzanne said, not comfortable thinking about her brother that way.

—Oh fuck, the bus's here. Pull out the transfers, Suzie.

—God, I'm tired all of a sudden, Suzanne said, yawning.

They walked to the back of the bus and collapsed. Suzanne secretly wondered why they hadn't just called a taxi. Ali closed her eyes. Suzanne looked out the window, admiring the residual sunlight in the sky that reminded her of vermillion powder used to paint kumkuma on the foreheads of Indian brides and Hindus performing puja. She liked the idea of the sun coming to the West Coast to sleep after spinning in slow, faithful circles around the galaxy, even though she knew the sun was just a star and the Earth did most the movement. The clouds looked like birthmarks on the sky's back, so lumpy and endearing. Ali napped while Suzanne watched the darkness unfurling to the ground like a supernatural banner.

Airwalk was a scene like every club in Capitol Hill. There

were glam drag queens, G-Star lesbians, athletic lesbians, home repair/grunge lesbians, drop-dead gorgeous lesbians with razor-line undercuts and choppy pixies (some of whom Suzanne found kinda hot), there were futuristic Asian and white ravers carrying LED stick lights, appropriative white Rastas in "Redemption Song" T-shirts, and a whole legion of students, bearded white hipsters, bears in jeans shorts, tank tops, trucker hats, and skinny gay boys dancing in "Wo ist Daddy?" T-shirts. The dancefloor was comfortable and sweaty, if sweaty could be comfortable. Ali disappeared and came back with two monster smoothies, a purple glass with green chunks and a maroon glass with shipwrecked nuts floating in a sea of fruit swirl.

—Here, Ali said, take it before I get frostbite.

Suzanne took a big gulp. —Raspberry-banana-orange? What are these nuts?

—Beeswax. Gives you mad energy.

—Ah yes, of course.

Suzanne took another gulp and then began shivering when the brain freeze hit. After people-watching some more, she sipped her smoothie until it was just a pink froth and then went to the bathroom. As she was looking in the mirror, a transwoman in a dark green and black lace vintage dress, platform shoes, and black silk scarf passed by. Suzanne thought her blond Betty Page wig was thing of exquisite perfection. The other women nodded at Betty Page as they applied makeup, talked on their phones, and shared a stinky bowl of Snowdawg. Suzanne got a contact high as she washed her hands. She returned to the dancefloor, wondering why she'd stopped smoking weed and why she hadn't kissed a girl since college.

After swimming through a crowd of people getting down on the dancefloor, Suzanne found Samir and Ali talking to each other under a blue ceiling light that made them look Matissean. Ali's eyes were bubbles, glistening, sparkling with love as Samir held her hand and told her a story, pausing to drag his joint or kiss Ali's temples. Suzanne could tell Samir loved her because he couldn't stop touching her hands, kissing her temples, and rubbing her cheeks. And Suzanne could tell that Ali loved him because she never looked away, her face flushed with halogen adoration. It was like nothing else mattered to them except their love for each other. They didn't need anyone to register their affection because they radiated joy, magnetic harmony, and a completeness that made everyone else feel deformed and disconnected in comparison. Their connection made Suzanne squint and stargaze, prompted her jealousy, fed her romantic fatalism, but also inspired her own counterfactual daydreams about parallel worlds with parallel lovers that might intersect and entangle with this one like the leashes of frantic purse dogs.

Suzanne saw their rapport for what it was, the Platonic reunion of lost selves, she saw their rawness and symmetry, their uncensored affection and their time-stopping devotion, she saw their unfolding into each other, and it enchanted and nauseated her, convinced her that humans could live on love and fresh air forever. It didn't matter whether her romantic interpretation was true or not, only that she saw it with her own eyes, that she'd witnessed something sublime, something she wanted more than anything in the whole dying world. It was addictive watching people in love. It was also deeply disfiguring.

When Samir started spinning his first set, Airwalk was an orgy of grinding half-naked bodies and pulsating subwoofers. Her brother mixed Jay-Z, Blondie, and Jedi Mind Tricks, Notorious B.I.G., Debussy, and Tupac, Nas, Coltrane, and samples of children playing, Handsome Boy Modeling School, Billie Holiday, and Eminem, Kendrick Lamar, Marvin Gaye, and Erik Satie. The songs intersected together brilliantly like three-part Bach inventions, the crowd shouting with each new mashup, in love with Samir's arrangements, astounded by his creativity as they raised their hands in the air and shook their asses on the dancefloor. Couples plugged into each other, their glistening, gyrating bodies suggested vertical foreplay, drag queens tossed their boas around like rhythmic gymnasts on platforms, performing long ribbon routines for make-believe judges. Ali and Suzanne danced together, sometimes, their hands spelled out clumsy words with their makeshift sign language, sometimes, their hands became cages to protect themselves from desperados and pick-up artists, their torsos moving slowly from side to side like two hula dancers in the Bronx.

Ali went to the bathroom when a muscular white guy moved through the crowd slowly. His pretty face looked contorted in the dancing sequin lights. Dressed in baggy jeans and a Tommy Hilfiger rugby shirt, his red hair curled into little designs that reminded Suzanne of crop circles, he was attractive but way too cocky for her tastes. Without a word, he came up and started grinding her, pulling her kurta softly from behind. She could feel his chub as he pushed himself against her ass. She gave him a dirty look and shoved her way forward a little bit, but she was stuck. The crowded dancefloor was filled to capacity with swarms of sweaty people making out and guys hawking the crowds for one-night stands and a white Rasta trying to make eyes with her, giving her that how-you-doing-baby-look, which made her want to vomit in his face. She turned around and glanced at Samir on the DJ platform, hoping he'd notice her potential crisis before it happened, but he was nodding to this music in his headphones, one earphone on, the other one straddling his temple like a Carpenter Ant. Samir was totally immersed in hip-hop they hadn't heard yet, always one song ahead of reality.

The guy with red crop circles for hair rubbed against Suzanne again, pulling her towards him by her waist.

She pushed him hard. —Please don't touch me!

—Girl, you look *fine* as hell, he said, dancing with an annoying smirk that she'd seen a thousand times on the faces of aggressive men who treated personal space like an inconvenience to overcome, not self-advocacy to understand. Suzanne detested men who treated dancing like a mating ritual instead of an act of jubilation.

—I'm not interested, she said.

—Baby, why you tripping? he asked.

—I'm not your baby and I'm not *tripping* either.

—What the fuck's your problem? he asked.

—I don't like men who pathologize me when they get rejected.

He gave her a nasty look. —What does that even mean?

—Google it, Einstein.

He pointed his finger at her. —Man, fuck you!

Suzanne's heart galloped in her chest.

—What the fuck's going on here? Ali asked, moving between them.

Suzanne dismissed the white Rasta with a wave of her hand before leading her away.

—Asshole, Ali hissed, raising her middle finger in the air.

He gave them both the finger and disappeared into the crowd. The two of them moved to the other side of the club and shared a bottle of mineral water before heading to a different part of the dancefloor. After turning their backs to a group of last-call predators, Suzanne slowly lost herself to the hip-hop, to the visceral masculine rhyme of the lyrics, to the female vocal samples that looped from chorus to chorus, to the simple basslines that strolled from chord to chord and the classical music melodies and jazz riffs intersecting with the MC's lyrical counterpoint. It was like Samir said once, bad hip-hop was boxed wine: it was one-dimensional, cheap, it went through your system quickly, and it hurt your brain. But conscious hip-hop gave you a soft buzz. It was smooth, deep, and balanced like a nice Sangiovese that kept surprising you with every sip. Ali and Suzanne smiled as they danced. In this space and time, they were now safe again to spell out words again with their legs, their hips, and their hands, they were free to celebrate life with their asses, their arms, and their lungs. When Samir put on "Like it like that" by A Tribe Called Quest for his signature last song, he winked at Ali and mouthed words of love and devotion to her, his eyes smiling with acknowledgement and exclusive affection. Ali recited something to him, something only she could hear, something only he expected. Suzanne felt happiness and freedom and desire and primal envy for what they had.

Ali was perfectly synchronized to the music, her shoulders covered in voluptuous pixies, writing love notes to Samir with her slender fingers, using letters that curved and looped in the air like indulgent Edwardian cursive. Ali turned around, her hands half-raised in the air, her waist moving like a tambourine. Suzanne didn't know whether it was hip-hop or meringue inside Ali's head, but she understood the euphoria in Ali's bloodstream because both of them kept sweating it out on the lyrical mile, the huge break beats and the crystal smooth flow, the cheap beer and the orange peels, the DKNY and the wet flowers, the bananas and the kiwis, the American Spirits and the lime pulp. They drank the rhythm and it poured out of them as they moved their bodies in tempo, sweat dripping down their thighs that curved and bent like sine waves as they swayed on the dancefloor in soft and graceless ecstasy.

25. THE MIDDLE ELEVATOR: A SELF-CONTAINED EXPERIMENTAL NARRATIVE ABOUT CORPORATE PUBLISHING CONTAINED WITHIN A LARGER ANTILINEAR, COUNTERFACTUAL NARRATIVE (AKA, AOJB) ABOUT THE PEOPLE WE WERE SUPPOSED TO FALL IN LOVE WITH BUT DIDN'T BECAUSE LIFE IS FUCKING CRUEL, MAN

WHEN AZIZ WALKED INSIDE the shiny, luxurious, and spacious Éditions Pont Neuf building the first time and spotted the reception desk, he got paranoid that he was in the wrong building. There was no room to make mistakes in French culture because Aziz's face was a remnant, a signifier, and a living critique of French colonialism, which was why Parisians had no problem letting him know he was in the wrong place (and every white space was wrong for North African immigrants in France when your skin was the color of macchiato and you rolled a single harmless R by mistake). Since he was a teenager growing up in Paris, Aziz had to know what white French people were thinking before they did in order to anticipate and avoid their anxiety, disdain, presumption, and criticism. This was how he'd protected his college scholarship, his freelancing gigs, his professional networking, and his translation portfolio by ignoring the tiny margin of error French society gave him and also pretending his double-consciousness wasn't a lead vest dragging him into the swamp of racial melancholia where many of his friends and relatives had drown.

—Bonjour, Aziz said to the elegantly dressed white woman at the reception desk.

—Bonjour monsieur, she said. —Je peux vous aider? She was a pretty brunette with smart eyes, dressed in an impeccable black suit with white buttons, black plastic frames, and a printed white foulard tied around her neck like a French cliché.

—I'm looking for the editorial department.

—Which subdivision?

—Translation.

—Très bien. Au vingt-quatrième étage.

—Merci, he said, hurrying to the elevator.

—Bah, monsieur, she said, holding out her manicured hand like a bored duchess.

Aziz turned around, his paranoia returning. Because he was used to being treated with suspicion, he felt ashamed (and then irritated) even though he'd done nothing wrong. He hated this feeling of wanting to exculpate himself for the simple reason that it presumed guilt, which he thought about constantly even though he knew it had no factual basis whatsoever.

—Votre laissez-passez, she explained, her arm extended in the air, her thin fingers painted in a subdued pink polish that was chipped off at the corners. A silver diamond bracelet dangled from her delicate wrist as she passed him an orange button with today's date like the kind people once wore in museums to gaze at the spoils of the French empire. In a flash, Aziz saw her life in montage: another attractive meuf he'd never talk to on the tromé, just another jolie française that would marry the first chatty dude to jump through the most hoops for her that would supposedly prove how important she was to him and how focused and dedicated he would be as a lover and future husband. Outside at swanky cafés and during dinner repartee, he'd act cynical and tender, stubborn, prolix, and compliant at just the right times. Her boyfriend, the one who bought her that bracelet and probably asked her to paint her nails in colors she hated, would soon become her fiancé, eventually graduating to husband. They'd move into a nice flat in the 16ᵉᵐᵉ arrondissement, just off the Bois de Boulogne where he'd become a successful avocat, prone to fits of jealousy, intellectual reductionism, and conservative rhetoric, especially after spotting gay couples, transwomen, and North African immigrants in his favorite haunts or immediately after the next terrorist attack in Europe. They'd have two children, both of whose names would have hyphens, that they'd take to le Midi each year where les petits gamins would collect sun freckles on their skin at the French Riviera like seashells, changing their license plates every August. By the time she and her husband had reached their forties, they'd have other lovers in Paris or Toulon or Genoa or Montpellier, but they'd stay together anyway, simply because isolation and silence were worse than suspicion and infidelity.

—Voilà monsieur, she said, her eyebrows raised in self-defense like she knew Aziz was psychoanalyzing her accoutrements.

—Merci, he said, pinning the visitor's badge to his one and only expensive tie. Inside the first elevator, he pressed the "24." As floor numbers flashed above his head like a reverse countdown, Aziz wondered if she was watching him fidget through the elevator camera. He wondered if she had anything better to do than watch him pray in Arabic to a God he had trouble understanding and definitely didn't believe in, especially when the world majored in crisis acceleration.

Inside the Translation Department office that looked like

a simulacrum of a university classroom for literature seminars with its fake stained-glass windows, long oak tables, photographs of libraries that covered entire walls, and columns of bookcases filled with in-house publications, Aziz handed his cover letter to the editorial assistant with owl glasses and a bob cut, along with two copies of his CV and his translation portfolio. She handed him a "supplemental job application for long-term translation assignments." He sat down at one of the empty seminar tables, put on his reading glasses, and glanced:

Formulaire pour la mission de traduction à long terme chez l'Éditions Pont Neuf

S.V.P. écrire lisiblement en lettres moulées de préférence

SECTION A.

Lieu de travail actuel :   *Poste occupé :*
Téléphone au travail : ( )
Adresse:
Téléphone à la maison : ( )
Portable: ( )
Duration d'emploi: ( )
Adresse précédente:
Poste demandé:
Avez-vous précédemment fait une demande d'emploi auprès de l'ÉPN?

Si la réponse est oui, mois et année:
Pouvez-vous travailler à plein temps?

J'atteste que les informations inscrites dans la section A sont conformés au dossier du candidat.

*Signature:*__________________________

en date du: ____________________________

Section B. Please list, in inverse chronological order, the past six projects in the field of translation, noting specific assignments, duration of translation projects, work translated (including word count, genre, target audience, international ISBN, and stylistics index number), project supervisor, publishing company, and target/base languages used for each project in the space provided.

                                       6.

                               5.

    77.

                                       3.

                            2.

                1.

Section C. Please complete the following:

Please follow the directions for each subsection. If you feel you cannot finish this application or choose to withdraw your application from ÉPN, please skip to the section called "End of Mandatory Application" and return your unfinished formulaire to the dull-looking editorial assistant at the front desk. No need to leave contact information, we'll reach out when the time is right (i.e., we've reached complete and utter desperation after all our editorial assistants quit in protest for subsistent wages and a glaring lack of racial, gender, class, and sexual diversity).

New Hampshire English Diagnostic Examination

I. Please circle the adverb in each sentence:

1. I'm hungry because corporate publishing doesn't pay me livable wages.
2. No.
3. My cat is the blue Siamese with the scabies. Yours is the ugly brown Tabby that keeps chewing on Grandma's ear.
4. [shhhhhhh].
5. ñ
6. ਇਹ ਪਨੀਰ ਬਦਬੂਦਾਰ ਹੈ
7. Yar, the scallywags be fiendish.
8. お母さんを話して下さい。
9. 3.1415926535897
10.

II. Please fill in the blanks for each incomplete sentence. If a sentence requires no additional words, write "yes" at the end of the sentence:

1. Quantum Mechanics is the underlying mathematical framework of many fields of physics and chemistry, including condensed_________and solid-state_________.

2. Atomic ginger snaps, molecular structure computer simulation, computational_______________, particle men and nuclear families, are the scientific foundation of quantum mechanics, established during the first half of the twentieth century after a meal of___________.

3. I eat my fingernails_________when I'm thinking about poop.

4. I like to break things__________when I'm angry, which makes me a dangerous employee.

5. I like to eat cheap cat food when_________people are mean to me, which is an admission that I'm not psychologically stable enough for this job.

6. *The first thing St. Peter said to our grandparents as they walked to the pearly gates of heaven was________________.*

7. *Their response in Aramaic was:________________.*

8. *Window-washing is________________as long as the steel cables are strong.*

9. *I want to________stick your toothbrush in my bum for good measure.*

10. *Pi, otherwise known as 3.1415926535897____________ _____ 2884197169399 3751, is a useless sum to remember unless you're a math geek (in which case, have at it).*

III. Translate the following sentences into Cantonese, Ukrainian, Chiac, Middle English, or Occitan:

1. *What the shite is that twat doing here bugging out like an ill-nana?*
2. *Yar matey, it's me shinklewad the shibboleth!*
3. *Gēmen, let's get ghost before the alphabet bois come!*
4. *Featherloin this be-atch.*
5. *I'm finna go go go to the show show show.*
6. *Spoodge à la Maylock begotten like a goo.*
7. *Your vibe tastes like Ass Cracker, my dude.*
8. *Thirsty Clickbait Fuckboys of the IG Influencer Militia*
9. *What the fuck is wrong with that fucking fuckface trying to fuck over my fucking bestie with this cheapass motherfucking facial moisturizer? I'm gonna fuck up that motherfucker's fucking face by calling those fuckers at Queer motherfucking Eye and have them do a motherfucking makeover on that fucking zit-faced piece of fuck.*

End of Section C

To fill out Section D, upload required documentation, and complete your application, please visit the following link at your earliest convenience: http://www.jacksonbliss.com/epnsupplementalapplication-because-we-are-quite-woke

Merci beaucoup! We thank you for applying to Éditions Pont Neuf Translation Team and wish you success in all your future endeavors, wherever they may take you (as long as it's far away from this department of privileged cishet white women who only know how to "fall in love" with books written by other cishet white women, especially when they translate other races, identities, and cultures for them in a way that feels safe but stills centers whiteness above all else. Now THAT deserves another million-dollar advance!).

Additionally, if you have chosen to give up on this application and/or you "don't have internet access," please use the middle elevator, which is basically safe to use and has a VERY low mortality rate considering it hasn't been inspected since the 1950s. But it's nothing to worry about it. And remember, we are quite woke at ÉPN. In fact, we might even change our motto to Quite the Woke Folk if our publisher okays it, which, being a white member of the French nobility, he absolutely won't.

After Aziz had wasted a good hour trying to understand what the hell he'd just read (both the hard copy and online supplemental application), he finally walked over the editorial assistant.

—This is just an experimental satire of corporate publishing, right? Like a choose-your-own-Robert-Coover short story about white privilege or something? he asked, handing her his finished application.

She smiled. —Bah oui, she said, though to be honest, you spent a lot more time than most applicants.

—Well, my Cantonese is rusty, to be honest.

—Quoi? You actually did Part III?

Aziz shrugged his shoulders. —It was either that or teach myself Ukrainian in thirty minutes.

The editorial assistant raised her eyebrows and shook her head.

—So, what's the point of this application anyway?

—To see if you have a sense of humor and I dunno, this is just a guess, to see if you can tolerate experimental, postmodern writing in an industry that publishes the same trite, realist drivel over and over again by white women and then pretends it's saving literature when it actually accelerated its demise.

—Oof. Ça fait mal.

—I have strong opinions on this.

—I can see that. It's like you're like a double agent working within the system to destroy the system.

—Something like that. The truth is that editors here reject almost everything that doesn't have a straight plot line or straight white characters fighting with their family or Asian women speaking in philosophical clichés. Basically, if white women don't like it, editors don't buy it.

Aziz stopped to think about it and laughed. —Allez va! There are Black women publishing brilliant SF right now. And what about literary fiction writers like Zadie Smith, Junot Diaz, Edwidge Danticat, David Mitchell, Lydia Davis, Chang-rae Lee, Toni Morrison, Aimee Bender, Sandra Cisneros, Min Jin Lee, Laila Lalami, Haruki Murakami, and Yiyun Li?

—I love those writers, but they're the exception to the rule.

—There is a lot derivative, inane crap on the co-op table of bookstores.

—Voilà.

—So, do you think they'll give me a call or should I give up?

—Depends. If your cover letter, clips, and CV are excellent, it's possible. I'll be honest with you though since I just scanned your CV illegally. You are WAY too educated for this job. They *really* like to hire twenty-somethings with licences. That way, the industry can get away with paying them €10,000 a year by bribing them with free books.

—Free books are my vulnerability, Aziz confessed.

—Mine too! Why do you think I'm here? But here's the second part of my answer: most editorial assistants are white women who come from money so they can afford to be under-paid for twenty years and still pretend they're working in the glamorous business of literary capitalism.

—I really like the way you think, Aziz said, even if it's scaring the shit out of me. I hope your friends and family can keep up with that amazing brain of yours.

The editorial assistant snorted. —You know, you swear a lot.

—Désolé.

—Je m'en fous. I'm not the one doing the hiring. Besides, I actually like a man who can swear when the situation calls for it. Only prudes are offended by changes in register.

—You know, Aziz confided, you're not dull-looking at all, whatever that application said, and you're obviously too smart for this job.

—Merci, she said, smiling. —The truth is, I wrote that application. I'm an experimental fiction writer, you see, and this boulot just pays my rent.

—Spoken like a true artist.

—A propos, don't take the middle elevator.

—Attends, I thought that was a joke.

She raised her eyebrows but didn't say anything as if silence was the only appropriate answer to a life-or-death question. Aziz took the left elevator just to be safe.

Outside, the day had ejected the morning sunlight like a passenger thrown through the window of an old Peugeot. It was the afternoon now and the shadows on the sidewalks were smaller, the air hotter and more oppressive. Aziz lit a cigarette and took a long drag. It burnt his lungs but tasted heavy and smooth in his mouth. With each drag he felt lightheaded as he exhaled. He looked down the bustling avenue, the yellow macaroon sun was high in the sky now. Aziz noticed some upscale boutiques, a guy in a bowtie unpacking books in a new librairie, a boulangerie called *Pain dans le Main Street*, the heavenly smell of melting chocolate, butter, sugar, and rye floating in the air, escaping through the window cracks, and serenading his opiate receptors. God, he loved the way Paris smelled. He wished he could bottle it and spray it in his bedroom before he fell asleep or whenever he traveled abroad.

At Hassan's half-filled café, Aziz looked for his friends, who were sitting at two adjoined tables, smoking cigarettes and arguing, an ant hill of butts in the sky-blue ceramic ashtray and a half of day of tea stains on the tabletops. Aziz felt bad for Hassan.

—Aziz! Michel said, how'd it go? He pulled up a chair for him, who went around the table shaking hands with his friends before sitting down.

—J'uis vanné, Aziz said, reaching for the ashtray.

—Aller va! Ousmane said, that's the first job you've applied to in a month.

Wafi sipped his tea and smiled.

—Aziz, what don't you sell your hair? Nizar asked, it's so thick and black.

—Ta gueule, Aziz said, don't hate me just because your bald head looks like a globe.

—You mean *boulder*, Wafi says.

—Fuck off, *all* of you! Nizar shouted.

—Well, at least this way, Ousmane said, when they don't hire you, you can say you tried.

—That's so dark, Michel said, it could happen, inshallah.

—Yo, it takes more than creds to score a good job in this country, Ousmane said, you've got to have *connections* to work in the EU. He opened a new pack of Gitanes and passed Aziz a cigarette and lit it before lighting one for himself with the same match. As Ousmane exhaled, Aziz saw Cyrillic letters escaping from the corners of his mouth, forming the word "стирания," which hovered in the air like stage directions for a silent film, the Russian word for "erasure," a detail Aziz kept to himself.

—Ousmane is right, Nizar said, it's like that English sign I saw once: NANNAH, North Africans Need Not Apply Here.

Everyone at the table nodded.

—The system is intentionally unfair, Wafi said, but you *still* have to try. Our neighborhood is filled with defeated people. I mean, *look* at us. Have we done anything all day?

—The system is literally designed to disempower former colonial subjects and protect the people who designed the system, meaning white wealth above all else, Ousmane said, how could systemic racism be any other way?

—Of course that's true, Aziz said, but it's still our job to overturn this racist system and reject our own disempowerment, even if there's a French bayonet pointing at our throats.

Michel nodded.

—But why should we have to work twice as hard just to get half as much respect? Ousmane asked. —Besides, every overachieving minority just ends up being part of the model minority myth, which white supremacy welcomes in order to deflect its own racism. So you lose either way.

Aziz nodded because his papa was a perfect example of what Ousmane was talking about.

Wafi waved his finger in disagreement. —Allah works in mysterious ways sometimes.

Nizar giggled at Wafi's naïveté. He lit a cigarette, puffing away with contempt.

—Wafi, Michel said, tell Aziz about your cousin.

—Oh, right, Wafi said, so Aziz, where is the ÉPN headquarters?

—New York, I think.

—So, Yankees, hot dogs, Brooklyn, and Jay-Z, Ousmane said.

—Écoute, Wafi continued, my cousin has an apartment in New York City.

—Hassad? Aziz asked.

—Hussein, Wafi huffed, and he told me last night that if any of us made it to New York in the next six months, we could stay at his apartment for free because he'll be in Rabat until the New Year.

—Damn, Aziz said.

—Oh la la, Ousmane muttered, on y va!

—Maybe, Aziz said, it's time you stop collecting advanced degrees and get a damn job just like I'm trying to. He took a drag from his cigarette.

Aziz's friends laughed as he exhaled into Ousmane's face. Ousmane told him to fuck off in the language of biceps and forearms.

—I want you to get this boulot, Wafi said, to help you get over your broken heart.

—That's very sweet of you, Wafi. Aziz stubbed his cigarette in the mountainous blue ceramic ashtray and then grabbed dirty dishes off the table before walking inside the café where he saw Hassan at the zinc bar, chatting with old customers. Aziz laid the dishes in the kitchen sink.

Hassan's face brightened into a pomegranate. —Aziz, ahlan biik. La baas?

—I'm fine. W'inti Hassan?

—Koshi Bikhir, Aziz. All praise be to Allah. Come and have tea, my son. The truth was, ever since Aziz was a kid, Hassan had treated him like the son he never had. Aziz's mom said it was natural for a Moroccan friend of the family, especially with three daughters, but Aziz always thought Hassan worried about him because his papa never did. Ever since he could remember, Papa was too self-consumed in his own professional failures and frustrations to look around. Or maybe Papa and Hassan simply wished they'd traded places.

—Merci, Hassan, but I should go home soon, Aziz said in French.

—You just missed your father, Hassan said in Darija.

—Comment va t-il?

—He's fine, Hassan sighed, you know how things are.

Aziz nodded slowly. Sometimes, he was tired of knowing.

—A Moroccan PhD might as well be a twenty-two-year-old white kid with a licence.

—Ouais, je sais.

—Anyway, enough of that. Comment va t-il l'entretien?

—Today was just the application stage and it was so strange!

—I've got a *good* feeling about this, Aziz.

—Hassan, you're an incorrigible optimist.

—That doesn't mean I'm wrong. Hassan patted his heart for emphasis.

—I wish I felt anything in my heart except pain, Aziz said, ashamed at how easy it was to fall through the trap door of his own sadness, which he'd been trying to avoid since the break-up, which had become impossible to avoid, especially when he took the métro at night or got lost in museums or skimmed through new paperbacks at Quartier Latin bookstores or speed-walked past Le Champo where he and Yesha used to watch movies together until late at night, the one place where they had complete privacy, sometimes falling asleep in the backseats until breakfast was served. Other times, Aziz felt the pain of longing when he passed boisterous bistros in Oberkampf overflowing with tipsy couples who held hands and laughed at each other's mundane stories, just like they used to, back when the illusion of love was worth fighting for. You never fought harder than when you were fighting for something that didn't exist.

—You're too young to understand your true convictions, Hassan said, laughing.

Aziz shook his head. —You're too old to be so idealistic.

Hassan roared. —Pas mal.

—En tout cas, Aziz said, I'm going home now.

—Peace be with you, my son.

—And you, Hassan.

—Oh, by the way, give these to your papa. Hassan handed him two giant loaves of houbz araby. —I forgot to stick them in your father's briefcase, he explained.

Aziz grabbed the bread with both hands. The loaves were dense, brown, and soft like the legs of a fat tanned European aristocrat. He didn't have to examine them to know what was inside. He knew Hassan. He knew how much he loved his papa, loved him enough to recreate the manna miracle every month of their life.

—Shukran, Hassan.

—Afwan, Aziz.

—Peace be with you.

—And you, my son.

Aziz looked at the old man's face, softened by the Moroccan sun and wrinkled by sixty years of incessant laughter, swimming with childhood friends at Plage Bakassem, and chain-smoking at Tangier cafés. Aziz felt an indescribable surge of love for him. It was irrational he knew, but he felt affection for this man like a deep pain in his stomach and a sharp contraction in his chest. It had something to do with his missing link, his absent father, and the way Hassan swaddled him with his affection even as a grown man. It would be embarrassing if he didn't like it so much.

—Aziz.

—Oui?

—Remember what I said about the golden thread.

—I don't *believe* it Hassan, but I remember.

—That's good enough. Memory is the love of details and love is the root of all true faith.

—If you say so, Aziz said. He tucked the warm bread under his arm, shook Hassan's hand, and walked outside into the scorching summer air where the streets seemed to be exhaling. He walked to Canal Saint-Denis and looked through the branches of forgotten trees, the evening sky resembling a Vaseline dream of scuffed prisms and incandescent pastel strokes.

26. DREAM LIFE OF VAGRANTS

It was the last hot day in August before the rainy season began in Seattle. Suzanne walked through SeaTac with her satchel and ladybug backpack, stopping once to unzip her sweatshirt and tie it around her waist in a double knot. When she found the baggage claim, Ali was waiting for her, snapping her bubblegum like a martial art. Dressed in tight jean shorts that were torn on the hip, a white tank top, and pageboy hat that brought out the pink in her cheeks, she flashed Suzanne a smile with a wad of pink lodged in her teeth before running over to hug her.

—God*damn* Suzie-Q, she said, her lip ring vibrating, aren't you the hottest bitch in town?

—Hey Ali. It's been forever.

—Girl, you look like you just woke up and somehow you're *still* hot! I don't get it.

Suzanne looked around the airport. —It smells like a rainforest here.

—I *love* that T-shirt, by the way, makes your tits look *huge*.

—I see your tats are coming along beautifully.

—I know, right? Most of it's filled in since I saw you last. You like the pixies?

—They're so cute! You're cuter though.

Ali smiled with all her gums. —So, how's Georgie McFly?

—Ugh, it's a long story.

—I want details, you little slut!

—Where's Samir?

—Outside. He's so excited to see you. We both are.

Suzanne grabbed her favorite satchel from Delhi and her suitcase while Ali snatched her ladybug backpack. They took the escalator upstairs, laughing the whole way. The electric doors opened and the scent of temperate rainforest, clean heat, and fertilized air filled Suzanne's nostrils. It smelled like a brand new day. Samir was standing in skinny jean shorts, a turquoise-black tank top, black hoodie, and White Sox cap because Chicago never dies. Ali shouted at Samir. He turned around and laughed, his lips expanding into a half moon.

—Suziiiiiiiiiiiiie!

Suzanne smiled big.

Samir grabbed the luggage from their hands, threw every-thing in the back of his Pathfinder, and gave his sister a tight squeeze, which made her laugh. He always hugged her too hard, like he didn't know his own strength, not even after all these years. Suzanne kissed him on the cheek and hugged him again. On the highway, Suzanne looked at herself in her cell phone and noticed deep fabric marks pressed into her face. Samir looked just as she remembered: cute, hip, pensive, and fidgety. Because he was the perennial DJ in the family, he was always nodding to music inside his head like he was mixing tracks for his next set. He changed lanes quickly and without hesitation, something Suzanne never did.

—You look sleepy, he said, accelerating past a white Prius.

—That's what I said, Ali said, snapping her gum like a tiny whip.

—I slept the whole way, Suzanne explained, and I had the craziest dream. I was flying through the clouds. No Freudian analysis, please.

—So, how's Mum?

—The cool thing was I could read people's minds.

—Did you hear about Lata?

—I know, Suzanne said, leaning between the front seats, she's dating some guy that sells spark plugs.

—Wait, which one is Lata?

—Oh, you know already. Ali, she's our dad's fourth sister.

—But listen, in this dream, I could read people's thoughts and there was this little kid who was playing with a red toy truck.

—Did Mum tell you about Papa?

—Jeez, can we go back to my *dream* please? Suzanne's voice was surly.

—Your dad's so cute.

—So *any*way, there's this boy.

—I wish *my* dad would talk to trees, Ali grumbled.

—And I could read his mind and he was wondering if it was true that you can dig all the way to Ceylon.

—I wish he'd do anything except cut those fuckers down with his chainsaw, Ali said, rimshotting her gum for effect.

—My mom thinks he's crazy, Samir said, but I think it's better he's missing a few cumin seeds, if you know what I mean.

—Okay, your guys are TOTALLY IGNORING ME.

—No, I'm listening, Samir said.

—Me too, Ali said.

—Goddamn *liars*.

—I just wanted to make sure you're up on the gossip.

—I think she is.

—Just forget it. I'm done.

—No, for real. Tell us.

—Doesn't matter. It was just a dumb dream evidently.

—I was listening, Samir said, pointing to his ear.

—Samir, you only listen to the music in your head.

Ali giggled.

—Here's what confuses me, that little boy, the one who was digging all the way to Ceylon . . .

—Yeah, what about him?

—Well, that's impossible.

—Why? they asked.

—Because Ceylon isn't a country anymore.

—Oh God, you're right, Suzanne groaned, how could I have forgotten? Somewhere, a hundred University of Chicago students were shaking their heads at her in disapproval right now.

—What is it? Ali asked.

—It's Sri Lanka, bitches!

They burst out laughing. Ali handed her a cigarette, Suzanne rolled down the window, and Samir played a DJ Krush album on car stereo. Suzanne was absolutely positive it was *Zen*, the same album she'd given him for his birthday on vinyl. Her brother was playing it for her, which meant he probably never listened to it, not even once, or he thought it totally sucked, which was worse. As the Auburn exit whizzed by, Suzanne took a drag and coughed. For the first time since she'd crashed into George's quiet and functional life, she didn't have to know what time it was because time was irrelevant. Time might have been the original slaver of humanity, but Suzanne was free now. She thought about what John Locke said, how freedom was the ability to suspend making decisions. She took another drag and looked at Ali and Samir, who were everything she and George weren't: affectionate, spontaneous, flexible, and passionate AF. Hanging out with them was joy porn. A few minutes later, Mt. Rainier popped into view in the distance—that transcendental mass—and Suzanne's eyes got wide and blurry as she peered at the white-crowned Buddha in the sky. She loved not recognizing her life. She was a stranger to this timeline and she loved it. For a few seconds, she didn't feel like a June bug committing suicide in Lakeview apartment windows, stuck forever to a smudged window in Hyde Park, or snagged in the screen of a new condo on Devon Avenue. She took a long drag, which made her hack since she never smoked. She liked the light-headedness though. Her cigarette reminded her of Catholic high school parties that she and her friends used to crash in the North Shore, where all the students were white and smoked Marlboro Lights and drank their parents' top-shelf scotch and played Lacrosse in their sculpted backyards and good and evil were cut into little hard slabs of rock candy, the kind Suzanne used to buy in large plastic bags in fishing towns, near boardwalks, and at overcrowded marinas on the East Coast when she was visiting colleges.

When the Zap Mama track came on the stereo, Suzanne flicked the cigarette butt through the window crack without thinking.

—Suzie?

—Yeah?

—We don't do that, sis.

—Whah?

—Litter, he said. We put our cigarettes here. Samir opened an odorless ashtray.

—Sorry, she shrugged, I wasn't thinking.

He shook his head and rubbed her shoulder. —It's cool, Suzie.

When they got to the outskirts of Seattle, Samir played the third track over again and turned up the music, igniting a series of whispers and break beats from the speakers. The air tasted fresh and crisp as it poured through her open window, the sharp light bleeding through the windshield like a deep cut slowly eating through a million layers of gauze.

Seven days passed by like a fleet of Blue Angels. Suzanne was still analyzing her dreams, searching for clues in their narrative distortion. She had a system that went something like this: She asked herself an important question about her life right before she fell asleep and when she woke up, her dream was the answer. The fatal flaw, though, with her experiment was that she couldn't remember her dreams. She couldn't pry their coded messages loose from the jaws of her dreamworld. Maybe, the answer wasn't supposed to follow her into the waking world. Maybe, there were no answers, just desires, fears, and obsessions masquerading as destinies that all dreamers selectively referenced when it suited their needs. When she woke up today, she couldn't remember a damn thing (okay, maybe her experiment was flawed), but she knew it was late in the day by the supersized shadows in the front yard. She was somewhere in the afternoon midriff, astounded she'd just slept for ten hours. Thank God for red wine, clean air, and good music.

Last night they'd gone out to the Sitting Room in Lower Queen Anne, the perfect Lo-Fi candle-lit bistro to drink earthy and dialogic Bordeaux from smooth glass carafes and nibble on Mediterranean olives, vegetarian panini, and Iberian cheeses. Besides a nice Indian buffet, last night was the closest thing she'd had to comfort food in months. Suzanne got reflective as she drank last night. She liked the communal nature of wine, appreciated its social interconnection, the way everyone took turns filling each other's glasses with fragrant hues of fermented fruit, but she also loved the slow, dedicated, implied labor it took to produce a single harvest, the slow trickle of blood from clusters of grapes (like terrestrial ovaries) squished by human feet (right?) and fawned upon by the sun and its massaging fingers, its vines rinsed by the soft showers of spring. As she'd sipped wine and talked about the things she hated about George until she hated herself, she kept thinking that wine was a miracle that neither humans nor the earth created by themselves, being the marriage of nature and industry, the confluence of intuitive grape pickers and temperate climates, the almost perfect interplay of human bodies interacting with the soil, cultivating, picking, and fermenting grapes, making every sip a triumph of production, love, and empathy. She loved the rich ruddy complex qualities of last night's Bordeaux, the way it had lingered in empty glasses and stuck to bottlenecks and stained her teeth and hid in the corners of her mouth, its scent released with slurping tongues and smacking lips. She loved that wine was the product of sensitivity, intuition, and patience, perfect conditions to liberate her mind and ignore the relationship she'd set on fire in Chicago with old candles.

After their second carafe, Samir and Alison tried to pry Suzanne open like a giant oyster. They wanted deetz, scandal, confessions, and gossip: What happened to her job at the Indonesian restaurant in River North? What about George? Did she miss him? Had he texted her or filed a missing persons report? How long was she staying in Seattle? Was she leaving him for good? Was their fight the coup de grâce? A pretext for her own metamorphosis? Did he fuck someone else? Did she? Was there someone else in her life? Had she fallen in love with Il Postino? The taciturn yogi at the Saturday market in Lincoln Park? Was the sex too formulaic? The cuddling too infrequent? Was George an All-Elbow-All-Star on the dancefloor? Was she queerious? Did she want the name of a great therapist in Seattle, one they both went to once a month? Was she interested in kickboxing? Going on a charcoal-cayenne-cucumber cleanse for a week starting next Sunday?

Once their benevolent inquisition had gained momentum, once she'd realized that she didn't even know how to talk about their relationship after leaving, Suzanne just shrugged her shoulders and changed the subject, only opening her mouth to throw back mouthfuls of smooth, earthy wine and laugh about trivial things. She couldn't talk about why she left George because she knew, because she'd *always* known, that in order to talk about one issue in her relationship, she'd have to talk about everything connected to that issue, because jumping around and isolating specific events, issues, and wrongs committed only distorted the sweeping patterns that she'd eventually noticed, and it was those patterns, those faithful and sparklingly clear patterns, the ones with an emotional aerial view, that ultimately pushed her to act on a whim, giving her the ability to fly through clouds and hear people's thoughts, if only in her dreams.

Samir and Ali were smart people. They already suspected everything and she didn't want to get into too many details of her breakup until she'd had more time to process everything, so she just sat there, drank all the wine, and listened to the sounds of glasses chiming and bottles uncorked and appetizer plates clunking on solid wood tables. There was something simple and satisfying about the soundtrack of red wine filling empty glasses, erupting laughter, and whispered conversations about nothing, something too intimate to trivialize with her own banter and heartache anyway. She rested her head on Samir's shoulder, held Ali's hand, and smoked their cigarettes outside on the sidewalk, listening to the saddest alto Suzanne had ever heard singing on the stereo in some trip-hop ballad she didn't recognize, her sleepy voice floating on top of the soft and nebulous bistro chatter but never cutting through it. For all Suzanne knew, it could have been her own voice singing such wounded songs of loss, intimacy, and raw despair. Only the wine made her forget all the things she couldn't deny.

EGG

27. A FIRE WALK THROUGH A VALLEY OF FALSE IDOLS

YESTERDAY, YESHA BROKE UP with Aziz out of nowhere and now he was sitting at a table outside at Hassan's place, deep in thought not just about the relationship he'd lost (for reasons that made no sense to him) but also about the world he'd been in denial about since his return from London, the life he now desperately needed to change, and the racism he'd tolerated for too long because he was in love (and love always destroyed his peripheral vision). It was as if the instant he got dumped, he woke up from a romantic daze and then hated everything around him. The frenetic and serpentine riff inside his head went something like this: *Paris is a love poem written in the language of black and white films, cigarettes, and bloodshed,* he thought. *Paris is the Alexandria Library, a dated masterpiece slated for cultural annihilation by future historians. Don't let the romantic accent, the butter-thick pastries, the cinematic skyline pierced with glorified staples (La Défense and L'Arc de Triomphe), and that giant puddle-iron middle finger deceive you. This city is predicated on Gallic nostalgia, codified Islamophobia, neocolonialist trade policies, and romantic propaganda, the country's wealth built on the backs of former African colonies in the Maghreb and l'Afrique Noire, the city's classism spatialized in both buildings and city grids (servants on the top floor, brown people in the suburbs). The pretentious cafés with their curt waiters, the bloated museums bulging with obscure self-portraits, French landscapes, and stolen Babylonian artifacts, the luxurious gardens (and other upper-class odes to French nobility), and the grandiloquent Seine, whispering the sins of the French empire, these things are the footnotes of Paris, the bullet points of magical thinking, the way Paris needs to see itself, which cultural tourism reinforces.*

On the outskirts, Paris is a stew of reinvented French words (verlan), intersecting multicultural identities and global languages, class immobility, racial and religious discrimination, stigmatized brown and Black skin, all silent victims of shriveled up egalitarianism. Paris wants to be a postcard in order to rasterize its class conflagration. Paris is a city of muted rage, a catastrophe always on standby. Away from the Musée de l'Homme, beyond the Jardin de Luxembourg, the gaudy Champs-Elysées and overpriced fast-food joints selling Royal Cheese and pizza newyorkais, past the urban sublimation and the chain-smoking, scarf-wearing, lip-locking boulevardiers, past the baby-fresh couples making out on every bench, near every historical monument, in every métro station, on every street corner, past the soup-slurping rent-a-philosophers and the musicality of the French language (the building blocks of our narcissism, the reflection in our Hall of Mirrors), is a broken mosaic of culture and colonization. Tweaking the panoramic widescreen lens and zooming 50X past the city limits, you'll see à la sortie de Paris, just beyond the magnificent aerial views of Montmartre rooftops and dazzling carnation-colored street lamps and black and white snapshots of first-kiss love, just beyond this elaborate Russian Ark of bustling immigrant culture in Belleville and the squeaky rollercoaster rides of mass inflation, there is another Paris, a complex, unadorned, and broken down Paris, a parallel Paris far away from the tourist purview with makeshift apartments, cement playgrounds, and tarmac streets full of pissed off teenagers drunk on cultural nihilism, hip-hop, and football. There is a parallel world filled with immigrant-owned cafés and shops, men in burnooses, tight black jeans, sale-rack suits, hoodies and faux cashmere sweaters, turtlenecks and sport coats, and Barça football jerseys, sipping on sweet green tea, arguing politics, and searching want ads. There is a shadow Paris where poverty is original sin, full of political junkies, scorned intellectuals, underpaid serveuses, low-wage retail clerks, working class factory workers, irascible sheikhs, du shit smokers, hopeless job seekers, permanent residents, and urban professionals stuck in French bureaucracy, all exasperated by years of invisibility, racial stigma, and cultural repression. There is a shadow Paris of alienated children of immigrants with college degrees and religious heartache, men of good pedigree and women with impeccable French grammar who are polishing shoes and cleaning toilets and cutting bread to make a living. This parallel Paris isn't in those Let's Go travel guides or included in glossy brochures with pictures of beautiful white twenty-somethings plastered on the walls of SoHo and Boston travel agencies. This shadow Paris isn't charming or romantic or picturesque, it will never be centered in André Bréton manifestos or mentioned in Edith Piaf lyrics or resurrected by a brave new urban renewal project in time for an upcoming election. This parallel Paris, this shadow Paris, this anti-Paris, can't even be blessed away by the Saint-Denis Basilica because the prophets in this neighborhood have dark faces and punctured hearts.

This reciprocal image of Paris, this centrifugal apartheid, this class divide, is a brain tumor in the frontal cortex of republican democracy, a tower of Babel in flames shining in the distance like a sacked Carthage. Those of us living on the outskirts of Paris (the literal definition of eccentric) have learned that we can document injustice with social media, using massive protests, City Hall confrontations, hip-hop music, street murals, and burning cop cars as the alphabet of the disenfranchised. We've learned that a smoke-filled sky can be a living cultural document for St-Denis to notarize its resistance to state-sanctioned violence with every barrel fire and citywide strike. The streets can be a cultural palimpsest that the voiceless can erase and rewrite for their own scriptures of survival. We've learned that a metaphorical auto-da-fé in the streets can be an incineration to burn away the colonial violence in our souls.

More times than I can count, the cramped apartments in this neighborhood have crumbled, torn, and shattered like prison cinder blocks, overcrowded with bodies stuffed in boxes and stacked on top of each other like grounded freighters for dead circus elephants. More times than I can count, I've thought to myself, we're stuck in this cultural miasma, stuck in the fun house mirror of the white French gaze, stuck in the smells of stale couscous and cigarette pathologies, stuck in the cultural gangrene of colonized, occupied, and racialized space, stuck in the lingering scent of sour concrete and internalized colorism and mental colonization, stuck in the cycle of unrequited frustration, self-hatred, and diasporic longing. More times than I can count, I've thought that the dimly lit streetlamps in this neighborhood buzz with sickly yellow light, which is why moths can't find their way, why plastic flowers live longer than brown teenage boys in St-Denis, and why rage is always free. Paris is a city of lost souls, a descent into hell thirty-four Cantos long, and this marginalized commune is my burden, my punishment, my joy, and my time-released agony. It's the place where I lost my oldest sister to polio, where mamie died after the flics slammed her brilliant head against a brick wall in a warrant-less no-knock raid as she was reading The Moor's Account, turning her brains to mush. The place where I discovered that language—my own language, my family's language, my neighborhood's language, my friends' language, the language we speak at home, the language I hear in the streets, the language I hear passing the local mosque, the language harnessed in every conscious rap song—could be a vast stockpile of explosives, a fuse waiting to detonate in the powder kegs of the French cultural imagination.

Suddenly, in the middle of his rumination, Hassan tapped Aziz's shoulder.

—Ahlan biik, Hassan said, la baas?

—Ça va. W'inti Hassan?

—Mzyan, mon fils. All praise be to Allah. Let's go in back and have tea. I just finished the atai.

Aziz looked up at him, the old man's cigarette burning between his fingers, and followed him to a table in the back of the café, the smells of lemon floor cleaner mixing with simmering harira, garlic, tomatoes, parsley being chopped on the cutting board, and eggplants slowly grilling from the kitchen. The smells in Hassan's café sometimes felt like the closest thing Aziz had to home. Hassan poured mint tea into Aziz's glass and smiled. As they talked, he practically shook in his jellaba as he nodded and stroked his mustache that looked like a dead caterpillar. Aziz know that patented smile could only mean one of three things:

1. Hassan was looking at the singles ads again and he (thought he) found the perfect wife for him:

Femme Maghrébine (36 ans)
Looking for a financially stable North African male between the ages of 26-36. No smokers, Sunnis, or playboys. No alcoholics, cheats, or scam artists. No Marxists, writers, or grandfathers!

Idéaliste (39 ans)
Love will save the day. I want a loving, caring, romantic renaissance man who's smart, kind, and mildly neurotic. Geniuses, composers, and mimes a major +!

Érudite Française (30 ans)
Where are the real men? I'm sick of dweeby intellectuals and misogynists. I need a dynamic, affectionate man who likes to travel, knows his roots, and knows how to live life. No savoir-vivre, no loving!

2. Like every other North African French person he knew, Hassan was furious that America still occupied another country in the Middle East (even an authoritarian one) based on sketchy,

fabricated, and cherry-picked intelligence while it lectured the world about human rights, democracy, and the war on terror. And he just read another article talking about:

A. How Iraq is a recruitment poster for thuggish Jihadists and how the Pentagon keeps trying to erase the Abu Ghraib prison scandal from memory

B. How America wasted a golden opportunity to promote global peace between 2000-2008 and has repeatedly failed, even with a progressive Black president with an Arab middle name, to help create a viable Palestinian state

C. How Osama Bin Laden, the rich kid terrorist, was hanging out with Pakistani warlords, living in a luxurious compound, and boasting about the billions of American dollars wasted trying to scrub him out like a food stain before he was eventually taken out (no thanks to the ISI), proving to copycat megalomaniacs everywhere that brainwashed socio-paths could defy an entire nation if they're rich, politically connected, and knew how to weaponize poverty, religious fundamentalism, and a bellicose American foreign policy

D. How Americans are living in denial about SARS, fossil fuel consumption, and global warming, which is easy to do when you never leave your country, drive your Hummer to the local Chick-fil-A, and consume half of the world's resources while shunning the Kyoto Protocol because you're mad Ghana isn't using enough solar panels

3. He found a job for Aziz.

Hassan opened up his backpack and plopped a folded copy of *La Gazette marocaine* on the table. Aziz glanced at the job Hassan had circled for him as an ÉPN translator and laughed. Hassan was always thinking of him, always trying to bail his family out. Since François Mittérrand was re-elected in '88, he had been Papa's best friend. They'd been class-mates in Casa and fought each other mercilessly for the atten-tion of Nahal Al-Shadda, the dark-skinned princess who played a lute made of imported cedar and sang songs in six languages from her window like a trapped sky lark. She was the first girl to entrap them, their hearts raw and furious, beating like broken tambourines, their skinny

> **Traduceteur d'arabe-français-anglais.**
>
> Looking for trilingual translator with 5 years of editing, translation, and publication experience. Advanced degree preferred. Salary BOE. Send clips, 3 references, and CV to:
>
> **L'ÉDITIONS PONT NEUF**
> 108, Rue de Campo-Formio
> 75014 PARIS
> Tél. 01.41.25.08.07
> Fax. 01.41.25.79.63

little bodies filled with fledgling romance before they'd learned that love was a double pike half tuck into an empty swimming pool. Before they'd learned that love was a gateway drug to anni-hilation. They'd moved to France at different times, and forgot about Nahal and the spells she'd cast on street waifs, lycée students, and desperadoes walking past her open window in the medina. One day in Paris years later, they ran into each other at a neighborhood mosque on the first day of summer and they'd been friends ever since. Now, every time Aziz's papa disap-peared at night, they knew he was at Hassan's little café smoking bummed cigarettes and drinking sweet green tea with his friends, arguing about Israel and Palestine, still mourning the Al Qaida bombings in Casa, and reciting their favorite love poems by Kabbani, Najmi, Majen, and El Bakouri, mashallah. And every time Hassan stopped by their apartment, they knew that he slipped their father cigarettes and ads for temporary academic posts en centre ville as they did the dishes together or Hassan put rolled up Euros wrapped in plastic wrap inside day-old croissants or loaves of houbz araby. Sometimes, Hassan pretended he just ended up in their neighborhood, but Aziz and his family knew the old man's gifts of honeyed pistachio rolls and bags of coconut-covered dates (with almonds in the center) were beyond reproach. They were pure and honest gestures of love, even as cover-ups for their papa who'd been struggling to find work since his lectureship expired at Sciènces-Po. Actually, *struggled* wasn't the right word because the truth was, he had simply given up looking for a job after the department hired a white PhD student to teach his Arabic classes because she had an Egyptian accent and was willing to work for slave wages. Kindness was Hassan's technique for protecting Papa who had completely lost faith in French egalitarianism. All of them had except Hassan who was irrationally optimistic about France, a country he believed had helped him become a small business owner instead of racial stereotype. Most men, Aziz noticed, didn't consider themselves emotional and yet they believed whatever they wanted to believe just because it felt better. In Hassan's case, however, he embraced his emotions. He saw them as a form of enlightenment. They had this in common.

Aziz read the job description all the way though, sipped some tea, and wiped his mouth. —This job is perfect, he finally said in Darija, too perfect.

—What's wrong with a perfect job?

—Hassan, you know as well as I do that they'll never hire me.

—You are too jeune to be that cynical. Smoke escaped from his mouth, twisting into gray Arabic letters above his head in long bold strokes of Rehali calligraphy.

—Young people are the *most* cynical.

—That's the irony.

—Et c'est quoi?

—You know so little about people and yet you are the most confident of what their motivations are.

Aziz smirked. —I'm just trying to be realistic. Hope's an expensive drug.

—Hope is better than fatalism. Anything's better than blind surrender, Hassan said, exhaling.

—Papa's been on the dole for two years now, the unemployment rate is 10%, and in case you haven't noticed, North Africans are the French underclass.

— I'm not arguing with you (though Roma have it even worse than we do), but all that can change in a single day, inshallah.

—Inshallah.

—Aziz, you're too educated to spend your days dinking around this quartier. When you were in London, it felt like you could do anything you set your mind to. Now that you're back here, you've lost your confidence and misplaced your ambition.

—There's no class mobility in France.

—It's much harder for us, we all know that, but it's not impossible. If it were, I wouldn't have this café.

—Hassan . . .

—Aziz, what I'm saying is, it's time you started using that glorious mind of yours. Allah gave it to you for a reason. To not use is a crime against the creator.

Aziz sighed sadly. —Sometimes it just feels pointless.

—It's time you figured it out, Aziz. If not now, when?

—Je travaille à ça.

—I know you are, Hassan said in Darija, taking another drag, but sometimes, you can't think your way out of a maze. You have to follow the golden thread. Wherever it takes you.

Hassan stood up, touching Aziz's shoulder and smiling before disappearing into the kitchen to help his sous-chefs. His cigarette still burned in the blue ceramic ashtray, turning to vapor before Aziz's eyes. He squashed it, imprinting a black smudge that mirrored his own state of mind. Aziz grabbed *La Gazette marocaine*, tucked it under his arm, and walked to the Saint-Denis Porte de Paris métro stop. Mostly, he wanted Hassan to see that he'd taken the newspaper. That gesture was enough to feed the old man's optimism for a little while. Considering everything he'd done for him and his family, Aziz owed him at least that.

An hour later, Aziz knocked on the familiar wood paneling, its surface painted in rough cerulean circles like sky stucco. He wasn't supposed to speak to her anymore, but he came anyway because his heart couldn't accept the rules of their breakup, especially those telling him that love wasn't enough, that arbitrary principles mattered more than lived experiences. Aziz rested his ear against the door like a seashell and heard a confused voice, a door slicing through air, a few sharp murmurs, and then the pitter-patter of slippers. Yesha's little feet made tiny sounds as she walked down the creaky staircase and opened the front door.

—Mais, qu'est-ce que tu fous là, Aziz?

—Shh, tais-toi.

—You're not supposed to be here.

—Désolé.

—Don't be sorry. Just leave before Papa sees you.

—Regarde-moi, Yesha.

—Aziz, she protested, her eyes filled with emotion.

He covered her mouth with his hands. Her lips were warm, leaving a wet suction on his palm that ignited a series of memories inside his nostalgic brain. There was a trail of little saliva bubbles on his hand, each bubble like an infinitesimal snapshot of their lost world together fully stored and recorded inside his body in tiny biospheres of lost time:

Their first kiss at Café de la Paix *pop*

The taste of fresh Za'atar when it came out of his mom's oven *pop*

The day they lost their virginity inside a two-star hotel *pop*

Taking the métro to the Cité station and watching silent movies at the Le Grand Rex *pop*

Feeding pigeons and giving New Yorkers wrong directions *pop*

Yesha laughing in her sleep *pop*

Watching midnight movies at Le Champo in the Quartier Latin, sleeping for a few hours, and then eating breakfast at the theater before going to work *pop*

The smell of birch, wool coats, and mothballs in her closet when he hid from her papa who was searching the house for *that fucking Muslim boy* *pop*

The sounds of Hebrew songs in her kitchen, the smell of hardboiled eggs, and sea salt as Aziz crawled down the fire escape to safety *pop*

Passing out stolen Daisies to old women on Bastille Day *pop*

Slipping love notes into her pockets as he kissed her goodbye in front of Gare D'Austerlitz *pop*

Yesha sobbing underneath his Adam's Apple when she told him that breaking up was better for "both of them," a conclusion he never agreed with or to *pop*

Aziz removed his hand and looked at her with devastated and devastating eyes she pretended not to see. More than anything, Aziz wanted to know why she got to decide for both of them, why their love had become suddenly so unnecessary and so negotiable. He wanted to know why their relationship had suddenly not been enough for her when she had relied upon it so much in the past year, especially when her papa broke her cell phone and snooped through her Facebook posts and tried to force her to marry a lawyer from their synagogue. Aziz wanted to know why their relationship suddenly meant nothing, considering they'd been talking about moving in together that summer to a tiny flat in Notting Hill where no one knew them or cared what religion their parents practiced. In one instantaneous flash, Yesha had decided she was done. The next day, she'd insisted they'd made the decision together. They hadn't. There had never been a conversation.

    —You have to go, she whispered, I can't talk to you.

    —Yesha. Je veux pas parler.

    —Whaddayou want?

    —I just wanna look at you one last time. Aziz peered into her plaintive eyes, which looked desperate for him to disintegrate. She blinked hard at him, her eyelids fluttering like spiders fleeing from running water. Her eyes became heavy, her lashes thick and sticky like she was trying to hold on to her tears as if that proved something. She wanted to stop her tears by squinting, she wanted to squash them with her lashes until her emotions were dead.

She's right though, Aziz thought, *I shouldn't have come. I shouldn't have knocked. I should have left her alone, but I needed to see her one last time. I needed to remember what I was losing. I needed to know these precious details for when I finally forgave her and forgot everything.* She stared at him one last time, trying so hard to follow her father's diktat not out of conviction but exhaustion, but her eyes, her eyes deceived her. She stood in the doorway and stared at him, speechless, guilt-ridden, and lip-locked, the air vacant like an empty hangar where fighter jets rested between dogfights. Aziz looked at her eyes as she wiped her face with the sleeve of her tan T-shirt, the one with the green block letters spelling BARCELONA, the R and the O swollen in the exact places that he remembered, a topography he knew so intimately and for so long before she exiled him from the only country he knew. But just as quickly as Yesha lost control of her tears, her face became dry like a maxim. She bit down on trembling lips and wiped her face and Aziz knew, he didn't know how exactly, but he just knew that's when she'd wiped him from her life, flicking him off her soul like crumbs on the table, like cobwebs in her hair. It was just a matter of time now before she developed immunity to the twin diseases of guilt and shame. She'd forget the taste of sorrow and mourning in her mouth like bitter Seder herbs. It was all written in her face now. Soon, she'd smile at other men at family gatherings (upstanding, professional, Jewish men dressed in tailored suits with traceable genealogies, practical careers, and perfect Parisian accents). She'd forgive herself for her weakness, rationalize her father's racist aphorisms at the dinner table, and forgive him by noticing how little conflict there was in the house now, even though he was the sole cause of it. Eventually, she'd learn to sleep standing up and Aziz would cease to exist in her world. It was already too late. He'd already lost her. She'd already set in motion the snowball of his erasure.

—Je t'aime, he said, and I know for a fact that you love me, and nothing you say, nothing you pretend, will change that.

She closed her eyes and bit her lips.

—I wish you had the courage to love me even if it destroyed you because it's destroying me and I still love you. Mais toi, t'es une lâche! You're a coward because you won't even fight for us! And you don't even realize that you'll never love like this again. Jamais!

Yesha started bawling into her hands.

Aziz's hands reached out to console her by instinct, but he stopped himself and looked at her for the last time. He wiped his eyes and kissed her hands before leaving, his cheeks covered in a braille of devastation and grief. He disappeared into his own darkness before she could shut the door on him, walking for hours on the cobblestone streets of the 9eme arrondissement until the night let down her hair and warm light slowly filled vacant windows, turning Paris into a Scantron answer key. Aziz didn't look back after he left, he couldn't bear to, he saw what he saw, his heart flickered, consumed by delicate blue flames, reduced to ashes like a biblical fable. Every street he passed untangled a strand of knotted memory, every circular block became a blood blister, a fire walk through a valley of false idols, a funeral of salt and incense, and a hospital bed covered in broken chrysanthemums.

28. AMNESIA OF JUNE BUGS

Seventeen Hours

Suzanne put the nail clippers on the kitchen table and placed the phone between her ear and shoulder. Dressed in a pistachio green miniskirt, purple hair tie, gray Chinese slippers with embroidered carrots on the toes, and a gray tank top that read:

Cryogenics:
We Be Chillin'

in frosty blue letters, she half-listened to her mum on the phone and sipped iced mango juice.

—Sandu finally graduated from uni. God knows how many years he would have loitered around in his PJ's if Papa hadn't *yelled* at him, and your cousin on your uncle's side, the smart one that went to USC when she was sixteen—

—Whah? Suzanne asked, knocking over her cup of mango juice, the orange liquid spreading on their new white wooden table like a hungry blob.

—Married a young man whose family lives in Lodhi Colony. For their honeymoon they're building an orphanage in Varanasi.

Suzanne ran to get paper towels and then returned. —Well, that's very selfless.

—Young lady, and Tara called me and said she'd contracted *typhoid* fever while in Madagascar.

—She didn't, Suzanne said, patting the orange puddle with thick wads of paper towel before realizing she wasn't being eco-friendly. Emergencies would be the death of her principles.

—Ha, it *wasn't* typhoid, but I guess the symptoms were identical.

Suzanne squeezed the wet paper towels into a ball in the sink and then tossed it into the trashcan. —Score!

—Ha, and your brother called a few days ago and said he and Ali have been fighting like Shah Rukh Khan and Salman Khan.

—Samir doesn't even like Bollywood movies.

—Well, the analogy is mine, but the fight is theirs.

Suzanne looked at her fridge with longing. —Maybe I'll go visit them.

—Samir would love that.

—So, Mum, there's something I wanted to tell you. I've been feeling—

—Uncle Padu called.

—Oh . . . but . . .

—Ha, he told me your cousin Lata is in Toronto this week. She met a man from Uttar Pradesh who sells car batteries for a living.

Suzanne smacked her lips. —.

—Young lady, and your papa is talking to trees again.

Suzanne laughed.

—Now, he thinks he speaks pine.

—Pine, maple, what's the difference?

—Well, now it's pine.

—At least he rotates trees.

—But why do I have a husband who thinks he can speak Tree?

—He's branching out. He's becoming North American.

—Oh Suzie, you're too positive to laugh and I'm just too sad to make a fuss.

—That's very good of you, Mum.

—Young lady.

—Okay, well, I gotta get going.

Her mum inhaled dramatically. —How is Gengé?

Suzanne became thoughtful, trying to decide how truthful she wanted to be and how much time she was willing to waste. It was the family calculus. —I dunno anymore.

—Why?

—I feel like he lives on one coast and I live on the other and by the time we finally hang out together, we're too exhausted for new experiences.

—I'm sorry, honey.

—If I didn't see his dirty dishes in the sink or peek at the vinyl on the turntable, I wouldn't even know George lived here.

—But you wash the dishes, right?

—Not always. Any suggestions? Suzanne asked despite herself. There had been a debate raging insider her head whether to ask for help since her mum's advice was typically sexist and simplistic and primeval, always centering George's emotional needs like they were more important, even when they were unreasonable, and always treating homemade food like the panacea for all relationship problems. It drove Suzanne fucking crazy. Still, their parents had been together forever. Surely, that counted for something.

—Suzie, the first thing you should do is make George a delicious home-cooked meal. Something he can come home to. Something he can look forward to. How about some nice sambar with chapattis?

Suzanne groaned. —You know George hates Indian food. I heated up samosas for him once and he got first-degree burns on the roof of his mouth.

Her mum snorted. —I know, you work at an Indonesian restaurant, why not make him Indonesian food?

—I have and he doesn't like it. He's a spussy.

—A what?

—A spice . . . puh . . . a spice wussy.

—I don't understand you, Suzie.

—He can't handle spice.

—Oh.

—But our problems are bigger than that. Food doesn't solve every problem!

—Well, it's worked with your father for fifty-two years.

—Yeah, and he speaks maple.

—*Pine*, young lady.

Suzanne huffed in annoyance. —You know what, forget I asked.

—George is such a good boy, Suzie. So hardworking. So honest and stable.

—I don't want *honest and stable!* I want *unpredictable, nerdy, and affectionate!* I want *ingenious, quirky,* and *passionate!*

—Suzie, calm down, please.

—Okay, Mum, Suzanne sighed, I gotta go. I love you.

—Love you too sweetie.

—I'll come over Sunday.

—Wonderful.

—Or next year.

—What?

—Main jaa rahi hoon.

—Acha.

Suzanne sighed again. Zydeco, her calico, gave her an accusatory look from the couch before he resumed licking his spotless paws. She considered throwing a blanket at his bitchy little face, but she loved him too much.

Sixteen Hours

George stood on Broadway in the shade, holding his phone close to his ear before glancing at his watch. His mom lit a cigarette and exhaled on the other end for at least ten seconds. —I just want you to understand women, she said, because your *father* never did.

—What are you *talking* about? Dad has a knack for women.

—He does. They flock to him and he destroys them. He's incredibly efficient that way.

—Mom, come on.

—You worry me, Georgie.

—Why? I'm stable.

—You are sweetie. And to be honest, that's what terrifies me.

—Women like stable men.

—Wrong verb, Sweet Cheeks.

He switched ears. —When did you become the spokesperson for womankind?

She inhaled. —After your C-section, she said, exhaling.

—I'm ignoring that.

—You would.

—I'd like to think I understand women in my own way.

—That's what men *always* say when they don't have a clue.

—This is asinine.

—So is that word, she said inhaling.

—Mom, *stop* it.

—You know, she exhaled, we spend a lifetime trying to understand you guys: we buy books, pester shrinks on the subway, attend weekend seminars, study elaborate diagrams, and you guys don't have a *clue* what makes us horny.

—Gross.

—We want men who know how to *thrive*, not just survive.

—In other words, *French* guys.

—They're *fantastic* lovers, I'll tell you that. I remember the first time I went to Paris.

—Oh God, not that story again.

—*Fine.* But the point is, women like complexity.

—But men are simple.

—You mean lazy. Men have more options than being just a lost-in-the-stacks acadummy, a chemically imbalanced artist, a child-molesting psychopath in a minivan, an ammosexual incel looking to blow crap up, or a Sumo plumber.

—What's wrong with plumbers? Plumbing is an honest job.

—So is putting a bullet in your brain.

—At least pipes are solid.

—Georgie, forget solid. If you don't want Suzanne to run off with a Greek sailor or get a "Fifty Shades of Gay" tattoo on her ass one drunken night, you're gonna have to revise your primitive views on gender ASAP.

—Mom, she's happy.

—Is that why she called me last week, asking about her green curtains?

—What? he asked, stumbling as he turned down Berwyn.

—Oh yeah, we had a *very* long conversation about aphrodisiacs.

—Oh my God. Suzanne called my own *mom* for sex tips? That's so humiliating.

She inhaled. —Not really, honey.

—Wait, why?

She exhaled dramatically. —Because she's not the *first* girlfriend of yours to ask.

George gasped, dropping his phone on the sidewalk like a severed arm.

Fifteen Hours

Suzanne hung up the phone with her mum, dumped her half-chewed fingernails into the trash can, curled her lips over her teeth in the bathroom mirror, and touched up her "Desert Rain" lipstick. She brushed her hair, which emitted tones of chamomile and dried orange peels, and then sprayed jasmine-sandalwood scent on her neck and wrists before stopping at the front door.

—Zydeco, Bossie, Samba, I'm leaving now. You guys need anything?

Bossa Nova and Samba, their two baby dachshunds, were sleeping on each other in the dirty laundry hamper in the kitchen, dreaming loudly while Zydeco stopped licking his paws, looked up, and meowed in accusation. He got up, walked over to Suzanne, and rubbed against her ankle in protest. She picked up the obese calico and kissed his eyes, who purred like a little motorcycle. —All right, she said before setting him on the sofa, I'll see what I can do. Suzanne shut the front door behind her and avoided looking back. Outside in the humid Chicago air, the sunlight was almost gone and the evening felt like an early guest. She walked to the Addison El stop, wondering why George wanted to meet her all the way in Andersonville. It deviated from everything she disliked about their relationship and that was promising.

Fourteen Hours

Dressed in a pair of slightly wrinkled khakis and a black button-down rolled up at the sleeves, George looked at himself in the window of Ann Sathers before walking to Kopi Café and sitting down where he nursed his vanilla soy steamer (no almond milk!), thought about the past year, and flipped through the news on his phone. A year ago, he'd come here to get away from his roommate who was having loud raunchy sex in his bedroom with a middle-aged woman down the hall who looked just like a former philosophy professor of George's at NYU, a similarity which freaked him out and also turned him on in a confusing way. He'd ordered a cup of Samoan Marriage at the counter (the coffee du jour), flipping through *Tech Geek* when he noticed a stunning Indian woman talking to her friend at a nearby table. Or was it her girlfriend? Impossible to say in Andersonville. They were laughing, chatting in some language he couldn't identify (Hindi), but two months later, George and Suzanne were an item. Twelve months after the Samoan Marriage and one pain-in-the-ass move from Hyde Park and Uptown to East Lakeview, nine months after adopting two Dachshund puppies and rescuing a forlorn calico from a condemned building in the South Side, and six months after spending a shitty Christmas with George's family in Staten Island where his uncouth cousins had asked her, "So what's it like being Indian?" and "What's up with that red dot and why aren't you wearing one?", George and Suzanne were surviving. Conflicting sleep and dinner schedules, disputes over washing the dishes or cleaning the toilet, and the epidemic of debt, specifically, the contagion of credit card, rent and utility bills, were all shock therapy to their romance, but they were stable. George was fine with that. Suzanne, not so much.

George told her to meet him in Andersonville because that's where it all began for them and he wanted to resurrect their relationship that had been faltering as of late. He didn't buy her naughty-nurse lingerie with a zip-crotch or a collection of heat-activating love oils as his pervy mom had suggested, but he did have a plan, and it involved Suzanne walking through that door.

Since they'd started dating, George's biggest hang-up was that Suzanne was too good-looking for him. Over time, he observed as teenage boys in dirty Cubs hats chimed their bike bells at her, construction workers shouted from rooftops, lawyers dropped their briefcases, taxi drivers pulled along her curbside, sweet-talking her in Wolof or Croat-Serbian even when he was there holding her hand, children ran to her in the middle of the street to hug her like a favorite aunty, old people walked across busy intersections to tell her about their marriages, where they grew up, how big their Studebaker was, why she should visit them in Naples, Florida and go skinny-dipping in the "no questions asked" jacuzzi. Over time, George started to feel like a stinky swamp creature shadowing a teen idol because that's how everyone looked at him. He wasn't nerdy, argumentative, or hypercreative like her University of Chicago friends, and he wasn't professionally egomaniacal, self-actualized, or rolling in it like her Indian friends.

George also hated Indian food, which Suzanne thought was subtly racist. He hated the scar tissue inside his mouth from trying to eat scorching samosas, he didn't know how to reheat Naan bread in the toaster oven without incinerating it, he didn't drive a luxury car, his hair was beginning to recede at the temples, his face wasn't ageing as gracefully as he'd hoped, and his lovemaking was a little formulaic and uninspired, but dammit, he gave stability and financial security to the relationship. They could never have bought new furniture for their apartment or traveled every year to London or Hong Kong or Paris without his income. But what if his mom was right? George hated to admit it, but she *was* a woman, a realization he'd made one day in high school when he'd watched her flirting with a stout security guard at the Whole Foods in Clark, New Jersey, only to find that same man sitting on their toilet three weeks later, naked and dozing off with his hand on the hot water dial, the medicine cabinet mirrors fogged up, a debilitating stench hovering in the bathroom that punched George right in the septum as he closed the door. But now George was in a dilemma. He needed his mom's knowledge of women because he (maybe) didn't understand Suzanne, but this meant humanizing his mom again and that was traumatic. He ruminated on the last thing she'd said before she hung up on him: Women love the cupboard space for its stability, but they love the spice rack for its sensuality, variation, and color. Supposedly, there was a reason why Suzanne was steadfastly late every day. His mom said the clues were somewhere in the spice rack:

Chili Powder: Suzanne probably fell in love with a guy emanating a passionate and fiery sensuality, a desi that made her legs wobbly and her lips perspire, a man that made her heart beat strong and steady like an Ibiza compilation, a Brahman gifted with a thousand secret amorous skills passed down from a family of Punjabi players. This man would be a sexual aristocrat, worshipped and yearned by women of all castes. He would be the great unifier of the subcontinent, a man who seeded India with everlasting peace, using his croquet hammer of a penis to the delight and pleasure of all straight women coupled with his insatiable appetite for obscure yoga positions and post-coital cuddling, he'd understood women effortlessly, treating their bodies like temples of worship and wisdom, ready to sacrifice his divine hard-on to Suzanne in the name of sacredkinkylove.

Paprika: No, Suzanne had met a man from Eastern Europe. Some hunky morose Serbian dude who chain-smoked Camels and peppered his sentences with "you know what I fucking mean?" His name would have only two syllables like Jovan or Anton or Sasha. He'd be extremely sexist, but his thick accent would smokescreen his antediluvian views, transform them, render them charming even to untrained ears. The less women understood him the more they adored him. He'd wear a black leather jacket, tight jeans, crusty fucking hair gel, and a permanent sneer. He'd live on cigarettes, B-side vodka, and pink canned meats. He'd survive on salty eggplant dishes and irradiated caviar platters—all gifts from his adoring majka—even though he was basically hypertension in a jacket. But none of that would matter. His accent was slowly breaking down Suzanne's resistance. And as long as he was alive (for fifty-four long years), he'd devote his life to chain-smoking, drinking plum Rakia with his friends, eating his mom's Ajvar relish, and making "beautiful fucking love" with the most stunning Indian woman he'd ever laid eyes on.

Basil: No, that's not right, Suzanne had probably met an Italian guy, some stereotypically pretty Mediterranean manchild with sculpted legs, a stomach like a turtle shell, thick lustrous hair, long girly lashes, opiate eyes, and MiracleGro-ing stubble that accentuated his machete jawline. Somehow flattering and self-possessed, boyish and assertive in all the right ways, he'd know how to combine his cultural romanticism, fleeting shyness, and animalistic sensuality into a flawless performance of the hot Italiangodchild. He'd be bathed in Armani threads and overpowering cologne named after a tragic Saint, his body like a DaVinci scribble of gold skin and compact biceps. His penchant for romance, like his erection, would never disappear. His lips would always cover some part of Suzanne's quivering body, always whispering, "Non trovo la pace" into her ear, a line he'd heard as a schoolchild playing calcio in the streets of Firenze (never Florence!). And when the two of them talked, he would tell Suzanne about his life using Italian inflections, occasionally mispronouncing words or inventing them, but that only made him more charming because he wasn't *American* and he didn't know how to be American. American men were so boring, simplistic, and predictable, everybody knew that.

Sage: No, no, Suzanne had met Mr. Soul Lover, a mindful, *spiritual* man who called all women—whether scabrous or divine—*goddesses*. He'd have a ponytail, an earring, a dog-eared bone broth cookbook, and an extensive incense collection.

A master of the art of listening, he would simply gaze into Suzanne's eyes as she poured out the undigested contents of her purging heart. *He's such a great listener*, she'd confess to Nina, *I feel like I could tell him anything and he'd understand.* He'd be the type of guy who *deliberately* elongated his name. Tim became Timothy. Tony became Anthony. Alex became Alexander. He would woo Suzanne with his silence and deep empathetic smile. His soft hands would graze her cheeks. He would hold Suzanne in his arms as she cried about the pain of being so beautiful and so brown in such an ugly whitewashed world. He'd understand though. Somehow, he'd understand every word she told him, even though he was the whitest dude on the fucking planet. He'd understand the grief of her beauty. He'd understand that the world was a savagely mundane and callous place for people of color. A place full of ugly and ignorant racists, a place full of selfish little people who didn't understand her and didn't deserve her either. And then he'd reassure her that *he* understood her. She'd always be safe and cherished and loved by *him*. She could always count on *him*. He'd promise her peacefulness and joy. He'd promise her an organic non-wheat-gluten-centered breakfast using local ingredients and served with freshly squeezed orange pulp that came from the lowest-income woman in all of Chicago who made a living selling homemade juices, her knuckles, scraped and bloody as she pressed orange rinds (that smelled like Suzanne's hair) against a piece of dull glass. And this destitute woman was only asking for $15.40 a liter. He'd bring home the OJ and then pour it into a non-child-labor BPA-free plastic cup delivered to her with semolina pancakes in bed every morning. And at night, because he knew that her beauty pained her, just as it pained everyone else who male-gazed at her with unaffected resentment, he'd offer her late-night massages using gentle lotions from sustainable sandalwood paste that wouldn't irritate her skin or contribute to deforestation. And Suzanne would cry out of gratitude, cry out of joy and disbelief, delighted that she'd finally found a man who understood her the way women did, the way George, her ex-boyfriend never could.

By the time George got to dill (right after coriander and right before celery seed), there was a vein pulsating in his temple when Suzanne sat down and pecked him on the cheek like it was no big deal.

Thirteen Hours

She forced a smile. —What's up, Gengé?

He gave her a resentful look.

—You okay?

—You're late.

— Sorry, she shrugged, I got stuck talking to my mum.

—.

—.

—.

—Are you sure you're okay? she asked.

—Let's just drop it because I don't think I can talk about it right now.

—Fine with me because I'm *star*ving. Where's the waiter anyway?

He sighed in frustration.

—What? she turned to him.

—Ugh. That tone in your voice really *bugs* me.

—What tone?

—You know *exactly* what tone.

—I don't have a tone. I'm the Schoenberg of girlfriends.

—Who?

—Gengé, I'm *always* late.

—That doesn't make it okay.

—You're right, she said, nodding, I promise to work on

that, but for the time being, can we get this date started? I'm starving.

—A date that obviously means *nothing* to you.

—Whah? I'm really happy to see you. So happy, I could *hurt* myself right now.

—Oh my God, it really irritates the shit outta me when you act all cute like that!

Suzanne's body froze like a catatonic mime.

The vein in George's temple began to pulsate again. Suzanne actually thought he might detonate right there in the café.

Suzanne swallowed and folded her hands inside each other. —If you're mad, we can talk about it and if you're not ready to talk about it, we can talk about it later.

—Do you know I've been waiting here for an *hour*? he yelled.

—Will you stop yelling at me?

—I'm *not* yelling at you. I'm just frustrated.

—You *are* yelling and those statements aren't mutually exclusive.

—Fuck you! George stood up and walked to the front door.

Suzanne tilted in her chair, too tired to get up. —Gengé!

—I can't *deal* with you, Suzanne.

—Why are you so angry?

—For one thing, that's a stupid-ass T-shirt.

Suzanne looked down at her cryogenics T-shirt. —I *love* this shirt, for the record.

—See ya.

—Gengé, wait!

George punched the café door open with his fist and walked down Clark Street in the direction of Foster. Everyone in the café looked up, startled. The servers gave Suzanne sympathetic looks she absolutely didn't want.

Suzanne took a tentative sip of his black coffee, which was cold, bitter, and metallic. *No wonder he's such in a bad mood,* she thought, *this coffee tastes like battery acid.* While she felt bad about everything (something she was extremely gifted at and something that George expected her to do), Suzanne tried to find the upside. At least she could skim *Lonely Planets* and novels about the insect world and books about relativity and maybe get back to her book about the prison industrial complex and text Samir and catch up on the news and dominate Words with Friends. Having some alone time at one of her favorite cafés in the North Side could be a gift, right?

Twelve Hours

After eating a Blue Cheese Tempeh Burger, Suzanne remembered the last time she'd come here. She'd met up with Nina, an entitled childhood friend of hers from the Gold Coast. They used to meet together once a week and talk in diffident Hindi, chatting about high school friends and random boy candy. Nina was married and unfaithful, she wore fake nails, loved her cell phone, and wanted to sleep with every man who looked her in the eyes. Suzanne was single, had never cheated on anyone in her entire life, loved foreign movies on Netflix, public libraries, electronic music, foreign languages, and cafés with exposed brick. She was attracted to shy, awkward men who didn't know the first thing about savage love. Her friendship with Nina was obviously limited, but they both lived vicariously through each other.

As she grew bored listening to Nina talk about her fling with the deli boy who'd made her an imperfect egg sandwich that oozed mayonnaise—a detail probably invented to symbolize the boy's virility—Suzanne looked around the café. She admired the clocks from Chicago, LA, Goa, and Timbuktu. Nina didn't notice anyway, she was operating on double espresso. Suzanne turned her head from table to table until she noticed a man with appealing bone structure in his face who was half-reading his tech magazine underneath the Goa clock and scribbling notes on a napkin. Suddenly, their eyes pulled toward each other magnetically. He blinked hard and looked away while she watched his body language. She saw him look down at the floor, check the Lima clock, wipe his lips with his hand, and then look back at her. She'd smiled at him, admiring the way his face flared into a smile. But then Nina broke their moment with a false dichotomy: *so, what should I do, Suzie? Should I fuck him or forget him?* When the two women had left the café, Suzanne wrote her number on a napkin and tossed it on George's table while he was in the bathroom.

George called three obligatory days later but didn't know who to ask for since Suzanne had intentionally not left her name, so he'd introduced himself and then began stammering. She giggled into the phone. —I didn't know if it was you, he explained, I mean, I didn't want to assume it was you. Thought it might be your roommate or something.

—Ta-dah, she said.

—So, uh, what's your name?

—Kavalishundapran.

There was a pause. —What?

—What, you don't like my name? It's a sacred Brahman name.

—It's beautiful it's just really um, long.

—Actually, I just made that up.

—Oh. You were fucking with me.

—That's right George, I was.

—So, um, what . . . origin. . . I mean, what . . . backgr . . . ethnicity . . . are . . . does your family . . . or their ancestors . . .

Suzanne listened to him ellipsis himself to death. —Indian, George. We're Indian.

—Okay.

—And the name's Suzanne.

—Suzanne? That's not Indian at all. You were *gypped*.

—Well, I'm Indian so my name is technically an Indian name, but you're right, it's not common.

—Oh, right.

—And by the way, you might wanna stop using the word, gypped, while you're at it. It's kinda racist.

—It is?

—It comes from the word gipsy.

—Oh my God. I didn't know that.

—Now you do.

On the other end of the phone, George dropped something on the floor that spun in a never-ending circle. Suzanne tried as hard as she could to suppress her laughter when she accidentally hung up on him, laughing until her diaphragm was sore. Their first conversation was a masterpiece of mistakes.

Now, here she was one year later sans Nina, wondering where her life was going and whether George was its centerpiece or simply an exercise of self-discovery. She was willing to wait for the answer. She'd always loved this café, loved glancing at maps, journals, and travel guides to cities she'd never seen before, loved touching the homemade earrings, worry dolls dressed in alpaca wool outfits and batik sundresses from Latin America. Maybe, the answer would come to her while she waited, skimming through *Time Travel in the Insect World*.

Eleven Hours

Or maybe not. Suzanne stood up to leave. The barista was sweeping the floor, inverted chairs placed upon tabletops resembled wooden fours. Suzanne put on her Cos hoody, looked down at the carrots on her Chinese shoes, and wiggled her toes. They didn't elicit laughter this time. Usually, she found them so damn cute.

George never returned. In his absence, she'd witnessed an influx of people: disheveled college students, a West Coast girl with short burgundy hair reading a book of Lesbian erotica with a naked Latina drawing on the cover, two fifty-something Turkish guys playing soundless backgammon games in their sweatpants, a plump man in stone-colored shorts and Australian Outback hat chatting on AOL Messenger with "hot4fatmen77," several shiny straight couples in the cellophane stage, glowing with a sleek naiveté, lost in the novelty of their own affections, their sexuality like a gift waiting to be opened with trembling hands. Suzanne felt envious and lonely every time she observed neophyte couples. With so little time together, lovers were always centered, always courageous about affection, always shy about aggression, always overjoyed at prosaic coincidence and untapped desire. Suzanne thought about that one chapter in *Einstein's Dreams* where couples had no memory and every kiss, every embrace, and every single moment was eternal. Meanwhile, she and George were completely stuck in nostalgic amber. It felt like there was an enormous metaphysical weight tied around their necks that they dragged with them whenever they were together, cutting off the circulation in their heads and grounding them into the hard earth. Suzanne wondered why they couldn't simply adore each other like June bugs, their entire romantic cycle condensed into the last seventeen hours of life.

Ten Hours

As she waited for George to return, she thought about a lot of things like walking through the streets of Mumbai or helping her show-off cousins (who were actually swingers in real life) build an orphanage in Varanasi, like driving to Mt. Rainier with Samir and Ali and taking photos of snow-capped mountain tops, like shaking her ass in a Capitol Hill club or drinking imported tea in a Wallingford café or applying to grad school secretly in London or jumping in George's Passat and driving to LA without a word.

She wondered why pain always changed the way couples saw each other like a Lomography camera. She looked up at the LA clock inside the café and thought about packing her bags and disappearing, a daydream that made her feel capricious and uprooted and hopeful. She hated fighting with George, hated the way that conflict poisoned every relationship, but she had her own issues that anchored her to this life. For one thing, she was afraid of being alone, of settling for less than she deserved, of acting brashly and then regretting every good memory she set on fire. She was afraid of tolerating misogyny and exotification in exchange for comfort and predictability. She was afraid of disappointing her parents, of crashing and burning the flight simulator of her life. Pretty much everything except death. She often felt like the act of breaking up with George (or anyone, for that matter) was the equivalent of killing a version of herself.

The incessant conflict they'd been having since New Year's made her crave harmony, simplicity, and amnesia, not reconciliation. When the barista turned off the music, haunting the café with silence, Suzanne went outside, lost in thought. There was a slight breeze in the humid Chicago air, the August heat exaggerated by the erratic lake effect.

—Suzie! Suzie! George shouted, running up to her and panting. He was bent over, his hands on his knees, sweat eating through his button-down. —Hold on a second.

She put her hands in the pockets of her hoodie.

—Look, he said, I've been thinking.

—Me too, she said. Part of her hoped that George had come to the same conclusion she had in her worst moments, that he loved her enough to be the bad guy for once and end their relationship, but she knew George wanted the happy ending, even if it was cinematically impossible.

—So, look, he said, at first, I was building my case against you. You know, accumulating all the reasons to be angry.

—You do that very well.

Anger flashed into his eyes momentarily. —I know, I know, okay? He took a few deep breaths. —Anyway, he huffed, as I was trying to figure out why I feel so pathetic and tiny in this relationship, it hit me that my attachment to you is a continuous source of shame and self-hatred.

—Gengé, that's like the sweetest thing you've ever said.

He ignored her. —I don't usually get attached to girlfriends. Normally, I'm too busy working to care, but you're so goddamn on point all the time that I find myself clinging to you like a kid on the Tilt-a-Whirl.

—Nice analogy.

—I guess what I'm trying to say is, I love you.

—Gengé, I love you too. She swallowed. —But I don't want us to settle.

—Is that what we're doing?

She kicked a twig down the sidewalk and sighed. —I don't know. She bit her lips. —The only thing I know for sure is that I want vertigo, Gengé, not stability, and if that's impossible, I'd rather be single.

—That's why I'm scared.

—Why?

—Because I've already invented our *whole life together* and now I'm afraid of losing it: the wedding in Calcutta.

—Mumbai—

—The honeymoon in Mallorca, the summer cottage on the Tambelan Islands—

—Gengé?

—What?

A look of deep and painful sadness blossomed in her face. —Just love me tonight. That's enough.

—Okay, he said, shrugging, I'll try.

—Anything else?

—One last thing. You know the story I told you about the Ugly Bright Green Curtains?

—Yes, and that's not their name.

—Okay, remember how I said they'd caught on fire from your Mango-Cucumber candles?

She nodded.

—I hid them in your attic along with your candles.

—Why?

—I hated how bright they were, but mostly, I hated the way you'd just decided one day to put them up without even asking me what I wanted. It made me feel like it became your bedroom, not ours.

—Gengé, those curtains came from India and they were literally the only thing in our apartment that you didn't buy. I don't have your income, so everything I buy comes from the Brown Elephant, which you have routinely rejected.

—But I never insisted—

—Oh yes you did. Not by saying the words, I insist—let's not be disingenuous—but by rejecting everything I could actually afford by claiming it was dented or janky or wobbly or that it didn't fit our apartment's aesthetic or that it didn't match the other pieces you'd already bought. When that technique didn't work, then you'd say that you'd *think about it* until I forgot. That's why our place is completely decorated by you, not us! You have money, so you got to make all the decisions, which made me feel like I was living in *your* space, instead of ours, and those curtains were my contribution and you just got rid of them because you *didn't like them.*

—Okay, okay, you're right. I'm sorry.

—.

—Maybe, it's just a coincidence, but ever since I hid them in the attic, we've been fighting all the time. I'm sorry I lied about them.

Suzanne moved towards him when a congregation of fireflies surrounded her in a veil of Christmas lights like fluttering celestial dots. She stood there in a daze, deeply moved by the soft buzz of their almost-broken wings, the flashing stanzas of their torsos, their fragmented conversation in the language of bioluminescence.

George reached for her hand, pulling her against him, their body heat colliding as the fireflies flew away. Their lips reconnected, crisscrossing desire and shame, guilt and confusion, sadness and resignation. Their mouths burned with the appetite of the damaged and the despondent.

Nine Hours

In the foyer of their Lakeview apartment, their kisses were hot, sweet, and heavy, burning each other's mouths. Bossa Nova and Samba wagged their tales furiously and barked for attention as Suzanne and George devoured each other in the hallway.

Eight Hours

Inside their komorebi bedroom, Suzanne undid her hair tie and shook her head as she looked down at George, freeing her long silky hair, which rolled down her shoulders and splashed George's face in the light-green penumbra, casting a spell of chamomile and Circe on him. As he undressed her, Suzanne felt both turned on and sleepy.

Seven Hours

Suzanne surprised Gengé by pushing him down and then climbing on top of him, something she rarely did, something he rarely wanted. As she straddled him, her brown body crashed down on his pale skin like a beautiful wave.

Six Hours

There were certain things Suzanne could only tell George with her own flesh, certain confessions only her body could make when he was disarmed and naked and silent, certain demands her muscular thighs made, certain stanzas her lungs recited, certain pleasures of flesh and fantasy, dilating heat and sexual electricity, that only occurred when George was inside her and the world disappeared. This was when sex became a sort of lockpicking of the self.

Five Hours

Her curved white fingernails clawed his clammy stomach, her strong thighs slid down his bony legs as she lost herself in the act of her body's recollection of its own power and strength. The soft and burning pleasure of their lovemaking became mysterious, like opening a tiny parenthesis.

Four Hours

Suzanne knew that Gengé loved her when he regained his memory of who they were and she loved him when she lost her memory of what they'd become.

Three Hours

He sobbed in her arms prophetically. As she held him, she kissed his temples until he fell asleep. Her dark arms were wrapped around his pale neck, her developed calves wrapped around his skinny back, consoling him with the soft force of her whisper. As his breathing stabilized, she cried on his sleeping face, cried at the intersection of her arms, cried on the thinning hair on his head because he was finally unlocked now, a mouth to her guilt.

Two Hours

Suzanne nudged her forehead against his, breathing in the scented candles and light green hues that her curtains cast on their bedroom walls. There was a shrine of mango-cucumber candles along the bed, the flames nodding like magi, bringing gifts of undulating shadow to the off-white walls. Suzanne's eyes felt heavy now, falling under the hypnosis of the flame as Zydeco scratched the door and cried.

One Hour

For one night, they both shed their dead memories, outdated roles, and compounding injustices. George was lost in his dreams, Suzanne was fully awake, their minds both clear and calm now.

Zero Hours

Three hours later, Suzanne placed a letter under his pillow and stared at him as flickering silhouettes danced on his serene face. She knew that as long as he slept, he would be weightless and infinite, his joy exponential until he woke up. She blew out the candles and kissed his face, tears welling in her eyes again. As she settled into the back seat, turned off her phone, and tucked it inside her favorite satchel from Delhi that covered her lap, she felt nauseous and dizzy as she wiped her face. When the taxi driver asked here where she was going, the letters lingered on her lips, the syllables stuck in her throat. She could barely say the directions out loud, could barely pronounce the "h" in "O'Hare," but when she finally did, her words were a cremation.

ADULTHOOD

29. MEC WITH A GAP IN HIS TEETH*

*TO BE SUNG TO THE SMITHS' "BOY WITH A THORN IN HIS SIDE"

I.

SUZANNE ANALYZES AZIZ BECAUSE she's trapped inside the C train and needs something to do besides worry about time (lines), which is all she's been doing for the past three days. Noticing Aziz's navy kaftan, grey linen pants, brown slip-ins, white kufi cap, macchiato skin, pretty bone structure, and French accent (dude mumbles to himself), she knows right away that he's French Moroccan. Suddenly, his satchel falls to the ground in an odd thump and lands on a passenger's foot. It's a gorgeous tan officer's satchel with gusseted flap pockets and padded shoulder strap (way nicer than the one her mum bought her in Delhi). Suzanne watches him ask an old woman in a crumpled purple sundress if her foot is okay. The old woman fans herself with her book, explaining to Aziz in rapid-fire Fluminense Portuguese that she feels faint. Aziz apologizes and she grabs his hand. He holds it and soothes her with soft, comforting words, speaking Portuguese with a perfect Brazilian accent that ignites something in Suzanne. She wonders if she misdiagnosed him, even though she's never wrong about people's origins. Ever.

2.

Suzanne is stunned by the quiet struggle for order inside the gloomy subway. She's also strangely moved by Aziz. The way he holds the old lady's hand as if it's nothing, the way he consoles a complete stranger, astounds Suzanne. Maybe, she was wrong about New Yorkers after all. As she watches Aziz, she feels the earliest stage of romantic time dilation, the stuff of time-stopping hallway crushes, intravenous sugar highs, and teenage arrhythmia. She drinks in the tension and clarity of the subway crisis, inhaling her confusion and wonder. The silent anarchy inside the subway is enough to make her heart explode. She is a prisoner of darkness, inappropriate desire, and coincidence, all wedged into the subway tunnel (New York's massive urban cavity). In a singular flash, Suzanne is captivated by the pointless humanity of a stranger with caramel skin just like hers. She is taken by the noticeable gap in Aziz's teeth and his killer accent. She swallows her thoughts and tries to meditate, but she doesn't even know how. She never did. Instead, Suzanne thinks about the stranger with the beautifully wounded eyes she told herself not to think about since there's nothing to think about since she's leaving New York in two hours and starting the next phase of her life in Wicker Park or Lower Queen Anne or Bronzeville or Wallingford or the South Loop or Capitol Hill, any place in Chicago or Seattle where people don't know her, where she has no pre-history. At some point, she might even sneak into her old apartment in Lakeview and kidnap the pups and the moody calico and pack up the rest of her clothes without a word of explanation. She tells herself not to think about the man with the beautiful officer's satchel (the one with the gusseted flap pockets). She tells herself to think about Seattle, the only city where she has family but no history. She tells herself to think about Chicago, the only city she has ever loved, the only city she's ever understood. But each time she fails. She fucking fails. She's never been good at muting the percolation of intrigue, desire, and fascination.

30. COUNTERFACTUAL PLOT LINES FOR HOLDING HANDS & FOR LEAVING BEHIND EVERYTHING YOU COULDN'T FIGHT FOR WHEN THE SUN PUNCHED YOU IN THE SEPTUM & YOU STOPPED LISTENING TO THE MIC-DRUNK PREACHER IN YOUR DAMAGED & MYSTICAL HEART

I.

THE COOL OCTOBER AIR and the smell of sterile rain slowly fills up the dark subway like a nerve agent. Passengers become restless. Some tap their feet or try desperately to text their friends, even though nothing is getting through. Others try calling their friends on their neutralized cell phones. A few even break the sacred rule of social ignorance on the subway and start talking with complete strangers. The silent fear and panic lingering in the background remains unspoken but felt by everyone.

2.

Two teenagers in Knicks jerseys (one white, one Latino) start yelling: *Get me the fuck out of here! Help us! Please help us! Call the cops! Has anyone called the cops? I don't wanna die in here!* They start shoving each other in the middle of the train, their faces shiny with sweat and piqued by druggy anger. One of them shouts something inarticulate and then smashes his fist into the other boy's face. Passengers roar in disbelief, which only eggs on the fighters. They slam their fists into each other's skulls like Mortal Kombat characters until their faces are disfigured, smashed apart, and bleeding profusely. They wrestle, their hands locked into each other's blood-stained jerseys, their broken voices screaming, fresh blood pouring down their faces, their legs swaying back and forth like a primal dance routine, their dripping bodies swaying back and forth, spraying blood and sweat everywhere, falling on passengers who stand up in alarm and shout, *what the fuck?* A Black grad student dodges the violent scrum by jumping out of the way, abandoning his mixed-race girlfriend in the white Beats, and moving to the other side of the train as the fight continues, turning passengers into captive boxing fans. A few passengers place bets, some cover their mouths in shock, others pretend not to notice. Winnie turns his Supreme cap to the side to protect his bandages from the teenage gangbang that Kwan Li rescued his ass from and joins Aziz who is rolling up the sleeves of his navy kaftan. Together, they break up the fight. People clap because it's easier to applaud than intervene.

3.

Suzanne watches as Winnie and Aziz slowly contain the teenage mosh pit. When Aziz had first entered the subway, he stumbled on her pensive and fidgety beauty in passing and bumped into one of her suitcases, dropping his tan officer's satchel on a passenger's foot who shot him a dirty look. Aziz was completely distracted by the synergy of Suzanne's presence, vibe, and beauty, her prominent cheek bones and glistening chocolate milk skin, her never-ending lashes, the glossy lusciousness of her purple lips, the pointy tips of her ears and her serial piercings, the thick luster of her braid, the hairpin curves of her hips, the jade circle dangling just below her clavicle, the tiny mole on her cheek, and the liquid caramel in her eyes. Aziz is a bit mesmerized by her but also weary. He is so tired of feeling alienated by New York's cultural mythology, its standoffish style and relentless beauty, its verboten class barriers, its thirty-dollar sandwiches, its stifling urban density, and its dirty streets. When it comes down to it, he can't afford the city's price tags. He can't afford anything in New York, least of all a crush on a complete stranger who'd probably break his heart anyway.

4.

Suzanne noticed Aziz earlier on the platform. He looked around confused, trying to find answers on his iPhone that would never come so far down below street level. She sensed his confusion and his panic, two feelings she'd experienced over and over again in New York. For a fleeting moment, she wanted to help him the way she wished New Yorkers would have helped her, even though she didn't know Manhattan from a plate of Chicago deep dish. When she sees him now in the subway, she feels homesick for some bizarre reason. It's hard to explain, really, but his face looks like home, at least for someone who doesn't know where home is anymore.

5.

Even though the teenage fight club is over, Ginger pulls out her cell phone and dials 911, but her hands are shaky. 911 ends up being 9-9-1-1-1. No matter. Her phone doesn't get through.

6.

Aziz becomes afraid suddenly that he's going to die in the company of complete strangers, buried underneath the Hudson

River by misguided terrorists who don't know how to follow YouTube videos. He can already read the subtext of his half-actualized life: another pointless and morally repugnant terrorist attack in New York. He's going to die inside this subterranean morgue alone, lost, erased, editorialized by foreign policy hawks and lamented by social media activists in the mass grave of American history he doesn't even belong to. All the dead passengers will be listed in the *New York Times* as victims of some once-in-a-lifetime natural disaster or some fanatical religious retaliation for another American occupation abroad. All of the soon-to-be-dead passengers will become cautionary tales about the dangers of cutting funding to urban infrastructure and public services or the accidental violence of drunk subway engineers and ridiculous mechanical glitches. Soon, the passengers' bodies will be devoured and swallowed whole by stinging darkness and polluted water, fodder for a million documentaries, internet sleuths, and conspiracy theorists.

7.

Ginger hasn't seen a fight since Kayisha started scrapping with that Vietnamese gangster back in high school, back when strong girls were worth fighting and cute grunge boys were worth every minor palpitation. But after Kayisha's hand accidentally smacked her in the face, Ginger got her first and last whiff of the blood-on-knuckle bouquet and it made her sick to her stomach, then furious. Ever since then, she's hated violence. It just happens too fast for her to protect her spirituality from that great primal descent. She wishes there was something she could have done for Winnie and the other passengers when they were struggling to separate the feuding ballers, but she knows Winnie would never let her help anyway. He's told her more than once that she will always be the hardest presence to replace in the world. Her void will always be the biggest tragedy. Graphies like him have a legacy, he told her, a body of work that will outlive them (if they've done their work and paid their dues), but Ginger's list of a 1,000 Good Deeds, her love and generosity, her empathy and selflessness, all make her a crucial life force of healing and reconciliation in this fucked-up world. Her absence will be the most devastating of all. She'll get none of the credit, of course, but she will carry the world on her shoulders like so many Asian, Latina, Black, and Native women in the world.

8.

Winnie nods at Aziz and gives him a fist bump for his help. They talk for a few moments, nod at each other in solidarity, and then go their separate ways. Winnie walks over to an old Black woman who waved him over from the other side of the train because he's got a soft spot for old people. Always has.

9.

After Aziz gives Winnie a fist bump, he walks to the other end of the subway and takes a few deep breaths to stop himself from passing out while Winnie walks over to an old Black woman in a massive hat. Even though he's lightheaded, Aziz turns to the mixed-race girl with the white headphones, who looks as him in disbelief. He doesn't say anything because she doesn't see him. She doesn't see anyone. He is cut up inside and out of breath, he can barely recognize his life right now, but he wants to help her, he's just unsure about whether compassion can be self-interested. Is he helping her to help her, or because unconsciously he thinks she's incapable of helping herself? Maybe, she doesn't want anyone's help. Maybe, she's not in shock at all, but just scared AF. Instead of talking to her, he prays in Arabic, something he never does, something he's exceptionally bad at doing since he's not actually Muslim. A few passengers exchange conspiratorial glances and whisper to each other before looking back at him, their eyes searching for wires or mysterious bulges under his kaftan. Aziz pretends not to notice, a trick her learned in Paris. He doesn't need to look at them to know what's happening now, to understand how fear always weaponizes prejudice. He's seen it his whole life from 9/11 to the London and Casa bombings. White people are afraid of everyone except themselves. That's always been their problem. Aziz can feel their Islamophobic glances even with his eyes closed. Maybe, he can just fall asleep praying until this nightmare ends. Maybe, he can just disappear for everyone's comfort.

10.

Suzanne watches Aziz on the other side of the train, talking to a French passenger in a Beatles T-shirt. She admires his beautiful satchel and the gap in his teeth and his Parisian accent most of all. Her ears perk up. Unfortunately, her hearing is bad and her French is a liability.

11.

After Winnie gives Aziz a fist bump, he walks over to an old Black woman who waved him over with her tiny, wilted hand. She's wearing a big Kentucky Derby hat and church clothes. Winnie pulls off his baseball cap and wipes the sweat caking his forehead. He checks to see if the Band-Aids on his cheeks are still attached, his hands grazing broken scabs that still make him wince. There's blood on his cheeks, but it's not his. He asks the old woman how she's doing and then realizes it's Mrs. Walker, his 10th grade lit teacher at St. Ursula's. She was the first teacher of his to teach Ethnic Lit, which Winnie didn't even know was a thing at the time. Mrs. Walker lit changed his fucking life when she assigned Octavia Butler's *Bloodchild and Other Stories*, Haruki Murakami's *Norwegian Wood*, Sandra Cisneros's *The House on Mango Street*, Maxine Hong Kingston's *The Woman Warrior*, and

Toni Cade Bambara's *Gorilla, My Love*. Until tenth grade, he thought literature was just another showcase for white people to center themselves in American history, but she changed everything. Her class taught him about the power of communicating your own history, of telling stories in your own voice, register, and imagination, of finding, sometimes even creating, your own language in order to carve out space for yourself in this world. She lit helped him understand that no one else could tell his own stories except him. Winnie smiles and says matter-of-factly, *What's up, Mrs. Walker? It's Winnie Yu!* The old woman grabs her chest like she's about to keel over and then breaks into joyous laughter. She pulls him close to give him a big hug. Winnie is so happy he's embarrassed. When Winnie looks back at Ginger, she's in hysterics.

12.

Ginger watches an old Black woman in the largest seaside hat she's ever seen in her entire life pull Winnie close and give him a massive hug like he's her missing grandson. Ginger laughs uncontrollably at the sight of a stranger bearhugging Winnie. She can't help it. And this isn't the first time she's seen someone hug Winnie out of the blue. He just brings out the doting grandparent in strangers for some reason. Maybe, it's his impeccably good manners. Maybe, they can sense his soft spot for old people. Ginger smiles. She's reminded of what an amazing dad and son-in-law Winnie will be when an emotional cloud suddenly blocks the sun inside her. She's reminded that her struggle to have kids has become a cage death match against time and genetics. Her prolactin, estradiol, AMH, and follicle stimulating hormone test results will be available soon and she's fucking terrified. Despite a history of premature menopause on her mom's side and unknown infertility issues on her dad's side, Ginger's reproductive endocrinologist tells her not to worry.

He says he's cautiously optimistic about her chances. But, he qualified, let's wait and see how the test results are first. With everyone else, Ginger is an incorrigible optimist. But with her own (insatiable, obsessive, impossible?) dream of being a mom, she has no faith. She's been off birth control for a long time now and nothing has happened. Her period has been erratic since college. There are—supposedly—just a couple branches in the family tree on her dad's side (but who fucking knows?). And her white mom took HRT for more than a decade to calm the effects of early menopause. But every time Ginger adds all the details up in her head, she feels like she's adding nothing to nothing to get nothing, and optimism has to be grounded in an integer. Something material. Something more than just counterfactual mommy fantasies. Ginger swallows her heart a little bit and tries not to cry, but it just keeps inflating like an infected limb.

13.

Aziz takes a few more breaths and stops praying. He barely knows the words anyway. He sees a Black grad student praying in French, his lips opening and closing like a pilgrim bowing his head at El-Mabka (the Wailing Wall). Aziz looks away so he doesn't feel self-conscious, so that the dude can have his moment alone with the universe. Everyone deserves at least that. Aziz walks to the other end of the train because he doesn't know where else to go, which is the story of his life.

14.

Aziz chats in French with a guy from Marseille who is dressed in a Beatles T-shirt, expensive Levi's, and a trilby hat with a peacock feather in it.

—Alors, t'es en congé? Aziz asks.

—Bah non, the man in the Trilby cap answers, —J'habite ici avec ma meuf.

—Géniale. Ell'est kainri?

—Non, italienne.

—Quel beau pays.

—Oui, oui. On a visité à Napoli pour la lune de miel.

—Félicitations, mon gars.

The man nods, grabbing the brim of his trilby hat. —Merci.

Aziz stops to consider his words. —So, let me ask you, does shit like this always happen in New York? C'est ouf!

The man in the trilby shakes his head. —Presque jamais.

—Oh.

—The crazy thing is, Lauretta told me to walk, but I was being stubborn and lazy, so I jumped on this damn tromé.

—Me too. Aziz smiles, but then his smile dies when he remembers the gap in his teeth. —We'll be okay, inshallah.

—I'm trying not to freak out, but it's hard right now.

Aziz nods. —C'est dur. But like they say in Burkina Faso, ça va aller.

—It's going to go?

Aziz nods. —You know, for the first time maybe in my life, I miss Paris.

—Pas moi. I don't miss that damn city *one* bit, he says, removing his Trilby hat and wiping his forehead. To tell you the truth, the only thing I miss right now is walking around Central Park with her. God, I miss her so much!

—You just painted a beautiful picture.

—New York is my home. Over there, my life was a French cliché: Macdo, boulot, dodo. But here, my options are endless. Granted, I can't afford to live in Manhattan, my Queens apartment is the size of a bathtub, and the rats are bigger than suitcases, but other than that, my life is great.

Aziz nods again. —For some reason, New York makes me feel lonely, excluded, and poor.

—Ah bon?

—Yeah. I hate to admit it because there's so many things wrong with Paris, but it's the most beautiful city in the world to fall in love in. It's a romance novel that writes itself.

—Mec, I hate romance novels.

Aziz laughs. —I'd kill for one right about now. My ex-copine dumped me because she's a coward, my surrogate father got killed by les keufs, my real father is a ghost, I lost two perfect teeth in a Parisian émeute, and now, I'm stuck on this damn tromé. This is quite easily the best and worst fucking month of my entire life.

The man pouts. —Putain de merde! That's brutal. I'm so sorry. Your situation is objectively worse than mine. Sorry for complaining about my bullshit.

—Eh, who's counting? Aziz says, feeling vindicated because he knows he's not the only person who thinks his life is a master-piece of tiny disasters.

15.

After they catch up, Mrs. Walker gives Winnie a Kleenex so he can wipe his bloody face and hands with coarse tissue paper decorated in antiseptic daffodils. She thanks him for breaking up the fight, tells him that the last thing people need right now is more conflict and drama when the world is already going to hell. Then, she talks about her seven grandchildren in Queens, Birmingham, and Wichita who she calls her *little dirt devils*. She tells Winnie she always knew he'd make something of himself. He tells her she was his favorite teacher in high school, that she changed the way he saw the world and the way he fought to tell his own stories. She blinks in quiet gratitude and waves to him, almost losing her gargantuan hat in the process. Winnie says goodbye and hugs her one more time, fighting the urge to cry.

16.

Ginger makes a simple promise to herself: if she and Winnie see the light of day again, she's going to tell him what she learned about her body when she stared at herself in the full-length mirror, a conclusion her reproductive endocrinologist said he'd confirm next week after all her test results come back from the lab at New York Pres. Shit is about to get real and Ginger knows she's not ready for it.

17.

After more than two hours, there is only mitigated darkness, constricted time, the insinuation of death, and the hint of slow suffocation in the subway. The opaque insanity of the city blackout and the lingering scent of 9/11 in the air encourages some passengers to open up and others to break down. After all, they share the same collapsed ecosystem. They share the same trembling fault line of mortality and regret. They share the same catastrophic vulnerability, citing paralysis and the crumbling mess of human desperation. Sentences bloom between strangers. Inside the chilly and dark train, there is nothing left except the crude therapy of talking, the redemption of em dashes, and the unclean space of butchered words, which keep dying in the air.

18.

Suzanne wishes she spoke French. She really wants to understand what Aziz and the French tourist are talking about. By their gesticulations, it sounds joyous and interesting, the way all secrets do when someone flaunts them right in front of you, daring you to break their cipher.

19.

After Winnie sits back down, Ginger wraps her arms around him and kisses his cheek.

He inhales her neck and kisses a handful of hair. She smells like cucumber deodorant, nori, acrylic paint, and sesame oil. — Yo, you're not gonna believe it.

—What?

—That was Mrs. Walker, my tenth grade lit teacher! She was like my fave teacher in high school.

Ginger smiles and gives him a look that is both joyful and wounded.

—Why you giving me that dreamy look, Ginger Snap?

Her eyes try to censor what they can't hide. —Oh, wouldn't *you* like to know, Mr. Yu?

—Hit me up, girl.

—Tell you later, she sighs, when the sun swallows us like a giant whale.

—Come here, you little sphinx, he says, laying a heavy kiss on her lips.

Ginger giggles. Winnie gives her a dirty look. She holds her hand up in apology and then gives him big sloppy kisses on his cheeks and forehead. He shakes his head. He's secretly annoyed with her mystery, which feels like a violation of their code of explicitness. He tells himself there must be a reason why she's withholding something. He makes a mental note to ask her again above ground, which he will forget.

20.

A few passengers watch Ginger and Winnie with low-key fascination because they assumed Winnie was a thug and Ginger a cholita. Their flash judgments misled them. Winnie and Ginger are a verbose crossword puzzle of affection when they're together: intersecting, interlocking, and contrapuntal. Their love is verbose and bulky. They have luminosity. There is a clear joy in their interconnectivity that makes some passengers feel lonely, confused, and resentful, but that's their fucking problem.

21.

Suzanne looks at her watch again, makes a few calculations, and realizes she's not going to make it to Chicago on time. She feels a sudden and enormous panic. Her mum will never understand. She'll never believe a story about New York falling apart at the seams unless there are exploding cultural landmarks and a massive body count. But sometimes, the lie sounds like the truth and the truth sounds like a lie. Sometimes, the truth is the most absurd and illogical story of all, better understood in small pieces and told backwards. The truth is, the C train has collapsed into darkness with passengers entangled inside these concrete fallopian tubes like a massive ectopic pregnancy.

22.

After their conversation comes to a lull, Aziz looks at the French expat who keeps adjusting his Trilby hat. Aziz stands there awkwardly for a moment and then shakes his hand.

—Du courage, mon ami, Aziz says.

—Cimer, the man replies, holding his grip.

—I hope you see Lauretta soon.

—I hope the world falls in love with you after all the pain it's caused you.

Aziz tries to smile but he can't pretend. He feels grateful, embarrassed, and sad about being understood by a stranger. He worries that his loneliness is an obscene advertisement of self-pity.

23.

Winnie tries to stop freaking out about his foiled meeting with *Adbusters*. Maybe, he has to surrender to the blackout. Maybe, nothing is happening in the city anyway since the power is out everywhere. He tries to convince himself that the only thing he can do right now is enjoy his time with Ginger. He knows he'll never have to choose between jamming and love, but if shit got real, if he were forced to pick one or the other by gunpoint, he'd pick Ginger all day every day every way. There'd be no hesitation. He grabs Ginger's hand and kisses it, lingering on the ring finger before he holds her hand like it's a delicate universe.

24.

Ginger smiles and rests her head on Winnie's shoulder. She tries not to question the way reality can fold into itself, the way time can warp reality, collapsing into imagination, daydream, inversion, and yearning.

25.

After three long hours, passengers inside the C train stand to stretch. Some try to use their cell phones again to call fiancées, dads, and girlfriends, supervisors and forty-year-old roommates. Others start moving around the subway to get the blood circulating in their legs like on transatlantic flights. Some passengers even start doing simple yoga positions or taking naps on the shoulders of friends. And still others, the ones who've become sick of sitting silently in semi-darkness for hours, strike up conversations with complete strangers (verboten in New York). This cultural cross-cleavage inside the subway is a transitory and tenuous truce. Underneath the streets and stuck in the subway tunnels, stasis gives new meaning to dead languages, especially for stranded passengers. Commuters blurt random words out like insect songs to reclaim language from the graveyard, to reclaim every lost verb and every banned noun.

26.

Aziz passes Suzanne and then sits down. He smiles self-consciously. There's a soft, awkward, and sensual warmth in his face as he smiles at her, but she doesn't understand its purpose, meaning, or origin. With one unwarranted smile from a complete stranger, her skin becomes a flesh burn. Suzanne wants to know why Aziz, with his broken eyes and broken teeth, just walked away, smiling at her with eyes that were both wounded and exquisitely tender. She feels confused, aroused, and powerless. As it turns out, the end of the world can be an aphrodisiac.

27.

A Latino hipster scrutinizes Suzanne. He's wearing enormous tortoise shell glasses, tight jean shorts, a seersucker blazer, strategically ripped T-shirt, and a yellow handkerchief with blue umbrellas tied around his neck like a confused French Eagle Scout. He looks at Suzanne and bites his lip.

—Hey, Suzanne says. Are you okay?

He shakes his head.

—Yeah, me neither.

He cogitates. —When I finally get off this subway, I'm gonna be single again and he's the fucking cheater. Not me!

—Whah?

—My white husband is a serial cheater who basically fucks his patients.

—God, I'm so sorry.

—Yeah, it's fucking terrible. I keep finding incriminating evidence in his office: ugly ties, boxer shorts, an Alabama driver's license, a Columbia student ID, car keys for an Audi, even a Mets cap. Who roots for the goddamn Mets anyway?

—I dunno, Mets fans?

—I used to wonder why he had four locks for his "office." I thought it was just paranoia, mostly because he groomed me to doubt myself.

—Well, being single has its advantages.

The Latino hipster scrunches up his face like a feisty pug.

—Says you. I'm not some hot Indian beatch, so I can't just date whoever I want.

Suzanne blushes. —No one can. I think that's the point.

He shakes his head. —You don't get it. My husband's practically a supermodel and I'm just an accountant from SF.

—Oh. Well, that shouldn't mat—

—When you love someone, you have a place to go to after things fall apart. When you love someone, you have shelter from the hailstorm. Just *knowing* where to direct your love when it starts accumulating inside you is a privilege. Now, I have to carry my love with me wherever I go, which is the heaviest weight in the world.

Suzanne wants to disagree, but after two months of confusing and tumultuous independence, she can't. She gets him. She feels the same way about dating that she feels about her life. She will never go back to George, but she isn't ready to move forward yet either. At the same time, she's also sick of feeling displaced (New York), stared at (Seattle), and unloved (both). At least in Chicago, she knows how to be herself, which is more than she can say in New York. Now, she's stuck in a web of double negative constructions and annoying counterfactual conversations inside her head. Sometimes, she just wants to be held, especially by someone who won't smother her or ask for permission all the time. Sometimes, she just wants to be with a (non-white) man who is mildly obsessed with the way she smells in the morning, with the way her mind sees the world, with the way her heart beats in her body. A man who celebrates her abstract reasoning, her strength, her memory, her voice, and her humanity instead of challenging everything she worked her ass for. Some passionate sex would be lovely too after a nice long bath and maybe some Peruvian dark chocolate and some Malbec and a little weed.

28.

Stuck in a tunnel where the air is heavy and cool like a storm cloud, Ginger feels conflicted about her test results but grateful too that she gets to avoid her reproductive endocrinologist for the time being. Being on the subway means being in the in-between of reality where every mixed-race person lives at some point. At the same time, she feels like love can be an enormous burden, like she's schlepping a gigantic weather balloon with her wherever she goes, struggling with its magnificent size and bulky shape. She's too ashamed to admit that sometimes she feels constrained by love, slowed down by fear and self-endangered by codependency, even though she feels mostly comfort, radiance, and joy when they're together. She feels grounded and balanced by their coevolving teenage love affair, which crushes them both, pinning their bodies to a shifting geography of desire. Ginger loves him with every cell in her hapa body, with every developed complex emotion she's got. When she imagines her life without Winnie, she disintegrates into table salt. Sometimes, she feels vulnerable and wants to choke from emotion when he says goodbye to her on the street. Sometimes, she wants to tell him, *Please don't die.* She knows her love for Winnie can't and won't solve all her problems, she knows that, she's always known that, but when she's with him, when he holds her hand and kisses her cheek and touches her hair like a greedy infant, she feels perfect by design, she feels heavy by the laws of love and meteorology, she feels immune to the armies of dark matter, where time/space bends backwards and folds and slowly collapses into itself.

29.

Aziz wishes he were back in Paris. It's a strange wish because Paris is a city he's never loved, a city that has never loved him or his brown face. Of course, part of him wants to stay in New York and fall in love, just like the man in the Trilby hat, but Aziz doesn't understand New Yorkers at all, especially the way they sacrifice their happiness for their careers, their human labor given up like a bribe to the American dream, their unsustainable lives crashing into the ground after the brief tailwind of their own hubris. Besides, New York doesn't want another over-educated French guy with a chip on his shoulder and multiple advanced degrees anyway. This city is the ontology of dreamers for everyone except broken-hearted Muslims and Asian grandparents. What Aziz wants, what he finds himself dreaming about since the C train stroked out, what he needs more than anything right now is impossible: he wants an alternative life in New York he'll never have, an alternative world in Paris that never existed. He can't stay in New York where everyone is too goddamn busy to be in a relationship. He can't accept the slow atrophy of the soul of the sixty-hour work week in America, but he can't accept the false cinematography of Paris either where everyone he loves is in mourning or in denial or crawling through the emergency exits of poverty, racial gloom, and self-hatred.

30.

Ginger and Winnie kvetch about everything that's wrong in the world. They just go off about Three Strikes laws and the prison industrial complex and no-knock warrants and qualified immunity and police brutality and Contract with America and the war on drugs and big Pharma and Wall Street and the 2000 presidential "election" and the Iraqi Occupation and cash bail and private prisons and Israeli war crimes and American interventionism and Russian hacking and heteropatriarchy and global warming and the two-party political system and Trump's failed 2012 presidential bid ("no way America is stupid and racist enough to vote for that motherfucker," Winnie declares) and Bloomberg's racist Stop and Frisk and the racist Electoral College that intentionally erases thirty million votes from California. Ginger complains that Americans dump their senior citizens off at Death Resorts. Winnie talks about going back to grad school, something he hasn't done in years. They talk about Ginger's new list of good deeds she's working on and Winnie's next culture jam and future trips they wanna take together: Paris, Dakar, Chicago, Singapore, LA, Seattle, Seoul, Helsinki, and Casablanca. Ginger asks Winnie what RTS stands for again (*Reformed Theological Seminary? Return to Sender? Ready to Screw?*). Winnie talks about his ba again but then shuts down. Gingers kisses his hand to encourage him to keep talking. When Winnie stays silent, Ginger talks about the deterioration of porn because of smart phones and working with kids to create raw and authentic art, something Winnie loves hearing. They talk about M-Boz's suicidal tendences and laugh again at the image of him parachuting off a skyscraper like a dumbass. They talk about the bad Feng Shui in her bedroom and the perfect cup of green tea and the so-called death of hip-hop and the perfect falafel. As they chat, time slithers by, but at least it moves. Their kong xu will always lock their souls together and their bold and incandescent love will always be a refuge. Even in their criticism, they can't help but to celebrate their lust for this fading world, which doesn't deserve all the love they give it.

31.

As much as she misses Zydeco and the pups, Papa and her favorite cafés, as much as she'd love to eat Thai food in Edgewater, bike up the boardwalk to Rogers Park, get lost in the Kandinsky room of the Art Institute, and reconnect with her stranded UC friends in the South Side, the truth is always more complex than the narrative tricks we use to capture it in our butterfly net. Suzanne doesn't want to stay in New York, but she's glad the city shut down, glad her flight is unreachable now. She's not ready to return to Chicago even though she craves it. In some strange and demented way, she actually appreciates the suspended animation of the C train. She prefers liminality to forced trespassing or contrived conclusions. She wonders how her life will ever be normal again after she watched the June bugs spiraling from the sky like bogeys shot down by enemy fire in Chicago.

32.

Aziz glances at Suzanne. He can tell from the way she speaks to the Latino hipster in the seersucker blazer, that she's intrepid with strangers but also quietly defensive about her own time. She strikes him as observant, intuitive, emotionally strong, and fiercely intelligent. She empathizes with other people's suffering without inserting her own problems into it, which is rare, especially for Americans. There's something about the way she lets herself become completely immersed in a singular moment, practically drowning in the nowness of human rapport, practically lost in the random design of conversation as if the man's words are just a series of grands jetés and her only responsibility is to catch his ideas in the air. Aziz feels terrified, inflamed, and moved by Suzanne, but he doesn't stand up or walk away because all his thoughts about timelines—the one he's living, the one he's imagining, the one he's hoping for, the one he lost, the ones he fears, the one he daydreamt about back in St-Denis— are all crisscrossing now. They're smashing into each other. A woman like Suzanne would never love someone like him, especially when his heart is covered with stiches and parables.

33.

When the time is right and she can hold Winnie's hand in the open air and feel his pulse between her fingers again in the polluted New York air, Ginger will tell him the secret of mirrors and the confessions of pregnancy tests.

34.

Just as passengers start feeling another wave of panic, anxiety, and paralysis, a group of fire fighters bursts through the emergency doors suddenly like bulky superheroes in raincoats. Passengers stop speaking mid-sentence like a palpitating colon: staring in confused adoration at the stocky angels of salvation in yellow rain slickers and coal miner helmets. The captain of the evacuation squad holds a walkie-talkie in his hand like a giant and powerful hammer. He is handsome and gruff. He is unshaven and covered in ash. His face is covered in dots of sweat and carbon grime, just like in the newspapers. —Ladies and Gentlemen, he says in a thick Brooklyn accent, if you will please folla us, wuh gonna get you outta hey. At least two passengers faint out of joy. One pees on herself.

35.

The train becomes frantically empty. The two teenagers in Knicks jerseys are carried away on stretchers like dead possums squashed by an old pickup truck.

36.

The passengers finally escape the steel sarcophagus of the C train. They flee from New York's underground necropolis with slow and steady footsteps, marching through the thick pitch and the post-apocalyptic dread of the subway tunnel with the help of LED flashlight beams and industrial power Streamlights illuminating their path like Virgil holding a lantern behind his back in Dante's Christian fairytale. Before the characters' paths in this backwards novel diverge above ground, fragmenting into a thousand shards of language, backstory, entomology, and willful forgetting, they share a fragile and singular moment together in their departure, which is the closest they will come to meeting. Winnie finds the air underground heavy, creepy, and ominous like playing *Fallout 3* without weapons. The smell of tar, gasoline, engine grease, and invisible mold in the subway tunnel is ubiquitous. Winnie follows Ginger with his hand on her waist. Aziz grabs Suzanne's hand even though they've never spoken a word to each other. This is their only time together, their one moment of fearless intimacy. It's not enough.

37.

Out on the sidewalk, gusts of wet wind slap their faces. The firmness of the solid ground and the perfect mobility of their bodies has a new meaning now. For a few days, not a single passenger takes their life for granted. All the passengers will go their separate ways now, their paths splintering into different directions, their thoughts eventually looping backwards to the moment before they took the C train, before Hurricane Sandy knocked out power in New York, before the world came to an end again for one week in the city. Their brief intersection inside the subway tunnel will soon be lost and forgotten in time. We are their only witnesses. We must do the remembering for every passenger who needs to forget.

38.

Six blocks from the emergency tunnel exit, Ginger and Winnie look at each other in disbelief, the rain and the wind taking turns sucker-punching their faces.

—Dinner? Ginger asks.

Winnie nods. —Hell yes, Ginger Snap, let's get inside before it rains again.

As they turn to leave, a mob of reporters in rain slickers slithers through small groups of passengers and surrounds them. *How long were you trapped inside the subway? Did you hear any strange noises? What's this we hear about a schizophrenic passenger and a jihadist? Was anyone harmed? Where are you from? Do you speak English?*

Winnie grabs Ginger's hand. —Yo, let's get the fuck out of this mosh pit.

—Okay, baby.

39.

Aziz and Suzanne let go of each other's hands. They walk in parallel lines now across the street from each other, protecting their heads with old copies of *The Village Voice* as the wind releases glass beads on the city. The brief intersection they'd shared underground is now gone forever. Both of them want to hold each other's hand again like they did in the subway tunnel, but they don't have a pretext anymore in the unlit city streets and the savage industrial air. They're strangers again to this city and to each other. They're displaced foreigners again, disoriented and turned on, stuck between worlds, and quietly alone after touching each other briefly in the forgiving darkness. Now, they're missing the amorality of the underworld, the implied mortality of broken dreams, and the possibility of a stolen future. Their fear and their brashness have disappeared. The vows they made to themselves when they were stuck inside the C train have lost their meaning above ground. They need a new reason to act audaciously or they will never speak again.

40.

In 2012, New York is trapped in the Eurocentric definition of the Dark Ages again, transported back to a time before the Industrial Revolution or Thomas Edison. It's fantastically anachronistic: one of the most modern, cutting-edge, and multicultural cities in the entire world (the unofficial *capital* of Planet Earth but somehow not America) is shrouded in the dark mystery of its own inexplicable collapse. It takes only a few more blocks for

Suzanne and Aziz to realize separately, and in their own way, that the city has already filled its sprawling void with millions of chatty locals sitting on the hoods of taxis and leaning against large trucks. Cops and civilians are guiding traffic. The streets are at a standstill, half street festival and half crisis management. Sidewalks are crammed, stoops overloaded, and restaurants overcrowded, many of them giving away free food to anyone with a death wish or a carpe diem tattoo or too much wine circulating through their veins. The city has become a never-ending block party, a festival of historical primitivism, and a celebration of the multiracial body politic. New Yorkers have never acted so laid back before. They haven't been this gregarious and open since 9/11, since the Northeast Blackout of 2003, and this time, there are no body bags or video loops of society breaking down.

41.

Both Winnie and Ginger try calling their family on their phones, but the circuits are still overloaded. Slowly, they make their way towards First Avenue, stopping now and then to talk to strangers on the street. There are enormous lines behind public phone booths as quarters rain from the sky, overflowing from people's pockets, held between twitching fingers, and eventually forced down the throats of pay telephones that haven't been fed so much since pagers ruled the world.

42.

Aziz watches Suzanne walking away and panics. He stops at a crosswalk and notices a large Buddha Mao dressed in aviator sunglasses, baggy jeans, muscle T-shirt, Nazca line tattoos covering both shoulders and forearms, and a wool shoulder bag hanging from the side with an Incan sun. The tattoos are Chinese characters for the words people, hive, love, and memory. A caption to the left of the Buddha Mao reads:

**More people means a greater ferment of ideas,
More enthusiasm and more energy. Never
before have the masses of the people been
so inspired, so militant, and so daring
as they are right now.
—"Introducing a Co-operative," (April 15th, 1958)**

Aziz reaches inside the pocket of his satchel to grab a cigarette and cross the street when he realizes his pack is gone. And so is his wallet. He sighs sadly. When Aziz looks up again, Suzanne is gone. He feels an exquisite and painful saudade—that's the only word that makes sense to him right now—for the life they could have had together and for the life they will never have together. He knows he has no right to wish for love when his heart is broken into pieces.

43.

Winnie stops at a crosswalk and points at a large billboard. Ginger smiles. She's seen this Buddha Mao twenty times in the past year: he's dressed in Ray-Bans, gangster jeans, surfer tank top, and Chinese characters covering his arms she can't read, and a shoulder bag with an indigenous sun. The tattoos are kinda dope. She doesn't need to read the caption to know what it says. After all, she's the one who gave Winn all the quotes for the Buddha Mao campaign.

44.

Suzanne stops once to look back. When she sees Aziz a block away, shuffling through his beautiful officer's satchel with the gusseted pockets, she realizes he's not following her anymore. She knows it's irrational and antifeminist to want him to chase her around New York like a treasure map, a city she doesn't even know, a city she doesn't even love, a city where both of them are self-conscious, sad, estranged, and completely stranded in a shattered universe where space has collapsed into time like a bad SF drama. She knows it's romantically fallacious to expect him to follow her to the nearest hotel, a man she's never talked to, a man who's not even her type, just because they held hands for twenty-five minutes in the emergency subway tunnel, too afraid to speak and too exhausted to cry. And yet, there's a smoldering speck of desire inside her that still wants him to stay with her in this city where streetlights have aneurysms, where trains get lodged in cement cavities, and where the expansive darkness is just a temporary plague of locusts covering every surface with vitreous wings. When she turns down the next street, she feels a deep and throbbing sadness inside her heart that lingers for a whole week, even after she flies over her favorite Chicago neighborhoods like a demoted angel.

45.

At Yaffa Café, Winnie and Ginger snag the last empty table inside (the wind is blowing too strong on the back patio), just as a group of professionals in matching khaki shorts and plaid polos are leaving. Ginger and Winnie take turns cleaning up in the bathroom, wiping the grime and industrial ash from their faces. By the time they both sit down, the sun has crashed to the ground like a snipered bird, ripping layers of bubblegum yarn from the gifted sky with its talons. To Winnie, New York looks caked in layers of pixilated charcoal and raspberry purée. The waiters at the café circulate through the unsolicited darkness, dropping off clusters of candles on the tabletops, picking up old plates that once carried free slices of Mud Cake and Sour Cream Apple Walnut Pie.

46.

Soon afterwards, Aziz walks past Yaffa Café and stops, completely entranced by the candlelit tabletops inside. The café looks like a field of solar flowers and a cave of unspectacular miracles. *It should be called St. Mark's Grotto*, he thinks. Aziz thinks about Hassan. He thinks about Suzanne who suddenly disappeared, his heart filled with sadness and confusion. He wonders if their paths will ever cross again, if he should have ignored the rules of personal space on the sidewalk and talked to her anyway. He also wonders if he'd completely misunderstood the situation when they held hands in the emergency tunnel, finding meaning in their proximity. He regrets not saying anything because now he'll never know. The flickering candles in the café bring him back to reality. They look like translucent slivers of Albuquerque moon, like flaming teardrops of a broken sun bird. Aziz considers waiting for a table, thinks he recognizes Winnie inside, though he can't say for sure in the semi-darkness. He questions his own judgment. He wonders where his imagination ends and his reality begins. In the end, he decides to walk over the Brooklyn Bridge, even if there's still a lingering storm. He wants to remember the feeling of being part of the metaphoricity of language one last time.

47.

Winnie passes Ginger veggie rolls and then she passes him salmon rolls that they bought at a bodega across the street. *Half price for half the world*, the sign said.

—Here's your water, two lemonades, and a cranberry juice on the house, the waitress says. She's dressed in a gas attendant's shirt and has a Tigger tattoo on her hand. —Oh score! I see you guys made out well.

—Sushi? Ginger asks the waitress, her mouth full of rice and avocado.

—Yeah, Winnie says, help yourself. We've got way more than we can eat.

—Maybe just one piece of salmon, the waitress says, com'ere little guy.

—Go for it like there's no tomorrow, Winnie says, because there might not be.

Ginger and the waitress exchange looks before laughing. Ginger accidentally spits rice everywhere and Winnie busts out laughing.

48.

Counterfactual narrative writing can be a cruel and presumptuous art form, but it's hard to dismiss precisely because all plotlines are possible, uncertain, contingent, and mutable considering every character could have made other choices, each choice with its own consequences that might radically change the novel's plot structure. At different times, both Suzanne and Aziz wonder whether they made a mistake letting each other go without a word. Their intersection inside the subway was a tiny opening into each other's lives, one they would think about and replay inside their heads again and again for years afterwards, sometimes fumbling, sometimes full of self-reproach. Someone had to violate decorum, someone had to act courageously and articulate their feelings in stumbling syntax, but neither did. If Suzanne had said something to Aziz on the street before she disappeared from his life or if Aziz had taken a right instead of a left turn when she disappeared like the electricity in the city, they would be sitting on a bench in Washington Square right now, talking about their exes and silently planning their first adventure to Ellis Island the next day, Fire Island a week later, and maybe even Paris in the spring. And even when their paths diverge, they still had one more chance. If Suzanne had shared a taxi at Penn Station with the girl in the NYU sweatshirt who was headed to DUMBO (where Aziz ended up) instead of the Bosnian family that was headed to Queens via East Williamsburg, she would have run into Aziz again in Brooklyn after she paid the cabbie. And this time, she would have found the courage to gamble on the uncertain design of their attraction (inchoate, undetermined, and unclear as it was). After waking up Aziz on the bench in DUMBO, something she would normally never do, his body curled up like a Styrofoam peanut, they would have walked together with the Manhattan and the Brooklyn Bridge as witnesses, dragging Suzanne's luggage over the planks like FOBs, watching boats bobble and hover about the dark harbor like seasick prophets, and gazing at the tens of thousands of cell phone lights throughout the city, all fluttering like fireflies, all sending their one-way love poems in tiny flashes of bioluminescent code:

```
•_ _        ••_         •_ _        •_          _••
••••        _ _         ••••        _•••        •_
•           _•_ _       _•_ _       •••         •_•
•_•         •_••        ••          •           _•_
•           _ _ _       •••         _•          _•
•_          •••_        _•_ _       _•_•        •
•_•         •?          _ _ _       •           •••
•                       ••_                     •••?
_•_ _                   •_•
_ _ _
```

49.

There are two conversations taking place inside Winnie's head at the same time. The first conversation is overt and rational, helping him talk with Ginger and listen attentively to her observations about people at the café. The second conversation is covert and irrational, returning again and again to the welfare of his family. He knows his mama, his uncle, and Tian-Tian are all together, probably eating dan dan noodles, spicy eggplant and watercress, jasmine rice, and roasted root veggies by candlelight now that Tian-Tian is a full-fledged no-hurt-atarian. They're probably nibbling on rice crackers and sipping green tea, but for some reason he can't stop picturing violence in his head. He keeps seeing Gambino thugs in black leather jackets, Flying Dragons wielding sharpened Tsai swords, armed-to-the-teeth Zetas, Tenth Avenue Gangsters dressed in camouflage pants, Hammerskins in steel-toed boots and suspender jeans, and Latin Kings in jean shorts and white tank tops, all breaking into his fam's apartment during the blackout and running off with their geriatric TV and their fancy turquoise china set from Hong Kong with the anthropomorphic camellias in the center and vines forming infinity signs in the perimeter. Winnie sees an international cast of criminals dragging the American Steel safe with them, its forbidden contents remaining an enigma for the rest of his life.

50.

Before he crosses the Brooklyn Bridge, Aziz wanders through side streets and ends up sitting on a bench in Main Street Park, wondering why his trip to New York feels like such a personal disaster, starting with his tragic departure from Paris and ending with his tragic departure from New York. He feels so far away from Paris right now, so far away from St-Denis, so far away from Hassan, Sakina, Wafi, Ousmane, and Michel, all the people who made his life intelligible. Now, he feels like they're minor characters in a French novel that someone else wrote and translated, that someone else is reading. His community in St-Denis has become a troupe of traveling ghosts, haunting his dejected mind and his ravaged heart. Aziz almost believes that New York is in mourning too because of him and he feels guilty about his egocentrism. He feels ashamed not only because he is useless to his family in Paris, but also because he feels personally responsible for dragging the darkness to New York with him after Hassan was killed and so many of his neighbors and their teenage sons were beat up, teargassed, stomped on, and arrested by the Gendarmes before being criticized by the French bourgeoisie for valuing human lives over property. Aziz feels like he inadvertently dragged a gargantuan veil with him all the way from the slums of Paris, ensnaring New York in a broken parachute of despair.

51.

When Ginger looks at Winnie, she knows right away that something is bothering him. She knows the meaning of the faraway look in his eyes, like he just teleported to another timeline and sent a holographic replica of himself in her timeline to make everything seem normal. She knows his eyes better than anyone, she knows their presence, conflict, joy, and duality. She knows when he's with her and when he's gone, when he's thinking about his next culture jam and when he's trying to remember something, when he loves her explicitly and when he loves her in quiet agony. Sometimes, she loves him even more when he struggles to regain the silence in his eyes, fighting the trauma inside him in order to avoid infecting her with his anxiety, racial melancholia, and barely contained anger at the broken world. She reaches out and grabs his hand, kissing it. She wants him to be feel grounded in this moment. Winnie smiles because he knows that she knows that he knows that she knows.

52.

From the taxi window, New York is a sprawling black-and-white photo installation that goes on forever. The soft brassy lights of Michigan Avenue and the illuminated rusty bridges of the Loop have never seemed so far away, so charming in their obsolescence, so distant in their emotional comfort as they do right now when Suzanne is trapped in another person's dream. She wishes there was some way she could get through to her mum right now. Her email is taking forever to refresh on her iPhone and her parents' landline has been busy for the past hour, something she didn't even know was still possible in 2012. Her mum has probably concocted a Hollywood drama inside her head involving hijacked Russian submarines, hacked North Korean nuclear launch codes, and a global jihad campaign. She's very talented at imagining the numerous ways that her family can die tragically. Suzanne wishes there was some way to let her know she is safe and perfectly healthy, except for her clothes that are covered in ash and soot. She wishes she'd said something to Aziz before he evaporated like a shooting star. She realizes that her freedom is also the cradle of her paralysis.

53.

Winnie keeps picturing made-up thugs with baseball bats attacking his little sister, smashing her fibula in a single swing that severs her tiny wrists that haven't even tasted the chilled dish of violence yet. He sees his mama getting pistol-cocked in the soft part of her fleshy nose with a glock, the cartilage split in two like a chestnut, he sees Ba's favorite cobalt plates smashed to fragments. Winnie has faith in his family, he just wishes there was some way he could know they're safe from gangbangers. He wants Tian Tian to be safe from this collapsed city and safe from his own hyperactive imagination that keeps spitting out graphic images of violence at the worst possible times.

54.

In the counterfactual world that could also have started in DUMBO, Suzanne looks at Aziz in a way that makes him feel like the darkness that once plagued his soul has been sucked out of his bloodstream, like a syringe of morphine after a nasty scorpion bite, slowly curing his spiritual sickness. In this alternate world, Aziz and Suzanne talk all night on a bench between two bridges until she falls asleep. Aziz becomes the short-term guardian of her dreams, the short-lived protector of archetypes. When she wakes up three hours later, just as the sun is napalming the cityscape with a chemical orange glow, Aziz looks at her with eyes that are corroded by delirium and heavy with the atomic weight of his unjustifiable affection. Suzanne reaches for his hand. The gentle and firm and warm feeling in her touch is the slow undoing of everything that felt wrong. In this timeline, however, Aziz is alone, sitting on a bench in DUMBO, staring at barges drifting by, his trench coat zipped and buttoned to the top. Aziz feels as if his soul is covered in a sticky patina of trauma, grief, and regret. He wants nothing more than to cleanse the sadness that's caked into his body now. His mind and his heart are both sore from the contingency of love and disaster.

55.

Despite his freak out session, Winnie and Ginger stay at the café for a couple of hours. When they finally pay their bill and leave an obscene gratuity for the "cool as fuck" waitress with the Tigger tattoo, it's almost one in the morning. The wind is still blowing hard, smelling faintly of melting freezers and candle wax. They walk up Avenue of the Americas, exhausted but still holding hands. They move slowly up the street, prolonging their moment of loss and reconnection.

56.

Eventually, Aziz and Suzanne would have gotten tired and sat down on the curb to share a bottle of Snapple Half & Half she'd packed in one of her suitcases. While they talked and kissed indirectly through the bottle, Suzanne wouldn't be able to stop looking at Aziz's lashes, which were longer than hers, longer than Cleopatra's, longer than the longest word to describe the chain of chemical reactions taking place inside her body every time he looked at her with his glazed, damaged, and fiercely tender eyes. In the joyful serendipity of their moment together, they'd reject every opportunity to say goodbye and invite fresh conversation with each and every new instance of precarious silence. This evening would have been the beginning of the beginning of the lovesick and the vertiginous. We are the only witnesses to their speculative love affair.

57.

Three days later, Ginger drags Winnie to a vegetarian dim sum restaurant on Pell Street. Winnie tells her that vegetarian dim sum is an oxymoron, but he shuts up once the food comes, devouring everything on his plate in humbled silence. Somewhere between the spinach dumplings, the fake shrimp rolls, the veggie steamed buns, and the sticky rice wrapped in Taro leaves, Winnie realizes he's the happiest he's been in years. Somewhere between Confucius Park and Union Square, Ginger realizes that people use their children to autofill their empty lives.

58.

In the parallel universe of contingent and counterfactual love, Aziz sees Suzanne one final time in New York before they leave. They meet at a Brazilian restaurant called *Obrigado, Senhor Descarnado* in Red Hook. The bilingual waiters are fabulously beautiful and full of attitude that can't be taught or learned. The male servers wear mascara better than the female servers. Suzanne asks their waitress—a chiseled Black transwoman in a Mozart wig—about the vegetarian options. The waitress rolls her eyes, says *merda!*, and walks away, returning with their bottle of Miolo Lote, two glasses, and a tiny menu for troublemakers. They drink their first glass in silence. Aziz pulls out a cigarette, but Suzanne gives him a dirty look and tells him he's not in Paris. He crushes the cigarette dramatically and flicks it inside his water glass. Small strands of French tobacco forms C's that break up underwater, spilling out like the ellipses in their own sentences. Finally, Aziz can't stand it anymore, so he takes a large sip of wine and says:

—You're the most beautiful woman I've ever seen, that's the truth, but beautiful women aren't my type because their beauty is a burden. Also, I'm terrible with long-distance relationships.

Suzanne blinks hard. —Excuse me? Who said anything about a long-distance relationship? The last time I checked, we were having dinner.

Aziz smirks, his eyes melting into dreaminess and embarrassment. —I'm just saying, I'm not attracted to American women.

—That's okay, I don't like short Moroccan guys with missing teeth.

—I'm not ready for a relationship.

—I'm not ready for a fling.

Aziz takes another big gulp of wine. —And I have to be honest: I think Americans are ignorant, hypocritical, uncultured, racist, self-righteous, and bellicose bubble babies. And your coffee is shit.

Suzanne blinks hard again and smiles. —All true. On the other hand, French people are snobby, homophobic, politically obsolete, neocolonial, incapable of shutting up, unfaithful, and culturally unimaginative. And your wine is overrated. She takes a big sip of wine and smirks.

He laughs hard. —I don't trust vegetarians.

She giggles into her hand. —I despise smokers.

—I'm flying to Paris tomorrow.

—I'm flying to Chicago.

—Will you come with me?

—I'd rather slit my wrists with a rusty butter knife.

—I know it doesn't make any sense because we just met today and we know absolutely nothing about each other, but I'm asking you to come to Paris with me.

—Okay, she whispers, on y va.

Aziz wipes his eyes and then touches her hand, the warm tears running down his fingers until they form a pool on her half-eaten fingernails.

59.

A couple days later, Ginger and Winnie are holding hands as they walk down Canal Street. On the corner of Lafayette, she stops and swallows hard. —Boo, I have something tell you.

Winnie gives her a confused look. —'Sbout time, yo.

—I love you.

He smiles, brushing a piece of imaginary ash off her cheeks. —Me too.

—Say it.

—Aw man, he says, smirking.

—Say it, boy!

—I love you, Ginger Spice!

The light turns green. Pedestrians stampede across the street like a herd of pursued oxen in gray suits, Adidas track suits, and rolled up jeans.

60.

In this world, Aziz looks up at the damaged sky and the resinous river and the bulky silhouettes of the Manhattan and Brooklyn Bridges and feels lost and invisible and sad. Somehow, in this city of immigrants, he feels like he doesn't belong, like a permanent foreigner with no place to go except inside himself. Aziz thinks about the last look Suzanne gave him before they parted ways. He feels enormous regret now. He should have said something before she disappeared. He should have asked for her name. He's exhausted, lonely, and ashamed of his own silence. He's embarrassed by his own nostalgia for a life in Paris he never loved. He misses Hassan before the street riot, he misses his mom and Sakina before they became an Amy Winehouse song, he misses Yesha before she erased their highlight reel, he misses New York before it fell apart, and he misses (the idea of who) Suzanne (could have been). Even though he doesn't know her name, he misses what they could have become, what they could have said to each other if they'd fought for more time together. Aziz feels hypothetically nostalgic. It's quantum nostalgia at its worst.

61.

Ginger's eyes radiate a soft brown glow backlit by private agony. She has her back to the street and she's trying not to sob. —Boo, I have something to tell you.

Winnie grabs her hand and kisses it. —What is it, baby?

Big chunky teardrops clunk on her collar like a pearl necklace breaking in slow motion. —I've been meaning to tell you, but I just don't know how. The instant I tell you, it becomes true.

—.

She kisses his hand and wipes her eyes with her wrists. —I don't know how to say this.

—Say what?

She wipes her nose on her sleeve. —Winn, I have the ovaries of a fifty-year-old woman.

—Wait, what?

—Reproductively, I'm middle-aged.

Winnie shrugs. —That's okay, boo, we'll just keep trying until we get good news.

—It's not gonna happen, Winn. Ever.

He gives her a confused look because they only stopped using birth control six months ago, so Winnie thought they still had plenty of time to start a family.

—It means I can't have a baby without an egg donation and you know I'll never be okay with that.

Winnie is filled with immense and sudden sadness. At first, it's mostly for Ginger, but after a moment, his sadness is for his loss too, even though he doesn't want to center his own devastation. Recently, he's been daydreaming about being a ba and carrying their gorgeous hapa daughter on his shoulders during Central Park concerts and going to her school recitals and watching her compete in spelling bees and competitive crumping and gymnastics and Academic Decathlon and spoken word and Chinese school recitations and fencing, he's been thinking about the unwarranted joy of waking up and finding their daughter nestled between them in bed, her little head resting on his shoulder, her hands gripping his T-shirt with quiet urgency. Winnie gulps hard and grips Ginger's hand tight. —Oh man, I'm sorry, baby.

—I'm an idiot.

—No.

—Yes, I am! I hadn't gotten my period in two months and I thought, I don't know why, I thought, *This is it*, so I went and got a bunch of tests done when I saw my reproductive endocrinologist, but instead of telling me I was gonna be a mom, he told me my ovarian reserve was depleted.

—What does that mean exactly?

—It means my ovaries aren't producing eggs anymore and my missed periods are the signs of premature menopause, not pregnancy. Ginger stops herself as black tears streak down her face like musical bars.

Winnie wipes them away with the back of his hand and kisses the teardrops on her clenched fingers. —It's okay, baby. It's okay.

Ginger's face trembles, the devastation bleeding out of her. —I'm sorry I can't make you a daddy, Winn. I'm so fucking sorry.

—Baby, I don't *need* that. My life's already complete with you. I don't need a kid to be happy.

—But *I* do, Winn. *I* do, she says, clenching her yellow button-down with her hand. —And I didn't realize it until the moment I couldn't be a mom. Ginger sobs quietly in the middle of the sidewalk, the grief and shame cycling through her like a hardy generator. Winnie squeezes her tightly and kisses her forehead and her temples, crying with her, furious about his own powerlessness, confused about his daydreams, and so incredibly angry at the world for crushing Ginger with its heel. If anyone deserves to be a mom, it's her (even if he's not ready to be a dad).

62.

After being forced to spend another week in Brooklyn against her will, Suzanne flies to Seattle with a heavy heart, a handful of unanswered questions about a relationship that never happened, and a shitload of disposable time, all of which her mum absolutely loathes (both the disposable time and the decision to return to Seattle). Suzanne looks through the airplane window and sees a fortress of wonton clouds. Passengers nap in their chairs or watch movies on their phones. When the stewardess passes, Suzanne asks for more orange juice because she can. Suzanne is worried that Seattle is going to feel incredibly tiny and nauseatingly white after New York. She's worried about the rain. She'll have to figure it out as she goes. For the time being, she'll stay with Ali and Samir in Capitol Hill until she finds an IT job or joins Médecins Sans Frontières. Maybe, she'll move to Lower Queen Anne, Columbia City, or Wallingford where she can have a backyard, a clawfoot bathtub, and a tiny pug named Shibboleth. Just saying the name out loud makes her smile thirty thousand miles above ground. She just needs a city that's cleaner and cheaper than New York with good mass transit, lots of local cafés, a thriving farmers market, green spaces, respectable vegetarian restaurants, and some tree-lined streets that are safe to bike in, and she'll be happy. Maybe, she'll work at a bookstore and flirt with stumbling, self-deprecating intellectuals. Maybe, she'll work at a French restaurant for a couple years, get burned out serving snotty libertarians and hyperactive environmentalists. Maybe, Seattle will be the perfect impetus for grad school. She could get her PhD in race and ethnicity, English and feminist theory, and/or sociolinguistics at U Dub, publish three monographs with Oxford University Press, and someday after she's made tenure (wait, does tenure even exist anymore?), she'll fall in love with a brilliant, complex, kind, and affectionate scholar who looks a little like Aziz and isn't intimidated by her beauty or resentful of her intelligence. Or maybe, the next two years of her life in Seattle will be like a MA in personal vocalization. She will learn to hear her own voice, project it into the world, and hurl it into the clouds like a sonic javelin. Maybe, she'll join the Peace Corps to teach math in a developing country in West Asia like Kazakhstan, Azerbaijan, or Tajikistan. Or maybe, instead of volunteering, she'll save up all her money and travel around the world by herself, taking the TGV from Paris to Budapest, then the Tran-Siberian railroad from Moscow to Beijing, and then the Shinkansen from Kyūshu to Hokkaido until she runs out of money (or contacts amoebic dysentery for the third time). In a few hours, she'll have a four-hour layover in O'Hare where she will order a large Earl Gray with almond milk in the international terminal, flags from across the world hanging from the terminal like the UN Plaza, and then she'll look at pictures of Chicago on her phone. She won't call anyone. She won't look for friends or classmates at the airport. She won't even text her mum. She'll just sip her overpriced tea and wonder how Chicago got so far away from her when it's the only city she's ever loved and the only city she's ever understood.

63.

Instead of spending a few more weeks in New York as his manager suggested on the phone, Aziz leaves New York on the first available flight back to Paris. In his first-class seat, he thinks about his time in New York. He thinks about the tragedy in St-Denis that followed him across the Atlantic to a tiny apartment in Washington Heights and then eventually into the New York subway. He thinks about the blur of women that passed by on the sidewalk every day in a dizzying spell of style, attitude, ambition, and beauty. He thinks about the majestic view of the city from the Brooklyn Bridge and the sounds of cars passing underneath the planks. He thinks about fresh Cubanos at his favorite restaurant in Washington Heights, the way he used to cradle the warm sandwiches in his hand and hold them against his forehead on the couch, carefully plying the tin foil open as the smell of melted cheese and grilled ham gushed into his nostrils like food poppers. He thinks about the breakdancers in Union Square doing head spins, back spins, and windmills on dirty cardboard to '80s hip-hop blasting from duct-taped boom boxes. He thinks about the plasticized darkness that draped New York in a shiny black layer. He thinks about his family dressed in layers of black. He thinks about Yesha's engagement party the following month that he wasn't invited to. He thinks about the negative space he's returning to in Paris. Mostly, though, he thinks about how he let go of Suzanne's hand by mistake. He was just being polite because that's who he is. He didn't want her to feel imposed or pressured. He didn't want her to think he was being creepy. But there was nothing he wanted more than to hold her hand, their fingers glued by nervous longing. They could have climbed up the staircase of the Empire State building a week later to see the bright lights of New York flicked on again like a divine light switch, the electricity spreading block by block through Manhattan and beyond like a panoramic metaphor of the Gospel. They could have shared cannoli in Little Italy as refugees of the necropolis and immigrants of the New York body, christening their displacement with white sugar and opiate dreams. They could have been so many things they never were, so many things they would never be now.

64.

After Ginger tells Winnie the results of her tests, his chest fills with metastasizing grief that expands into the future and the past. His heart is a giant wound now. They both sob uncontrollably, their tears thumping on their cheeks in the language of rage, devastation, disbelief, and social defiance. With their faces pasted with sticky, black, and thick tears, they make out like narcissistic teenyboppers while petulant New Yorkers pass them in every direction and huff and shake their heads in annoyance, protesting with impatient footsteps, passive aggressive sighs, and collective scorn. One Japanese tourist even takes a picture of them and posts it later on Facebook, getting fifty-eight likes. The two of them are a living sculpture of love and mourning for the family they already are, for the family they thought they were becoming, for the family they wanted to be, and for the family they'll never be, the ghosts of their imagined life trailing them like the specter of stale rain. Winnie grabs Ginger's head and cups her cheeks with his hands and kisses her salty lips that quiver. He holds her in his arms and kisses her head. As the mango-colored dusk silkscreens the tops of skyscrapers and slowly disappears in a quiet and merciful coda of sunlight, Winnie hugs her tight, kisses her cheeks streaked by mascara lines. He rubs her back and kisses her temples until her chest stops heaving and her hands stop clawing and twisting his T-shirt.

65.

Aziz realizes he doesn't know her name, or where she's from, or what she does for a living. She could be an economic hitman or a World Bank mosquito, sucking the blood from corrupt Third World dictators. She could be an officer for the CIA's clandestine services collecting intel from peaceful Muslims. She could be an industrial spy or a professional strikebreaker for Walmart (quel horreur!). She could be a psychopath who preys on young Christian mystics and stores their cubed brains in an industrial-strength freezer for holiday meals. She could be the exact opposite of everything he wants in his life and everything he needs his life to be. The truth is, he doesn't know anything about her except that her fingers were smooth and silky like the hands of a hypersensitive poet or a self-moisturizing intellectual. Her palms were clammy and warm to the touch like a baker's and there was subtle pressure in her grip that moved him like she was saying something to him through her touch, something he'd only find if he were looking for it. But the pressure was so subtle, he questioned whether it was even there, whether he simply mistook her fear for her attraction.

66.

Once passengers made their way through the subway tunnel to the street level, the spectral voices and the jabbing wind and the bursting raindrops and the transcendent sunlight poured down on everyone. That's when Aziz tugged at Suzanne's hand, became self-conscious and then hesitated, and when she sensed his hesitation, she let go to save face, to stop him from embarrassment. Aziz thinks about that liminal moment, about the beautiful accident he let go of, about the uncertain world he escaped, about the poignant moment of self-consciousness he misdiagnosed, and he wonders (still wonders, in fact) whether he made the whole thing up in his head. The truth is, he'll never know. We are his only witnesses now.

67.

Because time is a collapsible and invented thing, the ending in this novel ends at the same place it begins. When the stranded passengers pass through the steel sarcophagus of the C train and finally escape New York's underground necropolis, they march through the thick pitch of the subway tunnel with the help of LED flashlight beams and industrial power Streamlights illuminating their path. Before their paths diverge above ground, fragmented into a thousand shards of memory, longing, and forgetting, the characters in this time/space share a fragile and singular intersection. The air under the streets is heavy with the smell of tar, gasoline, engine grease, and mold. Aziz joins the line of evacuees. Halfway through the subway tunnel, he does something brash, something he would never do in Paris or Casa or even in the streets of New York. He reaches for Suzanne's hand even though he's never spoken a word to her. He fears the worst, expecting her to flinch or pull back or scream for help. Instead, she whispers a smile and holds his hand tenderly, but with pressure that feels significant for some reason. The two of them walk together in the slow exodus for an abbreviated eternity through the penumbral subway tunnel past signs written in code for conductors and water pumps and manholes and ventilation machines and miles and miles of bundled cables, every step like a frame in a post-apocalyptic survival movie that went straight to DVD. They march slowly until they reach solid land again, until they feel the natural light splashing their cheeks.

68.

Aziz and Suzanne pass through the birth canal of the subway tunnel until they reach the sidewalk where the New York horizon has burst into wet flames. Sporadic gales throw dead leaves and flyers for jewelry stores, knock-off purses, and exterminators into the gradient sky. October showers peg their temples like defiant children armed with wrist rockets. As sparkling orbs of sunlight glimmer in the stormy air, crowning their bituminous heads with celestial sequins, the fading sun consumes everything in its path, turning pedestrians into bronze statues and towering skyscrapers in the distance into totems of metal and mineral. After being trapped inside the shadow world of New York long enough for Suzanne and Aziz to abandon their lives and rediscover them again, the citrus punch sky is sublime now, practically religious. Before they let go of each other forever, their fingers linger, their fingers curl, protesting their inevitable erasure from each other. It's almost as if Aziz and Suzanne need to gather their courage and blow away the other worlds before they disappear into their divergent timelines and become strangers again, their heads throbbing in endless permutation of love and absence. For the rest of their lives, for as long as memory lasts, their ears will ring with the verses of the unsung and their lips will burn with the hallelujah of the storm. We are their only witnesses now. We are the only ones who can hear their songs.

ACKNOWLEDGEMENTS

I'd like to express my deepest love, appreciation, admiration, &
respect to the following people:

Baby Moonshine. Tu amor, apoyo, empatía, rabia, compren-
sión, alegría e incluso frustración son fundamentales para mi
propio éxito. Me animaste a nunca renunciar, incluso cuando
sentía que la industria editorial siempre me ignoraría y rechaz-
aría mientras tantos otros escritores estaban sacando cachita y
me sentí como un boludo completo por mi propia incapacidad
de publicar esta novela (la que está afuera en el mundo, che!).
Llevo mi amor para vos en el fondo de mi corazón, ahora y
siempre. Sos mi sirena peruana, tan inteligente y atenta con ojos
de chocolate derretido, gotitas de miel en los cachetes, y cintas
& oropel en tu cabello. Te amo, te amo, te amo, mariquita. Sos
rebella, sos refuerte, sos renecessaria. Nunca podés olvidar eso.

My **fam**, especially obāchan, Wickie, who has the gentlest soul
I know, and my mum, who has been the inspiration for many of
the strong female characters I've created over the years. You've
all humored me for years every time I got close (but not close
enough to) having a breakthrough in my writing career before
getting my heart broken again. I love you all so much.

Valerie Sayers, William O'Rourke, and Steve Tomasula, for their
insight, talent, support, and love at **Notre Dame** where I wrote

this novel for my MFA thesis. Thank you, Valerie, for talking to me like my writing mattered to the world even before it did. Also, big shout out to my gifted MFA cohort whose talent was inspiring and whose suggestions were insightful and generous, with a special shout-out to Renée D'Aoust (tu me manques, mon amie), Beth "Bee" Couture, Angela Mi Young Hur, Tom Miller, Shero Sheikh, Tim Chilcote, Lily Hoang, KPG, Jared Haley, and Brenna Casey.

Huge hug, many songs of praise, and massive shout-out to the brilliant, supportive, and demanding **Sunyoung Lee**, publisher at Kaya, who worked with me on this manuscript for years and fought so hard to get the board to publish it. You did everything you could, sister. Without her insight, intelligence, pushiness, generosity, and endless suggestions, this novel would never be what it is today.

A huge and heart-felt thank you to **Leland Cheuk**, my smart, insightful, brutally honest, and sharp-as-hell editor, for seeing the value, the flaws, and the importance of this novel when so many other editors and agents didn't, something I will never forget. You made me a published novelist, you gave this book a home, you saw its worth when no one else did, and you helped me make it better. I'll always be eternally grateful to you and love you for that, homie.

Last but not least, thank you dear reader for spending time with me in these pages. I can't tell you how happy I am to see you here and how grateful I am that you're alive, in this universe with me, taking time in your busy life to celebrate the tiny solar flares of our existence together. I appreciate you so much and hope we meet again.

ABOUT THE AUTHOR

Jackson Bliss is the winner of the 2020 Noemi Press Award in Prose and the mixed-race/hapa author of *Counterfactual Love Stories & Other Experiments* (Noemi Press, 2021), *Dream Pop Origami* (Unsolicited Press, 2022), and the speculative fiction hypertext, *Dukkha, My Love* (2017). His writing has appeared in *The New York Times, Tin House, Ploughshares, Guernica, Antioch Review, TriQuarterly, ZYZZYVA, Columbia Journal, Kenyon Review, Quarterly West, Joyland, Fiction,* and *Longreads,* among others. He is the Distinguished Visiting Writing Professor at Bowling Green State University and lives in LA with his wife and their two fashionably dressed dogs. Follow him on Twitter and IG: @jacksonbliss.